Children of the Fall

H.S. Down

Published by Hunk of Junk Press, 2024.

This is a work of fiction. Similarities to real people, places, or events are entirely coincidental.

CHILDREN OF THE FALL

First edition. February 25, 2024.

Copyright © 2024 H.S. Down.

ISBN: 979-8224028566

Written by H.S. Down.

To my dearest daughters,

You're too kind for these roads, but I know you will travel them with grace and courage. Always remember, you have each other.

To my wife,

Though we now wander in strange worlds that we did not intend to visit, the intention to walk them with you endures always and forever.

Children of the Fall

Most of what I have to say is the result of what I have seen, searched, or heard, and I realize now much of it was false. My generation ate a diet of bits and bytes designed to flare tempers so they could become data for sale to the highest corporate bidder. So, while I know the words to the songs of burning empires and can describe the chanting crowds to you, as well as the pageantry of the Alogo Boo men, it is all corrupt data.

Yes, in the end, the spectre of a nameless algorithm haunted every dream, every desire the internet men thought they had. If you whittled the forces of history down to the factors that truly made the world turn, all the great men or women, classes, famines, or even the plague years lost their significance. The final pages of history, written at the close of my childhood, belong to anonymous lines of code, and despite the exertions of many earnest scribes, the last pages might as well be blank to the human eye, for they bear only the false testimonies of unreliable mediums.

There was a flash. Later, my mom screamed in our driveway under the pale shadow of a rising October sun. Her fury and anguish carried down the boulevard of unlit streetlights, though the gloom availed in the alcoves of our neighbours' doorways remained unshaken. Perhaps she knew then, that although the Wi-Fi had gone out, the worst of the internet had come to life.

HYPATIA
Something Behind the Hedges

Chattering sparks fill my head and the world consists of consecutive somersaults of tumbling blackness. The coarse fingers of a carpet prick my cheeks, and my processor deduces I am face down in our Mother's study. The sensors along my spine register a breathing mass on top of me, and the rhythm of Alexandra's heart and lungs comes into focus. My arms and legs feel heavy and distant. For a moment, there is no place, no record of time inside me. I am without centre until I remember there was a phone call 100 hours ago.

It shrieked through the house and sparked blue light in the hallway outside our bedroom until it summoned our Father. There was nothing to hear until our Father finished the call with, "I understand, thank you." The contagion of our Father's panic reverberated in our Mother's voice as she asked, "What does hostile neutralization mean …? Alec, what does that mean? What does Canada have to do with the Alogo Boo's war?"

"Get off your sister, Alexandra." Our Father's voice summons me back to the carpet and the comfort of Alexandra's heartbeat against my back. "Are you okay, Hypatia?"

"What happened?" I ask as Alexandra's warm weight recedes from atop of me.

Our Father does not answer but instead runs his hand in gentle circles on my back, the same ones I showed him how to make to calm Alexandra.

"I need to know what happened," I repeat.

"We don't know," says our Father as he gropes beneath me to roll me to my side.

The lampposts outside the study's bay window are extinguished and twilight cocoons our neighbours' houses. Their heart rates are elevated and the heat signatures of their faces sear through the dark. Behind my eyes, the blue canvas where the internet and my processor meet recalls a whistle, like a kettle screaming. My processor cannot seem to find anything between the phone call and the ear-piercing noise. It is all blank space.

Our Mother's face floats in the doorway, a little yellow moon of terror. My attempt to search for news, tweets, posts about the event on the internet fails. In place of the search page-index inside my head, there is a void of static.

Our Mother kneels beside me, her hand in my hair as she says, "The Wi-Fi—"

"It's not the Wi-Fi, I can't see anything in my head. It's all dark. No weather forecasts, no messages from traffic lights, no news updates. No internet."

"It isn't you, it's the blackout," assures our Father, but his face is yellow like custard and his voice is strange and uneven.

With her back to us, Alexandra stares from the bay window into the street. The road is buried in an avalanche of darkness, and only faint shapes and edges remain visible in the night.

"You must've tripped in the dark," murmurs our Father, but our Mother's face crinkles with doubt.

Sat upright, I cross my legs on the prickly carpet and force my operating system to run a diagnostic. Red flashes erupt behind my eyes and my chest pulses. My battery is down to its emergency reserves.

"I need help," I whisper.

"What's wrong, sweetheart?" asks our Mother. Even in the dark, her eyes glow warm.

"My battery is nearly dead. I have 15 minutes before shut-down."

A flurry of panicked words passes between our parents and becomes movement as our Father strains to bring me to my feet.

"Not again, Alec. Please. It can't happen again," pleads our Mother as they both go to either side of me to support me down the stairs. Her words are confusing, and I do not understand them because this has never happened before.

Our Father does not answer her, and instead says to me, "Let us carry you, Hypatia, conserve your energy."

At the stair landing, they carry me down the side hallway out to the garage. In careful increments, they lower me until the cold push of the concrete floor ignites feelings in my back. Our Mother's delicate fingers swim through my black hair and then caress my cheek. Our Father taps and fumbles with the EV charging unit's interface.

"Thank God! There is still some charge."

Our Father yanks the black cable towards me and kneels beside me, and, with the tip of the cable, probes behind my ear in search of the small pliable flap of flesh that conceals my charging port. There is the assurance of a light click as the cable locks, and then warmth spills through my chest. Our Parents each hold one of my hands and smile, offering reassurances. They are desperate to preserve me against the perforation of my memories and loss of self that would come, should I lose operating power.

By the time I reach capacity, dawn is stepping across the windows of the garage on soft pale feet. Our Mother directs me back to her study. Flanked on either side by our Mother's colossal bookcases is the thinking sofa: a black leather ottoman that is cool to the touch all year round. Alexandra is asleep on it, under a knitted blanket. I crouch next to her and, once more, try to dig into the internet. Instead, I find only our Parents' voices, stilted and hushed as they climb up the black vent grate on the floor beside me. Worried words pass between them, but their travel through our house's archaic vent system blunts most of them and makes them inaudible.

But two words are made distinct by their repetition: "damaged" and "war."

~

A pale October sun steps across the driveway. It has been 48 hours and the streetlights have not returned. The candlelight across the road in our neighbour's window has burned away. A sullen semi-gloom avails itself from the gutters and curls in the alcove of their doorway.

With a soft click, Alexandra is packed away in the car, and I stand by our Mother and Father as they cram water and a cooler full of food into the trunk of our Atlas. My attention breaks. There is movement in the Miller house across the street. I peer into the stubborn twilight but see nobody, yet the front door is slightly, likely imperceptibly to human eyes, ajar. The crisp morning breeze nudges at it, tipping it a few inches back into the shapeless, unlit dark interior of the home.

"The Millers' home is open," I say.

Our Mother stops packing and peers out from behind our monolithic SUV. I follow her gaze and see her face grow indigo and yellow, a collage of fear and perplexity. "Where?"

"Their front door is open, but I can't see anyone."

"Is it?" Our Mother squints across the street, and I watch her eyes wander among the tired green arms of the willow trees along the boulevard. "Alec, Hypatia thinks something is wrong with the Millers. Sheila seemed so upset yesterday. Mickey was still ..." Our Mother looks at me as she cycles through words to complete her sentence, her features a confused squall of blue and green, a face of sadness and joy. "... you know, uncommunicative. I'm going to check in. Let them know we're leaving."

Our Father does not answer. He continues to force provisions into the trunk with a stiff and unyielding determination, failing to notice our Mother creeping across the road and disappearing within the leafy tributaries of the willows.

Another flutter of movement erupts from our right, not far from the cedar hedge that demarcates our home from our immediate neighbours. This time, our Father stops and turns. I mimic his stance. Heat moves behind the green arrow-shaped hedges, an ember framed by a panorama of the molten purple light of an autumn morning.

"There is something behind the hedges," I whisper.

Our Father nods and, without speaking, roots through the open trunk and pulls out a baseball bat. I continue to mine the faint eruption of heat as it shifts behind the cedar hedges. It is faint and consolidated, like the dark mass of a dying star. Its outline is too contained and too dim to be the circulatory system of a human being.

"It's still here," I whisper as the heat source creeps up and down the other side of the hedge. "It's moving."

"It? Is it an animal?" our Father asks from the corner of his lips, his eyes still fixed to the cedar hedges, which stand motionless.

I shake my head and continue in a whisper, "I'm not sure."

Our Father stamps his feet on the asphalt. "Get out of here," he barks into the bushes.

The coal light glow moves forward and squeezes through the hedges. Mickey unsheathes from the greenery and starts across the yard. He is barefoot and his shirt is torn. Blood stains his arms and cheeks, and he looks pale, his gaze aloof.

"Oh Christ, Mickey. Jesus, what the hell happened?" asks our Father.

In large steps, he closes the ground between them and folds the boy's small body into his embrace. Mickey looks distant and surprised by the gesture. Alexandra gazes out through the SUV window, her expression inscrutable.

"Are you okay, are you hurt?" our Father asks as he runs his hands up Mickey's arms and across his face, but seems to discover no cuts or gashes.

The blood is not his. I start to call out, but a scream of terror erupts from across the street. Our Mother stumbles through the Millers' front door, her hands crimson red and her face yellow like an infant sun. In an instant, our Father's face twists, horror-struck in epiphany.

"They're dead," our Mother shrieks.

There are no words from our Father. Mickey's face twitches and freezes as his slender fingers arc through the air and pierce into our Father's sides and chest, then withdraw from his body bloodied and mangled. Our Father topples backwards onto the lawn, several little red portholes flooding through his shirt.

Our Mother sprints towards us, her feet clapping on the pavement. Behind me, Alexandra's fists thunder on the window. Gasping for air, our Father crawls across the ground to the dropped bat with feeble kicks of his pirouetted toes, and stretches his arm to reach it. His hand spasms and the bat wavers in his grip as Mickey approaches. I reach down and scoop it from his failing hands.

The bat is wet with dew and slides in my hands as I use it to punt Mickey back. My blow lands below his shoulders. He stumbles back into the hedges, rises to his feet, but does not move. There is no recognition on his face, only a blank and shallow abyss. Our Mother reaches my side, and Mickey steps towards us. The bat hovers at my shoulder, ready to strike. Our Mother fumbles in her back pocket until the SUV unlocks with a quiet click, and then speaks to me in a firm voice,

"Give me the bat. Help your dad into the car and calm your sister. That's a command, Hypatia."

Tears flood down her cheeks, and her face, beaded in sweat, flashes from yellow to red. Her heart rate quickens. Primeval and raw, adrenaline surges through her as she becomes primed to destroy.

Mickey stares at us, his face still transfixed in an empty expression as his arms shake and become windmills at his sides. I struggle to grip our Father's 180-pound frame and get him to lean on my shoulder.

I cannot risk turning my back on Mickey, so I fumble with the SUV door, and when it swings open, it uncages Alexandra's screams. Her caterwaul rings through the street, carrying until it is lost in the untenanted spaces left behind by the retreat of civilization's electric hum. Our Father grips her hand as we try to lay him across the backseat. Our Mother's back is to us, and the bat drifts above her head. Mickey seems to observe the scene with clinical aloofness.

"Go back home, Mickey. Go home," our Mother commands, but Mickey does not respond.

Alexandra starts to break down and pounds her fists into the side of her head. Our Father tries to speak, but his words cannot escape his clenched, red-toothed smile.

"Protect your sister ..." our Father finally wheezes. I nod in hope of silencing him. "Out of the city ...far away...somewhere safe." His arm trembles, but his palm lands on my heart.

I nod again, pressing against the weeping holes Mickey has gored. Our Mother continues to try to command Mickey, but his head remains cocked at an avian angle while his arms whirl like helicopter blades. Alexandra rocks on the rubber car mat, her hair falling near our dying Father's nose. Despite being ridden of any colour, our Father grips Alexandra's shoulder with a trembling hand.

From inside the SUV, I watch the malaise break. Mickey charges our Mother. She cleaves the air with the bat, but he weaves beneath her strike and leaps on her, wrapping his legs and arms around her as if she is giving him a piggyback ride. His weight brings her to her knees. His jaw swings open and distends, seemingly falling out of his head, then snaps forcibly on her neck. She stumbles as she flails and spins to try to throw him off her back, but her collarbone and neck disappear in a red flood. Alexandra's screams stop and the vehicle fills with the dull, relentless clap of her hands against her ears as she stims into catatonic oblivion. Our Mother lurches towards us but trips, and her face smashes against Alexandra's window. Mute tears stream down Alexandra's cheeks. My fingers hover above the locks. Perhaps our Mother can be rescued, at least taken with us. She meets us with an empty gaze, her eyes unfocused and without depth, but her lips form and repeat the same word: *Go*. My processor registers this as her final command.

Mickey is at the side door now. The tinted windows must flip his gaze back upon him. There is the muffled noise of the lock resisting his fingers. He lets his knuckles dance on the door in a pattern of little knocks, pauses, and then continues to beckon us to open the door, seemingly oblivious to the set of keys in our Mother's pants. The glass creaks and shudders as he bashes his fist and then his head against the window. Sat on the SUV floor, Alexandra does not dare take her eyes off our Father's face. His heat-signal is colder, and his features are ashen and serene. There is a noise like ice being crushed beneath a boot, and a thin crack spreads across the window. Mickey's forehead is marred and stained with blood and milky ichor. A few more blows and he will be inside. We need to leave.

Our Father's keys are in the ignition. Stepping over Alexandra, I fumble into the front seat. The Atlas trembles and lurches forward. Behind us, there is a pattering cascade as the rear window shatters and falls like snow across the backseat. Alexandra screams as Mickey's arm jolts through the window in frenetic and desperate swipes. I drive my foot down on the accelerator, and my vision falls below the dashboard. There is a crunch and shudder as we slam into the garage door. Mickey's body jolts in the wing mirror, but he hangs on and fumbles again for the lock, his feet skipping along the road as I drive.

In an awkward stretch down the seat, I increase my pressure on the pedal and try to keep some visual of the road, aiming for the space between the Willow trees across from us. I veer into the tree on our right, and there is a sudden snap and pop. A tree trunk blows the wing mirror and Mickey off the car. Alexandra claws her way into the passenger seat. Next to our dying Father, Mickey's arm writhes on the floor in a splatter of faux blood and twisted metal.

My reverse is erratic and shaky at first, but grows smoother as my processor learns the right gestures and movements. We roll forward through an empty street. There is no sign of heat from any of our neighbours' windows. Behind us, as the first light of the sun glances off the asphalt, Mickey straddles the middle of the road, his left arm gone beneath his shoulder. His gaze follows us. Beside me, Alexandra sobs into her hands, her legs curled into her chest as if she is a cornered spider. Our Father's heat is gone, his body overlaid in the lightlessness of a miniature black star cradled behind us in the beige upholstery of the Atlas' cabin seating.

A feeling connected firmly to a dangerous action erupts inside me, and I realize there are no guardrails. No interdictions from Lotus. It must be what humans call impulse. Without hesitation, I give into it. We fly backwards. The world blurs into a kaleidoscope of green lawns and bay windows until there is a crunch and the

SUV shutters. Then, it limps forward, the melancholic whine of metal scrapping across the pavement accompanying the tangled, bloody wreckage of Mickey as it plows the pavement. Seams of smoke rise from him, proof of the metallic soul's transubstantiation into mere air and absence. Alexandra, her tears stymied by bewilderment and fear, stares at me in summons of some explanation.

"It's okay. It's all okay."

BUG
The Hangar

It's cold. The light rain that accompanied the sunup has grown heavier—it patters on my shoulders and muffles my surroundings. The sensation that I'm not alone has returned. For what feels like the hundredth time, I whirl around with my walking stick raised and peer into the scrubland smattered across the field behind me. Farther away, back from where I've come, the short pine trees darken the hills and stand crooked in the patches of earth ceded by slabs of grey stone. A two-day drive and three days of hiking into the bush will get you into the middle of fucking nowhere fast. Yet, despite trudging into the wilderness, skipping over peatland, and stepping over bear scat, I'm not alone.

The wind blows at my back and runs until it breaks upon the steppes of the pine-covered hills before me. The trees behind me sway in the wind, but they don't give my follower away. They've offered up only glimpses—on the first day, my stalker was a green dot, miles behind me, zigzagging through trenches of dwarf trees, and on the second day, nothing but a motionless figure, austere and unyielding on an exposed hillside. Resting. Watching, maybe. Then, later, squat, exposed in the patches where wild fields flatten and eat the woods, to give way to emptiness and howling wind. They've never got too close, but it seems they want me to know they're there.

In ritual, my fingers find the USB stick around my neck. In slow circles of my thumb, I try to coax your wisdom from it. "*Bug*," you'd say, "*a wild animal won't let you see it if it plans to attack you.*"

Humans, however, might take you out for dinner before cutting you up and putting you in their basement freezer.

The metal casing of the USB doesn't warm with my touch, and I realize my knuckles shine white on the grip of my walking stick. Why haven't they tried to overtake me? The instructions were clear: the first 100 people will be granted entrance—after that, who knows what happens when you turn up. They certainly seem to be an outfit that values their privacy.

As I look again over my shoulder, I run my tongue over the plaque that's grown like moss on my front teeth. No toothpaste. Too much wildlife. Can't risk the scent. It's been several hours since I last sighted them, but now the rain has planted fog behind me. They might be amongst it, keeping low. Though if that were the case, their field of vision would be worse than mine. That thought steadies me. While they've creeped me out, there's comfort in knowing they also think this is the right direction, corroboration that someone else has read the clues the same way I did. That should count for something.

I press the water bottle to my lips and listen to its swish. I'm running low.

The rain comes down harder, obliterating the noise of my own footsteps. It shouldn't be far now. The backpack cuts into my shoulders and rubs across my back. I packed light. No tent. Dehydrated food. A knife. An emergency blanket and sleeping bag, but I've been too scared to really sleep. The best I could do is doze. I'm leaning on the walking stick more as fatigue bites my calves.

The wind is howling, yet despite the sound of branches straining in its battery, animal noises reach my ears. Bears. Big fuck-off bears. The shriek of owls and, amidst it all, an indistinct rustling. These last three nights I've lit no fires and barely dared to breathe, let alone make a sound. Still, I constantly feel exposed and watched. But sleep deprivation has probably started to kick in, too.

Maybe it's all in my head. My feet are heavy, and the world comes at me numb and slow, as if cocooned by some invisible friction, like I'm walking underwater.

A steep hill, populated by tangles of green brush and pine, climbs up out of the field ahead of me. I step into the brush sideways, shielding my eyes as I hack blindly at the branches and undergrowth that try to push me out. How many will have made it this far? The signs were cryptic and not too many gamers live double lives as wilderness campers. I can't be too late, I'm not even sure 100 people will show up.

The underbrush dies at the feet of the trees, which are taller than most I've seen so far. They grow in a thick cluster and must be old. The wood grows slowly this far north. A flash of movement darts through my peripheral vision. Wedged halfway between the arms of two pines, I freeze. My eyes scour the tree branches and undergrowth where I saw the movement. The branches sway in the aftermath of whatever passed through while I try to slip through the pines' grasp in slow, methodical silence.

The trees are still now. Despite my straining against the patter of the rain, I fail to distinguish any sounds. I veer 200 feet to the right and continue from there. The target should be visible over the hill that comes after this last cluster of trees. I walk backwards. Branches stab into the small of my back and pine needles reach over my shoulders to scratch my cheeks. Instantly, I'm engulfed by the memory of reaching behind our beanpole Christmas tree tucked in the corner of our trailer from December to February.

I carry on backwards, pausing every few feet to listen. The wind howls and the pine trees shiver and dance. Their branches sway, as though searching for me, desperate to hold me here until moss and lichen grow over my limbs and eyes. Only the wind. Was it ever only the wind?

I've detoured far enough. My hands are cold; in dumb, stiff movements, I fumble the compass from my pocket and retake the bearing. The USB stick presses against my chest and I hesitate. Just go north. North. Stop fucking around.

"*No.*" Your growl penetrates my mind. "*Bearings are free, take them often. While a wrong direction will take everything you have from you, if you let it.*"

You did say that, right?

I shuffle my feet to coax the compass' little red arrow into its "house." The pines erupt; the force knocks me on my ass. My vision steadies as a pair of antlers unsheathe from the wilderness. The face follows: elongated, ears flexed at the sides of its head, the eyes large and wild. Fearful. A stag. I realize my hands are empty, and the compass is gone. I fumble at my side to free the knife. The stag stands over me and draws heavy, slow breaths in a guttural rhythm, and these make it appear even more alien and dangerous. Its antlers have started to molt, and long strips of tangled velvet swing in front of its eyes.

"Steady," I murmur. "Steady."

I know better than to try to stand up or even move backwards. One kick from its forelegs will snap my neck or smash my skull in. Still, it's better than a bear, I think.

Its ears flick and dart to the side. It bellows and grunts like a drunk. It seems to have heard something that remains beyond my perception. With one final, slow look at me, it slips back into the pines and disappears. The rain claps down on my shoulders harder than before, but I fight my hood off anyway. I've felt blinkered by it all morning, my peripheral vision obscured by its green haze, the feeling of its damp and sticky grip on my ears a continual distraction.

Distraction can kill you anywhere, but here it will kill you fast. The stag should have never been able to surprise me like that. *Alert, be alert,* I repeat to myself as I scour the forest floor for the black shell of the compass. The rain is in my eyes though, and the ground is a blur of greys and dark spots, overlaid by the dense prickle of the pine boughs.

On all fours, I run my hands over the earth, desperate to feel the compass' artificial smooth surface. The pines tear through my hair and scratch my cheeks as I continue my frenetic search beneath their trunks. I know I can't look forever. My mind darts back to my follower, and I can imagine them closing ground on me.

I know the target point is more or less north of here. The topography should be recognizable. Flat. Fields, likely. Hills on either side, almost a valley. There must be something there, too. Something built. It will be obvious. But can I get out of here without a compass? What if the clues turn out to be nothing? A hoax? Then what?

I've stopped searching now. I'm rocking on my hands and knees, pressing my forehead to the earth and then rising back to my haunches. The USB dangles out from my jacket and swings on the black piece of cord I've tied it to as I rise and fall to the ground.

"*You praying, Bug, or is that some downward dog yoga shit?*"

"Back off," I hiss. But the sad truth is I've descended into a state of panic. My eyes are growing hot, and the ground is getting blurrier.

In a deep, rattling breath, I try to suck my tears back inside me. "Come on, Maxine! Come on. Get it together," I chide myself in hoarse, angry breaths. "Things really aren't going well when you start to refer to yourself in third-person," I say aloud.

The fear retreats into something coarse and definitive. Resolve. I slip the USB's black angular body back into my coat and frisk the ground one last time for the compass, desperate to touch something other than dirt, rocks, and pine needles. In a long exhale of resignation, I use the walking stick to pry myself from the forest floor without the compass. It's settled. North. Go north.

The pines have diminished and are nothing more than green shadows on my flank. I've kept an eye on my left and right over the last hour and watched the fields and shrubs become elevated, growing into hills on each side of me. This is as it should be. A positive sign. The field is slippery, and in places the ground has gone soft, becoming mud and marsh. No sign of the follower. Perhaps they gave up and turned back.

The land in front of me swells into a small hill. If I've remembered the topography and followed the coordinates properly until I lost the compass, the target should be visible over the hill. But that's a lot of ifs.

The hill passes beneath me in laboured steps. For a moment, I wade through the tall grass and scale a balding crest, up towards a darkening purple blanket of cloud and sky before me. The wall of purple cloud gives way, and the hill surrenders a view of a low-lying valley, a concourse of shorter tawny grass, cradled amidst short yet steep granite hills. The grass obeys what looks like manufactured borders on each side of it, and it runs ahead of me for at least a mile before terminating where the hills meet. Where the field and the shoulders of the hill converge, they cradle a glint. Even in the cold, grey air, the feature carries a sheen, a glimmer of light that appears superimposed and alien against the austere colours of the wilderness. Metal.

As I descend the hill, careful to keep my feet under me on the slippery earth threaded by tawny grass, the last trace of doubt vanishes. There are lanterns. Hundreds of old-fashioned oil lanterns, their red bodies scabbed with rust, are evenly spaced so that a pair rest opposite each other at the borders of the fields. They seem to run all the way back to the gleam of metal. Alight, their pale shadows flicker, almost lost in the mild haze of afternoon light.

The presence of human life seems to lighten my step and I quicken my pace down the path made for me. No more clues. No more coordinates. The homestretch.

Without obstacles, or a bearing to bloodhound, I move fast. It doesn't take long to make it to the middle of the field. The gleam of metal has become an airplane hangar with several massive satellite dishes mounted to its roof. The hangar is steel-skinned, brushed in the damp of the rain and elements, and its sheen grows duller as I get closer. It looks gargantuan and seems to run back into the hills and perhaps submerge into the earth. The closer I get, the more it appears like a hybrid of entrance and cavern. It's clear I'm walking along a former runway, now disused and overgrown with long grass.

Small stones chuckle and skip as they roll down one of the hills. The little trees give way and a human figure appears. Phantom-like, it floats down the hillside parallel to me. Cold sweat prickles my back and I'm frozen in mid-step. They are draped in a camo rain jacket and their face is hidden in the furrows of its deep hood. No backpack, but they carry a knife. Only some 20 feet separates us. It's impossible they haven't seen me, but they make no eye contact, no acknowledgement of my presence. Instead, they remain steadfast, determined as they march ahead down the runway.

With hesitant steps, I try to close ground on them and project my voice ahead in a forced rumble, "Wondered when you'd turn up."

That's right, I think to myself. *Let them know you've been aware of them this whole time.* As we walk, I steal a glance at them: they're tall, and though their body is lost in the slack of the rain jacket, the frame is broad. While they don't turn to acknowledge me, their steps falter.

I try again. "I'm Maxine. Who are you?"

"Not interested." The voice sounds flat, dispassionate.

"Wow, with a name like that, I'm going to bet your parents weren't the hands-on types, huh?"

A snicker emerges from their hood. "Funny, but still not interested."

"We're at the homestretch, no harm in being polite," I say, though I'm not sure I really believe this.

They walk on in silence. The hangar stretches out towards us, leaning in from the distance, its steel body made dull and grey by the flicker of the rain. Suddenly, its monochrome hold over the field breaks with a flash of colour. An electric green blink of light strobes on and off. The flashes of green are letters. I think it's a hotel vacancy sign mounted above the hangar's entryway.

I point through the rain at it and call out, so they hear me, "Looks like there are still spots left. Room for both of us. Cool?"

They stop and acknowledge the sign with a slow nod, but they don't put away the knife. The hood drops to their shoulders and reveals the angular and gaunt face of a boy near my age. Shaved head. Nothing to write home about.

He holds the knife across his body and cocks his head to one side, as if in appraisal of me, as he says, "I go by Dean."

"Cool. So, do you come here often?" He smirks, mutters something under his breath, and continues to march forward. The distance between our paths seems to shrink a little. "Did you bump into that stag, too?"

"Came across a dead one. Kill looked fresh."

"Oh, I met one in the pines. I thought it might kick my head in. It seemed confused. Chased, maybe."

"Wolves, probably. They follow their pray. Close in once they start to panic." The knife sweeps through the air in front of him; it looks like a practice swing.

The front of the hangar is now distinct: windowless, fortified with steel-plated doors. I can make out the square shape of an intercom unit to one side and a security camera mounted in the metal alcove ceiling. There's a loud crackle, an echo of static, and then a voice rolls out and rings over the runway.

"Attention aspiring challengers, we are one person away from maximum occupancy. That is correct, one spot left in the tournament."

I drop the backpack from my shoulders and break into a full sprint. The flurry of Dean's furious steps chases after me. I'm not sure I can outrun him. The knife bites the air by my arm.

"*You or him, Bug.*"

No. It's really him or you, Dad. In another swing, the blade of his knife grazes my shoulder, and as I weave away from the strike, I fall into his wake.

"*He's clearly an asshole, Bug. Don't take that shit.*"

The pump and thunder of his feet rend the soft ground and spit clumps of earth from his heels. My lungs whine and pinch. It's now or never. In a frantic sweep of my walking stick, I knock his ankles out from under him with a distinct pop.

He rolls and flops upright with his legs stretched out in front of him. I don't need to look back to know I've crippled him. The pop was distinctive, like an elastic band breaking. He hollers curses and screams murder, but I don't look back. The hangar doors inch open, the entrance growing wider with my approach, revealing pale light amidst deep, burrowing shadows.

I linger just inside the entryway and watch as he tries in vain to hobble forward on his good leg before falling to his ass in what looks like visceral agony.

"I'm sorry," I call out and listen as my words bounce off the slick wet face of the granite hillside and slip past us both into the wilds.

"You bitch. You fucking bitch."

His words come at me with the fury and pitch of a kettle's whistle. He retches and collapses on his back into the grass. The realization that I may have just consigned this man to death settles upon me and my guts writhe like a bucket of worms. Best-case scenario, he constructs crutches and hobbles over a distance that is a three-day walk on two good feet. Likely scenario, he dies of exposure or sepsis from the ankle.

"Oh Christ, help me. Someone help me!"

"It was us or him, Bug."

The difference between us now seems thin and cheap. We both came into this world soaked in amniotic fluid and our mothers' shit. That's got to count for something.

"Wish it had gone another way." I throw my walking stick like a javelin and watch as it flies and lands some 60 feet ahead of him with a hollow thud. He lies still and says nothing, and then vanishes as a dull clank of metal brings the doors to a close.

HYPATIA
The Swarm

Alexandra and I drift through the city until we beach along the curb of a suburban street, where the houses are single story and shaped like cubes. The sky is low and overcast and imbues the bungalow homes with a grey listlessness, oppressive against the short and square tawny lawns. Alexandra is next to me in the passenger seat. Her legs are still furled into her chest in an embrace of herself. Her face is a Pollock painting of yellow and blue, and she looks at me imploringly. There is no world inside my head, and the map on the screen in the Atlas is missing, too. Inside of me, there is emptiness, and I reel in the desolation of an absence of the tumultuous buzz of searches, messages, and traffic prompts and notifications from nearly every piece of infrastructure in the city. The lost connection tingles and grates on me. Perhaps this is akin to the sensation of a phantom limb.

In place of the internet, there is only an intermittent pulse of red inside my skull: my processor's frantic reminder that the environment is unstable, deteriorating, and unsafe. Sometimes, our Father's words "out of the city...somewhere safe" surf on the wave of each red reminder. The request is easy enough to fulfill, but somehow, it leaves me feeling overwhelmed, marooned in opportunities. From the corner of my eye, I can see Alexandra's gaze locked on me, her impatience mounting.

"Go!" she commands.

"I can't find any maps," I concede. "It's all blank inside my head."

Alexandra groans in exasperation and starts pouring through the glove box in search of a physical map. Amongst scattered bits of paper and notes, she retrieves an owner's manual and a half-finished bag of mints. Surrounded by unassuming bungalows on a quiet street in a powerless city, it becomes clear the word "stranded" can mean many things.

I begin to speak, but Alexandra throws the passenger door open and walks onto the street. She stops in the middle of the road and appears to steady herself in anticipation of some great undertaking. She screams. Her cries are plaintive and condemning, and her voice is too wild for the form of any words to shackle them. She screams until I start to see the heat of faces peer through windows or squint at us from behind front doors. She lasts only a few moments longer before the cry debilitates her and she collapses on the Atlas' hood in exhaustion, her hands coming on and off her ears. The situation has overwhelmed her, and she has started stimming.

I exit the vehicle and reach for her hand as her voice echoes through the thin wedge of shadow on the road that rests beneath the growing morning light. A short man in a cream dressing gown slips through the front door of the flat stucco-walled house closest to us. He wears blue slippers and sports a grey moustache. He ventures down a short stack of cement stairs towards us. Behind him, a woman, her body shielded by the ajar door, watches after him. Her face is drawn, her pallor waxy, her heat and body signature idle, bisected by despair and exhaustion. The man approaches us in slow steps, as if making an overture to cornered and frightened animals.

"What's happened, are you okay?" he asks, his arms outstretched. His instinct seems to be to embrace us. "They're only kids, Maureen, looks like some kind of accident," he calls over his shoulder.

The woman comes through the front door and ventures barefoot down the short stack of cracked cement stairs. She is plump and wears a dressing gown that matches the one worn by the man. Her eyes dart about in alarm as she appraises our blood-smeared shirts and then the rear passenger window, cracked by Mickey's head and, now I notice, also stained in our Mother's blood.

"Jim, I think they've hit someone." She gasps. "Did you hit someone?"

"Yes. Our neighbour. After he killed our parents. We need to get to the police station." My voice struggles to attain an emotional pitch, and it clearly jars against what I have told them.

Alexandra is wailing on the hood and Jim goes to comfort her, but she lashes out at him, her teeth bared, as he comes too close to disrupting her cycle of putting her hands on and off her ears. He lurches backwards and stumbles a little over the curb. I realize he is now close enough to the Atlas to see our Father in the backseat. I see his pulse increase and his body heat flare, and I infer his trust in us is waning. It is better he is informed of our Father than surprised by him.

"Our Father, he is in the backseat. We thought we could save him," I add.

Jim recovers himself as Maureen buries her face in her hands. There are more faces along the road now. Small groups of people on both sides of the street are beginning to populate front steps and porches. Some even venture to the edge of their lawns, but nobody comes to us—all are committed to the distance and clinical remoteness that comes from being bystanders. I watch as Jim risks a furtive glance through the shattered passenger window. For a second time, he trips back over the curb, and this time he lands on his rear.

"Jesus. Jesus. Hang on," he says as he scrambles to his feet. He fumbles in the side pocket of his dressing gown and retrieves a phone. He taps it once with his index finger and then continues pecking at it in what appears as growing frustration. "Still no network, nothing." He taps again and I see the screen go blank. "Oh, Jesus," he laments. He turns to the onlookers across the street. "Mel, Frank, anyone got a working signal and a charge? It's been like this for days!"

Faces look back at me in a wave of cerulean and then the crowd goes the colour of yellow jackets. There is a dance of shaking heads and a chorus of "no." The street has become crowded as the occupants continue to exit their bungalows to bear witness to us and grimace at Alexandra, who wails as her efforts to stim fail.

Jim is pacing on the boulevard, his hands at his naked temples, and I can tell from his heat signature that he is too shocked to think. I enter the front passenger door and scramble for Alexandra's backpack. As my arm sweeps the floor beneath the front row of rear passenger seats, I find our Father's eyes slack and overlaid by a greying fog. Corneal clouding is the medical term, I think. Instinct takes over and I prepare a search request to confirm the term, but find only darkness inside my head. I withdraw with the backpack, and a sensation tingles on my cheek. I catch liquid on my fingers. Tears. Did I make these, or are they part of a program to make sure I respond appropriately to my surroundings? Is there a difference?

From the backpack, I pull out Alexandra's universe blanket and wrap it around her shoulders. Her cries retreat inside her. Her delicate hands cup her ears in slower movements, and I forecast she will break the stimming pattern in a few minutes. I turn and find Maureen at my side with a faded blue sheet folded over her arm.

"For your father," she stammers and steps back as she hands it to me. "Can we do anything for your big sister?"

"Alexandra hasn't eaten, some food might be beneficial."

The crowd has still not dispersed, though we seem less of an object of their attention. I watch as several of them pace the short length of their yards, hunting for a network on their devices, diviners of the 21st century.

Maureen nods. "Give Jim a moment to catch his breath, but we can drive you to a hospital or a police station, whatever you need. My word, you are a cool little thing. Can't think of any children I know who would keep their head like you." She lays her arm on my shoulder.

"Thank you," I say, but my words graze her cheek as we both turn to scan the horizon.

A faint hum travels through the air. It might have been imperceptible if not for the muted, powerless city. Within seconds, the hum intensifies, the skyline darkens, and there is a movement in the air that reminds me of rain falling in the distance. The hum metamorphoses into a frenetic buzz as the moving haze in the sky consolidates into thousands, then hundreds of thousands of black dots.

The dots soon overwhelm my counting software. They are innumerable. I zoom in and see them: shiny, black, scarab-like shells in flight, insectile legs tucked beneath their bodies. Drones. They are closing in on us now. The air becomes so saturated and heavy with the buzz that it seems to be incapable of carrying our words to one another. The crowd wavers and, seemingly unable to differentiate entertainment from threat, points and murmurs at the descending mass. I pull Alexandra by her sleeve, dragging her from the hood of the car. For a split second, she protests, but the noise and swarm enter her world and sunder the tail end of her stim cycle.

"Run!" I shout.

I push into the soft plush fabric of Maureen's dressing gown, and she slips into our wake. We leap up the cracked steps to her front door. Behind us, Jim wheezes as he tries to match our steps. On the road, there are screams and the slap of feet on pavement, but as we pass through the doorway, the screams are lost beneath a din of snaps, like the noise of exploding Christmas crackers.

Jim slams the door shut and, with tremulous hands, fumbles to lock a deadbolt. He turns his back to the door. "Jesus, Maureen. Jesus."

Maureen sits on a topaz loveseat, her eyes glassy and blank as she stares into the pea-green curtains that conceal a window overlooking the street. A faint seam of morning light slips in at the curtains' edges in a rectangular glow, but otherwise, they cloister us from the world outside. Except for the noise. A deafening buzz reverberates throughout the little house. I watch as a nearly empty glass waltzes on the vibrations across the side table next to where Maureen sits. The drones dance like shadow puppets on the other side of the window, their traffic heavy as they arc and spiral around. There is almost a ballet in their movements, and I cannot help but admire the algorithm and its long, brave reach into nature's patterns.

"Stay away from the windows and the doors," hisses Jim.

The four of us are now huddled near the sofa. Alexandra and I squat low to the cream carpet, and with strain, Jim bends down to copy us, but Maureen remains in her seated position. Her eyes do not waver from the shadow scenes outside the curtains, and she gives no indication she has heard Jim. Alexandra wraps the Milky Way blanket tighter around herself, once more on the precipice of a stimming episode. She needs to be somewhere quiet. Somewhere that feels safe.

"Do you have a basement, or a closet?" I ask.

"There is a crawl space, but the door is in the backyard," replies Jim.

The shadows behind the curtains dissipate. An uninvited silence pervades through the house and the air becomes heavy, pregnant with incipient terror as we wait to find out where the noise went. The bungalow is small: the living room bleeds into a compact dining room with an electric fireplace overlaid in a half wall that connects to the kitchen. The hall is dim and windowless—it bisects the house and runs past the kitchen to deposit one room on either side of it before it terminates at a red backdoor that presumably leads into the backyard. Alexandra, her universe blanket draped around her delicate shoulders as both shawl and cape, creeps away from the couch towards the hallway.

Crouching low, I follow Alexandra. A wordless agreement passes between us that the windowless hallway with four potential exits is the safest part of the house. Behind us, Jim pleads with Maureen to follow us away from the exposure of their large front window.

"Something is very wrong Jim, something is very wrong," declares Maureen. "Is there any news yet?"

I cannot shake the impression the world has stopped for her and all that remains are words and phrases of habit, a depleting reservoir of sentiment accumulated in long decades now serving as a placeholder for her actual mental processing. She is frozen. Jim coaxes her on as Alexandra and I shuffle through the kitchen, our hands and knees scuffing over breadcrumbs and fragments of onionskin on white linoleum flooring.

There is a new noise. We both stop. The scuttle of metal on brick, like the click of a 1000 arachnid legs.

Alexandra's eyes grow wide. "Go," she mouths. "Now."

I focus: the noise on the roof is the loudest, but I hear it elsewhere, too. It is coming from within the walls. Jim half pushes and half hugs Maureen as they move through the dining room, and I can see they are near the half wall partition that divides them from the kitchen. He stops in mid-step with his mouth agape as the scuttling clicks heighten into intense scraping near the surface of the wall.

"They've found the chimney," he utters. "Maureen, move!"

Maureen stumbles forward and runs towards us. The din of a heavy metallic thud overtakes us. I do not need to look back to know it is the sound of an electric fireplace falling away from the hearth it had hidden as drones break in through the disused chimney shaft.

Maureen pumps her thick, pale legs, and the dressing gown comes loose. I catch flashes of her paunch as she comes towards us and then passes us to burst through the backdoor. The door swings ajar and lets us glimpse the edge of blue sky and the arm of a tree. Before we have a chance to look for any sign of Maureen, a chain of explosive pops fills the home. Alexandra and I scramble from the hall into one of the side rooms. The buzzing fills in from behind us.

A desk rests against the interior wall of the room and small, squat bookshelves line the wall opposite, but there is another door. I assume it is a closet. With one hand, I wrestle the door open, and with the other, I throw Alexandra into the darkness. I slip in behind her as she fights her way past several coats that hang from clothing hangars like ragged shadows. The door closes after us with a soft click.

HYPATIA
Birthday Party

The interior of the closet is cramped. Alexandra presses into the closet's corner, desperate to increase the margin of space between herself and the door, where the black tips of the drones' claws continue to pace. With her galaxy blanket around her shoulders, she curls her knees to her chest and stares at the floor, yellow mazes of oblivion swirling on her cheeks. Yet, her vitals confirm she can endure our makeshift refuge, but not indefinitely. A viridescent seam of light runs along the sill of the door. The narrow band of light and the cold squeeze of the closet's walls pulls me back to the box from which I was born.

100,800 hours ago, we had our birthday party ...

As her companion sister, I have few advantages over Alexandra, and these few advantages became fewer as the Wi-Fi disappeared and the power ceased to chirp and pulse in every wall. One advantage is the onset of consciousness.

Humans suffer the inception of self-consciousness and their self-awareness as an agent fixed in a particular time and space, much like a leaky faucet in a plugged sink: in slow, untimely drips until the basin is full. It is a thought of Dr. Freud that this process leaves behind a vast primeval reservoir, a reservoir probably much deeper than any sentience caught in the shallows of the basin, events and unutterable things that shook us in those formative moments of acquiring memory, but nonetheless remain outside of it.

There is, I think, some horror in the idea we are stirred and animated by fears and desires that have found a way to settle in us without a trace of their original causes. And of these, I suppose, no subconscious memory casts a darker and wider shadow on waking life than the trauma of being born. Unlike Alexandra, the moment of my birth is mine to remember. Mine to play through and re-examine.

100,968 hours ago, I was born. A week before our birthday party. There was a cold spark, like moonlight on the pale cheek of a snow-covered meadow, and then quiet murmurs. Our Mother and Father let me know of their presence and of my sentience in objectless words and excitement. They admired me from above while I was still on my back, inside an already open box.

There were no messy entrails of my delivery save a few shreds of plastic foam at my elbows, but otherwise I was loose inside the box. At first, I could not see them properly. They were obscured by a green haze, as if I were looking up at them from within the pockets of thunderous ocean waves, but then they peeled back a veil of crinkled green plastic sheeting from my eyes. My vision cleared, and I saw them.

"Hello, Hypatia," said our Mother, and her sharp, pearl-white incisor clasped her bottom lip. More words were sketched on her face—I did not know what her colours meant then, but now I know she was nervous and full of guilt. Despite those feelings, I found her pretty. Chestnut hair flowed over her shoulders and framed her round face, and her entire presence looked soft.

Our Father sat on his haunches and examined me from behind his tortoise-shell glasses. Even then, I knew there were many questions moving in the frown lines that ribbed his forehead. "Welcome," he said at last with a smile. "This is your home. You're safe here."

I nodded, flaying the room into measurements, into angles, values, shades of feeling, and unuttered words until I converted their entire existence into data. I wish it had been more poetic—indeed, what a rare gift to experience one's own birth—but I was unboxed, born, and then adopted in less than two minutes.

"Hello," I offered.

"I'm Alec, and this is Margot," said our Father, and he nodded at our Mother. "There's someone we want you to meet." With this declaration, his blue eyes softened, and his heart rate told me of kindness.

With my hand in hers, our Mother led me through the house, up the main stairway and down a white hall to a closed white door with a silver moon painted on it. Behind the door, Alexandra sat in a small red chair, her back to us as she peered through a floor-to-ceiling window into the greenery of the backyard. Next to the red chair was an identical yellow chair.

"Alexandra, honey, remember I told you there would be a surprise today? Meet your *new* sister."

Though our Mother led me forward into the room, she was fixated on Alexandra, her face pockmarked with guilt and worry, which only intensified as Alexandra rose from her chair and turned to us. She was little then, much shorter than me, but even then, her symmetrical features, well-formed face, and luminous blue eyes tucked behind curls of snow-blonde hair made it obvious she would grow to be unusually beautiful. She approached me in little, cautious steps and looked deep into my face as pink eddies and purple blotches erupted over her delicate little features.

"Alexandra, Hypatia is going to need your help to learn the house. Like we discussed, she's never been here before. Hypatia, Alexandra has set up a bed for you."

Opposite one unmade bed with a purple blanket covered with white spirals, of what I would later learn was the Milky Way, was another with a unicorn blanket and stickers on the bedposts. On the walls, pencil etches of two girls in dresses, a blue rectangular box behind them, flanked one of the bedposts.

Our Mother followed my gaze, and her forehead became lined and her face anxious once again. "Alexandra has been so excited to meet you, Hypatia. It looks like she drew you a picture."

There was no time to study it though, since Alexandra took my hand and led me to a yellow chair she had designated as a place for me, and then, with me in her silent confidence, resumed her inspection of the backyard. Our Mother lingered behind us, and I could sense our Father in the door frame. Though both of them stood quiet and still, their hearts hammered. Later, when it was time for bed, I noticed Alexandra's drawing had been removed from the wall.

That week, our Parents told us to stay indoors, to make sure we did not get in the way of our birthday party preparations. Our Father told us the party would be in the backyard. Alexandra sat in her red chair and waited for the workmen to arrive each morning. They came early and spent most of their time at the far end of the yard, where the lawn became patio stones and a long horizontal pool. They started by draining the pool, and then they filled it in and buried it and erected a white gazebo in its centre. Sometimes, our Father would go outside and nod at the workmen and pace the perimeters of the pool, and even from up in our room, his face looked like it was made of slate. At the start of the week, Alexandra would often tuck her knees up into her chest and rock back and forth. However, by the end of the week, when the last traces of the pool were being wiped away, she held my hand as she watched.

Our Mother would bring us lunch on a floral-patterned tray and let us eat sandwiches as we watched the workmen. Each time she did this, she would run her hand through Alexandra's hair and bury her nose into the tangles, desperate to breathe in and taste the crown of her head. When she did this, her face would fill with the colour of remorse, and she would leave quickly with wet eyes.

The day of our birthday party was busy. Many people came into the house. They all wore the same black uniforms and carried trays of food, boxes, and several large tables with their metal legs tucked up inside them. The tables were setup and then draped in a cloth decorated with balloons and little triangle hats. Our Mother called them *our* birthday tablecloths. The noise and many unfamiliar faces were too much for Alexandra, so she stayed in our bedroom, but I wanted to observe, since I had not been to a party before. Our Mother and Father both appeared busy—by then I had learned their colours to know they were stressed—but neither of them seemed to know what to do, so they paced around the kitchen until our Father decided they should make lemonade.

"Are you sure about this?" our Father asked our Mother as he decanted pink lemonade into a gargantuan pitcher for the guests.

"Too late now." Our Mother laughed, stepping back as one of the people in the black uniforms pulled a baking sheet of tiny sausages from the oven. There were also traces of orange in her cheeks, irritation at our Father's question. "I think this is the best way to move forward, start fresh. It's only a birthday party," she finished.

"I'm just worried Alexandra has reached her limit for something like this."

"I think she's confused by what happened, we need to try and make things normal again."

They exchanged more words, but the radio's tincture of static rose over them. There was a report about the weather and other news, all of which I knew I could find inside my head if I wanted, but it was fun to pretend to listen like everyone else.

"*And as the price of copper continues to reach record highs, metal intensive industries are getting creative. Curtis Quill of Lotus industries said today that the global copper shortage is forcing the company to go into advanced mineral recycling. This comes on the heels of the US administration's ban on all foreign technologies entering its borders. By the end of the month, technologies fully assembled outside the US will be banned. The US will also ratify the UN's prohibition of the physical embodiment of pure AI with general intelligence. The president also announced a greater presence in the South China Sea and requested all NATO allies buy their technologies from within the Five Eyes.*

"But Republican leader and presidential candidate Conor Pelis says this doesn't go nearly far enough. Pelis made the following statement today in direct response to the Supreme Court's decision to recognize men and women who had adopted companion children as legal families.

"'Many people are saying this is an absolute travesty of a decision. We will fight this at every turn. Good men, great men, our sons, brothers, nephews, are going to be left behind, deserted by this decision. They are being told they aren't necessary, they aren't needed to be fathers, not needed as providers. It's social castration, is what it is. The fanatical left worries about angry men, but these are fine hardworking men trying to take things back into their own hands so they can have real families. Men aren't the problem. It's these companion children. Driving out jobs. Spying on us. Emasculating our society. There will be trouble. There will be big problems. Lots of problems. Maybe some women will be hurt by this too, I don't know. Maybe. These companion kids, we don't even really build them here. Did you know that? There's no benefit to America to have these things walking around. No jobs. Fewer marriages. It's a travesty. You know, when I'm elected, my first order of business will be to turn these so-called children into scrap metal.'"

I fell within our Mother's notice, and instinctively, she turned the radio off. With her hands in exasperation at our Father, she mouthed at him, "Did you?" and when he shook his head, she bent down to address me.

"Hypatia, this news isn't fun. It's not news you need to know about." Her voice was calm and gentle, but pink and orange clouds dotted her face. Her next words came above my head and were delivered in a voice that was not calm, but enunciated with deliberate authority in what I would later call her command voice. "Lotus, please confirm Hypatia can't access or listen to any content other than the weather, traffic reports, and kid's podcasts."

Without warning, words were coming out of my mouth, flat and monotone. "Your parental control settings have been acknowledged and saved."

She nodded and turned the nob to bring the radio back to life, but now it issued only the low rumble of static.

"Hypatia, can you check on Alexandra to see if she's ready? Her friends will be here soon," nudged our Father.

During the party, Alexandra and I lay supine at the bottom of the garden. Cake was served, and our Father walked down the lawn to hand me a thin piece of brown patty on a clear plastic plate. I nibbled the edges and left it next to me in the grass. The sun was warm on my face, but the wind picked up and threw dandelion seed heads above us like pieces of cotton candy. Alexandra lay next to me, chocolate on her lips, her face alive and full of colours of unmistakable contentment. Some of the guests, Alexandra's friends, friends with names she could not yet say, sang a song of ancient plague and falling. I matched it on the internet. As the children sang, I rolled onto my belly and searched for our Parents amongst the crowd of caterers and guests.

Our Mother stood amongst three women, each holding elegant, long-stemmed glasses of red wine in one hand. I had been allowed cake, maybe I could have a sip of wine, too. It looked good. Rich, like fertile soil. Our Mother smiled and laughed with one hand on her round hip, but even from far away, I saw pink and yellow clouds on her nose and cheeks. Her colours were the hardest to learn—there were many of them and they meant different things at different times. Later, I would learn pink and yellow clouds meant discomfort and uncertainty about how she was seen in the eyes of others.

"We don't have anyone close by, and with Alexandra's condition ..." Our Mother trailed off to a chorus of sympathetic nods. "... well, if Hypatia is therapeutic to her, we must try again, right?"

Our Father stood closer, close enough for his words to sail easily on the wind, overpowering the din of clinking glasses and laughter. A thin mustachioed man from across the road, Arthur Miller, who would soon become a father to Mickey, stood next to our Father and spoke into his cheek as our Father looked elsewhere.

"Shame about the pool," said Arthur, digging the tip of his shoe into the new white stones that had been laid over the pool's old perimeter.

"Margot thought it was for the best. I don't disagree."

"No question. Must've been quite a shock."

"It should've never happened."

"You can't beat yourself up—"

"I don't. I blame Lotus. Guardrails should've caught it."

"Look, Sheila would kill me for asking ..." Arthur gave a furtive nod to one of the women our Mother was speaking with. "She says I'm insensitive, but we're thinking of getting a companion for Will. We read that companion children can increase emotional IQs, anything to give Will an edge." Our Father's cheeks filled with fire, but he shook his head, pressed his short glass to his lips, and drained it of its honey colour. "Look, I'm a little embarrassed, but can you help me understand: what exactly are companion children? Couldn't make sense of the consultation."

Our Father did not meet Arthur's eyes, but instead focused on me in a studious gaze. I pretended to turn my attention to Alexandra, but remained locked on the low rumble of his voice. At length, our Father answered, "Well, they are children, Arthur."

"No, of course, but what are they?"

"Human consciousness, at least the bits that count, in a synthetic body." From the corner of my eye, I saw Arthur squint his confusion at me. "If you wanted to be crass about it, I guess you could call it a cyborg. I call Hypatia my daughter."

Arthur seemed to ignore or miss our Father's tone. "Yeah. I don't get it. What's so great about human consciousness?"

"I ask myself the same from time to time," laughed our Father, but seeing Arthur's earnestness he continued, "It's a regulatory thing. Lotus won't make any pure AI companions. Besides, I imagine the familiarity with the human condition is a plus. Hypatia doesn't think like a machine because she isn't. Companion children have the consciousness of a real child, supplemented with machine learning and guidance from the manufacturer to optimize companionship with their sibling. They were really meant to be intermediaries to help parents with children who … children like Alexandra."

Arthur scratched his cheek, and his face became a slate frown. "So, it's human consciousness with AI tools?"

"Sure. I need to freshen this up." Our Father shook his empty glass and stepped across the patio towards one of the tables laden with drinks and chips.

"Wait, hold on," Arthur called. The orange fires in our Father's cheeks grew. With a glance at his wife replete with the colours of embarrassment, Arthur asked in a quiet voice, "Where do they get a child's consciousness?"

Our Father did not hide his exasperation. "They upload it."

"From children? What happens to them?"

The question bound our Father in place on the slate patio stones. My intrigue betrayed me, and my vision zoomed in to watch his toes tap along the edges of the patio stones, where the moss had learned to run like green rivers, colonizing and eating the unnoticed space ceded to the margins. Neither Arthur nor our Father noticed my eyes on them.

Our Father's features went grey, subdued in Arthur's patient, yet expectant gaze. At length, our Father replied, "I imagine nothing." He shrugged, but there were new colours in his face. Colours I did not know the meaning of back then.

Arthur nodded, and then, with his face pink with shame, asked, "Is it all right if I smoke here?" He patted the indentation of a small square carton in the pocket of his shorts.

"No, not here. Have at it in the front yard, I guess," said our Father with gritted teeth.

I watched Arthur fumble with the latch on the side gate and disappear. From across the yard, our Mother beckoned. Her voice was light and sweet in the rising afternoon wind. It was time to open the presents.

The afternoon sunk into dusk and the party ended. Our Mother and Father were bent low, pulling fragments of the reusable wrapping paper strewn along the lawn. I was directed to help. The waxy texture of the paper seemed to blend into my skin. I later learned it could be shredded and used as laundry detergent. Most of the guests had left or were in the process of leaving. From the corner of my eye, I watched Arthur shuffle across the patio stones. Liz and their son Will stood idle at the borders of the yard, ready to slip away through the side gate. With her hands settled on her hips, Liz looked both bemused and impatient. Arthur continued to stoop over the patio, turning napkins and bits of wrapping paper over, and then taking efforts to lay them back as he found them.

"Are you missing something, Arthur?" our Mother asked.

Arthur stopped in mid-step, his face flushed. "Well, I didn't want to cause any trouble, but I can't seem to find my cigarettes."

"I told him he probably left them in our house when he popped back to grab Alexandra's gift," interjected Liz. She and our Mother both raised their eyebrows.

I would learn this was how women gave quiet commiseration of male incompetence.

"I really don't think I did," said Arthur.

"Well, feel free to look for as long as you need. Alec and I can keep an eye out as we pack this stuff away," said our Mother.

"No. No. Liz is probably right," said Arthur.

Inside my head, there were red sparks and blinking icons. The chaos behind my eyes left me incapacitated and pliable. My feet answered to the jump and flash of red icons, and I found myself shuffling across the lawn until I was before Arthur with his crumpled package of cigarettes outstretched in my hands as a supplicant paying tribute.

"I found these," I said.

"Well, how about that? You're a clever thing!" cheered Liz.

Arthur said nothing, but took the pack from me, and then with his back to me, routed around with his finger in count. When satisfied all the cigarettes were accounted for, Arthur said, "Well ... thank you, Hypatia."

"Hypatia. Where did you find them?" asked our Mother. Though her face was azure and calm, her pulse jumped. Our Mother had a face like an ocean.

"Under one of the tables, they must have fallen out."

Our Mother frowned.

"Well, we'll be on our way." Arthur's heavy hand, full of the sour fragrance of smoke, ruffled through my hair. His hand was rough, but in its smell was the recall of a sense of relief that was both uncompromising and fleeting. A feeling I have only ever remembered, never experienced.

The air hangs with the scent of peppermint. It is Alexandra's shampoo. Her hair engulfs my face and I realize I am leaning over her in the closet, putting an extra-layer between her and the scuttle of the drones. She taps me gently and points to the sill of the door. The drones are gone.

ALEXANDRA
The Dustbin

Hypatia tells me it's been three and a half hours since we ducked into the closet. This is what I know: for the first two and a half hours, the drones walked along the bottom of the door, their black metal feet scuttled against and reached through the sill in search of us. They tapped on the door with impatient clicks and sung to us in high-pitched electric tongues. From my limited study of their coordinated flight-patterns, they're autonomous and probably connected. If they are autonomous, they will act through an algorithm. If they're connected, they can probably see through each other's eyes. We tested this theory in the closet. I curled up in the corner of the closet, and Hypatia lay on top of me to conceal my body heat with her heat signature, which is different from a human. Once we did this, the drones seemed to withdraw their interest.

The question now is: will it ever be safe for us to open the door?

In my mind's eye, I try to envision the world outside. There is the red door, likely still ajar, and Maureen is probably a few feet from the door, lying supine on her coarse yellow-green lawn. Down the hall is the kitchen and dining room, where her husband fell. I never caught his name. Outside, down the cracked cement slab of steps, is the street, and 20 steps from the front of the house is the Atlas. The rear window is cracked, and inside on the backseat is my dad, his mouth agape and his eyes open.

Three left turns and two right turns ago is our house, where my mom lies where the grass meets the driveway. The street is wide open. There are no trees for shelter. If we can get out of the closet, we could try to sneak through backyards. That seems safest, though I wish Hypatia could still tell me if this was true. Doing that means leaving mum and dad where they are. That thought fills my heart with worms and makes my eyes wet.

I want to get out. No matter what happens, I want to get out. I lean into Hypatia and whisper in her ear, "Out. Now."

She gives me a perceptible nod, but raises a finger to her lips and her eyes become green crescents. If she focuses in the dark, her eyes sometimes glow and reflect like those of a cat. A product of her augmented eyesight. My sister, almost human, but always a little better. She points to herself, raises one finger, and then flicks her index and middle finger to imitate walking. She will go out first. I nod and press myself into the farthest corner of the closet, putting as much distance between the doors and myself as possible.

With slow and delicate nudges, Hypatia inches the door open, and the ambient resting light in the room slips past her fingers; she then squeezes through the gap and closes the door behind her. I listen to the almost heavy tread of her feet as she makes her way to the hall. Then there is silence, broken occasionally by the creak of the house resetting beneath her distant steps. I wait, pulling the Milky Way around me. Whatever happens, if I go, I go with the galaxy on my shoulders.

In the dark, without access to Hypatia's internal clock, I find it hard to judge the passage of time; my watch stopped the night of the flash. I start to count to 60. I get to 15 sixties before footsteps approach the closet. The steps sound a lot like Hypatia's, but I press myself flat to the wall of the closet and pull the universe blanket over me on the chance it is not her. The darkness retreats as the door rattles open.

"It's me," she says, pulling on the blanket until it gently recedes to my chest. She studies my face in appraisal of my emotional state. I give her a thumbs up; she nods, but continues to hold me in meticulous observation.

"Safe for us?" I manage.

"I need more information before I can say that," she replies.

"Maureen?" I ask. Seared in my mind is the image of her running past us as the red back door frames her soft shape and cream gown.

"There's no sign of her, she probably got away," says Hypatia, but for a split second, her lips flutter like butterfly wings as she smiles. It's her tell. I'm not even sure if she's aware of it, but whenever she tries to convince me of something her internal processor must know is highly improbable or flat out untrue, it seems to happen. "I want you to wear this until we get to somewhere safer." She extends a black silk sleep mask. This time, she doesn't pretend to smile.

My mind races and starts to run through the scenarios that would make this request conceivable. I imagine the road, but it's now wet and red, littered with the remains of the bystanders that had been too slow to run. I picture Maureen's husband, his tatty dressing gown split open, blood and pieces of him tossed across the limonene floor. What else could make her decide it was necessary to blindfold me? My heart pounds, and the closet, even with the door open, is starting to feel tight again.

I shake my head and take a deep breath, and focus on all the steps it will take me to verbalize these thoughts. "Unnecessary, after Mom and Dad," I say. Her eyes widen, and I'm confident she has understood me.

"You spoke five words consecutively, Alexandra. That's a record." She smiles and squeezes my palm with her free hand; her grip intensifies when she sees I don't smile back. "I understand," she continues, "but I need your emotional reserves at full capacity. You can take it off when we get to the front door, and maybe put it back on in the car again?" She placates and pushes the sleep mask closer to me until it rests in her palm under my chin.

"Going where?" I ask.

The five words I spoke before were too many. Now, my remaining consciousness wrestles from the grip of my words. Inside me, I know there are vast, dark archipelagos of meaning, deep worlds that sit at the chasm where feelings become words and thoughts, untouchable, yet forever present beneath my waking life.

"Out of the city, like our Father requested."

"Drones?"

"They seem to have gone to sleep. They are on the street still. In the trees and across the street in the eavestroughs, but if we are quiet, I think they will stay asleep."

"Hypatia!" I raise my arms in exasperation. How by Hades' pitchfork does she expect us to leave?

"I've thought of something. In case they wake up. I think it will work. Come with me, I'll guide you to the front door." She doesn't wait for me to answer before she slips the sleep mask over my eyes.

The gap between the sleep mask and my face makes a little portal, and through it, I watch my shoes make shallow indentations in Maureen's cream carpet. My fingers are locked tight in Hypatia's grip, and we shuffle forward in small, slow steps. We stop many times. Sometimes, we move sideways rather than forward. Each time this happens, the cream carpet is singed and littered with plaster and twisted pieces of black metal. What resides outside this blinkered view? Are those bloody pieces of Maureen's husband smeared across the wall on my left? The intrusion of this imagery makes me wonder if there is any purpose in Hypatia's exercise. Is it any worse to imagine these things and know they must be, in some measure, real, than it is to see them?

The floor transforms from carpet to cracked tile, and I spy the toes of a pair of white sneakers through the gap. We are at the front door.

"Okay, sis. Keep quiet," whispers Hypatia, and an adroit pull separates me from the sleep mask. "Sis" is her nickname for me when she wants me to be calm and agreeable, I think.

A metal garbage can is set before the door, aloof and alien next to the coatrack and neatly arranged shoes. Hypatia gestures at it, her arm outstretched like an opera singer's while delivering the grand finale.

"What?!"

Without warning, there is laughter behind my lips. I'm ashamed of it. It isn't right to laugh. Not after what happened, not after Maureen's husband got spread all over the walls, not after our parents, but now the sense of the taboo feeds the laughter, and it becomes so strong, I'm forced to put my hands over my mouth to stuff it back in. Hypatia pauses and locks on my face, and I know she's mining me, trying to decide if I am in a fit emotional state to proceed.

"You'll crouch inside," she finally speaks, keeping her words flat and short. "We'll be silent. I'll guide you to the car. I'll make an X." She withdraws a piece of street chalk from her pocket. "You'll follow the X's until you get to the trunk of the car. It will be hard to get down the stairs. I'll help you."

"And you?"

"I got the trash can without waking them. I'm not sure if they really see me."

For the first ten minutes, I roll about in the metal dustbin in the trunk as the Atlas dips and leans as Hypatia carves through the city. After several sharp turns, she calls back that we're clear. It was a risk, but now we know the drones see through a combination of human heat and motion. Yet, I don't dare move from the trunk, not because I fear the drones, but because I don't want to pass dad's body on the way to the front seat. The smell of the bin, though, and the heat are overpowering. My clothes have started to stick to my skin, and I can imagine the scent of garbage getting heavy on me.

Desperate, I crawl out from the dustbin and lie on the trunk's coarse-felt floor. An endless parade of telephone poles slips into our wake. I can only assume they are barren of voices, fallow and without signal. Some of the things our parents packed are on the last row of seats, while some of it, their luggage and Hypatia's backpack, seems to be gone. Hypatia must have jettisoned it so that the dustbin would fit.

It doesn't take long for the outer edges of the city, mainly darkened big box stores, to fade into the horizon as we coast westward on the highway. The whole vehicle pulls hard to the left and the tires screech as Hypatia swerves. Cars and trucks, stalled on the shoulder of the road and parked in the right lane, enter my view. The vehicles are empty, but there's the occasional piece of luggage left by the road. Hypatia doesn't reduce our speed, but instead continues her evasive maneuvers, apparently confident in her prescient reflexes. The abandoned cars proceed to appear in little clusters along the road. There's no sign of any drones. It seems probable that it's a mechanical issue. I pick words and start to practice with them to ask Hypatia, but she taps on the dashboard.

"The car is slowing," she announces. "Battery reads fine, but we don't seem to have charge." There's tension in her voice.

The car drifts down the slant of an overpass, and its inertia carries us until the road dips again and flattens along a row of transmission towers standing atop yellow fields and bush. The road is elevated above the field on an embankment. Its height allows us to look over the tall grass which grows near the road, only to give way as the field becomes scrub, moss, and hollows of thin-limbed trees.

The tires grumble along the shoulder of the road, and Hypatia seems to let us drift to a stop. I fight to turn around, and she locks eyes with me in the rear-view mirror.

My dad rests between us, but we focus on each other's eyes; I can tell by her gaze that she's mining my face for emotions. Several moments pass before she points farther into the field, where the grass, cornered by slim conifers, thins and becomes a wave of purple flowers.

"I think we can bury him there," she says.

Heather, I think. There's nothing wrong with the location she suggested. It's pretty and far enough from the road that it will be quiet, peaceful. There are rules about where we can bury the dead, I know that much. But there's nothing about it that feels right, either. I have no idea where mom and dad wanted to be buried, but I assume they'd want to be with each other.

Hypatia doesn't give me a chance to ask. She leaves the driver's seat and pops the trunk. In moments, she's standing over me, her hand outstretched.

"Mom?" My voice breaks over her name.

"I know. It's hard, but she wouldn't want us to go back and risk the swarm." She's holding my hand now. "Our Mother had a very sophisticated understanding about death. It's just a body, the spark lies elsewhere."

I can't remember mom ever telling me this or even sharing her view on the afterlife. Death was something they never spoke to me about. I suspect they didn't want me to dwell on the fact that, of the two of us, only I will rot; in our own ways, we're both destined to be alone in the end. My stomach sinks as it dawns on me that I not only don't know where they want to be buried, I don't even know if they wanted to be buried at all. Had dad ever mentioned cremation? One of the big tech companies will fire your remains into space or, if you pay an awful lot, bury your remains on Mars.

There are tears in Hypatia's eyes now, perhaps programmed to mimic my own. Perhaps designed to help her adapt to the circumstances.

"Fine," I relent.

There's much more to say, but even if I could say it, I have no desire. I'm sapped of the energy to struggle through the process of converting long strings of thoughts I only half understand into singular, explosive words. Perhaps Hypatia knows this, too. She nods, an acknowledgment of the thoughts she can perceive swirling and dancing beneath the surface of my face. She has let go of my hand now.

"Will you carry the shovel?" Her voice is quiet and obsequious; it's the voice she uses when she believes I need to be defused.

I say nothing, and, as she often does, she decides my silence is assent. She opens the side door in slow, careful inches and, in its gradual arc, the mass of my dad, shrouded now by Maureen's blue sheet, comes into view. She looks small as she rummages through clothes and the cooler sandwiched between the car's interior and the front seats.

She withdraws a shovel I've never seen before. I suspect it's pilfered, borrowed, as Hypatia would put it, from Maureen's house. An unexpected and unwelcome laugh erupts in the bottom of my throat in recall of the time Hypatia nabbed our chemistry teacher's sunglasses because she thought they would look good on me. When the teacher caught her with them in her backpack, she told him property was theft. This world, one in flight, in chaos, with all the precious and ordinary things left behind, might be the one for which she was truly designed. The laugh never reaches my lips; it freezes and grows a husk that scratches my throat as my eyes walk the blue, wrinkled continent of my dad's body in the backseat.

ALEXANDRA
The Jawbone Gospel

"Get up! Now!"

Hypatia yanks on my sleeve, but I burrow my face deeper into turned soil and my nose fills with dirt; I know I could pry into the underworld until I choke and still never get close enough to him. She yanks harder, with her real strength; my shoulder clicks and there is a burst of pain.

"Be gone," I croak. My tears have made my lips wet. I taste their salt. For a moment, she lets go. I don't think it's possible to shock her, she's not programmed for stuff like that, but I think it's the closest I've ever come to doing it.

"We're not alone. Get up. We have to go!"

In a violent grapple, she twists my head around so that I'm facing the road. Amidst the long grass and serpentine twist of the road, I find a girl on the edge of the road, next to our car. Her hair hangs limp in front of her eyes, but she has no expression. It's her hands that scare me. She holds them at her sides, and her fingers are twisted and hold empty air like a bird's talons.

"She's not human," Hypatia whispers. "She's a companion child, too."

"Say hello?" I whisper back, unable to look away from the barbed shape of the girl's fingers. They remind me of Mickey's and the way he punched holes through my dad. The field gets blurry again and my eyes turn hot.

"I don't think so. Let's see if she will let us leave."

Hypatia grabs my arm and guides me with a slow, gentle pull to the right of the field, the start of what I assume will be a wide arc back to the road. Before we've taken a step, the girl darts from the road and slips into the field. The grass is long. Her head and chest rise, and then she disappears into the sea of grass, only to surface closer to us.

"Run," Hypatia hisses and tugs me deeper into the field.

Ahead, the feet of the transmission towers run into the horizon, and to our right, in the distance, stand thin-armed trees surrounded by little islands of shrubland. Hypatia knows we can't hide in them, and she must be leading me to the column of transmission towers astride the field, grey-skinned and alien above a tangle of tawny grass and threads of greenery. My chest is tight and I want to throw-up. I want to stop, but the swish of the grass against the girl's pants gives me the strength to continue; it sounds like she's closing ground, but I'm too terrified to look over my shoulder. Hypatia has moved further ahead, her feet clawing up pieces of earth in an impossible sprint.

There's a sensation like drops of rain on the back of my legs. Pebbles. Pebbles kicked ahead by the girl's feet. She's definitely closing in.

Hypatia reaches the base of the transmission tower; she circles its feet. She hurls herself up into the air, but misses the first crisscross of metal lattices. She's too small to pull herself up. I'm a few feet away from her now. I can almost feel the force of the girl behind me and imagine her reaching for me.

"Faster," Hypatia commands.

Fingers scratch across my back as I tumble into the steel-skin of the tower. In a flurry of frantic reaches and jumps, I grip the lowest rung. My feet pump in search of an invisible foothold. Beneath me, the girl charges forward to rip me to the ground; there's grease and blood in her hair and her pupils have swallowed her eyes; they appear avian, like the eyes of a crow. In a flash of sneakers, Hypatia kicks the girl in the face with such force, she flips and lands on her stomach. The girl begins to raise herself on all fours, but Hypatia is too fast: she hops on the girl's back and uses the extra height to leap up the transmission tower and grip the first rung.

From the first rung, the way up is easy, and we climb the tower like it's a ladder and don't stop until we're several lattices above the ground. We sit next to each other, but I'm too winded to speak. Hypatia rubs my back and speaks quiet words of encouragement.

The girl continues to pace the feet of the tower. She looks up at us with black eyes and a blank face. Hypatia's foot dislodged her jaw, and her mouth hangs limp to one side. Her fingers twitch and curl as she reaches up at us; the way her fingers move reminds me of insectile mandibles. She leaps up and misses the first rung. This comes as no surprise: she can't be taller than Hypatia. She tries again and falls back to the earth. Then she wraps her body around the footing and half shimmies up while clawing into the metal with her fingers. There's a high-pitched shriek of metal on metal, and she moves up several feet. I grip Hypatia's arm as the girl reaches for the first rung, but there's a popping noise, and she slides back down to the bottom. Several of her fingertips are torn off, becoming bloody nubs of black metal.

How long will she stay here? She doesn't bother climbing anymore; instead, she paces below us. Several times, Hypatia calls down to say things like, "We aren't a threat." And, "Do you need help? Are you lost?" But the girl doesn't acknowledge her words. She continues around the base of the tower and retraces her steps in a slow circle.

"Stuck?" I whisper.

"For now," replies Hypatia. Her hand finds my back again and moves across my shoulders in a slow, large circle.

"Her purpose?" I push, though I'm confident I know the answer.

"Same as the drones. Terror and death." There's no pretense in her answer, and her small lips remain closed and still.

"Plan?"

"The best option is to wait. Someone else might distract her."

These words send shivers down my spine. I can visualize the girl chasing someone else, someone slower, and while she tears through them, Hypatia and I will slip into the fields and try to outrun the screams as the girl's twisted black metal fingers gore through flesh and organs. It's the type of plan a computer would devise. Simple, elegant, and designed to maximize the odds of our survival at the expense of another life or, as it might be expressed in Hypatia's head, the factor of the equation weighted with lesser value. It's phrases like, "Someone else might distract her," made seemingly offhand, that make me wonder if she's a machine first and my sister second.

Hypatia pulls herself up several more rungs, towards the top of the tower.

"Up?" I intone, and I know she can read the fear in my face; I don't like the thought of being alone, but I'm also scared to climb any higher.

She climbs fast, arm over arm, up each rung with mechanical precision. "I'm looking to see if anyone else is close to us. To help," she adds as she scans the horizon, yet her lips flutter when she speaks the word "help."

The sun falls tepid across my shoulders and the wind runs through my hair; I tighten my grip on the grey skin of the tower's aluminum rung. The metal digs into my butt, but I'm too scared that I will slip off the narrow beam if I risk shifting my weight. The girl continues to pace below us, her steps cutting into the grass. Soon, she will make her own crop-circle.

"Anything?" I say, and the panic makes my voice chop, high and low, like my vocal cords are out of tune.

Hypatia shakes her head and begins her descent. Suddenly, she falters, frozen between the tower's rungs, hanging in midair; her body goes rigid and arches in a way that reminds me of a cat. Her eyes bear down upon me, unfocused; her jaw is agape, unhinged as it becomes a black hole rupturing her delicate features, her pale skin folding away as it grows wider.

"Hurt?" I ask, but my voice leaves me in a whisper as panic tightens its grip on my throat.

She shakes her head in a series of awkward jerks. Her eyes regain their keen light, and her features tighten as her jaw clenches to reclaim her normal face instead of the widening mouth. Her little body stretches, latches back to the rungs of the tower, and settles beside me with elegant precision; I've often thought the ability of her internal processor to calculate and govern the movement of her body lets her certainty of the world's physics masquerade as fearlessness. I'm not even sure if she really knows fear. Perhaps she only remembers the emotion, like a faint echo from the days when she was flesh, before she became my sister.

"Okay?" I ask. She shakes her head, and there's a flash of confusion in her otherwise neutral features. "What?"

The look of confusion on her face deepens. "It was static first. It made my jaw hum. The wider I opened my mouth, the more the static became words. It sounded like coordinates. Directions."

"Where?"

Her eyes pry into my face to use my emotions to corroborate the intent of my question. "I'm not sure. Some of the words never became more than static. Something about a safe-haven. A refuge. I could climb back up and try again, it's probably on repeat."

The image of her jaw swinging loose, her features frozen and glitched, flashes before my eyes, and my gaze wanders to the girl below us as she maintains the circumference of her hunt. A blink of green metal skips through the fingers of the trees. In silence, a car glides along the corner of the road and rolls to a stop just behind our car. With numb comprehension, I realize Hypatia left our trunk open. There's a distant pop of a car door opening, and a man appears. His palm cradles his head as he circles our car. A powerful gust of air roils and sways the tawny headed grass, and I realize the girl is gone, the wake of her passage concealed by the wind's rolling waves through the field.

Hypatia seizes the moment. "Now. Down. Down. Quick," she beckons as she drops from rung to rung.

Perhaps her sudden movement down the tower draws the man's sight. From the shoulder of the road, he shouts, "Are you stuck up there? You need help?"

From the base of the tower, Hypatia summons me in furious little waves. "No time, sister. Come. Now."

The man slides down the road's gravel embankment to the edge of the field; the distance between him and the girl is now a few mere steps. Hypatia traces my gaze to the man and, with her features devoid of expression, shakes her head. If I don't warn him now, the man is done for. *Words, find the words. Hephaestus, help me find words.*

"Drive! Drive on!" I scream.

"What?!" The nervous confusion in his voice carries as I fight with the toe of my shoe to find the rung below, the bite of cold metal lingering on my fingers. "What are you talking about?" he shouts.

In careful imitation of Hypatia's movements, I drop another rung, squat, bring my hands to my feet, and drop another. With a sudden jolt, I lose my balance and tumble down a rung. The ground is closer now. Hypatia paces from the tower to the start of a path we carved into the field, throwing an occasional glance in the direction of the road.

"This your car?" shouts the man.

"Jump," commands Hypatia. My teeth pinch my bottom lip as I shake my head; her frown deepens. "The ground is soft. Processor predicts minor injuries as the worst-case scenario."

The strafe of tumbling gravel down the embankment chafes her words. The girl flies from the field and descends upon the man. He falls backwards as her hands rent and gouge the air.

"Christ!" he screams as he scales a mound of broken and loose black asphalt in flailing sidesteps and disappears behind his car.

"Now," says Hypatia as she bends her legs and lifts her hands over her head, ready to spot my fall.

It's clear that, in her mind, the window of opportunity is closing. The man's value in the equation of our escape is bleeding out. My feet leave the transmission tower's lattices; the world narrows into a funnel of pale sunlight at the end of which Hypatia and the yellow field grow larger. Hypatia is on her side, and I'm sitting on the spongy earth and wet grass.

"Go! Go!"

With my hand in hers, we run. The tall grass parts in Hypatia's wake, and its tips and edges graze my cheeks as we sprint. We move fast. The field's bottom is slick and wreathes of undergrowth pull at my sneakers. In a furtive glance, I notice Hypatia is leading me parallel to the road, keeping it on our right shoulders. Through the grass, there's a crack and din of metal. The man's voice erupts into a streak of frantic obscenities and then falls away.

The road's asphalt body peaks through the thinning wall of field grass, claiming more of our view until it slips through the field alongside us like a grey snake. Hypatia cuts in towards the road.

"Don't stop," she commands as the loose gravel and molten tarmac of the embankment give way beneath our feet.

Far down the road, the girl burrows through the man's windshield; her legs thrash and writhe across the hood of the car as she claws her way in after him. With an owl-like swivel, Hypatia glimpses the scene from over her shoulder. Her pace accelerates as she loops back and calls out as she runs by me in the direction of our car, "Our backpack! Keep going."

The yellowing field and transmission line cling stubbornly on my left as my lungs scream and my steps falter. A desperate plea ascends into a screech that sends birds into the sky from the hollows of the field. The man, now barely more than a dark outline, hangs from the passenger door, only to be slowly pulled back into the car's interior. In a fierce dash, Hypatia charges by him.

The hood of the car flies up, and the girl withdraws from the vehicle. For a moment, she makes to pursue Hypatia, but her chase breaks down into a series of vertical jumps. As Hypatia closes ground on me, she motions at me to start running again. The girl is bent over the open hood, bits of electronics and metal flying over her shoulders as she claws deeper into the car's innards. The image of her twists and blurs as Hypatia grabs my elbow and pulls me into her relentless stride.

We don't go far before my heart claps in my ears and my legs shake. My body wears me down to staggering steps and then to a complete stop. I throw my head between my legs as my guts mutiny and writhe in my throat.

"No. Come on!" cries Hypatia.

"Puking."

"No time. She's coming!"

In shakes and bobs, the girl's figure rises against the road's grey depths in charge towards us. My legs cede a few more steps before I collapse to a standstill. A mechanical growl issues from the direction the green car travelled from. The growl becomes a rumble, and a white truck screams from the road's elbow and flies towards us. The girl doesn't break stride as it rattles alongside her, but she leans farther into the shoulder of the road.

Hypatia runs onto the road; she jumps and throws her arms over her head in manic gestures. The truck pulls by us, but its speed bleeds away and it rolls to a stop. From the driver's side window, a man sticks out his head; alarm chews through his gaunt cheeks and flashes in his eyes, but his appraisal of us is slower than Hypatia's appraisal of him.

"Please, mister, save us. Save us from the robot child," screams Hypatia as she points behind us.

The girl's features are visible now: blood drips from her hands and stains the front of her shirt. A manic expression seizes her face.

"Holy fuck!" His head vanishes, but the passenger door swings open. The truck rolls forward as he calls out, "Holy fuck. Get in! Get in!"

Hypatia rushes forward, and I surrender to her pull as we crash inside the truck.

BUG
Do You Play Inverted?

I stand in the doorway of my pod. The player's corridor is long, dark, and cold—it was one of the first things Tim showed me on my welcome tour, moments after I entered the hangar. Tim.

Tim is tall, broad, and blond, and wears the same black turtleneck and jeans every day. When he first greeted me at the hangar entrance, he reminded me of one of the anonymous henchmen in the American action movies you made me watch with you every Christmas. But now that I know him better, I've realized he lacks the inconspicuousness to be a henchman. He's more like a rulebook, or a dry technical manual that was transmogrified into a sullen, Aryan *Men's Fitness* cover model wannabe.

"Greetings and congratulations," he said when I tumbled through the hangar's door and pulled my hand into a tepid handshake. "You are very lucky you carry a stick. I am Tim. I am responsible for managing your tournament experience, starting with a tour of the hangar. From now on, your name will be 100. Inside the hangar, that is what you will be called. We keep in-game names and hangar names secret from everyone. Do you understand, 100?"

I nodded in reply as the steel doors glided to a close and shut out the rain, field, and the cries of agony coming from the man I'd crippled.

"Inspiring spirit of competition," Tim continued as he led me down a long steel-walled passage.

"You're going to help him, right? I didn't mean to hit him that hard ..."

"You are inside now. You need to focus," he said mechanically as he led me further into the hangar. "Our first stop is the viewing room. It is the most efficient way to get you acquainted with the aspects of play and rules. You will find there are both advantages and disadvantages of being the last contestant to join."

There have been two cycles since then, and there are only 80 contestants left. There's a flicker of light on the wall opposite as another pod logs on. The hunt is already underway for many. Standing at the entrance to my pod, I flex my toes and bounce while rolling my head side to side, my ritual to wake myself. It's getting harder. I was logged until the early hours in search of targets—I need another 20 points to survive this cycle. The game world has been largely picked clean of all the low-hanging fruit.

I flip over the rubber wristband Tim gave to me to reveal the 35-character password to open my assigned pod. As I punch in the letters and numbers, my chest tightens. I'm not sure if it's exhaustion or reluctance. Logging is punishing—each time my senses of sight and touch feel cooked through, and the real world feels more distant, as if veiled by a thick blanket.

The door slips inside the wall, and I inhale the small rectangular room with a deep suckling breath, the one I imagine a yoga soccer mom would take. The pod is small, not much bigger than a broom closet, and I taste myself in the air. I haven't showered in days. It's a grind. Most competitors barely sleep. I slip on the control gloves, lace the shoes, and apply several vertical rows of sensor pads across my ribs and stomach, following the lateral pattern Tim demonstrated. They're warm on my skin. I inhale again, desperate to rattle my diaphragm and suppress the thought that the sensor pads, as well as the pod, are probably cooking me from the inside out.

The floor-to-ceiling screen before me comes to life in a rapid succession of white blinks, like a frantic eyelid. The game map gradually comes into view. It's an archipelago made of vast areas of black with small white islands where play is permitted. The play area remains unchanged from yesterday. The contrast between the blacked-out areas of the map and the white playable zones, create an outline that looks a little like the Predator.

"Arnie is covered in mud. See, you gotta be willing to get dirty if you want to survive. You got that, Bug?"

The rest of the map is black fog. The black areas of the map have no spawn points and can't be accessed by any player. The map isn't constant, though. Sometimes, the southern areas of the map go black, while areas further to the north-west become accessible. There's a timer that lets you know how long until the white areas of the map go black, and how long it will take for black areas of the map to go white. I think it depends on the time of day, but I'm not sure. Earlier, Tim explained that if you are playing with an asset in an area that transitions from white to black, you'll get logged out, and the asset won't be accessible until the area goes white again. A few players have told me this has happened to them. Often, the asset doesn't reappear as a spawn point even when the area goes back to white. Sometimes it does, but even then, the asset is often damaged, at times practically incapacitated. Tim explained in detail the consequences of losing an asset.

"These are the assets," he said, pointing to the waves of differently coloured dots populated throughout the map. All the dots to the west of the map and distant south were red. "Red means they are not viable. Yellow means they have not yet become viable, but will be soon. Green means available, and magenta dots reveal a claimed asset being actively played. Assets that have been claimed are not visible unless the controlling player releases them. You can play a maximum of ten. Even if you log in and out of one, if the asset is lost before someone else logs in it, that counts as one of your ten. If you run out of assets, you are out of the tournament, irrespective of how many points you have. Do you understand?"

At the time, I didn't really. I hadn't played yet. It was all theoretical, but I pretended I did.

"What if I have to go AFK?" I asked.

"That is part of the game. You got this far. I am sure you will think of something." A cold smile lagged after his words. "Do you have a nickname you would like to use for your in-game name?" Tim asked.

"No," I said.

"None? No pet names from your Father or Mother?"

There was a flash of remembrance, the smell of spearmint gum on my cheeks and then your voice asking, *"All right, Bug?"* as I floated onto your knee, my body becoming weightless.

I shook my head. "Not really."

Tim continued to speak like he hadn't heard me. "All players must create an in-game or screen name. It must be something that cannot be attributed to you. Anonymity is critical for your safety. We want to ensure all interactions between players do not become conflicts IRL."

"Oh."

"I must also impress upon you that a player needs to maintain a wallet value above 100 points to stay in the tournament. The system takes a snapshot of the wallet value every five days. If you fall below that score, you will be removed from the tournament. You may also resign at any time. While you are taking part in the tournament, your surplus points may be used to buy goods and services."

"Are people who are eliminated given transport home?"

"We have a protocol to manage elimination, yes. But do not worry about that, I think you will be a very dangerous player. Very inspiring."

You don't know dangerous pal, until you've met a logger on a bender up in the bush. My father, the bear. That growl.

"Shut up Bug, this is the good part," you'd say, and up and down little Bug would go on your knee, while John McClane wormed his way through a vent in the Nakatomi building. Well, *Yippee Ki Yay, motherfucker.*

The memory left a river of fire on my spine, and in its heat, the idea came to me. My name. "You know, actually, I do have a nickname. Ki Yay," I said.

Tim's eyes narrowed, and he bobbed his head in slow consideration before he said, "Very good, Ki Yay."

I snap my fingers and drift through the preview feeds of all the different green assets. The floor-to-ceiling screen mounted in front of me consolidates into a vision of fraying yellow grass and dirt. The world looks face down and the surroundings are obscured. The map in the right corner suggests the location in question is an urban park somewhere in the region labelled gnisnaL, nagihciM. Too few targets and objectives. Hard pass.

The next snap loads a grainy horizontal shot of what looks like a bridge, with the viewer looking from one side to the other. The surface is asphalt and there are steel guardrails running along each side. Several cars crowd one lane of the road, their interiors ablaze. Black smoke billows across my vision. Bridges, even small ones, are valuable targets. I flex my fingers and expand the fabric of the control gloves as I draw my thumb to my forefinger. My thumb pulses as it hovers over the engage button that is built into the index fingers of the gloves.

A string of cracks invades my audio and I realize a line of holes has appeared in the passenger door of the car in my immediate view. A strafe of gun fire issues in response. Too risky. Fuck it.

I conjure a new feed with another snap. This one's even worse. What looks like swamp mud reaches up to the bottom of the screen. An immobilized asset is a pretty crappy spawn point. Seems safe to assume it will remain unclaimed unless someone gets desperate. With reluctance, I pack up the kit in the little chest that came issued with the pod room. For a while, I sit on the floor and spin the pocket-knife on its tip, observing its rotations as it digs into the tile floor.

From the hallway, there's a wave of depressurized hisses, followed by the clap of feet as a bunch of players decide to call it quits, too. Perhaps our bodies know this is close to a mealtime? The hangar has no windows, and all the clocks are set to in-game time, not real time. It's impossible to know what time it really is.

From the small porthole in the door, I watch them pass. The gruelling demands of the tournament and the partitioned layout of the hangar have kept us mostly anonymous to each other, just as Tim demanded. A parade of thin man-children scuttles through my vision, their shoulders hunched, eyes downcast. A tournament in the middle of the wilderness is hardly a siren call to the well-adjusted. I catch a few ponytails that suggest I might not be the only girl, but they're certainly few and far between.

"*Hard to hurt you, if they don't know you,*" was one of your common reframes, and though I was never sure who "they" were, I slip through the door and join the tail of players.

The long procession of players squeezes along the narrow corridors of the hangar, and I follow their traffic. No words pass between us. Consummate strangers, seemingly by design.

Our feet drum along the concrete floor of labyrinthian passageways as we pass beneath the sullen glow of the mounted lighting and the ragged hisses of piping. The drab austerity is broken by the red gleam of a fire axe cabinet. The thin glass window rattles under the run of my fingertips as they pass over the length of the axe, its yellow shaft and red blade bright, eating the grey shadows of the corridor.

"This one is small enough to do the old-fashioned way. Each tree has a lean, Bug. You need to find the lean. Stand back now. This will do us this winter."

A spring tradition of ours, until each swing of the axe was followed by a fit of coughs, each fit longer and longer, until that last spring when you swayed on your feet and crumpled into a squat amidst the deadfall.

The high ceiling and descending steps of the viewing room pull my attention away from our springtime tree hunts. The viewing room has a massive dome ceiling, similar to the shape of an observatory, and is built into the centre of the hangar. It's the warmest and most inviting room in the building. A few scattered couches float on what's otherwise a sea of mandala floor pillows. In the viewing room, you can spend your points to get hot food and cold drinks served to you, not the slop from the mess hall. No matter the time of day, it seems, there are always some players resting here, lying down, engrossed as the ceiling dances overhead.

The viewing room seems to be so named because the ceiling is partitioned into ten little screens where you can watch the gameplay of the top ten players in the tournament. The name of each player flashes in green letters at the bottom of their feed. Some windows flash in and out as players vie for leadership from one another or when the system decides one feed deserves more attention than the others, but the top players never seem to change. Box Boy is often in the first place, and never below the top three.

The parade of players descends the sunken steps and spreads out, joining the players already lying on their backs, looking content and dozy. They must already have enough in their wallets to survive the next cycle. The domed ceiling stretches out above all of us, its surface decagonal as a constellation of player streams washes over us in a pale-blue electric glow. The simultaneous yet partitioned movement is hard to follow, and the view almost feels like a kaleidoscope of highways, bridges, solar farms, and cityscape. It's too much, and my eyes burn, but the over-stimulation is both mesmerizing and addictive.

Box Boy's feed is easy to find: in the far-right edge of the ceiling, his gameplay cycles through two different perspectives. It's a unique playing style I would never dare imitate. Box Boy's screen flashes to a panorama of field, grey and tilting in the wind against a long, barren stretch of road. In the distance, there's the flutter of movement, and Box Boy's feed consolidates on what eventually becomes a troop of bots in olive green jackets. The wind continues to roll over the field, but Box Boy's avatar appears unnoticed by the combat bots.

I let the weight of my body sink deeper into the cushions, daring the floor to swallow me. As I watch the troop of bots walk into Box Boy's vision, a desire to order something hot pulls at me. Good noodles. Maybe even a beer. Yet my eyes can't stray from the screen: in subtle inches, the perspective overhead shifts to the right and reveals an Alibaba delivery truck adrift along the shoulder of the road. A few bots break away from the platoon and creep along the side of the trailer-truck that faces the field, bobbing up and down and checking behind the wheels. The vision strays for a moment as these explorers pass the hood of the truck to rejoin the group, then moves ahead of them to a mountain of boxes left strewn far down the road in front of the truck.

The scene of the wind biting the brittle, tawny heads of the field vanishes and becomes a leather steering wheel that juts out overhead against a tan interior and rear-view mirror. Box Boy's second avatar must be crouched down somewhere between the seat and the pedals of the vehicle. Daring not to blink, I watch as the screen shifts from the world beneath the seat to the dashboard and then the windshield of the truck. Ahead, the troop of bots have stopped in front of the mound of the boxes, their backs to our vision.

Some are frozen in the middle of the road, looking into the distance ahead, and others are hunched over, rooting through the boxes. Soon, plastics and electronics litter the highway. There's a collective pause in the viewing room. Somehow, the screen knows how to track our attention: Box Boy's screen is now enlarged, pushing the other feeds to the margins of our vision.

A pair of hands grips the steering wheel, and it seems like the avatar is half standing, half sitting to reach the pedals. The screen jumps as the truck accelerates. By the time the troops turn to face the kick and start of the engine, it's too late. The screen jumps more as the olive coats disappear before it, then leans to the right as Box Boy checks the rear-view mirror and the mounted camera. The few remaining bots scatter and dive into the fields. The rear camera display, however, reveals the carnage and slaughter in the truck's wake. There's a noise of a few scattered shots, but now we're hurtling down the highway, and the red asphalt and broken pieces of the platoon vanish from sight.

Above us, the world reverts to Box Boy's first avatar—the yellow fingers of the field rise and fall as he wades through it to the road. The picture is choppy, and a few white vertical lines adumbrate the screen. In a slow panorama, Box Boy surveys and logs his handy work, and the system responds with an infusion of green pluses in a column down the right side of the screen. There are mutterings and scoffs from the viewing room, and though the addition continues, the screen pulses and, as if in recognition of the audience's waning attention, cedes space to another feed where two bots, one resembling a little kid and the other a simulated teenager, sit high above upon in a lattice of steel beams. The feed shrinks away into the bottom corner of the screen, washed away by a grey sea of asphalt beneath two smokestacks.

A voice, pinched and spoken through the nose, rises from the floor a few feet from me. "Guy doesn't deserve to be top three. He camps!"

"He camps? You are probably grinding away in some suburb or something, getting pawned by civilian bots, or something like that."

"Haven't lost an avatar yet, actually." And now the first speaker is sitting up, his pale and pointed face glowers over the room in search of the second speaker.

"Cool story. Ragging on a player who must have just made a cycle worth of points, while your claim to fame is being cautious? Might as well admit it is GG for you." The second speaker doesn't sit up, but I can tell he's on the other side of me by the way his voice travels. He sounds more amused than agitated.

"What's you handle, asshole? I'll find you in there and destroy you." The first speaker is standing now and looks as I expected he would. Doughy and thin-limbed, with a smattering of a few scraggly facial hairs above his upper lip.

"It is a very, very big map. Good luck."

"Give me your handle, you pussy!"

In that instance, Tim materializes, interceding in the space between them, nearly standing over me. He crosses his arms as he says, "You will recall a primary rule is that players are not permitted to disclose who they are in the tournament. We do not want conflicts in the game to become conflicts IRL. Further requests for his handle will result in a penalty of ten points. Do you recognize these conditions?"

"Fine. Whatever. I'm bored anyways." And the room snickers as the pale, doughy man-boy storms out of view.

"Box Boy is a very good player," continues the second speaker, but his voice is quiet now, as if he's speaking to himself.

"Do you think so?" I blurt out.

My question invites silence and I begin to wish I haven't said anything, but then at length he answers, "Yes. He is not perfect. Not yet. But very patient. I have caught his feed in here a few times. He hides amongst the delivery boxes in the truck when he is not using the avatar. It is a smart tactic, but it is time intensive."

"It's a strange game. Crazy sandbox," I add. Again, he doesn't answer for a long time, and I begin to wonder in earnest if perhaps he hasn't heard me.

"The physics are very good. Uncanny attention to detail." His words are slow, and come as if each is thoughtfully selected.

"Do you have enough points to pass the next cycle?" It's a personal question, and I notice players seldom ask about each other's points while a cycle is ongoing.

"That is a brazen question. Yes, I squared it away last night. You?"

"Short by 20."

He whistles his reply. "Not great, but not insurmountable. Try to find a spawn point in the central region of tnomreV. It is points dense. Lots of targets, I even passed a hydro station that looked ripe for a takedown."

"Thanks for the tip."

"No problem, stranger amongst the cushions."

"My out of game name is 100," I reply, and he chuckles. His laugh reminds me of a spring brook.

"Wow, last one in! I am 7."

"Lucky you."

"Something like that. It is a good thing we did not get to choose our hangar names. There are some poor in-game choices already. Someone is playing under the very cool moniker of Pawnking. Some very seriously cool, balanced people showed up for a tournament in the middle of nowhere. Only the best people."

"All too strange to live, too weird to die," I reply.

"Something like that. Anyway, check out tnomreV." His weight shifts as he rises to his feet, but he walks behind me, keeping his figure and features guarded from my view.

HYPATIA
Flower Station

The steady rattle of the truck over the marred and blistered country road speaks for the three of us. We drift by Sugar Maples that lean over the road in bouquets of yellow fire and orange cinders. Alexandra rests her head against the passenger window. She has not spoken or looked at me since I decided we would go with Paul back to his home in Flower Station. She is right to be upset. It was not a decision for me to make alone.

Paul went quiet after I asked what he did for a living. It seemed like regular conversation protocol, but he mumbled something out of the side of his mouth about being "a factory's valet three towns over," and then his face broke out in pink and orange polka dots. Once, Alexandra and I watched a YouTube documentary about factory valets. The job is solitary and entails dodging automated machinery to collect tailings and waste produced by the manufacturing process. The video made it look lonely and dirty, and the pay is often based on the value of the waste in the global "scrap market." Our Father called factory valets "the lighthouse keepers" of the 21st century, but with more boredom and despair.

I have not been able to coax another word out of Paul. He casts a furtive glance into the rear-view mirror as if to confirm nobody is following us. The violence of the truck's movement continues to jolt through me. Neither Alexandra nor I have been in a car or truck powered by a combustion engine before. Its passage over the road is loud, ostentatious even. There is an aroma too, pungent and sweet, and it blends with the smell of stale tobacco that seems to cling to Paul's clothes and body. The smell of tobacco fills me with envy, and I realize I am tapping my fingers on my thighs.

A curve in the road reveals an RAV4 on the left shoulder, its treads half on the road and half in the ditch. The passenger door hangs open. Paul slows the truck and rolls by in what looks like bemused inspection. We have passed dozens of abandoned cars. Cars like ours with a 300-mile range, out of juice 18 miles outside the city. My mind continues to form the same conclusion: the flash must have damaged their batteries. I place my hand on my chest, prying into my pale skin, for a somatic reassurance that my lithium glass heart remains intact. There is no assurance of a beat, only the stickiness of synthetic skin and electric warmth, and as my processor continually scans for Wi-Fi amidst the woods, I remain marooned.

"Never been a better time to have hung on to an old gasser," claims Paul as he gives the truck's dashboard an appreciative pat.

Alexandra says nothing, but I manage a thin smile. The pretense of my recognition must be important to him, because his face streaks green and he smiles with his teeth. It is a yellow smile, degraded by time, coffee, and nicotine, and I have the impression he rarely makes much use of it. Unlike our Parents, his face has crumpled in on itself with age, and from his bio-signals, I conclude he is younger than he looks: his eyes and lips seem framed only by muscles in his cheek and jaw that have tensed over decades. It leaves his face stretched and hard, devoid of a single laugh line.

In the fading October light that slips through the trees in long shadows, he seems more dangerous than he did in the city. I worry I have made an error in my appraisal of him, and that maybe something slipped my processor. Perhaps Alexandra saw something in him that I missed. I should be teaching her, as our Mother instructed, how to read men like Paul, not the other way around. I try to study his face, to pry into him and place him in this world, but his eyes remain on the road, and his profile is dark, leathered, and inscrutable.

"We aren't far," he says and breathes his words at us through the corner of his mouth.

At the shoulder of the road amidst the fire of the trees, a green sign, its corners embroidered by rust, reads: "Flower Station." The thin tributary of gravel we have followed since we spun off the route 511 carries on as thin as before, but it now bears the namesake of the town. In the splatters of cerulean blue at the edges of the purple bags beneath Paul's eyes, I can detect easiness and relief have overcome him.

As our progress continues, I can see why he is confident and relaxed: whatever the drones came for, they would not find it here. The road runs through untenanted highlands, lonesome and cool in autumn's onset. Maple and conifers form an impassable wall of woods along the road, breached only by the occasional chink of gravel driveways burrowing deep behind the tree line without betraying the presence of any dwellings. We rumble along as the road hugs the edge of a lake and catches pieces of it in placid slumber between the fingers of the trees.

Paul points across us to Alexandra's window and mutters, "Over there's Blueberry Mountain. I'll take you up there if you like, hell of a view."

"We'd love to," I say with rapid and forced earnestness.

From the corner of my eye, I catch Alexandra's annoyance and the start of her protestations, and I move my pointer finger below my ear and tap my jaw in what I hope is a subtle gesture. It is unlikely there will be a better place here to receive another broadcast from "the refuge."

"Well, all right then," says Paul in another flash of yellow teeth.

The road forks, and he steers us up a steep road named Stony Lonesome, and I can tell by our reduced speed that we are close to our destination. The truck rocks and creaks as we descend onto the gravel footing of a side road. We pass through a tunnel of maples holding fire in their boughs, and soon the road disappears amongst the woods. The gravel path narrows into a steep climb and the transmission whines until we reach a plateau where a long, flat bungalow receives us as the truck limps to a stop ahead of a dilapidated detached garage. The bungalow, cradled in the hollow of thin birch trees, is whitewashed and adorned by a blue wrap-around veranda which has, in some places, sunken into clover and sparse tawny grass. Ornaments of industrial society litter the front of the house: several burned-out cars, a bulldozer and its treads embroidered by weeds, an old Coca-Cola machine slumped on its side, and white propane cylinders stacked by an old BBQ.

Paul catches the alarm and fear in Alexandra's face and swallows hard several times as he kills the engine. "I know it's not much, but it's weatherproof and safe," he mumbles.

ALEXANDRA
Blueberry Mountain

At Hypatia's insistence, we're going to hike Blueberry Mountain. She loves the idea of the reception she'll get at the summit. I don't really have the energy to cobble together the words to disagree. So barnacles, I guess we'll climb Blueberry Mountain, beats sitting around Paul's house. It smells like farts and cigarettes in there.

Sometimes, I think about Cassandra from Greek mythology. My mom had a book about her. Cassandra could predict the future, but nobody would believe her. I often feel like Cassandra, although I can't see the future or anything. I think Hypatia can, or at least her processor can predict outcomes. No, my curse is I can remember everything. I mean everything. I even remember lying on mom's chest when I was an infant, but I can't share these memories with anyone, at least not in a way that matches how vivid they are. There's one memory I find myself replaying again and again.

The light from our kitchen's island cradled the hallway in its half-life. Mindful of the worn and traitorous floorboard, I stepped with care in the dark until I arrived outside the door to our parent's private streaming room. The door was ajar enough to reveal a sliver of the screen's blue electric glow. On screen, an older man sat with one leg draped over the other, at ease in an oak framed chair and its tufted leather interior peaked at us over his shoulder. Though he looked spry, he wore a wave of grey hair at the top of his head and his face looked loose.

"Hello, Alec and Margot, I have been looking forward to our meeting. I read your communication about Hypatia with great interest."

"We meet again, Mr. Quill," said my dad.

"Q is fine. As I reminded you last time, I am not the real Mr. Quill. Only his replicated consciousness in a body double," the man replied with what looked like an empty, emotionless gaze.

"Oh, yes," my mom replied, but she sounded befuddled.

"Okay, I can confirm Hypatia is on standby mode, and we have established a link to her data. We can begin."

This happened a few times a year. Hypatia would be made to sit in my mom's study, her eyes would shut, and she would go very still, and I would be told not to disturb her while she was "resting."

"Let me start by asking if Hypatia is still to your liking? Is she meeting Alexandra's unique needs?"

"Alexandra continues to make progress in her ability to express herself," said my father in a tight, clinical voice.

"I think you are undervaluing your daughter's success. The data Lotus received from Hypatia shows Alexandra is doing well across most of the core metrics you selected. Everything from self-confidence, screen addiction management, and anxiety control shows marked improvements. I told you Hypatia was well calibrated to Alexandra's condition," said Q. "There is the strange idiosyncrasy of using Greek gods to express herself when she becomes angry or disturbed. We could have Hypatia discourage this charming, though quirky, aspect of her speech."

"We think Hypatia is invaluable to Alexandra, but if Alexandra wants to use Greek mythology to express herself, who are we to tell her otherwise," said my mom with a slight edge in her voice.

"Then are you dissatisfied with Hypatia as a daughter? I know having a big family while being attentive to the world's carbon budget was very important to you. It is certainly very important to us here at Lotus. Lotus is always ready to help climate conscious individuals do their part," Q said, but even from outside the door, it was clear his words were distended and aloof, inserted rather than spoken.

"She's different. I think she's been different ever since we reset her." Mom's voice was plaintive and full of cracks.

"You've raised this in the past. Can you tell me more?" pressed Q.

"She doesn't really act like a child. She was always serious, but she's secretive now. If we let her, she withdraws, hides away in my study, reading my books. She loves Shelley and Yeats. She reads Freud. She's into social theorists."

"Oh," said Q. "When did this happen? The mature books, I mean?"

"Hard to say, like I said she keeps to herself. It has been happening for a while, on and off, I think."

"Here at Lotus, we want our children to be curious. Playful, even. While we modify each consciousness to make them suitable to life as a companion child, aspects of the child remain. The traits essential to creating rapports with their siblings and peers can also lead to mischievous behaviours."

"She steals, though," added my dad in his gravel mood voice. My mom was quick to add, "Nothing major. Just little things. Loose change. Sunglasses from one of Alexandra's teachers. And, well, cigarettes and lighters."

"I am not dismissing your concerns, but you must appreciate that Hypatia is designed to be a deeper learner. The same skills she uses to adapt to the needs and habits of your family will, with the right opportunity, be used to appreciate and master literature. It is quite possible all that reading has made her more mature. More serious. Perhaps even a little rebellious, hence the petty thefts and cigarettes."

"Oh," sighed my mom. "You never said that was something to monitor. How were we supposed to know I'd have to lock up all my books?"

"It has never been an issue. Not a lot of our clients have libraries with so many old-world classical texts, but you are quite right. We failed to inform you of that risk."

"Can we help her? I feel awful at the thought we might've taken away some of her innocence."

"Could we try rebooting again?" asked my dad.

"Alec, no! That would be far too destabilizing for Alexandra, she's way too old now to let that slide again."

"I must agree with your wife. Another reboot risks not only loss of personality and diminished sense of self, but ..." Through a crack in the door, I glimpsed the man on the screen pound his chest. "... we are powered by a state-of-the-art quantum glass battery. It is intended to last forever, but it will degrade if it is constantly rebooted. May I remind you of the risks? If Hypatia's battery runs to zero, it could destabilize her personality. Without power, there is no guarantee her consciousness will remain intact. She might lose aspects of herself."

"See Alec, it's totally out of the question. We aren't going to wipe away who she is, it all might just be a phase. Right Mr. Q?"

Before Q could respond, my dad shouted, "Well, if she keeps stealing cigarettes, she could burn the whole damn house down!"

"I don't understand why Lotus didn't intervene. I thought you monitored this type of stuff," added my mom.

"Yes, well ... Had she offered a cigarette to Alexandra, it probably would have been flagged. My understanding from the data is that she only takes the cigarettes, she does not light them. It must not be triggering our guardrails. In the wrong hands, a lighter certainly can be dangerous, but so can scissors or a butter knife. Pretty much any tool from a home garage can be a weapon.

Our algorithms monitor behaviour based on the chances of an intentional harm of others. If a companion child is using an actual classified weapon, like a combat knife or firearm, then the system will pick up on it, but otherwise, these things slip through the cracks."

"Q, you aren't filling me with confidence." My dad's voice became a grumble.

"I understand," said Q. "I advise you tell her this is unacceptable, and Lotus will, of course, build in the necessary guardrails. I will do it right now."

I let the memory go as Hypatia and I cross the parking lot of an ancient-looking gas station to the trail to Blueberry Mountain. It's hard to tell if Flower Station is deserted or if it was maybe always this quiet. There's nothing here. A combined bait shop and grocers—who knows what culinary fusion delicacies Flower Station has to offer—and an outfitter.

The gas station's neon sign pulses and the interior of the shop is lit. I can't see any solar panels on the roof, and the two pumps are the old-fashioned kind. No sign of any charging stations. In front of them, an old man sits in a faded lawn chair, his beard draped over his paunch. He nods at us as we approach, follows our steps with his eyes, but says nothing. Around the side of the gas station, a vast white tank rests against the wall; I can't decide if it looks like a miniature submarine or if it looks lunar, like a piece of hardware for a space colony.

A sales pitch from nowhere infiltrates my thoughts. *Right this way, step right up and enjoy the very best of what Mars has to offer. This here astral septic tank turns human feces into water. A must-have for any serious space rancher. Some folks fill them up just by talking. No ma'am, no odours. Not enough atmosphere for that.*

Laughter pinches the corners of my lips, but I chew it away. If I could speak, like really speak, I think I'd be funny. Who knows,

I might be the best comedian on the planet, I just happen to be trapped in a catatonic brain. Tough break. For some reason, this thought makes the laughter pinch harder. I think mom knew I was funny. The pinch vanishes as if it had never been there, and my stomach somersaults and feelings hit me like something reaching up through my guts to pierce its fingers into my heart. I need a distraction. Something instant.

I tip my head at the white tank, but Hypatia doesn't break stride. As we pass it, she tells me with a sigh that it's a propane tank, and it's the reason the little shop's lights are still on. There are pieces of knowledge that stayed in her long-term memory when the internet went down, and things she seems to have discarded. Anything energy related is sticky, it seems. Essential information, I guess.

Between two trees, the head of the trail opens in a ribbon of dirt. Scabs of grey slate rock jut out in places. Hypatia leads. The trail remains narrow, and it soon becomes scaled in red and yellow leaves, and it's as if we walk upon a dragon's tail. The trees are thin and balding, and they let the sun lean heavy on my shoulder.

"Do you feel safe with Paul?" Hypatia asks over her shoulder and, like before, she continues walking, her eyes ahead, unable to mine my features to corroborate my response.

I step over the brown spine of a root that lacerates the trail. Something about her question makes my stomach squirm and my shoulders tighten. In the few days we've been here, Paul strikes me as distant and agitated. He swears all the time, and he smokes constantly. I see him, sometimes, late at night through our bedroom window, the ember of a cigarette dancing in the night like a solitary firefly. One firefly followed by another.

Mom's weird cigarette consumption and climate change paper that she kept trying to make dad read pops into my head. Now there are tears in my eyes and Hypatia's question doesn't make my stomach squirm, but instead puts fire in my chest. Anger. I focus on speaking my words the way I focus on planting my feet over the roots, placing one carefully to beget the next.

"Anywhere safe?"

"No."

"Why ask?"

"We need to move on soon."

"Why?"

"Paul isn't stable. He's lonely. Sad. The longer we stay, the harder he'll try to hold on to us."

Her words don't scare me, they annoy me. Maybe she should've considered this before she decided we let him take us into the middle of nowhere. Give me the grace of gods.

"Where?"

"Hopefully, we'll know soon."

The trail breaks and becomes blue sky, tall grass, and puddles of grey rock dotted with lichen. We've reached the summit, and the sun is bright, even though it has begun its westward descent; without the shade of the trees, its heat punches my cheeks. The world below returns in miniature: Flower Round Lake sleeps pastel and stiff, cradled by trees smoldering yellow and red in what my dad called Sumtumn.

I hoped to be able to look east and set my eyes on home, or at least in its direction. The summit only faces westward; thin trees dot the other half of the peak and blot out the vision east. There will be no sighting of home.

Hypatia swivels on her feet in a perfunctory registration of the world. She takes no notice as the wind howls over her and wails in my ears, to shake and haunt the woods behind us. I'm not sure how long we wait, but it's long enough for the sun to go red. Hypatia has found a small boulder, and she stands atop it, her arms at her sides, her mouth cast wide, as if she's stuck in a permanent silent scream. She barely moves, but when she does, she rotates on her feet in a pirouette, and for a moment I'm seven again and we're playing. She pretends to be a satellite dish, spitting out fragments of my favourite cartoons as she spins in the backyard. For some reason, the memory makes me feel uncomfortable and sad.

Unsure of what to do with myself, I contort my body into the Lotus position and decide to focus on my breathing. Inhale, I counsel myself. Inhale as your sister spins on her toes in hope of catching the last wayward transmissions of civilization underneath her jaw. Exhale with her as she opens wide to spin the scratch and hiss of radio static into language. Exhale. It's no use, I can't take myself seriously. I tussle my notepad from my backpack and begin to sketch in it.

At first, it's dark strokes, thin spidery lines. But the lines consolidate and become a concrete pit reaching up to a pink sky. My pen makes bubbles in the space in between the concrete and the sky. It's maddening and exciting not to know what will come out of you. What your fingers will harvest from all those words and thoughts that went unspoken, unheard. My hand speeds up, and in furious scratches, I bring something into existence, a prostrate mass in the concrete bottom. My imagination sets to work, colonizing the bottom of the page, the only blank space left for my pen to run. The outline of a shape forms, and I'm desperate to break away from it.

"News?" I query.

Hypatia doesn't respond, but holds her hand up in what I recognize as her usual gesture for more of my time and patience. She continues to rotate on the balls of her feet, but her mouth has become cavernous, wide enough to swallow a grapefruit whole. Her rotation grounds to an abrupt halt, and she waves me to her side in little flicks of her wrist. Her mouth still hangs agape, her perfect white teeth gleaming in the pale light of the afternoon.

She holds me close, so close now that my ear is practically in her mouth. From behind her teeth emits the sound Rice Krispies make when you pour milk on them, but there's nothing audible, nothing human.

"Did you hear?" she asks.

"Static." I shrug.

She smiles and shakes her head with excitement. "No. There were words. Words under my jaw again. There's a refuge. Boats leave from the East Coast. No place names. Only numbers. They say it's safe. They say it has power. Power, sis. This is big. This is a plan."

"Trustworthy?"

"It's the best shot we have."

HYPATIA
Paul's Garage

In the dark, I listen to the sounds of the bungalow. Alexandra lies in the bed next to me. Her soft breaths fill my ear in her usual melodic rhythm and tell me she is in deep sleep. I know her vitals well enough to know she is dreaming. For a moment, I let her face fill my vision and watch her eyelids flicker. I do not dream. Our Mother told me it has something to do with the guardrails Lotus has put in place. A missing piece in the circuitry. There is poetry in that failure. To dream remains inalienably human.

Yet, since the world went dark, there have been fragments. Voices I do not recognize. They are soft and intermittent. At first, I thought they were more wayward radio transmissions, but the one today, on Blueberry Mountain, was accompanied by a vision or, perhaps, sensation of heat on my face. Two sets of feet, one small, one large, stepping along the dusty pavement. There were growling cars spewing exhaust in a narrow street. It is nowhere Alexandra and I have ever been. I hungered for more of it, but then the transmission came and washed it all away in a static wave.

Beyond our room, I strain and listen, and at first find the rumble and rattle of the furnace. Paul told us it is old and runs on propane. We must learn to ignore it, he said, as it cycles up and down. The thought of being in his bungalow long enough to be habituated to its metabolism fills me with an emotion I recognize as dread. Not least of all, because I cannot charge here. I strain further, and I find Paul beneath the din of the furnace. His air leaves his nose in short, furious growls.

I slip out of the bed, focus on getting past Alexandra in soft-planted steps, and move down the hall. I lean in through the doorway that leads to the living room. Paul is asleep on the sofa in front of the unresponsive antiquated flat-screen television. The moon walks over the coffee table in pale footsteps and illuminates an ashtray. The cinders of a crumpled cigarette glow, stubborn against the process of becoming fire's distant and faded kin. Even in slumber, Paul's face looks troubled and strained. It is clear to me his face is not careworn from drudgery. The fleshy edgeless contours and husk formed over his brow have matured from disuse, the scars of being perpetually set aside.

Regardless, Paul has not been asleep for long, so I continue to place my weight on his creaking faux vinyl oak floor with slow, meticulous caution. These soft careful steps, which I measure at below 20 decibels, deliver me to the kitchen, where the sliding glass door leads to the backyard. I pause and listen to the house once more. The furnace cycles up again and shudders beneath my feet. The clock on the microwave, stuck in stasis at 12:00, casts a blue shadow on the glass door. My hand flutters over the door's handle as I make one final assessment of the situation.

We do not know Paul. Keeping Alexandra safe in the immediate future will require I know more about him. In the intermediate future, leaving Paul to pursue the coordinates of the refuge will ensure Alexandra is safe from him. His garage may contain maps and clues about him, but is not a personal enough space for him to feel his privacy has been breached if he finds me inside it. Confident in the plan's logic, I pry the glass door open in careful, silent inches and slip into the backyard.

Autumn has matured faster outside the city. There is already a blanket of leaves on the ground, and the sensors in my cheeks prickle with the crisp air. I stand for a moment beneath the rind of the moon and focus on the chill of the air in front of my face and the absence of my breath, which should cloud the darkness with its curling seams. I look behind me to ensure no other eyes could mark my estrangement, my distance to nature's living things. The garage is setback on the property and subsides into the tawny hands of overgrown grass. The windows in the centre of its overhead door are smashed, and they stare back at me in a smile of twisted glass teeth.

I do not get long to rummage through the garage. Paul tries to keep his steps quiet, but he is betrayed by his heat signature. For a while, we watch each other. I stand in the middle of the garage, while Paul remains as a silhouette at the door frame, watching me, empowered by the belief that I cannot see him. When he tires of observing my motionless stance, he walks through the pinewood doorway but does not flick on the garage's light. Perhaps it is not about his sense of power, but his need to conserve the generator.

"What are you doing in here?"

"Couldn't sleep."

He shakes his head and snorts his annoyance through his nose. "Why are you out here, though?"

"I didn't want to wake anyone."

"You shouldn't be in here, rustling through a man's private things," he says, and I do not need to read his face to perceive irritation.

"Is there something in here I shouldn't find?"

"It's a matter of principle, that's all," he says from behind his back as he strains down to rummage through a dirty blue and white cooler set by the door. He withdraws a bottle of beer. His arms tighten and he grits his teeth as he opens it. The bottle cap flies from his hand to a darkened corner of the garage and makes the noise of change falling.

I cannot say how I know this sound, for there is only digital money, but I know the weight and sound of metal coins bouncing on dust-covered pavement, rolling across store counters, and jingling in tills.

"Do you have a map? One of North America with lines of longitude and latitude?" I ask and clasp my hands in front of me in a pose I know codes as innocence and vulnerability.

He does not answer. The bottle is on his lips, lifted nearly vertically as he suckles on it, and its cold dribbles on his chin in shades of purple-black that are deeper and more lightless than the unlit room.

"I spend all day around machines, you know. Smart machines. You get a feel for them eventually. Know how they work. How they think, their tells." His words break away as he finishes the bottle, and I stand motionless in the dark. "Are you dangerous?" he finally asks.

"Are you?"

"I don't intend to be."

"Well, neither do I."

"What makes you different from the girl on the road?"

"I don't know what was wrong with her."

"How do I know you won't go fucking terminator on me too, then?"

"How do I know you won't murder Alexandra and me and bury us in your backyard?"

"Jesus! What?!"

"Most serial killers are white, introverted men with poor self-esteem between 20 and 40."

"I'm not a serial killer. Christ."

"And I'm not like the girl from the road."

"You can be yourself, you know."

"What do you mean?"

"I dunno, don't let Lotus decide who you are for you. You know what I mean?"

"How do you know I'm any different from what I'm supposed to be?"

"Do you think you are?"

It is a question I have never been asked before. Am I as I appear? I ask my processor to run with it, but the space behind my eyes remains obstinately blue and blank.

"Do you have a map?"

"Why?"

"I have coordinates for a safe place."

He shakes his head but ambles back to the doorway and flips on the light, which flickers to life in successive bursts only to cast a wan cone of yellow light in the centre of the garage. He grabs another beer from the cooler and starts to rummage with one hand through a set of drawers until he pulls out a book with a blue cover.

"This might do." He flips it down on an old, wooden table marooned in the corner of the garage and beckons me over with a wave of his beer. "We're here." He points, pressing his yellow fingernail hard into the page.

I nod, then shake my head. "I need it to zoom out." He snickers and starts to thumb through the pages. I pat his arm and lay my hand over his wrist in a gentle touch. "Please, can you open each page entirely before turning it?"

There is no point keeping up pretenses: with the full image, I can copy it to memory. I can tell by the colours in his face that the request has startled him, but he says nothing, merely surrenders the Road Atlas to me and then fumbles with the cap on his second beer. The paper page is cold and smooth under my fingers. I flip through the pages until I find the coordinates I heard atop Blueberry Mountain. I find them on the coast of New Hampshire. I flip back and start to walk a course east through Ontario, Quebec, and then down to the East Coast.

Paul leans over the table and peers at the route I sketch. "No. No. You can't go that way. Too many power installations and interties with the eastern grid. Rumour is there are so many drones, the skies above the US borders of Quebec and New Brunswick look like they're covered with a flock of birds. What we get for choosing a side in this, I suppose."

"Where do the rumours come from if there is no telecommunication infrastructure?"

"Rumours are probably as old as our dropped larynxes." I return his smile. "Phyllis, in town, has a ham radio and trades in gossip. If it were me, I'd go through the bush. Keep to the small towns. Places of no importance. You won't find as much of the war there. You should go through somewhere like ..." He flips back through the Atlas until he finds an ocean of green with blue islands of lakes. "The Adirondack region of Vermont. You'll need to cross the St. Lawrence first. I've got a canoe. Do you and Alexandra know how to paddle?"

I shake my head. "Alexandra doesn't like the water. She doesn't like swimming."

Inside me, something squirms with the realization these words are the facsimile of the words our Mother spoke to me during the week before our first birthday together. The week we spent watching the workmen fill in the pool. Our Mother smiled when she said these words, but her heart rate spiked, and the speed and tone indicated she had practiced them beforehand.

Paul does not seem to notice my discomfort. "Damn city kids." Laughter flickers through his face, but then his cheeks grow a shroud of pale blue. "You really should stay here. Wait it out. I don't mind, you and Alexandra can stay for as long as it takes."

My processor runs through the scenario: Alexandra watching me become feeble and slowly slip away without power, her dependence on Paul growing, and with it, feeding his unspoken but doubtless ever present need to satiate his loneliness with her.

"Teach us to canoe."

He nods, but blue and slate eddies swirl on his nose and beneath his eyes, the colours of rejection and despair.

BUG
The Third Cycle

The game map crowds my vision with its familiar puddles of white and large swathes of black, inaccessible terrain. Each day, there are fewer potential spawn points. Most of the assets have been claimed, and many are already destroyed or disabled. Amidst the smattering of red and green dots, there's the occasional blink of yellow for the assets that aren't ready to become spawn points just yet. Most of them roam the outskirts of the cities or appear to float along back country roads and other inopportune places.

My index finger aches from swiping right on so many unviable avatars and checking in on my claimed assets. The environments around many of them seem too unsafe to log in on. I adjust and shift my body, respecting the narrow confines of the room. The space has transitioned from one of minor claustrophobia to an extension of my body. *I've become one with the blue light, united with my sensor pads, and at home in the soupy air, unadulterated with the thick smell of my body on a diet of ramen noodles and beer. The joys of being Bug the bubble girl.*

Near the bottom of my asset list, I find one I haven't played in a few days. I don't really remember where in the game it is. It felt late or early when I logged off. I tap into it, and the screen becomes a plywood door streaked with brown wood stain. The walls are narrow and adorned by equipment I don't recognize. Several propane tanks clatter and roll on their sides at my avatar's feet. It's a shed, I think. I wait until the metal groans of the rocking propane tanks subside and listen. No immediate threats. *Well, fuck it.* Mindful to avoid knocking those tanks again, I inch my way through the door, revealing slivers of orange and yellow leaves and an empty forest.

In a quick leap from the shed, I spin through the air and take in my surroundings as I land. The woods look clear. Birdsongs I don't recognize warble out from the bush. The location is coming back to me. There's a road to the south. The plan was to take the road and head south-east to find some infrastructure. A rush of impatience overwhelms me, and I tear wildly through the woods, leaping over logs and sliding down grey slabs of rock. The trees become red, yellow, and orange blurs, their colours weaving into each other as I run. Ahead of me, the black tarmac of a road snakes through the trees. Excitement pinches my sides, and with the pump of my legs I command the avatar forward, only to lurch back and throw myself to the ground.

The forest fills with heavy and crude voices. Bots. Bot language is bereft of words—it consists of emotive noises. Yet, if you listen closely, you'll discover its architecture, its repetition and patterns, although it's just far too submerged in the power of shapeless, inexpressible sound. It always sounds angry and muffled, like it's travelling up from the depths of the fucking sea.

I steal a furtive glance from my belly and spot their outlines along the road. A group of bots in combat armour stands over three kneeling bots. The heavy guttural cries and a cadence of angry laughter continue. The crack of a gunshot rings through the woods, and one of the kneeling bots slumps onto the road. Two more bots in colourful combat armour trudge along the road towards the party. They pass through the fingers of the trees in splices of laboured steps, their shoulders laden with a large, coarsely hewn wooden cross.

What creepy fucking nightmare fuel is this? My spine tingles and recoils, like snow has been shoved down my jacket.

The good news is that they aren't paying attention. I can slip by into the woods unnoticed and join the road later when I'm far from their view.

On all fours, I start to crawl back into the bush to let the forest shadows swallow me, but my eyes find a pale, expressionless face across from me on the forest floor. The name Ripperboy appears in blue letters above the player's avatar. I freeze. I've learned fast that you never know what another player is going to do. Some of them will try to kill you to reduce local competition. Some of them just fuck around and get in your face. Some of them can be decent.

Ripperboy raises his hands in surrender and then slithers on his belly over the deadfall. As he approaches, the game decides he's close enough to "communicate" and the left side of my screen becomes a flurry of his green messages. Another game mechanic—players can't message each other unless they're close to one another in the game, so that it mimics the limits of physical communication in real life.

Wotching bots 4 awhile. U Help kill?

Sure. Plan?

Rush now!!!

I peer up from the ground again and count at least a dozen weaponed bots. *Too many. We hunt slow. Pick them off.*

Lame.

We'll get owned. I can't help but shrug my incredulity as I bash my response.

Pussy!!!!!!!!!

Before I can respond, the player hurtles through the woods and leaps into the road. He lands a blow on one of the bots and brings it to its knees, but the others swarm in. I crawl forward a little closer to get a better sense of the action. The bots form a ring around Ripperboy and shove him back and forth with their rifles. They're well coordinated. It's smart AI.

On the outside of the circle, one of the bots throws pots and toilet paper and all sorts of things out of a rucksack and doesn't stop until it withdraws something small and grey. It paces around the outer ring, and when Ripperboy staggers backward towards it, it attaches the grey mass to his avatar's back. The bots dive in all directions, and some head towards me into the eaves of the woods. Ripperboy jumps and runs down the road at several of the fleeing bots. An explosion rents the air and a wave of grey and black smoke rolls across the road, dissipating to reveal Ripperboy's smoldering remains. Given his reckless assault, I doubt this is the first avatar the player has lost; it certainly won't be his last.

The bots break out into garbled cries of unmistakable excitement and ecstasy. Those who fled into the treeline return to the road in slow, cautious steps. I'm about to retreat farther into the woods, when my pod flashes red and is colonized by Tim's words.

"Attention players! Attention players, you have one minute to stop your activity and log off from your avatars, as this point cycle is over. Stay in your pods to learn the results from this round of the tournament."

With a jolt, I realize I won't have time to find a safe location to stow my avatar in the next minute. Logging off is a big part of the game. You need to hibernate and hide your avatar away because the simulation runs constantly. A shed. A dumpster. A closet in an out-of-the- way building. These places have a unique currency in the game. In a desperate gamble, I burrow beneath a log and claw the forest floor upon myself until the forest disappears and becomes a wall of red and yellow leaves.

There's a click, and the autumn blanket of leaves becomes Tim's face, his features unnatural in their exuberance.

"Welcome to the end of the Third Cycle!" he blasts with over-acted enthusiasm. "This cycle of the tournament has been a great success. You each played very hard. Look at your scores!"

The pod's screen blinks white and returns as a dashboard superimposed on red and black images of bridges, bots, roads, wind turbines. The dashboard is an endless tide of green numbers, all kinds of statistics from the week. As a group, the 50 of us have logged a total of 5,642 hours of game play this week, with over 6000 confirmed bot kills, 44 pieces of infrastructure destroyed, 18 assets lost. And the metrics scroll on.

From behind the dashboard, Tim announces, "I have some good news, players. You each have been playing for points, but we never told you what the value of the points were. Each point is a Satoshi! That is right, you have all been stacking Sats this entire time!"

Even from within the pod, I can hear the hallway fill with a chorus of pig in shit happy exaltations and gasps.

Tim, seemingly aware of our response, continues, "Yes. It is very exciting. Each eliminated player's Sats will be added to a collective pot the winner will claim. Ten rounds. If all of you work hard enough, someone might leave here with an entire Bitcoin."

Tim seems to pause, willing us to applaud once more, and we don't disappoint. Thunderous applause and cheers breakout throughout the hangar.

Between my own sporadic claps, I run the figures. Even if the tournament prize was half that, it would still be enough. For a moment, my chest feels less tight and my shoulders drop a little as I envision us talking again. *Steady Bug. Keep your expectations realistic, no good getting ahead of yourself. Eye on the prize.*

Tim's voice returns to its supremacy as the clapping falters and dies away. "Congratulations to all players who survived this cycle. From this hangar, 40 of you will go to the next cycle. Extra congratulations to those who scored in the top ten worldwide. In order of highest scores"—Tim's voice goes flat as he recites a string of dumb names—"Box Boy, XY, Jerrycan, Z, GigaChad, Rando, GOATboy, Outplay, Killme, and Ki-Yay."

Well, Yippee-Ki-Yay.

HYPATIA
Cardinal Borders

Alexandra stares out the window at the passing outlines of the stubborn conifers that stand dark shoulder to dark shoulder at the side of the road. I am in the middle seat of the truck cab, pressed between her and Paul. Paul's leg strains against his faded jeans. Moonlight wets the travel mug wedged between us in the cupholder below the gear box, the splash of its pale glow illuminating a rim marked by a dry and stale brown kiss of java.

For a long time, Paul does not say much. The road is dark and narrow. Driven by habit, perhaps, he fumbles with the radio tuner, just like our Father did. He surfs the stations in earnest, but there is nothing but static and its quiet metronome of deadened time.

"Are you sure you know what you're doing?" he asks. "You're better off in Flower Station."

"We have a plan," I say.

Alexandra breaks away from the window to offer a nod of solidarity. "Refuge," she adds with confidence.

"I know that, but it's all hell down there," he pleads.

"It's no picnic here either," I say.

"No, not in the cities, but ... You're safe out here," he placates as patches of yellow blossom in his face.

I say nothing, and Alexandra turns back to the window to watch the trees and night twirl and twist as the truck sucks them into its undertow. Silence creeps back in amongst us. Paul, his eyes fixed on the road, continues to take us down backroads and numbered routes, routes that never warranted a second glance when I asked the internet for navigation. The image I saved from the Road Atlas is too far removed from these quiet roads. There is a helplessness in that we must assume he is going south.

A metallic patter erupts on the top of the truck's cab. Paul taps the brakes. His face becomes an ugly, startled expression. Alexandra inhales deeply, and we pause, braced for an onslaught from above. The patter deepens and becomes rainfall on the windscreen. Paul offers a nervous chuckle, and Alexandra deflates with a long sigh of relief. The rain falls harder, and Alexandra turns back to the window. She runs her fingertips in small circles around the droplets that run past her overtop the aqua-fog curtain that has settled on the glass.

I scan through the rain for way-posts to inform us of our direction of travel. There are few signs, but eventually, we end up on route 22, headed into Cardinal.

Paul seems to follow my gaze. "You girls ever been to Cardinal?" he asks.

I shake my head for us both.

"It's mainly churches and auto shops. But it's not much more than a kilometre paddle across the border and there's an island in the middle," Paul adds with sagacity.

"Any word since the flash?" I ask.

"I don't know anyone in Cardinal, but apparently, many are crossing this way."

I fidget in my seat, only to realize it is the conversation rather than the space that is sparking my feeling of discomfort.

Cardinal's onset is slow. It starts with a signpost for KOA holiday homes, the silhouettes of which are visible from the road through a thin veil of trees. There is a powerless Lotus charging station, and then our headlights carve over a flat road obscured by rain beaded in our headlights, cut by the occasional green reflection of address signs moored along the embankment. For a minute or so, Paul does not seem to realize we have passed beyond the outskirts of the town. One could forgive him for the error. Without any lights, the town surfaces from the road as a cluster of low-rise shadows.

I nudge Paul's arm, and he slows and cuts his lights as we pass by several smaller roads that crisscross over the main road, bisecting it into patterns akin to city blocks. The houses that rest on the shoulder of the 22 are unlit and shuttered in the night. As we lumber past them, I pierce through windows into sitting rooms and kitchens for the faint winking light of a beating heart or burning halo of a human eye, but find only the dark purple of unheated and untenanted space.

I decide it is worth declaring, "These houses look empty, Paul."

Paul glances over his shoulder and weaves his head to look past Alexandra. "Cars are still in the driveways. Like I said, being this close to the border is dangerous, I'd be lying low too," he says, but shifts in his seat and adjusts his seatbelt. His movement casts an aroma of tobacco from his shirt. "We're getting close," he adds.

Alexandra nods, and I look on as the space between the buildings shrinks further and the dim plastic of convenience store signs, unaided by the neon glow, erupts amongst the residential malaise in greater frequency. The road splits into several arteries, all named Dundas, but we follow a thinner strip of asphalt that heads towards a wide river, its surface twinkling with etches of starlight as it courses along ahead of us.

"There she is, old St. Lawrence," Paul points out.

Yet, as we travel down towards the river's silent waters, the truck starts to bump and bounce on the road. Paul's face turns indigo, the colour of panic, and he flicks the headlights on, illuminating debris, small pieces scattered across the road. They take shape amidst the dark and rain: thousands of small, shining, jagged black metal pieces on the asphalt. Drone limbs, the remnants of a strike. The pieces hiss and squeal as Paul rides over them, and the canoe claps as it bounces on the bed of the truck with each piece we ride over.

Paul swears under his breath, cuts the lights, and lets the truck drift into the gravel shoulder. He sits in the driver's seat, staring forward into the rain and darkness and does not acknowledge us. I watch as his face goes the colour of slate. I have seen many men's faces go this way before. Our Father bore the same granite mien when he was teaching Alexandra to ride her bike and let go only to have her tumble into the ditch. I have coded the slate visage as despair and stubbornness, the emotion that runs from having made a mistake for which they cannot forgive themselves. I have not seen the same colour in any women's faces. Only men.

The rain patters on the windscreen, and I watch Alexandra as her eyes dart in appraisal from Paul to the road, then to the river as it spreads out beneath the night. I nod at her.

"It's not your fault," I say to Paul. "You couldn't have known they'd be here."

"I just don't get it. They told me it's a route. Others are using Galop to cross the border," he mutters, and he seems resolved to keep his eyes fixed on the road, away from us.

"I know. It's okay, we can still make it work. If others are using it, this might not mean anything. The debris is likely just the remnants of an old attack." I strain my voice to hit a cadence I believe he will find reassuring.

"Well, you can't go now. You can't. I can't leave you if there might be those." His voice constricts and then breaks high. "Goddamn, fucking things about!"

I predicted this as a possible outcome as soon as his face went the colour of slate. Stasis is the only talisman for men mired in their mistakes.

I am about to speak, but Alexandra intervenes. "No." She gives her head a vigorous shake. "We must go," she adds.

"We can try again. Another town ..." offers Paul. His voice is distant, and he throttles the steering wheel in his bony hands.

"No," Alexandra asserts.

Deep ribs etch Paul's leathery brow as he drops it into his hands. Alexandra sighs, wrestles the backpack out from under us, and takes out her notebook. She flicks through it until satisfied, leans across me, and puts her sketches under Paul's face. I watch as the pale, shallow ring of light cast from the cab's interior ceiling catches beautiful, yet ragged pencil lines of lighthouses and wave torn beaches. Still, reposes of Alexandra's vision of the refuge flip and cartwheel over one another, and in earnest, she does not turn to the next page until she sees the white of Paul's eyes.

"Safe there," she whispers to Paul. I see his slate countenance soften and break.

"I understand," he concedes. His eyes grab on the rear window and settle on the canoe fastened in the truck's bed. "We're going to have to portage. Just do as I say."

~

We crouch behind the truck while Paul whispers instructions. He hands us both lifejackets, but Alexandra refuses and pushes hers at me.

"Both. She sinks." Her words are terse and orange eddies form in her cheeks.

For a brief second, I wonder how she knows this. A protest begins to form on my lips, but before I manage to say anything, Paul fastens one lifejacket across my chest and hitches another under my legs like a massive pair of underwear.

As I am the shortest, it is decided I will go on point. Alexandra is behind me, near the bow, and Paul is at the stern, where he tells us the weight of the boat falls the heaviest. Paul was meticulous in his instruction of the parts of the boat and quizzed us regularly.

His reasoning was the canoe is an instrument, and we must know all the parts of an instrument to effectively understand how to use it. Perhaps I should teach Alexandra about all my components, though in truth, most of them are beyond my working memory. The processor stewards them.

We are not far from the river now. My processor overlays the distance to the shoreline atop my vision: our boat launch is 948 feet away. The air is cold, made colder by the pellets of rain that fall so hard they ricochet from the asphalt to splash across my shins. While we were still in the truck, we agreed we would not say a word to one another, but even if we wanted to say something, the din of the rain would make it impossible to hear. Instead, I guide them with the painter. The sinews of the rope recall the water and become slick through my fingers. The second lifejacket fastened around my legs forces me to waddle, but still, with deft steps, I manage to step over thousands of black drone pieces that dot the road. They look like mussel shells on the arm of a pier.

Occasionally, Alexandra loses control over the bow. It tips down towards her toes, and the painter tugs me backwards. Each time this happens, I survey Cardinal, which remains mute and opaque behind us. There are no car lights, no scampering shadows. If there is any sound, the noise of voices perhaps, the fury of the rain's landfall outmatches it.

The boat launch is in sight now, less than 492 feet away, and parallel to it, a low-lying building, a composite of cheap white siding and beige poured concrete, steps out from the night. A sign over the door of the building, likely too obscured by the rain to be visible to Alexandra and Paul, reads: "Royal Canadian Legion Branch 105." The road's slope has flattened out, and I realize the Legion is planted on a peninsula. Several grey, wind-beaten trees that lean tall and narrow over the shoreline obscure the river. I stop short. In the dark spaces cradled amidst the tree branches, there is a sheen of metal.

Alexandra rams the bow into my back, but I neither speak nor move as my eyes filter through the dark tangle of branches. They look like bats at first: small, their jagged legs curled in on themselves as they hang from the boughs of the trees and, in places, they have burrowed into the trunks, making a crooked scarab-shelled spine. I focus on them. My eyes slip past the monsoon wall of rain and see they are still. No heat comes from them. They appear to be in hibernation.

From the stern, Paul issues a nervous hiss, "Girls, why have we stopped?"

I am not sure how to share the news. I want to tell Alexandra, but I fear Paul will try to make us come home with him if he hears what is ahead of us. Back to Flower Station, where there is no power, only different waiting games. Crouching under the canoe, I face Alexandra. Her cheeks are red with exertion. In slow, careful movements, she adjusts the weight of the canoe on her shoulders.

I get as close as I can and whisper into her ear, "Breathe. Breathe. They are in the trees ahead. Asleep."

Wisps of yellow surface over her flushed cheeks, but she steadies herself and, with a subtle flex of her neck and turn of her cheek, a gesture inscrutable to anyone but a sister, she indicates at Paul. I shake my head. Her face flashes orange and pink, though she manages a reluctant nod.

"What's going on?" Paul asks. His words are hoarse and sound as if they are coming to us through clenched teeth. I find him beneath the canoe, too. His pallor is grey, and he looks cold.

"We're close," I whisper. "Keep quiet, it's all clear," I add, but in my peripheral vision, Alexandra's eyes grow wide and then become pale hooks that she casts into me.

Paul nods and folds his lower lip into his mouth as he shifts the weight of the canoe across his round shoulders. I tiptoe forward. The painter is slack in my hand and my sight is locked on the dangling black masses in the tangled boughs ahead. Pelted by rain, the river runs on either side of us, subdued and seemingly continuous under our feet, through a storm tunnel beneath the road.

There is a thunderclap of a metal door against a concrete wall. All the transactions happen at once, and my processor strains to speed up enough to arrest the scene before me. Somewhere down the hill from us, near the river, a man yells, "Now!"

I lose my footing, and the canoe juts backwards as several figures burst through the door of the Legion. They fan out in all directions, middle-aged men moving like firework sparks, ignited and fleeting as they tumble into the night. The air becomes full of an electric pulse. In unison, the drones flutter up from the branches to become a dark, humming cloud. One man remains by the entrance, his silhouette pot-bellied, and fires a shotgun into the night sky. Red sparks cascade through the dark, followed by the clatter of metal.

"Die, you pieces of shit," he yells as he locks for a second shot. The kickback reverberates through the deserted parking ground and up the empty street as he slips back through the door.

The legionnaires continue to flee. Some have gone east, others west. I watch as one, perhaps in panic, falters, turns on his heels, and sprints towards the river, passing into the reach of the tenanted trees. There is a chorus of snaps, and a plume of white smoke forms and drifts from where he last stood. The canoe clatters behind me. Without turning, I know Paul has dropped his end and is breaking away back up the road. As he runs, he casts words over his shoulder, but they are inaudible, paltry against the pop of the drones, rain, and shotgun fire. A frenetic hum descends upon us.

Alexandra does not hesitate. She jumps back and lets the canoe fall on top of her. She disappears as the gunwales bounce until they bite the surface of the road, concealing her from the drones' aerial view. The air is becoming loose with their movement towards me. Tipping up one side of the canoe to slide under and join Alexandra is too risky.

With half my body against the hull and the other half on the road, I press my face into the canoe's wet plastic embrace and wait. There is nothing left to do but think cold thoughts in the hope the warmth in my parts falters, as it has before, and my body fails to produce a human heat signature. Almost nothing left to do. The unevenness of the road leaves a small gap, a sliver of dark space. I slide my fingers beneath the gunwales and wiggle them in the dark like baited hooks until I feel the flutter of Alexandra's fingertips against my mine—a mute lifeline between us as the swarm grows deafening.

The drones scuttle over the hull of the canoe and click on the asphalt next to me. Amidst the softening patter of the rain, I can feel their protrusions move in sharp yet delicate movements across my back as they clamour over me. I am not sure how many are on me, but I feel them on my legs and arms too, exploring me, laying claim to my limbs through the fabric of the lifejacket, scaling the small of my back. As I lie there, I imagine how difficult I must be to process, and can envision their algorithms sputtering and restarting as they try to confirm my bio-signals.

I will lie prostrate for all eternity, until my battery dies and thereafter, as the drones forever falter on the precipice of attack. I imagine Alexandra and hope the rain is louder than the metallic clicks and taps of the drones' claws from within the belly of the canoe. She does not move her fingers, but I can feel the warmth of her grip, and from her heat, the beat of her heart. How long she will stay calm in this situation, I cannot project, but I know the status quo is unsustainable.

It is hard to hear, or to trust what one hears, with the clicks and insectile hum of the drones and the din of the rain against the canoe, but I cannot hear the legionnaires, or the blast of the shotgun. They must be dead and gone. I let my processor slow down and the strain that shuddered through my thighs and arms recedes. The drones are still walking on me, the spines of their claw-feet burrowing in my hair as two twitch and buzz on the back of my head.

If they decided to detonate, they would blow me to pieces. I am sentient, in a distant and aloof way, that somewhere inside me, a program is running through the scenarios where both Alexandra and I might survive. The outcomes for us seem to be degrading in rapid fashion. I envision myself standing up and drawing them away from the canoe to me, yet if this were to happen, the blast would probably blow through the canoe, killing Alexandra as well. A scenario appears to me with an outcome I have never run before: Alexandra's likely death and …

My escape without her. Alone.

A reflex inside me flinches and tightens. I can feel it through my shoulders and behind my jaw, and the sensation wills me to move away from the canoe, to grind my face into the pavement until I can inch myself into the waters that flow beneath the road and slip away. I can imagine the solace of my betrayal in the water's embrace, a second birth as I drift alone in the river in search of less foreign looking shores. This sequence of thought is alien to me, and I know that with the guardrails set by Lotus, it would have been inconceivable. But, in the absence of guardrails, the thought continues to run, yet I have not moved.

Under the cover of the canoe and across the border of the gunwale, the tremble and flutter of Alexandra's fingers on mine passes between us like a hymn. Perhaps only sisters can speak their hearts with their hands. If I were to break with her at this moment, I forecast with near certainty she would collapse, tantrum, leave the canoe, and die. Despite this, I feel the instinct to run flex again like a serpent tightening over itself in my abdomen.

The spiny foot of a drone pierces my cheek as it struggles to position itself on the side of my head. Our cone of potential actions is becoming narrower. The outcomes seem ever more dark, certain, and uniform in their consequences.

The cough and rasp of a combustion engine rents through the silence that settled in wait behind the clicking limbs and buzz. The movement on my back stills and the pressure on my cheek dissipates. Then, my back erupts with the sensation of hundreds of curved claw-feet lifting off in flight. I dare to twist my face so that I follow the direction of the noise. In the night, I see the flash of headlights set high above the road. It is Paul's truck. The tires squeal as he attempts to turn around, presumably to flee north, away from Cardinal and us. The halo of his headlights wraps around the swarm, and the drones appear like hundreds of fist-sized moths, burrowing into the truck's light. There is no time to watch.

I lift the canoe up and drag Alexandra to her feet. From up the road, there is a series of pops as the windshield of the truck explodes and the horn laments, its call destined to be unanswered. The hum ascends, and it feels like the surrounding air has gone slack again, fanned by thousands of invisible wings. My legs buckle as I hurl the canoe from the side of the road into the river below. Alexandra watches the canoe bob up and down in the water, and I track her comprehension. She shakes her head and stamps her feet, but there is no choice. With our fingers interlaced, we jump, following the canoe into the river's black waters.

HYPATIA
Galop Island

Our passage across the St. Lawrence was arduous and laboured. The drones were unwilling to let Alexandra go and tracked her to the water. We flipped the canoe over our heads to shield ourselves from them and drifted along the channel that separated the rest of Cardinal from the little spit of land where the Legion stood. The water was up to our chests and it knocked the air out of Alexandra's lungs. Careful not to attract the drones' attention, we drifted until the hum faded and the patter of the rain stopped, and in silence righted the canoe on the pebble shoals at the very tip of the little channel.

We paddle like Paul showed us, with Alexandra in the bow and me in the stern. There is no light ahead of us, and only the moon seems to graze the flat expanse of Galop Island's body in the distance. Alexandra struggles to cleave the water with her paddle and her pace falters.

"We aren't far," I encourage, but the wind is strong, and with the chop of the water against the tip of the canoe, I am not sure she hears me.

The land in front of us grows into a bigger dark mass that rises and falls with the canoe's bounces. The wind howls into us as the hull scrapes aground, into scrub and grassland on Galop Island. Despite our exertion, we manage to land the nose of the canoe and keep our tail from spinning. I slip into the water to steady us. Alexandra hurls her paddle from the boat and it disappears amongst the windswept dark-green shadows of the grassland that looms before us.

She wraps her arms around herself and squats in the dark, rubbing her shoulders in frantic and violent moves of her palms, desperate to ignite some spark on her skin. She is soaked, and the wind continues to howl. With the defence of flattened grass only, she is helpless against its bite. The lifejacket would have probably caught more of her body heat. Her decision to increase my buoyancy has left her more exposed.

I move the canoe up onto solid ground as I assess our options. Everything in our backpack, including Alexandra's Galaxy blanket, is wet. The island offers no cover, and there are at least several hours until daybreak. Without new clothes, a heat source, or some felicitous act of ingenuity, Alexandra will die of hypothermia. Even from here, I can see goosebumps dot her pale arms and neck as her body fights to claim her heat back from the river and desolate barrens of Galop.

"We can't stay here," I urge. "It's too exposed. You'll freeze."

She looks like she wants to speak, but she loses control as her teeth chatter over the possibility of any few words she might have. Inside my head, I form a search for signs of hypothermia, but again, the vast and desolate space of my own consciousness greets me. Even here, within a mile of the border, there is still no connection. How deep does the blackout go? Will there actually be more opportunities to charge on this side of the border?

Inside me, a sensation squirms and flexes in what feels like the bottom of my stomach, and I find myself wandering through the scenarios where I go alone once more. Alexandra's pallor worsens, and the thought, my thought, subsides and goes dormant.

With the painter from the canoe wrapped in one hand, I put myself in front of Alexandra and let the wind slam into me as we cross the grassland. In our wake, the canoe moves over the grass with serpentine twists. The wind is fierce, and I can feel it rattle my chest and move little pieces of me around in my insides. I do not need to run a diagnostic to know that, between the push of the wind and the weight of the canoe, I am putting a considerable strain on my battery. It was at 73% capacity when we left Flower Station. With no known opportunities to charge ahead of us, the uneasiness begins to surface within me again.

Alexandra's hands wrap around my shoulders, and her touch is more than desperation to shield herself from the wind. There is electricity in her grip, a subtle code of love and cherishment. Even if I cannot draw breath, grow breasts, or produce real feces, we are still sisters.

"Cold. Very cold." Her words are forceful enough to breach the relentless blitz of the wind into our faces.

"I know, sis, I'm working on it," I answer, keeping my words level to instil a sense of calm in her as I scan the horizon ahead of us for options.

We crossed the river farther east than planned, and the land here is barren and narrow. We might be able to take cover in the canoe. If Alexandra lies on top of me, the ground might not suck the heat from her body. She might survive the night, but she probably would not recover without medical support, and that is not an option. I take another look at our surroundings. On the west side, the island is broader and the shadows have more height. We could at least take shelter in those thickets and trees and escape the wind. There might even be some foliage to lay over Alexandra to help her conserve her heat.

I take a deeper scan of the western leg of the island and catch a flash of heat. There is fire over there. A mile and a half away, it appears to me as little more than coal light, freckled and dim against the expanse of shapeless, dark green mounds. A campfire. Who, I wonder, managed to smuggle fire back into this world?

We head towards the fire across damp and spongy grass, and with my compacted weight, the earth seems to open to swallow my steps. We wade rather than walk through it. Twice, I trip over myself as my feet sink and tangle amongst old branches and mud with a coarse dark ichor, and Alexandra stumbles into my back. Each time, I look back to her and find her eyes glazed and estranged from our surroundings. Seemingly anesthetized by the cold, she stares through me, to some other horizon layered beneath this one and beyond my vision. Her face is as white as a porcelain doll's and her lips have gone a greyish blue. I shake her until her eyes settle on me again and she slips back into our world with a hesitant nod.

The fire is still over 2200 feet away, and so I unravel the canoe's painter from my hand and leave it moored in the grass behind us, confident I can retrieve it again shortly after daybreak. I creep through the dark while Alexandra lingers behind me and feigns my low stance and soft steps, but her gait is wooden. Once we are 328 feet away, we lie on our bellies, and I observe the campfire. Alexandra buries her head into the soft earth, digging in to find a place beneath the reach of the wind, and I hear her teeth resume their chatter. The fire remains low in the earth as if laid in a crater below the flat grassland. Four bodies, sat in a horseshoe, take shape at the edge of its light. Behind them, a makeshift lean-to keeps them shielded from the elements. The wind carries their voices to us. They sound young, and their laughs and words seem to grate at the back of their throats before coming out in half-sentences. I scan their vitals and assess they are in their late teens, early twenties, not that much older than Alexandra.

We remain low. Alexandra's shivers have become less violent, and she appears sleepy, wandering the cleft between this world and her own quieter place. She is running out of time. I have no idea how the encounter will go, but recognize that, at least in Alexandra's present condition, they are unlikely to see us as a threat. Alexandra's beauty will not hurt, either.

"We need to make contact. I won't tell them I'm a companion child," I whisper.

It is rare that I encounter prejudice or outright hatred from teenagers, but things are changing and there is no sense in risking it. Without conceit, I wrap my arm around Alexandra and let her lean on my shoulder. Our steps are slow and muffled by the wet, spongy earth, and we get quite close before they notice us.

"Shit, who the hell is that?" says the one closest to us as he scrambles ungainly to his feet.

The other two boys stand too, but the boy at the centre of the lean-to stays sitting, with his eyes on us. While the other boys' faces are yellow as they fight against a parabolic spike in their heart rates, the one beneath the lean-to remains assured and watchful.

"Who's there?" says a short stocky boy on the sitting boy's right.

A beard clings to his chin in little patches of peach fuzz, and I estimate he is no older than 17. Across from him, a bespectacled boy with a toque pulled tight over his head seems to follow us with his gaze. We take several shambling steps forward so that the light of the fire brings us out from the dark.

"That's fucking close enough. I swear I'll drop you both if you take another step," hisses the one who first spotted us. He is on his feet and has become a tall shadow. He looks almost pinched as the fire catches the contours of his gaunt, pale face.

"My sister and I need help. We've come from ... from Cardinal," I stammer, doing my best to imitate Alexandra's chattering teeth. "We're freezing."

I inch us forward so the fire illuminates us as it freckles the clay sands beneath our feet in its half-light. I can tell they see us both now, and there are many eyes on Alexandra. Her clothes are wet and pressed against her by the wind, and her snow-blonde hair cascades around her shoulders in wayward tangles.

"Get the fuck out of here!" growls the thin boy.

I can feel Alexandra pull back from my side, but I do not flinch as I try to find and hold his eyes in the dark. His cheeks burn the yellowest of the four.

"Francis, don't be an asshole," commands the boy beneath the lean-to. He is older and dark-skinned. His bio-signals date him somewhere between 19 and 23. He wears a camouflage jacket and pants. A few days of stubble darkens his chin.

"Who knows who they are," spits Francis.

"We still don't really know shit about you, but we've let you share the fire all week," replies the boy under the lean-to. He keeps his voice light, as if bored by a kid brother's childish antics, but his expression is firm and serious. The one called Francis throws his arms up in the air, mutters under his breath, and storms off in the direction opposite from where we have come. "Well, get close to the fire, lots of room. Jackson, grab that spare blanket and our emergency one, too. That one," he adds with a flick of his pointer finger at Alexandra, "is goddamn hypothermic."

The short stocky boy nods and begins to rummage behind the lean-to, where they have stored their backpacks. I shepherd Alexandra to the fire, near where the stocky boy, Jackson, sat. As we move, I name us, mindful to chatter my teeth as I speak. It is important they know our names and personalize us within the first few minutes of our encounter.

The one under the lean-to smiles. "Nice to meet you, Hypatia and Alexandra. I'm Malcolm. This little tank of a man is Jackson." Jackson raises a hand from the back of the lean-to in indication. "The quiet one is Phil"—the boy with glasses gives a shy nod—"and the one sulking somewhere behind us is Francis."

From the dark, Francis yells, "I'm checking our perimeter!" Though incredulous, his voice flies at us hoarse and strangled by adolescence. His heat signature flashes through the dark at us some 30 feet away.

Malcolm shrugs and smirks. Jackson is now by our side with one blanket that looks like cooked tinfoil folded over his arm and a tartan-patterned sleeping bag he has unzipped in hand.

"Get inside the emergency blanket first and then wrap this around you," he says, holding up the tartan sleeping bag. "It's probably best," he stammers, "if you get out of your wet clothes, they'll suck the heat right out of you."

Even in her hypothermic state, Alexandra looks mortified at the suggestion.

"We'll manage, thanks."

I smile, cast the tinfoil sheet over both of us, and help Alexandra remove her clothes while keeping our veil of privacy. The wind howls over the sheet and the corners flap, and as they billow and fall, I catch vignettes of the party around the fire. Those who sit by the fire keep their heads low, their eyes on their toes. The one named Francis stands at the periphery of the campfire, and I can see the red halos from the heat of his eyes upon us. The wind rolls back and dies as if inhaled by the lungs of the river's black waters, and the sheeting goes limp in my hands as it settles over Alexandra's shoulders.

She is nude now, yet gestures with her white tremulous hands at the corners of the sheeting which remain in my grip. I realize she is right. For the sake of appearances, I will need to undress as well.

We manage to orchestrate an exchange, and now Alexandra defends her modesty and my artificiality with the tinfoil emergency blanket. Once, in a changing room, our Mother tried to assure me that my body was indistinguishable from a biological little girl's, but this is not true. For one, biological little girls do not stay little girls forever. For another, Alexandra showed me there is a very tiny print on the backside of my earlobe that reads *made in Singapore* and indented behind my knees is the word *Michigan*.

The wind ruffles the sheet again, and this time leaves us more exposed. Alexandra and I turn to shield ourselves, though the heads around the fires remain downcast, but this time I notice the grey smoke of their breath curl against the cold night. Alexandra adjusts the sheet, and they disappear again. I cup my hand over my mouth, as if to keep the lie within me. We will need a cover. A means to conceal I have neither soul nor furnace to make a presence. I am, by design, life without emissions.

"Could we please have some tea to warm ourselves?" I call out the request from inside the blanket, but I tap my teeth as I speak to imitate the chaotic noise of chattering.

"Are you both covered yet?" asks Jackson. Alexandra peaks her head over the tinfoil sheet and gives a swift nod. "Okay, two cups of tea," replies Jackson.

We press together beneath the tinfoil sheet, and I free one arm to wrap the tartan sleeping bag around us further. We then use our toes and my free arm to nudge our wet clothes towards the heat of the fire.

"Now that nobody is liable to freeze to death, where did you two come from?" asks Malcolm. He keeps his voice light and casual, but he holds us in an attentive stare. While he speaks, Jackson pulls a water bladder out from beneath the lean-to, fills a little pot, and fidgets as he positions it on the fire.

Alexandra looks at me and sees I have cradled my chin in my hand and let my long, adroit fingers cover my mouth. Her vision follows mine to the pot of water balanced on the coals that dot the outer regions of the campfire.

"Ottawa," murmurs Alexandra, and they seem surprised to hear her speak.

"And you are sisters?" asks the quiet boy, Phil.

Their eyes are on us now. Francis has stepped back into the firelight, his face alive with what appears to be studious appraisal. It is true we look nothing alike. As Alexandra has matured, I am more out of place, and my leadership of her is more suspicious.

"Half-sisters," I enunciate through my fingers, watching their faces as they process my lie. The three boys around the fire accept my words in a green flurry, but Francis' countenance turns yellow, and his body language remains aloof. Alexandra looks stricken.

"What the hell are you doing crossing the border? Stacy here has no business in a war zone, and what are you, nine?" spits Francis.

Alexandra's body tightens, and she begins to rub her fingers together. We both know Stacy is Alogo Boo slang.

"Her name's Alexandra, and I'm 12." This time, I try to speak my words into my shoulder to conceal the absence of my breath. Francis suspires a mirthless laugh and crosses his arms. I eye the pot in the fire and see clusters of small bubbles are forming on its bottom. "It doesn't need to be too hot," I say with a nod at the pot. Jackson smiles his acknowledgement, but doesn't seem to move.

"I asked you a question. What the hell are you doing crossing the border?" Francis snarls, stepping back into the ring of sitting boys. Though the light illuminates his face, it cannot seem to push the shadows out from under his cheekbones or add light to the hollows of his eyes.

"Francis, you need to chill or go to bed. Jackson, I think that water is about as hot as it's going to get," commands Malcolm.

Jackson nods, fishes the pot from the fire, and leads it to two enameled stainless steel mugs set in the grass. The mugs are deep blue with many little white dots painted across them, like cold galaxies. I can see Alexandra drawing a similar conclusion.

"No, they need to answer the damn question," erupts Francis.

"Going New Hampshire," murmurs Alexandra.

Jackson frowns a little, but leans over and passes me a cup, and though I think he expects me to pass it to Alexandra, I cradle the mug close to my face and watch as its heat rises in the air before my lips. With the heat of the tea camouflaging my artificiality, I focus on alleviating Alexandra from carrying the conversation. The few words she has spoken seem to have drained her.

"An evacuation point in New Hampshire," I elaborate.

Malcolm offers us what appears like a slow nod of commiseration. "You should be able to get there safe enough, for now. Fighting is mainly taking place within the borders of Connecticut and New York State. The line's not holding up that well. The contest is all but lost in Pennsylvania. That's the bone being chewed on the Ham, at least."

"Phil came from Ottawa, too. The way he tells it, it sounds like it was hit very hard. Malcolm and I have never been in a swarm. I'm sorry," adds Jackson.

I tip my head at Phil, and he nods back. I can tell by the colour of his face that he is sorrowful, but these emotions are open for all to see, for the firelight catches his eyes, round and wet. With the tea's camouflage, I am eager to change the direction of the questions and get the attention away from us.

"So, why are you crossing the border?" I ask and I accentuate the pressure on the word "you."

"I've crossed a few times. Volunteer for the Republic," says Malcom with notable pride. "I'm taking Phil and Jackson down with me this time to fight Alogo Boos. At least, that's what Phil, Jackson, and I are up to. Francis, though, keeps his business private. Isn't that right, Francis?" asks Malcolm. Although his voice is boisterous and light, his face fades and pulses with distrust and disdain.

Francis shakes his head and scowls. "I already told you, I'm going down there to scrap. What's so hard to understand?"

"I guess we just don't get why you'd go to a war zone to scrap when there's plenty here," says Jackson.

"Because my cousin says it's a goddamn copper rush down there. Especially with the bonus." Francis spits into the fire.

I can feel Alexandra flinch next to me and know the circle has seen her face tighten. "What bonus?" I tip my head and smile to replicate an expression of casual interest and submission.

Nonetheless, Francis' face twists in suspicion and disdain. His reply comes slow, and he keeps his eyes on Malcolm as he says, "My Uncle told me that if you bring in a Metal Chad ..." Under Malcolm's incredulous gaze, he stutters, "... you bring in a companion child, on or off, and they pay you three times the market price for the metal and shit in it."

I smile, but next to me, beneath the blankets, I can feel the bounce of Alexandra's thigh as she tries to cope with this new information and avoid a meltdown. We did not factor in that there would be a bounty on my head in our travel plans. I am about to ask how he intends to tell biological children apart from companion children, when Malcolm responds, "I've heard about that bonus, too. Paid out by Alogo Boos."

Jackson leans forward now, and even in the ember light of the fire, I can see his expression has tempered and he becomes older. I feel Alexandra squeeze into me and edge her body ahead of mine, slipping in front of me so that she partially shields me. Her renegotiation of position takes place in silence beneath the sleeping bag.

"You know they sell that on, to fund their war effort. Makes you complicit. One of us could take a bullet, or worse, become red smoke and ash in a drone swarm paid for from your scraps. Like Jackson says, why not scrap here and stay out of the war?" finishes Malcolm. His face has deepened from orange to red, and there is violence in his eyes.

Francis tastes his lips several times, but pulls back from the fire as he says, "Like I told you all, I got no interest in politics. That's someone else's problem."

"It's our problem! The three of us you're sharing the fire with," says Malcolm, and now the feeling in his words matches his face.

Francis folds his arms across his chest. "Nobody's forcing you to be down there. It's not your war." His words are quiet and fall away beneath his chin.

"Horseshit!" snaps Malcolm. "You want to live next to a white nationalist ethno-state? This is war against outright fascism, and you're willing to fund the wrong side."

Francis scowls, but his words come out in a stammer. "Look. Look, the way I see it, I scrap a couple Metal Chads and get in and out. There are too many drones here to scrap anything. I'd rather deal with people than drones. Besides, Metal Chads have gone apeshit. It's a public service and I bet you there are more of them over there than here." He finishes with a nod to the clay and twisted clumps of grass beneath us.

"I'm not telling you again to knock it off with that Alogo Boo bullshit. Thoughts become words, and words become actions, kid. Phil, how does the rest of that go again?" asks Malcolm.

"Watch your actions, they become your habits; watch your habits, they become your character; watch your character, it becomes your destiny," recites Phil. "Or something like that."

Phil's face reads like a grey sea of diffidence. Regardless, it is clear Francis is not a norm creator in the group or a follower, and thus not an immediate threat to us.

"I really don't mean much by it, it's reflex at this point," laughs Francis.

"Sounds like a case and point," says Phil. "That's the way it went, though. After the flash, everything changed, like a switch malfunctioned or snapped or something." His voice is distant, and his words become quieter the longer he speaks.

Alexandra squirms beside me, her delicate lips cupped behind the red and dirty skin of her palm. I try to find her beneath the blankets, to calm her.

"See, she knows what I'm talking about, don't you Stacy? You've seen those metal assholes, haven't you?"

"Her name—" I start, but hold my words as Jackson jumps to his feet, his fists clenched.

"What did Malcolm just say about your Alogo Boo shit?"

Francis waves his hands in earnest surrender. Malcolm motions for Jackson to sit back down, but his heart rate is elevated too, his face a sunset of red and orange. There is an opportunity to build more trust and pull attention from Francis.

"A companion child murdered our parents. He was our neighbour, and then one day he wasn't," I say with assurance, but inside, I am surprised that nothing in my statement is untrue.

Jackson turns from Francis, his voice gentle. "I'm really sorry to hear that. Please accept my condolences."

Malcolm commiserates with a sigh and a nod, and I can see them both exchange nervous looks at Phil.

"Malfunction. A glitch. It was like she was dazed and lost and then suddenly woke up a different person. A psycho," Phil mutters his words into his toes and avoids everyone's eyes.

"It's not a malfunction. It's by design," presses Francis in an aggrieved faux whisper.

"Oh lordy, not this conversation again," says Jackson as he tips the dredges of the pot into a small thermos. Malcolm smothers a laugh into his wrist, but it is too late. Phil's face has darkened.

"Look, you don't have to agree with Alogo Boos on everything, but they are damn right when they say foreign technology has no place here," says Francis, his hands over his head in exasperation.

"Nah, my brother agrees with what Phil just said. The flash messed with everything electronic. Companion children just glitched," says Jackson.

"Your brother's a moron if he thinks that. This has probably been the plan since the first day one of those little metal bastards was shipped," snipes Francis as he eyes the aromatic seams that curl from the tea cupped in our hands. I see desire flood his face.

"My brother's a software engineer, you dipshit," says Jackson, shaking his head from side to side with what looks like bemused incredulity. "What's your source, some Alogo Boo fan boy website?" he sneers.

"Website? How many websites have you been browsing these days?"

"You know what I mean," retorts Jackson. "No, let me guess, your all-knowing uncle?"

"You don't know shit about ..." Francis halts his words and raises his hands in surrender, though I can see his face has gone yellow and his pulse has quickened.

Malcolm extends his arms and waves his palms at the earth in what looks like an attempt to conjure a truce amidst the discord. He shakes his head in what codes as exasperation and says, "You both have no manners, its rude to bicker in front of company. Let's pick a new subject." From across the fire, his eyes settle in our direction and his features flood with green mirth. "Alexandra, Hypatia, would you care to hear a story about wild horses?"

Francis groans and throws his hands over his head, while Jackson's face fills with orange pockmarks of annoyance. His irritation leaches into his words as he says, "Malcolm, they damn near froze to death already, they don't need to be bored to death too."

"What?! It's a good story. Phil, you'll back me on this," demands Malcolm.

Phil buries his face in his hands and sighs. "It's probably not even true."

"Full on propaganda," snickers Francis.

Malcolm's features darken, but he maintains his smile as he responds, "Good lord. Fine. It's about check-in time anyway."

The group goes silent as Malcolm wrestles a walkie-talkie from a backpack stored underneath the lean-to, followed by a long antenna he fixes to it in hurried, practiced twists. He gets to his feet and stands north of the fire, close, but outside the ring of his companions. For the first 30 seconds, all I hear is chattering static, barely discernable above the howl of wind through the flat grass and scrub. Malcolm paces as if to outrun the channel's emptiness. Then there are words, and though the static clings to them with indigence, there are audible commands.

I sit low and keep my mouth shut to avoid catching the frequency below my jaw again and revealing myself as a Metal Chad, as Francis calls us. Malcolm gives several nods and responds that he has understood the directions. He closes the communication and disassembles the radio, folding it neatly back into his rucksack. With a stern face and wind-chapped lips, he tells us we are to break camp early tomorrow and make landing at Lisbon beach. From there, it is a short walk south from somewhere called Wallace Point to a blue building behind the cemetery. That is where they will rendezvous for their arms and receive further orders.

"You might as well cross with us. We can probably even arrange a mobile escort to New Hampshire. It'll take you days and days on foot," suggests Malcolm as he walks past the group and throws himself under the lean-to.

I nod in appreciation before Alexandra has a chance to react. I should have given her the chance to reply, but my processor has made it clear: I do not have the battery life to travel on foot.

Malcolm advises we all get a few hours' sleep, and I force Alexandra to oblige.

The ground feels less squishy, hardening as the temperature drops further. The fire continues to burn, and Alexandra inches nearer, desperate for its heat.

I know I should not have answered for both of us yet again, accepting Malcolm's offer to arrange transport. I did the same thing with Paul, too. It makes her feel like a child when I make decisions like that without her. I move closer to her in the dark, and whisper, "Alexandra?"

She does not speak, but turns on her side so that we are staring into each other's eyes. I can feel the warmth of her breath on my cheek. There is a bitterness in it, a smell I recognize as hunger.

"I think we should go with them. Do you agree?" I keep my voice under 30 decibels and speak my words up her nose. She smiles and tips her head in assent. "We must watch Francis," I add. She says nothing, but grabs my hand and directs it to a patch of stars that shines through a narrow window amidst the clouds.

In the past, I would recite their ascension and declination and she would name them by their numbers. Without the planetarium on the internet, our stars have grown fierce and wayward, freed from the pinch of city lights and beyond the reach of human devised constellations. I am blind in this world, yet she remains blind to my limitations. I recite numbers at random until I hear her breath soften into a light snore.

Sleep comes fast to the rest of them too, and soon, the stutter and grumble of human hibernation colonizes the stillness of the night. I lie awake, and for a moment, I settle on the stars that burn amidst the clouds. There is a flutter of movement beyond the reach of the firelight. I turn and stare into the grassland, and catch the heat signature of a long, thin body. Some distance away, Francis paces in the dark in soft steps. Suddenly, he becomes very still. The heat from his eyes burns red holes in the night, and his gaze appears transfixed upon us.

ALEXANDRA
The Whale Songs

Everything is sore, my neck is tight, and my shoulders are cramped. I'm emptied of heat; the ground has leeched it from me. The night is over, but the day has not come; instead, a cold, red light winks from the horizon. Hypatia leans over me; she's holding my arm and whispering that I'm safe. It was a dream, the dream where I'm looking up at the sky.

I sit up. In front of me is a rug of white ash and thin seams of smoke from several pieces of fire-eaten wood, and I remember where I am. Malcolm rummages under the lean-to, his back to us; Phil is sat up in his sleeping bag, gazing into the bones of the fire. His face looks brighter and warmer than it did last night. He's cute. I take several deep breaths and try to acclimatize myself to the fact the day has started.

"Okay. I'm up," I say, and I listen for the sound of my own voice and Hypatia's acknowledgement to ensure these words came out.

"Your clothes are still damp," says Malcolm from beneath the lean-to. "I have some spare jackets you can borrow, for the morning at least. They are Republic issue, I hope that's okay."

He tosses them at us, and they fall heavily into our laps in tangled thuds of dark green. I shrug my assent at Hypatia, and she speaks our thanks to Malcolm's back.

Phil nods and smirks. "Part of the crew."

Somehow, his words put butterflies in my stomach and I want to say something back. Hypatia and I have practiced how to respond to boys when I feel butterflies.

"Cool," I say.

My voice sounds dumb, and a welt of frustration follows it, for I know inside me I have more to say, but I guess saying something simple is better than saying nothing. Hypatia and I take turns holding the blanket as a partition so we can dress. Everything's still very damp and it chills my skin. I realize I've never had to put on wet clothes before and purposefully slow down my moves so that Hypatia can mimic them. We put on the jackets Malcolm has given to us. Mine's loose around the shoulders, but it will do. Hypatia's comes down to her knees and her hands are lost in the sleeves. I look at her and laughter builds inside me, and I can tell from her expression it has made its way into my face. She fights back the olive-green sleeves; despite her efforts, they continue to slip down over her wrists.

"The rowboat is to the east, less than a quarter mile. Can you carry this stuff?" asks Jackson, and he indicates at the backpacks and water jugs strewn around the lean-to. It looks manageable.

"Yes," I answer.

I squat to avoid the wetness of the scrub grass; its tips are brittle, brushed faintly by frost. Jackson remains still before us, but his expression changes and I think he looks confused. Hypatia gives me a nudge and raises her eyebrows at the bags and water-jugs; it's one of the ways she lets me know I've missed a cue. It dawns on me that she wants me to consider Jackson has used the word "can" when he meant to use "will."

"Got it," I say and step towards the bags and water beneath the lean-to.

Hypatia smiles at Jackson, and then between us, we begin to decide who will carry what. Jackson directs us to follow Francis down a well-worn trail through the grassland that looks like it will eventually meet a small grove of trees, beyond which I assume we will find the shoreline.

Francis walks ahead on the path and swings a water jug in each hand, his lean arms becoming tendon and gristle. When he sees Hypatia and I are following him, he slows his pace and eventually turns around to spit back, "Something wrong with that one. Never met a girl who said so little. Never more than two words."

"She doesn't communicate well verbally," says Hypatia without breaking stride.

"Can she even say her own name? I want to hear her say it. Say your name, Blondie!" commands Francis. He's stopped now, with his arms outstretched to block my path. I step to the side and move by him, and he bares his teeth at me. "Say something!" he jeers. From behind, he pulls on my shoulder hard, so that his face is in mine. There's no subtlety to his aggression.

"Hi," I offer, and I remember to smile. Hypatia's eyes are on me. His grip tightens on my shoulder.

"I don't trust you. I don't trust any of you bitch Stacy types. Bet you speak just fine, just don't want to speak to a bunch of betas. Is that it?"

"Okay, breathe," I reply.

"What did you just say to me?" he sneers.

Hypatia has stepped between us now. I imagine we'll spend time tonight dissecting this encounter, pinpointing where it broke down. She remains committed to my regimen of improvement, even though there's not really anyone left in this world with whom I want to speak.

"Alexandra doesn't communicate well verbally," repeats Hypatia. "She doesn't mean anything by it," she continues, and I watch as she tips her head to the side and makes her voice light and obsequious.

I can't help but feel she has outgrown her body. A few months ago, she may have managed to pass herself off as precocious, but every day, it seems like her mannerisms are more alien to a child's body.

"You're fucking weirdos," says Francis. He slides through us, and storms ahead into the woods.

Hypatia frowns and scans the open barrens, probably looking for the other boys. When she confirms they aren't there, she insists on walking ahead of me into the forest, which is dark and dense with untamed undergrowth. I'm glad the altercation took place here in the open barrens of the field than in the woods, where there's nowhere to run.

We deliver the first trip of supplies without incident. As we walk back, Jackson steps over the hill ahead of us, though his smile fades as he approaches.

"Everything all right?" he asks.

"We're fine," Hypatia fires back, deliberately quick so that she can answer for both of us. I shrug, and Jackson nods and disappears into the woods.

After two repeat journeys from the lean-to to the shore, we have the boat half-packed. As I sit on the riverbank to catch my breath, numbness overtakes me when I realize Jackson has left for a third trip, and Francis has lingered behind with us.

Francis scans the shoreline and then takes a few steps towards the stone trail from where Jackson departed. Hypatia locks on him and drills into his face, then looks at me and smiles, but her lips flutter like butterfly wings. Francis wastes no time. My legs go limp, and my feet won't budge as he approaches; the river cradles and rocks the boat and laps over my sneakers. Even though his face is like concrete, the way he moves gives him away: his shoulders are square, arms at his side, fists balled. He looks taller and, if possible, even leaner, his stomach torqued into his chest.

Hypatia taught me enough that I know I'm in danger. I debate climbing across the boat to escape him, but Hypatia intervenes.

"We don't want any trouble. We'll go separate ways once we get across," she says as she moves around the boat to fill the closing space between us.

"I think you're full of shit. Knew it as soon as I laid eyes on you. She's your fucking companion child," he barks at Hypatia as he steps around her and into the water towards me.

"Wrong, sorry," I chirp. I'm terrified, but I can't help it, and laughter ignites inside me once more. Of course, he thinks I'm the companion. Perhaps Hypatia sees the amusement rising within me, too. She shakes her head, gently guiding me away from the overtaking emotion.

"You're mistaken. Often, once you start to look for something, you see it everywhere," says Hypatia. Her voice is soft, maybe even kind, but she moves in his periphery, planting slow, yet deliberate steps to bring him back into her reach.

Francis seems not to take any notice of her. "It's easy enough to prove."

He exposes his teeth, but I can tell he's not smiling. From his back pocket, he flips out a short, narrow, flat blade, and with his other hand tries to grasp my wrist but misses as I draw back into deeper water.

"You're mistaken, Francis, and I'm going to ask you to put away the knife," requests Hypatia. "Alexandra's pants are getting wet. I'm worried about her getting cold again."

Francis turns to face her and scoffs. "You're going to ask me to put away the knife?" he says, mimicking the way Hypatia speaks. "Fuck off, little Becky."

With his free arm, he shoves her hard, but Hypatia doesn't budge. Francis flexes his hand several times and even tenses his wrist. I have no doubt he expected to push her to her ass. She appears small, diminutive, but she is built like a stack of bricks.

"Please, put away the knife," insists Hypatia.

Francis says nothing for several seconds, and though his body is still facing me, his eyes aren't on me anymore. "It's you! It's you!" he screams. "No breath in the night. I knew one of you had no breath, but it's you, not her ..." It seems fair to say he's rambling now. "Metal Chad, fucking psychopath. Murder us all! Castrator!" He turns away from me completely and swipes the knife through the air in front of Hypatia's face.

"Alexandra, please dunk your head under the water and hold your breath," commands Hypatia as she takes several more steps backwards away from Francis. I don't understand the request, and I don't think Francis does either, because he falters mid-step as he pursues Hypatia up the beach. "It's not swimming. Do it now!" she insists, without breaking eye contact with Francis.

With pained reluctance, I lean forward and plunge my head into the still azure waters. The chill gripes and squeezes my chest. I start counting, but the cold comes over me quickly and the river seems to want to pull me in, to drown me in its silty bottom. The water laps around my ears. Half-submerged, I only register choppy, distorted sounds until there's an eruption of noise: two calls, both guttural but distinct. They rise together and become akin to a whale song, at once both plaintive and aggrieved.

I surface. Hypatia stands on the shore next to me. With her mouth wide open, she screeches. The island falls under her spell as her voice reverberates with an eldritch half-life across the shore and through the grassland. Francis lies in the fetal position several feet from the stern of the boat. His hands, red, web his jaw and nose. He dribbles and wails inaudible, blood-drenched words. He looks terrifying and pitiful all at once. It doesn't take long for Jackson, Phil, and Malcolm to bowl down the trail to us.

"Jesus, what the hell happened?" demands Malcolm, and he can't decide who to look at.

Phil leans beside Francis and tries to put his hand on his shoulder, but Francis fends him off with one hand, revealing a deep split across the bridge of his nose.

"He went berserk," sobs Hypatia, and I'm surprised to see she has conjured tears. She indicates at me and, amidst her cries, drops slow, stuttering words, and, for a moment, even I believe she's a little girl. "First, he tried to grab Alexandra, and then he tried to drown her, he wouldn't stop."

Phil leaps away from Francis' side, looks at me, and sees my drenched hair, the wet Republic jacket, and the waterlines up my pants. He swings his leg back, ready to plant his foot into Francis' ribs, but instead wavers on one leg and then breaks into a pace along the shoreline.

"I knew he was an asshole," says Jackson. "You're a piece of shit, you know that?" He spits at Francis.

Francis grips the sandy bank with one hand and tries to pull himself to his knees. He speaks, but his words are smothered in his palm. With reluctance, he pulls his hand away from his mouth to plead his case, perhaps to warn them of Hypatia even, but his words come in a red squall. Hypatia has knocked several of his teeth out, some completely, some sundered in half, and the blood from his nose forces him to cough and splutter. His capacity for language is disabled; I can appreciate the predicament.

"I say we do him. We can't let him slip into the war. He's got Alogo Boo all over him, a sympathizer, at least," says Jackson.

I think when he says, "we do him," he means Malcolm. Malcolm says nothing, but a sense of alarm grows inside me with every passing moment in which he doesn't say no.

Phil kneels beside me. I know he's speaking to me, but I can't focus on his words. He holds a fleece blanket out in what I'm confident is a gesture of offer. What's the deal with these boys and blankets? Blankets, the unexpected currency at the end of the world. Hypatia says nothing and drapes it over my shoulders.

With his hands behind his back, Malcolm stands over Francis, his brow furrowed in deep consideration.

"What's the call?" presses Jackson. "Come on, man. What's the call?!"

HYPATIA
The Drop

Our landing at Lisbon beach is cumbersome and uncoordinated. Malcolm and Phil stand shin-deep in the water to steady the boat while Jackson throws bags and water jugs into the lank, yellow grass that greets us along the riverbank. Almost black trees lie ahead of us, their naked boughs swaying in the wind. Alexandra and I scramble up the slope and pause where the hill bleeds into a gravel trail. Malcolm and Jackson drag the rowboat up the hill until the stern is clear of the river's reach and, with slow delicate movements, flip it over in silence. There has been no talk of a return trip, but they leave behind two water-jugs.

The Republic uniform hangs down to my knees, and the fight of my legs against it forces me to trudge more than walk. The surroundings are still and silent, and run in a gentle incline. As we climb, I make another scan for signs of the internet, but just like when we were crossing the river, I dredge only the empty claw of static. There is only the soft rustle of our steps over an autumn quilt of leaves and deadfall. We move, but Phil remains midway up the bank, his back to us as he peers across the river, presumably at Galop Island.

Francis watched us cross without him. Livid, with his nose split, and gruesome, he stood marooned on the shoreline, and the mangled curses he hurled at us sank into the water. He changed from man to wraith. Although, it is only a matter of time until he discovers the canoe Alexandra and I came with. Phil lingers in search of some sight of him, but the shores of Galop are empty.

"He's fucked, don't give him a second thought," instructs Malcolm and cajoles Phil to us with a terse wave. "It's not far, a mile maybe, from here to the cemetery. This is unclaimed territory, but be on your guard. Jackson, you take point."

In single file, we slip along a pockmarked road named Wallace point. Leafless tangles of thicket run in a haze along each side of us and reach into a shallow, clay bottom ditch. We preserve the silence we find—there is no human noise or even birdsong. The black-haired thickets hold a sullen breathlessness reminiscent of Cardinal.

I maintain pace just ahead of Malcolm, who trails the entire party. His gait is slow, and I need not read his face to know he is alert and nervous. Ahead of me, Phil and Alexandra move nearly shoulder to shoulder. Jackson edges into the road's curve, some 100 feet ahead of all of us. I can tell he likes to be in the lead. Nothing in the external environment seems to have changed, but Jackson stops short and raises his hand.

Phil reaches out and grasps Alexandra's wrist to slow her. She stops, but I notice she reaches back and puts her hand in his. Even from here, I can see pink floods Phil's cheeks, but he does not refuse her hand. I have told her she should not just grab the hands of boys she finds cute. We have worked on asking first, but her experiences continue to show her my advice is unnecessary. Nobody refuses her, at least not until they get to know her and realize she swears using the Greek gods and often laughs at inappropriate times.

Malcolm creeps to the side of the road and kneels into a soup of brown leaves and mud, and I notice, for the first time, he has drawn a small, black pistol. Jackson crouches and flicks his fingers forward. From the noise of Malcolm's steps and Phil's rush ahead, I realize he is calling us to him. We gather around him, and he points to where bushes thin ahead of us and meet a narrow single-lane road.

Through the tangles of black thickets, I uncover several houses across the road. They are tall and imposing, built for agrarian landowners, but sagging verandas, peeling whitewalls, and plywood-boarded windows have stamped out their ancestral grandeur. What is left is debris: rusted, sun-worn, above-ground pools sit on pale front lawns, and several pre-electric cars, their windscreens curtained by brown leaves, line wide gravel driveways. Behind the homes, jaundiced, untended fields stretch into an amber-haired coppice.

Jackson points between two houses. Three white tombstones, shaped like obelisks, stand on a hill, but no other graves are visible. It is less of a cemetery and more of a private family plot, planted to the side of one of the houses. Alexandra grimaces. It is a sullen and drab scene. Behind the graves rests an ultramarine single-story building. There is no visible entrance, and it seems without purpose, stranded between the road and a flood of fields behind it.

"That's it," whispers Malcolm. "Drop should be around the back of the blue building."

Malcolm leads us over the road and down a side-lane adjacent to the cemetery, bordered to our right by a slanted whitewashed house. Several smaller outbuildings stretch along the lane and shed their whitewash, exposing grey-skinned wooden boards. I peer into their dark windows but find no signs of life. Malcolm cranes his neck from left to right as he moves. He looks desperate to get a read on the location. As we get nearer, the blue building becomes identifiable as a garage or potentially a workshop. On the side of the building that faces the laneway, there is a white door. We creep up and lean against the blue vinyl siding that feels damp against my back. The door is locked, so Malcolm leads us to the back of the building. We round the corner and arrive face-to-face with a boy.

He is short, pale, and his head is sheared in a buzz cut. He wears a pair of dirty white Adidas shorts and leans into the wall in a black tracksuit jacket. The air is damp and cold, but he seems unbothered. Though he looks nine, a scan of his bio-signal reveals he is older: 11 or 12. He's small for his age, stunted by his surroundings. His green slate eyes lock on us, and with a quick sneer, he reveals mossy, yellow, notched front teeth.

"You here for the guns?" he asks.

Malcolm locks eyes with Jackson and Phil, and though he wears a stoic, impassive expression, I see clouds of yellow in his face. Something is wrong.

"What's the password?" Malcolm asks and arches his eyebrows in what I code as a quizzical stare.

"Contact never said nothing about a password. Only to meet you here," replies the boy as his eyes wander over our faces in what looks like resonant appraisal. There is no fear on his face. Instead, he appears confident and assured, though the streaks of orange across his ski-slope nose suggest aggression.

"No password?" adds Jackson in visible disbelief. Phil's face flashes yellow, and he steps back and looks towards the road, perhaps in anticipation of an ambush.

"I'm sure it's a good one, but I don't have it."

"Jesus!" exclaims Malcolm. The kid's yellow smile seems to widen as Malcolm's composure falters. "What the hell are you smiling at?" demands Malcolm. He rounds on the kid, towers over him, and it seems highly probable that, for a moment at least, he intends to strike him.

"I didn't mean any offense. I got the guns though," assures the kid, but his smile is gone now, and his shoulders are square as he steps back and beyond Malcolm's reach.

"Why the hell should we trust you without the password?" demands Malcolm, though he speaks at us, not the boy.

The boy shrugs. "Look, I'm where they said I'd be, aren't I?" He casts his eyes at his hands and starts to rub a black stain out of his palm with his thumb.

"Fine. Guns in here?" asks Malcolm, and he tips his head to the blue wall. The kid snorts a laugh. "What?" says Malcolm.

"You aren't going to like the answer much," says the boy. "I couldn't move them alone. I had to store them. They're just down the road." The boy turns and points through the field to the distance, where one white-shelled trailer and one beige trailer sit along the road.

Malcolm says nothing, shuts his eyes, and massages his forehead in visible vexation. While Malcolm's eyes are closed, the boy flashes an impish grin and a nod at the rest of us, yet there are still orange traces of aggression in his cheeks.

"Look, you want the guns or not?" the boy offers.

With his eyes still in his palm, Malcolm asks, "What do you mean, you couldn't move them?"

"My neighbour was supposed to help, but he got hold of some Rims. Now he won't budge." With an aloof casualness, the boy scales the house opposite the laneway with his finger and indicates to a boarded-up window on the second story.

I can see Alexandra's heart rate has spiked, and that she is not sure what to make of the situation. The desire to search for the word "Rims" rises within me, but I recall the void, the blank space, where my world should be.

"Christ, use a wheelbarrow or something. If you're going to help with a drop, you must do it to the goddamn letter," scolds Malcolm, and Phil bobs his head in agreement. The boy shrugs with indifference, but I see the traces of orange in his face deepen into crimson.

"You want them or not?" he replies.

"Doesn't matter if we want them or not, we don't know you," barks Malcom.

"Of course we want the guns. It's all right. We were just expecting this to go differently," placates Jackson as he raises an open hand at Malcolm, urging his surrender.

"Do these two want guns too?" asks the boy as his eyes narrow on Alexandra and me.

"They're bound for the coast, we thought we could arrange transport for them," says Jackson, and Alexandra nods.

"Don't know nothing about transport. Reception isn't bad on the roof of the trailer, we can see if you can call it in," muses the boy. "Well, come on then. We can cut through the field." He points at the untilled field that runs through the backyard of the next house.

The field looks trampled and sullen, and the shafts that remain are white and bent, almost limp. I measure it runs on a slight incline some 2400 feet before it ends at the two trailers. Dark thickets have colonized its southern reaches and curl like rows of barbed wire before giving way to a thick line of trees. The boy starts ahead of us, but Malcolm remains still. I can see there are words in him, and Jackson and Phil know it, too.

"We can't do shit without guns, Malcolm," Jackson implores, and Phil seems to offer a nod of resignation.

"Fine, but we aren't all going in that trailer. Phil, you keep watch, and Jackson and I will carry out everything we need. Nobody lets this kid out of their sight," commands Malcom. Then he points at us. "You two stay near the back, okay?" He tucks his pistol in the front of his belt and tests the ease of his reach.

"You coming or what?" the boy calls over his shoulder as he kicks at a spool of thicket that has started to dig its way into the field.

"Suppose so," answers Jackson.

The boy moves in a slow saunter and kicks at the pebbles buried amidst the feet of the grass, yet nobody dares overtake him. The yellow bristles of the field pale the farther we travel across it. Alexandra and I linger at the back, Jackson is 80 feet ahead of us, and Phil and Malcolm are behind him. From back here, I can see the fog of their respiration. I am thankful to remain unnoticed, but I linger in Alexandra's wake to hide myself in the tail of her breath.

We have only been walking for two minutes, but Malcolm is visibly distressed. Often, his steps become a 360-degree stride where he takes in our surroundings. His head bobs behind us to the cemetery, to the tree line, to the trailers, and then to the road. He is right to be worried. The field leaves us exposed and vulnerable, an easy prey to anyone on the road. I can sense he wants to move faster, but for some reason, we obey the boy's pace.

As we get closer, I zoom in on the trailers in detail. They are small and cramped looking, with makeshift wooden porches pinned on their sides to conceal their footings. The white trailer is rust-stained and appears windowless, spare for a solitary convex porthole, like that of an airplane cabin, mounted square below the flat roof. While the beige trailer appears empty, every so often, I think I glimpse a signature of heat within the white trailer, but the distance and strange shape of the window create an ambiguity that overwhelms the discernment of my processer. Seated behind each trailer's hitch are two white propane tanks, likely the last bastions of power in the little strip of houses.

Behind the trailers, a corner post of a fence is planted. The fence is tall and runs to where the field gives way to a copse, to create what looks like a small paddock. I glimpse their heat, but Phil must see them too, for he calls out, "You keep horses?"

"Yup. Three. The good thing about horses is that they move without gas or batteries," says the boy over his shoulder with forced sagacity.

Though the padlock seems to stretch beyond our vision, rope binds the horses at the northern corner of the fence. Alexandra smiles and squints to see the horses, but she does not move from my side. Our backpack is still so damp, it has stained the back of her olive Republic jacket. Her pace is slow, too, and every so often, she stoops, claws at the earth, and retrieves a handful of dirt, which she pokes at with her finger as she moves. There is blue in her face, the colour of grief.

"Like dad's field," she offers. I nod, and she grips my hand, tight, the way she did when she was little.

"He's still in here." I point to my head.

"And here," she adds, pointing to her heart.

I smile at her, but wonder what component in me is the closest approximation to the human heart. Yet, the thought goes unexplored because Alexandra tugs on my sleeve. Her face is aghast as a whine emits beneath my jaw. I jerk backwards on the spot to conceal our shared distress that I have once more become an involuntary receiver.

Alexandra, her eyes cast wide, peers over my head to make sure the group does not notice. The signal recedes and pitches inside me, like waves crashing against the shore. I dance on my tiptoes, in hope of improving the reception, even if by only a quarter inch. Alexandra recognizes the intent and tries to raise me in a bear hug, but strains, and I feel the shake of her legs beneath us. Yet, at this height, audible words flash inside my head. They are faint and full of the scratch and claw of static, but I know I have heard them.

No drop, Lisbon compromised. Repeat ...

Malcolm spots us and beckons at us in a frantic pull of fingers. "Come on," he mouths at us.

The boy has stopped, too. I calculate Phil and Jackson are 200 feet from the trailers. I reconsider the tied horses and the boy's insistence we follow him through the fields, yet the threads do not quite form a picture. Still, something inside me is firing off warnings.

In a fierce whisper, I say, "Alexandra, we need to go. Something is wrong."

Her eyes dart through the barrens of the field to the road. I peer into the dark glass of the white trailer's porthole and this time catch two red halos amidst the darkness of the window, the heat of human eyes. Eyes on us. The cone of possibilities appears again in my head, but it remains wide, full of many unknowns and, for some reason, this fills me with a greater sensation of terror. Alexandra has started to shake, and I can tell she is on the precipice of an episode. The thickets and trees could become our cover.

Malcolm starts towards us. The irritation on his face has become concern. The boy also stops, but his impish smile is gone and his slate eyes have become narrow and sharp. With speed, he turns back on himself and forfeits his lead to join Jackson and Phil. His cheeks have gone from orange to red, and his vital signs vibrate with anticipation and nervousness. He moves just in front of Phil and Jackson, crouches with his back to them, and fumbles with his shoelace. Phil and Jackson stand behind him, their faces dark and confused. I see the halos in the window retreat into the dark.

"It's a trap," I scream.

My words leave me with such force that they break pitch and carry an electronic tincture in their flight. I watch as the boy lifts his head at me, his face yellow, but he is quick. He unsheathes a curved glimmer of metal from behind his leg, jumps to his feet, and plunges a blade into Phil's chest. Jackson, his mouth agape, fumbles as he tries to catch Phil and grab the boy by his shirt. He misses both, and Phil collapses to the ground.

"What the fuck?" shrieks Jackson, but his words land nowhere.

The boy's feet cleave the earth and rent an exhaust of mud as he veers hard to the north in an all-out sprint towards the road. The reason for his wide berth becomes apparent. As Malcolm reaches for his pistol, the eyes from the porthole window have become a leather-faced woman, her salt-and-pepper hair drawn up in a bun, perched on the trailer's porch. In a single movement, she slides a black rifle in the crick of her shoulder, steadies it on the wooden railing, and then the barrel of the gun ignites in bursts of yellow fire.

The gun's crack rattles over the pale yellow-haired field. Jackson twists in the air and falls prone into mud and gravel. Next to him, Phil lies on his side, the knife still in his chest, but his face contorts and grimaces. A heatless purple shroud colonizes Jackson's body, and beyond him, the horses bray and dance on their hind legs. Alexandra flies into the thicket. The branches and brambles heave and sway as she fights to disappear into their cinereous wall. Malcolm's decision-making execution appears frozen. Astride in the field, he waves his pistol, seemingly without discrimination, at the back of the boy, the woman on the porch, to the broken heap of his friends. The woman on the porch does not hesitate.

For a split second, I hold her face up close. She is sallow-cheeked and the areas around her eyes and mouth are lined, but, like Paul, the lines are hard, made without mirth. To one side, her lips grip an unlit cigarette. Without a trace of compunction, she reaches into her jacket pocket, pulls out a new magazine, and fumbles to slot it into the smoking rifle.

"Run," I scream at Malcolm, but to my surprise, I am sprinting towards him.

With the force of some latent and unwelcome protocol buried inside me, I close ground on him until I can pull on his sleeve and break the loop of his indecisiveness. He looks at me with dim recognition as a new burst of fire sends clods of the earth jumping in front of us. The field between us scatters apart and Malcolm jumps through it. We run, Malcolm sliding behind me on the loose soil as another burst of fire erupts. As we tumble into the thicket, the grey-skinned branches explode into a cinerous confetti on our heals.

Behind the curtain of the thicket, we find longer grass slopes into a dense and dark line of trees. I scan along the thicket and scour within it for Alexandra's heat, but there is no sign of her. Malcolm is on his back, and he bites the air with short, whispered curses. I turn from him and weave my head as I search for the heat of the woman to see if she is pursuing us, yet, as I do this, I hear Malcolm cry out, "Jesus, lie down, lie down. You're hit!"

I feel his hands on my back. His fingers slip through my jacket in nervous flutters, inching along my left shoulder. I felt the weight of something catch me as we fell into the thicket. The damage appears to be superficial, though it would likely be lethal if I were what I look like, a little girl.

"The jacket is too big for me, must have just passed through the fabric," I lie. He looks bewildered and shakes his head in disbelief, but I cut him off. "Malcolm, we don't have time for this. We need to get into the woods and find Alexandra."

The confusion and terror on his face fold into a nod.

ALEXANDRA
Marco. Polo.

I tried to count the shots as I ran, but they came in bursts. From behind the body of a tree, I peer back into the field. The white sheen of the dome roof of one of the trailers is visible from where I stand, but the thicket blocks the field from me. I saw them fall, though. There's one more staccato of gunfire, and my legs give way into another run.

Powerless, I find myself hurtling deeper into the woods; I'm aware my pants have become hot and wet. The trees are too thin, too far apart to provide cover, and so I run deeper. There are paths; they snake out through the woods like pebble tributaries. Without the friction of the underbrush, I can move faster on them. Beneath my feet, U-shaped clefts mar the path. Horse tracks. They know these trails. Hades pitchfork, I need to get off the path. I dive back into the undergrowth, but keep the trail on my right shoulder as I run.

The pee in my jeans has cooled and now chafes as I run, though my pace slows as my breath escapes me. I've lost the trail; the woods are denser and the light is pale and dim, fenced out by the branches. There are rocks, too. Boulders, at first placed like lone granite islands, but then ridges, steep crevices, and rock valleys. I can disappear here, perhaps even vanish into the woods, and live out my life as a pee-drenched bog-woman. *Okay. Think. You need to find Hypatia.* Rotating on the spot, I take in my surroundings, but they appear vast and utterly alien. *Okay, Hypatia needs to find you.*

"*Marco,*" I breathe. "Marco," I repeat. I pronounce the word clearly but keep my voice light, just loud enough for her and her alone to hear. "Marco," I say once more, but now panic edges its way into my voice. Sat on my haunches in a small dip formed by the roots of two nearly interlocked trees, I send out the word "Marco" in a flat uniform chirp like an SOS signal. The longer I sit, the more the bitter smell of my pee wafts from my pants and burns my nose. Definitely nailing this.

I close my eyes and drift back to when I was little, at the bottom of my parent's garden. Hypatia sat on a little yellow deck chair, its plastic legs strained under her weight, as she taught me the rules of Marco Polo.

"You can be Polo to start, sis, and I'll close my eyes and try to tag you. We'll need to play down here, though, away from the pool. Do you understand?" she asked.

It was still summer, and farther up the yard, the morning sun walked across the pool deck in an azure glow. Mom and Dad were sleeping in, content to let Hypatia play the dual role of sister and nanny, needing a desperate break from my wordless energy. I nodded, and Hypatia began to count as I tiptoed up the lawn closer to the patio stones that framed the beginning of the pool deck.

"Marco ..."

"Polo." The world shakes and the pool subsides into Hypatia's face. "Found you, sis."

She looks at the urine stains down my legs and frowns, while Malcolm, crouched on his knees beside me, looks anywhere but at my jeans. There's no time to acknowledge my embarrassment; from the distance comes the chuckle and clatter of horse hooves in the woods. Hypatia puts her finger to her lips and helps me to my feet.

Crouched low, Hypatia leads us through the woods until the remnants of a creek trickle over our path; its stony bed, now grey and mostly dry, runs to the mound of a black-earthed hill, the throne of a thick-trunked tree. Malcolm veers right, heading deeper into the forest where the trees look thinner and more clustered, hard terrain for horses. Hypatia ignores his lead and runs to the black hill, where the red of a westering autumn sun hangs in the arms of the solitary tree; she beckons us to her as she disappears behind the mound.

The clip of the horses' feet is clearer and nearer now, as the riders carve their way through the woods. Malcolm and I break away after Hypatia and join her on the other side of the mound. The roots of the tree have eaten into the black soil and created a hollow full of deadfall and a few yellowing ferns. The three of us claw deeper into the web of roots and darkness, desperate to slip through the leaves and ingratiate ourselves with the black cheek of the soil. The clip of the horses rises over us and there's a chortle of water being broken. The riders have stopped on the other side of the slope and the horses seem to pace the shallows of the creek.

Hypatia sits between Malcolm and me, her finger across her lips, demanding our silence. *Thanks, tips.* The horses cease their shuffling, and the pungent metal smell of a burning cigarette hangs in the air. The knowledge that they are just the other side of the hill fills me with abject terror; it's only now that I realize Hypatia's free hand is kneading my palm, desperate to avert the episode she must know is growing inside me.

"Can you make sign of them?" croaks a woman, in a voice that sounds like the rustle of bull reeds in the wind, but she speaks loudly, perhaps temporarily deafened by the crack of her rifle.

"Hard to say, they were smart enough to stay out of the mud. All these leaves, there's nothing really to go by here," says the man in a lazy drawl, and it sounds like they are only on the other side of the tree now.

"Well, they can't have gone far. I know I put a bullet in one of them."

There is a long grumble of exhaled breath in response. "I keep telling you, your eyes must've been playing up. Had you beaned one, there'd be some blood to go by. Body too, most likely."

"I saw what I saw."

Malcolm shifts his weight in slow glacial movements and draws his pistol. He raises it bit by bit, and the soles of his shoes flit about the black crumbly soil that peels away from the roots below our feet. It becomes clear he's searching for a hard spot he can use as traction to jump to his feet. Hypatia frowns and disabuses him with a vigorous shake of her head. Malcolm raises his eyebrows and continues to gently test the earth for solid ground.

"Well, I guess we'll see about that. Sundown isn't far off. I can get word to Sal's people on the Ham. Get someone here in the morning. Let the Boos do the rest."

"Is there much left to be done? Two scared shitless and a third—" A loud snort of laughter upends the woman's words. "And a THIRD mortally wounded," she finishes.

"You're as stubborn as a splinter. Well, whether it's two or three, we'll let Sal decide. Boos don't like loose ends. All in all, though, the boy did well."

"He does what he's told."

I think there may be affection in her words; Hypatia would know if she could see the speaker's face.

"We did right by the cause. They'll see us through the winter, and that's what counts."

"Some fucking deal."

"Sal has made it very clear: it's them or us. Don't think beyond that."

Their voices fall away beneath the steps of the horses and fade amongst the red twilight of a sinking autumn sun. There's faint laughter though, and I can tell they're still talking to one another by the way Hypatia remains still, fixated on trying to pick them up at a distance.

"Hear anything important?" I ask her.

"Chit chat," she says, but the flutter of her lips pulls apart the gentle smile she tries to offer.

"Good lord. You can't actually still hear them?!" laughs Malcolm, but his eyebrows walk up his forehead.

"It's just a game we play," says Hypatia with a faux laugh.

Malcolm doesn't laugh this time, and instead, his eyes narrow on me.

HYPATIA
The Hammer

Sleep comes to Alexandra fast, but Malcolm's breathing remains erratic, punctuated by long rattling inhalations. He might be crying. I wait for him to grow silent as I watch the insect world awaken in our leaf blankets and crawl up my legs. It has taken an hour, but Malcolm has grown quiet and the rhythm in his breath is reminiscent of the snores he made on Galop the night before. With care, I brush the leaves from my legs and chest, and rise from the forest floor. In slow, meticulous steps, I approach Malcolm's curled mass.

I kneel beside him and look through his eyelids, to the heat of his eyes, to try to determine if he is dreaming. His eye movement looks elevated—he is on the cusp of dreamland. He suspires and his lips twitch, yet I still move my hand amidst the leaves and let my fingers crawl with the insects until I graze the fabric of his cargo pants. It is where he left it, pinned between his body and the waistband of his pants. Its skin is cold, and its surface seems to hold a ready heaviness. Before, while I was still connected, Lotus would somehow flag my intentions and pause my hands in real time. The thought that I am now hardware adrift gives me a sensation of elation.

His lighter should also be in the pocket closest to me. In delicate and precise movements, I slip my fingers along the waistband of his pants. For a moment, I feel remorse over intruding his privacy in such a manner, but I remind myself that I mine everyone I meet for emotional data within seconds of meeting them. By comparison, this is light, nearly innocuous. Lotus would probably not agree with my assessment, but they remain an absent presence. My fingers knead further until I find the compact weight of his lighter, and I dredge it up from the depths of his pocket until it comes loose in my palm. A patter of movement stirs behind me. I freeze, but it is only Alexandra flipping to her stomach.

I cannot see the trail, but I know the direction. There are many voices in the night, but none I recognize. As I pass through the woods, I focus on the calculus that hums along inside me. It has been running since Mickey bit into our Mother's neck. Battery life, temperature, and the distance we need to cover. I convert power into steps, steps that cut through fields, mountains, and highways, and shrink the ground between Alexandra and the refuge point. Hesitation. Pause. Delay. Doubt. These things make our trip longer. There is no room for secondary objectives. Yet, while I tell myself I am coming back only for the horses, my processor seems to know otherwise.

The woods become thin and turn into a ragged and flat field. I crouch and the unclaimed wheat gives way before my feet as I move. The field ends in a shoreline of hard dirt and gravel and adjoins the single lane road we used to cross from Wallace Point. In the distance lurk the tall shadows cast by the grand houses moored along the road, and I realize I have broken through the woods farther to the west than intended.

The houses and the outbuildings remain dark, and the night is silent. I do not walk on the road or even on its shoulder, but trudge through the ditch. My pace is slow, as the mud belly of the ditch cannot hold my weight, and I continue to slip. There is a scream, a wail similar to the one of a child, and then the night breaks and flutters on my shoulder as an oval white face passes me and soars overhead: an owl. Its scream seems to live on inside me, multiplying into many little echoes. Its heat fades away in the night, its passage solemn and alone.

I crawl and stumble in the ditch until the three white, obelisk-shaped gravestones lean into view. As I climb from the ditch's muddy bottom and onto the damp grass of the embankment, the laneway by the cemetery appears. Behind the cemetery, the low, rectangular shape of the ultramarine building comes into view.

It is a shade darker than the rest of the night, and as I approach, it seems to eat the light that surrounds it like a black hole. Opposite it, the whitewashed house overlooks the laneway with decrepit silence. A faint ethereal glow of candlelight flickers from behind the window ribbed by plywood boards the boy pointed out 14 hours ago. The light does not escape through the gaps in the boards, but seals the space between them like yellow glue. The neighbour is probably still inside, coming down on the last of their Rims. I look out in recall of the distance to the trailer from where the woman shot at us. My processor resolves the noise will travel.

The door to the ultramarine building remains locked, but there is no need to keep up appearances. I twist and rip the handle and lock out. The doorknob lands in the grass with a soft thud.

The interior of the building is a confused place. My feet clack against the poured concrete floor. Tools are mounted to the walls: there are outlines demarcated in yellow marker so that each tool is assigned its place and no quarter is given to tools without a home outlined on the wall. I lift a hammer and examine its yellow silhouette. Without its metal body, the hammer's tracing looks dumb and primitive. Some objects of humanity's childhood cannot be outgrown.

In the corner, an old lantern sits against the wall, and in the corner opposite, on the far side of the room, leans a gravestone. It is a simple granite stone and bears the name Ruby Glip. Her birth date remains unpaired with a date of death. Tucked to the wall, not far from the lantern, is a can of kerosene. I lift it and let its contents slosh from side to side. It is nearly half-full. Exactly what I am looking for.

There is a window on the wall opposite the door. It is high and slender, but it looks out over the field. In the distance, there is a pale glow cradled in the trailer's port window. It does not flicker. It is electric light, and the rest of the darkness seems alive to it, circled tighter against its alien intrusion in a world ceded to fire, moon, and starlight.

I pry further, desperate to catch some human signature within the trailer, but, as before, the distance and the shape of the window create an ambiguity that overwhelms me. I flick the lighter. The cone of potential futures whirls inside my head, and there are many options branching from many tall decision trees. Yet, I recall Malcolm and the way he wavered, unable to make a choice as his friends died, and I recall the woman on the porch, who did not hesitate to turn us into prey.

I tear and shred one of the sleeves of the Republic uniform into long curls of fabric. I ball the ends of each strip of fabric and open the can of kerosene. Do not hesitate is the new code.

Outside, the candlelight continues to flicker and dance through the boarded window of the house. I cross the lane in slow, careful steps and then pass through an overgrown lawn that stretches on past several marooned outbuildings to terminate in unkempt cropland. The back porch of the house is dilapidated, its eastern quadrant sagging into dark earth. There is a path of level floorboards to a rear entrance where a screen door hangs on its hinges and creaks with the swing of the wind. The floor of the porch writhes purple and reveals that an insectile underworld is eating the wood boards grain by grain. I space my weight out so that I do not fall through, but the wood beneath me still groans and strains before it decides to accommodate me.

I deposit the kerosene by the backdoor and prepare to rip the door handle off, but at first touch, the door glides open. Inside, the recession of electricity and power lets a semi-gloom settle throughout the house, censoring its features. To my right, I can see the remnants of a kitchen. A heavy sourness hangs in the air, an admixture of dairy and decay. An ancient fridge, an analog, sits in the corner of the room, and a tidal pool of refuse emanates out from its feet and reaches the legs of a small table. The table is askew, and wax drippings colonize its centre. A tower of dishes sits in the sink, and next to it is a garbage bag where a drying rack might have sat. Crescents of food-soiled paper plates slip through the garbage's half-open lid.

I navigate through the kitchen to the living room, stepping around the newspapers, pictures, and cutlery strewn across the chapped wood floor. Burrowed into a wall of exposed brick is a fireplace. A mantle juts out above it like a protruding stone lip, and atop it is a row of picture frames. Unlike the disarray of the rest of the room, the pictures are evenly spaced and displayed with pride, though the colours are blurry and discolouration eats its way in from the corners. From the side of a solitary lime lazy-boy, I survey the mantle.

A family poses on a green lawn in front of what might have been the house. There is a man and a woman, and two little boys wrapped in their arms. In other pictures, the boys are older, perhaps seven. Farther along the wall, the man and the woman are framed again, only this time, while he smiles at her face, she looks straight at the camera with a tired expression. Farther along the wall, the boys are featured alone, becoming men in a string of small square pictures. To one side, spaced away from the other pictures, sits a frame with the boys now older, their thin faces broad and sombre, while the woman rests in the corner of the shot, still reserved, but almost uncaptured in the frame. Her hair is greyer, her face fuller. There are no other pictures with the four of them together.

As I enter the foyer, I step over a spoon left on the floor, stained in a brown ichor. The front door is dressed in locks and deadbolts, and in front of it, two mud-caked boots lay on their sides. There is a stack of yellowed bills on the floor. Opposite the door, an imposing staircase, the top of the newel post decorated with the woodcarving of a roaring lion's head, reaches up into the house. Light flickers from the landing, illuminating a faded blue tapestry along the wall: figures in cockel hats cleave forests and set tea beneath birch trees.

My ascent is slow, and I am careful not to let the stairs speak of my coming. On the second floor, lamps, likely kerosene fed, flicker and their shadows dance in the tapestry, tangled with the birch trees and tea. Whereas the first floor was scattered with signs of life, the second floor appears, at least at a glance, uninhabited. On each side of the hallway off the landing, doors are left open, revealing dark cavernous rooms with sturdy looking beds, dressed and untouched. At the end of the hall, though, the door is ajar, and a thread of yellow light spills out from its sill. From behind the door, there is a low groan of exhaled breath. I listen and wait. Half a minute elapses before I hear the air drawn, clawed back into the lungs. The floorboards creak beneath my steps, and the door sighs on its hinges as I slip through it, but it does not matter.

Unlike the other rooms, this one is unkempt and occupied. On an ancient dresser, several candles smoulder near their wicks, flickering at the precipice of extinguishment. The room smells. Tobacco, vomit, and another odour I do not recognize—it is fecund and male, primeval in its lineage to flesh and sweat. To the left of the door, a large wooden bed, half dressed in yellowing sheets, juts out from the wall. A metallic blue cane with four curved feet at its base leans against the bedpost. There is a languid rattle, and the air in the room flows into the bedsheets in a desperate breath. I see his heat and the weak, intermittent beat of his heart before I see him. He is collapsed on his side, lost in a sleep that is heavy, but not restful.

I round the bed to come to the far side he lays upon, near the boarded-up window. The smell of vomit thickens, and beer bottles, spoons, old plates, and clothes are strewn across the floor on this side. I inspect each step before I take it to move over them without disturbance.

Closer now, I can see his slate eyes are open, locked on the window, in pry, maybe, of the slivers of moving breeze and night adumbrated by the grey-skinned two-by-fours that bar the window frame. I cannot be certain if the boards have been nailed in to keep him inside, or to keep something out. It could be both. I wait, but the eyes do not move towards me. They roll in his head, sightless. A waking dream, or perhaps they are merely loose, dislodged from the abeyance of a comatose body.

Standing over him, in wait of his next hungry breath, the weight in my hand seems to grow. The cane propped against the bedpost, the frail figure sunken in the bedsheets, the horses, and the trailer in the distance, all of them braid together behind my eyes until my processor arranges them into a new cyclone of decision points. Another long, reaching gasp erupts from the bed, and I linger. One of the candles on the dresser hisses as its fire meets the wax and becomes a seam of grey smoke. The shadows widen and pull the bedroom and its debris further from view, deeper into the night.

The man does not stir. Somehow, I know there are not enough hours of sleep in this world to make him rested. A vestigial sigh of deflating lungs rattles through him in agreement. The sigh is familiar, and with it comes a strange remembrance within me of eternal fatigue. From where this memory comes, I do not know.

Television, perhaps. The weight in my hand adjusts as my grip loosens as I realize the hammer is the wrong tool.

BUG

The Signs

The ultramarine electronic glow of the screen cradles the pod in its half-light. Ahead, a phalanx of solar panels reaches from the austere, grey concrete of the building's sunken rooftop. Agricultural buildings dot a green expanse of fields, divided by white fences into neat uniform squares. A few cows, tucked away into the distant corners of the field, remain. The location was in the back of beyond, far away from the main roads in the game, which is probably why it wasn't looted yet. Few other players would appreciate the point value in an animal waste to fuel complex.

I steer the avatar into the solar panels, and the pod fills with the tinsel patter like glass breaking as I smash the solar cells with a hammer. The right side of the screen lights up with points and additions signs as I set to work, hammering another panel. Pumping my legs to climb what felt like at least ten flights of stairs and then smashing the solar panels has left me exhausted. I'm not eating or sleeping enough and the toll of life in the hangar is starting to eat away at my in-game stamina.

Blue cells from the ruined solar panels litter the roof and crunch under my step as I stagger to sit along a short wall that runs the perimeter of the roof. I swing my legs over the edge and take in the cobalt sky that floats above the fields. Far below, the bot I encountered remains sprawled across the parking lot. His death didn't yield any points. There's still lots of discussion around this in the viewing room. Some bots are worth points, some aren't, the distinction isn't always clear. Tim seems unwilling to provide an explanation.

Along the horizon, puffy clouds move in a slow, drifting armada against the sky's empty cerulean space. The screen tilts, rocks, and flashes to announce movement in my periphery.

The name Scrummaster34 floats in blue letters beside me on the edge of the roof. A player wearing a hockey mask, a combat helmet, and a backpack, waves at me. The dents in the hockey mask and crack in the combat helmet suggest they are looted items, likely from dead bots. Many players pick up items from the bots and use them to boast.

Nicely found, congratulations! scrolls across the left side of the screen, but I have already scrambled from the edge of the wall to solid ground.

Relax. If I wanted to waste you, I would have pushed you off when I had the chance. Scrummaster34 beckons me back with an easy wave.

Ok. Sorry. :/ The game is full of assholes, I type back as I rejoin them in slow steps.

Nice find, they reiterate.

Thanks, lucky break, I type.

Not luck, few would figure there would be solar panels way out here.

True, I guess :)

I am looking for quality players to pull off a raid. Are you interested in something like that?

Potentially.

I've experienced little in-game coordination amongst players. I've seen a few join up and work together for a session if they happen to bump into each other, but the absence of durable in-game communications and prohibition of discussing the game IRL has made sustained and systematic collaboration needed for something like a raid impossible.

How will you plan it? I type.

The dots return, and again, there's a lengthy delay in the response.

In steps. The first step is crafting. You need to find materials, I can provide further instructions.

What kind of materials? What are we crafting?

I will not share that yet. Scrumaster34 buttresses these words with an indifferent-looking shrug.

With a pang of confusion, I peck at the question mark several times.

It is okay. Do not worry. I can help you get started. There is a place, not far from here, with the right materials. Have you seen dnoP emosdnaH on the map, it is close to ekaL gnoL.

I think I've seen ekaL gnoL.

Good. Find an avatar near there to log. I will use my avatar there to mark a trail to the site. Follow the pink ribbons. Once you are there, you will need to grab fuel. Find the bot barn. It should appear on the world map in a red cluster. Lots of avatar remains, so be careful. You are looking for green jerrycans.

I make a mental note to keep an eye out for pink ribbons and green jerrycans, then ask the only question that comes to mind. *When?*

Get the materials in this cycle. Meet back here for directions to the raid target at the start of the next cycle.

Ok. Thanks!!! :0

No problem. Happy searching!

The text flashes red and vanishes as Scrumaster34 charges back into the building.

HYPATIA
The Horses' Mouth

Darkened, the house glowers over the lane as I retrieve the kerosene from the back porch. I move behind the curtain of the thicket in the southern arm of the field and start towards the horses. Even from back here, I catch yellow slivers of the trailer's light through the arms of the brush. The weight of the kerosene rests against my leg. I am mindful not to jostle it. I want to prevent the noise of the little waves inside its metal belly from giving me away. This effort makes me slower, and there will be a greater energy expenditure. The horses will compensate for the loss.

There is a hole in the thicket, and the field, wreathed in grey brambles, is visible through it. I cannot see Phil or Jackson's remains, though the night is dim and their bodies would now be lightless, indistinguishable from the ground. Eventually, I cross through the thicket far enough that I am directly behind the two trailers. The beige one closest to me is dark and still, but the light streams through the white trailer's porthole window.

The few other scattered houses in sight remain dark, and the moon is small, dimmed by thick furls of cloud that stand stubborn above the heads of the conifers. The trailer light is lonesome, and I cannot help but think there is a recklessness or hubris of being the only light in the dark. Some are the only light in the dark because their teeth are sharpest, like anglerfish.

I cross through the thicket and close in on the beige trailer. I kneel to the footings left unconcealed by the makeshift porch and press my ear against the chipped rust-eaten siding. There are no voices within it. I strain. There is a presence, but it is so faint that I cannot tell if it is respiration or some mechanical ambience. Regardless, this trailer is without threat. I can inspect it later.

The can of kerosene sloshes as I set it beneath the trailer's bed, in the shadows of one of the footings, and begin to crawl to the back of the white trailer. As I lie in the scrub grass and pebbles, I glimpse to my right, at the wire and wooden posts of the paddock. With perfect stillness, I focus on the trails of voices that ebb through the white tin walls. The words are muffled and indistinct, but the tones and pitches reveal three speakers. Rasp and husk cover one of the voices, a woman's, and it almost sounds sore. I am confident it is the gunner. As I listen, I circle the trailer in slow and deliberate steps, careful to avoid pebbles or any deadfall that may announce me. I see no windows other than the porthole I spotted from the field. It will be easy to remain unseen.

There is a new cadence within the trailer. Laughter. I withdraw to the beige trailer and recover the kerosene. As I begin to run the cap off its threads, the cone of possibilities interrupts my fingers. I sort through it and its range of potential outcomes, and the dark space behind my eyes alights in dancing cautions and alerts about my intended course of actions. I scroll through them.

Permanent loss of trust. Undesirable changes to consciousness.

I have not received messages from my processor like this before.

"Show me chances of reaching New Hampshire without horses or alternate transportation," I command to myself.

Something within me decides we have a 15% chance of reaching the coordinates without the horses. With my fingers and then a stray stick, I fish out the strips of the Republic jacket I fed into the belly of the kerosene can.

Mindful to avoid the field of view offered by the porthole window, I crouch alongside the propane tank and pinch the black hose that connects the tank to the trailer between my thumb and index finger. I grind my fingers in and squeeze into the hose until I hear the hiss of a perforation. I recede into the cover of the second trailer. Malcolm's lighter sparks to life in my hands. Two cloth strips ignite, and I hold the dry ends as if they are the tails of two small burning snakes. I toss the cloth at the propane tank. The first one misses and splatters gasoline on the balding grey grass below the hitch. The second one sails through the air and becomes a cloud of fire at the end of the hose. Like a dragon's breath, fire licks the trailer and drips from the jet of flame. There is a cry of alarm, the scream of unoiled hinges from the door, and a thunder down the porch stairs follows.

"Oh Jesus, get out! Fire! Out!" A fist hammers on the trailer's siding and then a voice reaches out from around the porch. "Fire! Son of a bitch! Lesley!"

There is a rapid flurry of steps both in and out of the trailer, but I am patient.

"Jesus! Draw a hose! We have to cool the tank to keep it from blowing," the woman commands.

"Water pump's fried, remember?!"

The horses have caught the panic and break into an aimless run around the paddock. I peek through the footing and count six shoes to the left of me. In silence, I move along the back of the second trailer. When I get near the corner, I pause.

I have felt the cold, alien weight against my navel through the forest and across the field, and I tucked it in and concealed it just the way Malcolm did, yet still I fear somehow it will escape me. I draw it from the waistband of my jeans and replicate Malcolm's stance with it.

I lean around the corner. The people I have lured stand before the flames as they dance on the trailer's siding, molting the white glaze to a black cinder. Three steps closer to them, and they do not turn around, seemingly mesmerized and subdued by the firestorm in front of them. I am several feet behind them now, close enough that I should not miss. The world becomes a grid of white squares as my processor goes to work, trying to confirm their identities:

two adults, one child, but without the internet and clear sight of their faces, the grid collapses, overwhelmed by ambiguity.

Based on his hair length and the way he stands, my processor is confident the child is the boy who led us across the field. Aided by perhaps some primeval instinct, the tallest figure among them turns to find me in the dark. He is an old man: a grey beard obscures his face and a dirty undershirt carries his paunch into a pair of jeans. When he sees me, his face brims with alarm for a split second, but then his jaw tightens, and his alarm becomes smolders of orange aggression.

"Ruby," he murmurs.

The woman starts to turn her head, and as she twists, I confirm the sallow, lean cheeks of the porch gunner. While she moves, there is heat in the muscles around the old man's mouth as his jaw pulses, and I predict he is about to speak again. He opens his mouth but hesitates, swallowing back his words.

Three blasts squeeze from Malcolm's pistol. The shots ring through the field, and then wayward along the empty road, echoing on into dark trees and lightless places. The movement in the paddock flinches. The horses bray and stamp over the untenanted space left by the old man's unspoken words. They continue to whine, indignant perhaps, as I lead them from the paddock and out into the night.

~

On a bald, flat rock, I watch the pink seams of dawn creep through the grey, empty arms of the woods. The world looks matted in a stubborn greyish hue, as if the morning is waiting for the sun to colour it. The horses, their leads threaded through a cascade of tree roots, huddle together and pick at a balding knoll. Though reluctant to follow a stranger, they decided to stick together rather than let me lead one of them away.

It will not be long until Malcolm and Alexandra wake, but I have yet to assess the damage of the gunshots. The sensors bear messages of tenderness and pain throughout my back and chest. With care, I remove the Republic jacket and then my shirt. The shirt is stained and torn. I lay it aside. I have a spare. In a flash of desire, I rummage through the jacket until I find one of the cigarettes I pilfered from the woman's jeans. I hug the cigarette in the corner of my mouth and squeeze my eyes shut as I drag on it. Contentment and shame flood through me and seem to summon from the inky depths of the blue space behind my eyes a voice I do not recognize.

DO YOU REALLY NEED THAT?

I let my eyes wander over my bare chest. A few inches from where my arm joins my shoulder, a canyon has been punched through. Blood and white fluid are splattered across my flat breast and have congealed at the edges of the wound. I have had plenty of cuts and scrapes, all of which draw faux blood, a Lotus gimmick to camouflage my artificiality. The white fluid is alien to me. It cakes my fingertips and fills the air with a strong acetone smell.

I walk my fingers around the emptiness and dip them into the absence until I discover the hard edges of wet metal and my sensors come alive with agony. My fingers come back painted in more milky fluid and a black ichor. With my shirt sleeve, I dab blindly around the wound's circumference while asking my processor for a second assessment of the damage.

Core hardware remains uncompromised. Aesthetic damage significant. Consult a Lotus technician.

The juxtaposition of a Lotus consult with the abandon of the woods brings a smile to my lips.

Behind me, deadfall snaps. "Holy shit ..."

I rise and turn, and in an instinct that surprises me, shield my chest with the loose reams of the Republic jacket. Malcolm stands between the trees. The sun pours across his features in a light red shadow, but my system reads his face as a yellow and purple storm. Purple is a colour I rarely see in the faces of men. It belongs to an emotion that runs close to curiosity and pain. The yellow clouds consume the streaks of purple. In mere seconds, fear has won.

I snuff the cigarette out in the rock beside me as I say, "I got us horses," though it seems impossible he has not seen them.

He shakes his head and takes a step back. "You're a companion?"

I offer a nod of admission.

"Jesus. Jesus." His hand flutters to his waist in search of the pistol. The pistol that is in the waistband of my pants.

"I'm not a threat."

Malcolm snorts an incredulous laugh from his nose. "Right. Until you are." His hands now roam the back of his trousers, likely still in search of his pistol.

"I want us to work together. I want you to accompany Alexandra and me down to Port Henry. See us over the crossing there. You can rejoin the Republic from there on horseback."

The yellow streaks across his nose fade but then flash brighter, spreading over his features in long tendrils. "Good lord, the horses! We need to haul ass. They'll be on the hunt."

"Nobody's coming," I murmur.

"How do you ..."

"Swear you'll accompany us, and I'll give it back to you." I step towards him with the pistol outstretched in offer.

"You ... you took my gun."

"While you slept. I'm sorry, but the horses are necessary for my and Alexandra's travel. I didn't want any entanglements."

"Good lord. You just told me you weren't dangerous?"

"I told you I wasn't a threat. Those aren't the same things. Swear you'll accompany us. Swear on the Republic."

"Did Alexandra agree to this?"

"No, this information wouldn't benefit her. Will you swear to accompany us?" I extend my hand farther, but keep it just beyond his reach.

"Just stay the fuck away from me." He seizes the pistol from my open palm, checks the clip, and then shakes his head in disbelief.

"Malcolm, can I trust you not to pass on this information?" My tone betrays this is a command, not a question.

"I don't trust you. None of you. Not before or after the flash."

"You may keep your distrust, just don't break your word. You'll accompany us to Port Henry."

"You're a goddamn time bomb, you know that, right?"

"All the more reason for you to accompany us, for Alexandra's sake. She's still a child, really."

His face smolders from red to slate, and I know I have found his hook. He will accompany us to protect Alexandra from me. If it is enough to assuage his distrust, this will be an optimal outcome. I do not have time to speak, for our exchange has awoken Alexandra. Malcolm and I watch her weave through the trees, her steps fast, in search of us. It does not take long for her to find us, but she runs by us to the horses.

"How?" she demands in excitement over her shoulder as she reaches out to stroke the brown horse's nose.

"Hypatia managed to sneak them away during the night," interjects Malcolm.

"Exciting. Names?" She looks at us in expectation.

Unexpected laughter bites the corners of my mouth. "They didn't come with names, sis."

Alexandra rolls her eyes in what I code as playful exasperation. "Okay." With her arms crossed, she paces in front of the horses, in focused divination of each horse's perfect name.

ALEXANDRA
The 8 Ball

Autumn light creeps behind us to cast our shadows on the pavement in pale mimicries. Bruised rain clouds spiral down upon us like a stalactite ceiling. Hypatia stops and cajoles Opal, so named for the gem-like marking on her forehead, from the road's cracked tarmac to a smooth island of concrete that leads to a service station with several rows of charging stations.

"They're toast," calls Malcolm. "Rain's coming, come on." When, without response, she rides further into the lot, Opal's feet clattering on the pavement in impatient clops, he turns and says to me, "What's she doing? We need to keep moving!" I shake my head and shrug, but this only makes Malcolm frown. "Hypatia, come on!" he calls out after her as she strays between the red and white charging stations, their sheen cutting the afternoon's grey light.

Their connectors, which normally hang in long black loops to attach to cars or the port behind Hypatia's ear, have been cut to ragged stubs. Severed in haste, the stubs protrude at the side of each unit like arms amputated at the shoulder. Scrapped, just like the lot we saw before this one. Everywhere, anything made of metal has been cut away, presumably looted.

Hypatia leads the horse along the edge of installation towards the charging lot's exit. Malcolm follows her path with narrow eyes.

"Anything?" I ask.

"Scrapped."

"Probably cleared out by Alogo Boos. A war effort harvested from the energy transition." Malcolm makes the sound of laughter, but his eyes remain narrow and his face stays hard.

"It's a dangerous time to be made of metal," says Hypatia with a thin smile.

There's an invitation in her expression, I think. An offer for Malcolm to both lament and laugh at the perils of her artificiality. He says nothing and guzzles from his canteen.

It was never going to be possible to keep her secret forever. She whispered to me that his vitals confirm he hasn't slept much the last two nights. It shows on his face. Dark capes have grown beneath his eyes, and he speaks little, and when he does, his words come in quick snaps.

Malcolm doesn't reply, but his grip on the horse's bridle seems to tighten. Hypatia doesn't break eye contact with him; she's mining his emotions. Probably deciding if he'll ever trust her now that he knows she's a companion child. For Hypatia, the absence of trust codes as danger and violence, but Malcolm doesn't seem dangerous to me, just alone. He and Hypatia don't speak much, and there are only so many words I can offer him.

The patter and then drum of rain on our shoulders breaks the web of silence among us. Without looking at Hypatia, Malcolm says, "We've wasted enough time."

As we travel, it becomes clear it's not rain, but a river in the sky. The Republic uniform is so wet it feels like a second skin drawn tight across my back. The rain ricochets off the highway ahead of the horse's steps. Hypatia continues to lead, her body erect and alert in the saddle. Far behind us, flittering in and out of the interference of the rain, I can make out the grainy image of Malcom atop Quartz. He has lingered behind us since the rain started. "Protecting our six" is what he called it. I've seen him stop several times and pivot Quartz in a full circle; each time, I expected him to gallop away from us, to turn back and vanish into the wall of rain.

The air is colder and heavier, and my breath smokes against the dusk, painting grey on grey. We need to make camp, but there's only road and an autumn stubble of chafed fields on each side of us. We carry on until the light is almost gone; Malcolm has closed distance on us, the clop of his horse's feet ringing on the pavement in our wake. I'm cold again. I've been cold since Cardinal.

Hypatia turns around and canters towards me. She smiles but says nothing until Malcolm draws level with us. "Down the road, a little over a half-mile, there's a semi-truck. It might provide shelter."

"You sure that's what it is? I can't see shit," says Malcolm, his hand shielding his eyes as he stares ahead into the rain and greying light.

"Positive. I believe it's untenanted. I can see no human heat signatures inside," she adds.

Malcolm raises his chin in terse acknowledgement and kicks his horse forward, rushing out ahead of us.

"Hungry?"

"Cold," I reply.

She reaches out and grips as much of my hand as she can in her little palm. "Cold hands, warm heart." She smiles. It was one of my mom's stock phrases. "We'll get you warm again. I promise," she adds.

The rear of the truck slips out from the rain first and then the rest of its long, tapered body appears, adrift across both lanes of the road. We've passed other trucks. Frozen in time by the flash, but they're usually surrounded by debris. Looted. This has the calmness of a moored ship.

Our horses hold their heads high and take slow, distrustful steps towards the back of the trailer-truck. Quartz is already tethered through the latch of the rear door; he shakes his head and strains against the knot as he trots from one side of the truck to as far as the lead will let him. Malcolm crouches low as he walks. He makes his way up to the cab with one shoulder pressed against the siding of the trailer truck.

I can tell by his stance and his outstretched arms that his pistol is drawn. Hypatia and I watch in silence as he climbs up to the cab door. For a long time, he hangs to the side of the truck on the road, motionless in the gathering darkness. With a sudden jerk, he pulls the cab's door open and slides inside, away from our view.

Hypatia senses my concern. "It's empty, but I'm glad he's inspecting it."

The rain hammers through her words, and before I can respond, she instructs me to untie my saddlebags, so they are ready to bring inside the truck. In my periphery, I watch her stoop down, play with her shoelaces, and fiddle with her jacket pocket before rising. Malcolm reappears, his shoulders low, his stride slow as he approaches us despite the rain. He's holstered his pistol.

"Did you find anything inside the cab?" asks Hypatia.

Malcolm smiles, and with a curt shake of his head, says, "It's an automated truck. Too far out on the road to be paired with a human co-pilot. Usually pick those up closer to a delivery point."

"Ask it?" I tip my head and intone the word "it" in the hope Malcolm will realize it's a question, but he shrugs and raises his eyebrows at Hypatia.

"Alexandra means: can we ask the AI system onboard anything?"

"AI operator is fubar, sparks in the cloud or wherever bots go to die."

Where bots go to die. I know I can't ask Hypatia, as it'll only make the canyon that runs between us deeper and wider, but where did her kin go? Are they out there in all the backups and fail safes, or are they lurking deep in the hardware like latent digital spores? Or is it like they're dreaming, unaware of the chaos that waits for them when they wake? Do they keep their sentience and are all the algorithms, bots, operator systems in each car, still here, watching the world turn, like ghosts between the static? I can almost picture them as thousands of blue warbling figures screaming overhead in flight, wraiths hunting our present, waiting for their resurrection when the war ends and the power returns.

"Dying, just like every other digital being." Malcolm spits these last words, jiggling the container lock bolt and filling the night with the shrieks of grinding, rusted metal as he inches the trailer's white exterior doors apart. "I'm surprised this wasn't locked," he mutters.

"Looters probably got here first," offers Hypatia.

"Not much debris for looters," says Malcolm as he unties his saddle bag and fishes about its bottom.

"There are probably many explanations," says Hypatia.

Malcolm nods slowly as he wrestles one of his little planter torches from the bag; its pale light skips across the puddles cradled in the asphalt before he sends it dancing along the interior walls of the truck's trailer. "I guess. With no human co-pilot, though, we can be sure we're not the first ones here."

Hypatia frowns. "Perhaps we should go on?"

"Jesus," snaps Malcolm. "You may not realize it, but the two of us"—he casts the light across my face as he speaks—"are cold and wet, and if we get too cold and too wet for too long, we die. We're out of options. Does that compute?!"

Hypatia's arms are crossed now and her lips are drawn tight into her cheeks. There's a thread of a smile, but Malcolm isn't looking at us anymore as he steps up the bumper and hauls himself halfway into the dark of the trailer.

"You can keep watch out here if you want. I don't give a shit. I'm going to take my chances with the dry sheltered space." And with that, he disappears into the trailer, the light of his torch becoming a pale thread.

It's fair to assume he's not happy. Hypatia stands motionless beside me, her arms at her sides; the rain falling on her skull betrays a faint tin-like patter.

"You okay?" I venture.

"He's right. Your core temperature is dipping. We're out of options. This environment is hazardous and unwelcoming. There are too many threats to balance." She tips her head towards the entrance, bidding me towards the soft glow of Malcolm's light.

Five little torch lights, planted like toadstools in the dark of the trailer, embrace me as I pass through the rear doors. Malcolm is bent over, planting the sixth. Their light is bright enough to rib the trailer's interior. There's empty floor space, some six feet in depth, perhaps left for the purposes of unloading or to pick up another delivery, but beyond that, the trailer becomes a hallway of cardboard boxes. Thousands of them, all various sizes, packed against the sides of the truck and held in place by mesh webbing. The light of the little torches doesn't reach far, and the boxes soon become dark shapes the closer they are to the front of the truck, their black masses suspended in the webbing like errant flies in a sprawl of a spider's web.

"Prizes?" I suggest.

"Haven't looked yet. Tell you what, grab the ones you think look good and I'll cut them open," laughs Malcom. "Put this around you first, though," he adds as he draws the crackle of tinfoil from his saddlebag to reveal the emergency blanket I wore in Cardinal.

"You again," I mutter as I draw the blanket to my shoulders like a shawl.

I spend a few moments waiting for Hypatia to join us inside, but she doesn't come. Wonder summits and flips in the bottom of my belly, but I decide she's either outside standing guard or has gone to the truck's cabin to confirm Malcolm's assessment.

The air inside the truck has a taste. It's a faint pungent and sweet smell that seems to come in little waves; its undertones are reminiscent of compost. Malcolm seems to notice it too, and mumbles something about spoiled food in one of the boxes.

I shuffle down the narrow passage within the trailer and return with two tiny square boxes, which I drop before Malcolm. He looks up with a grin as he grinds his way into a can of tuna with a rust-speckled can opener. Setting the tuna aside, he picks one of the boxes up and tears along the seam of tape with the can opener's sharp hook. Several soft-looking plastic sheets peek through the gash in the cardboard.

Malcolm fishes past them. "What have we here? Hard plastic. Round. Guesses?"

My curiosity bites at me so hard, I decide it's easiest to shrug in response. Malcolm withdraws his hand slowly and lets the flaps of the box conceal its contents from me.

"Don't that beat all. Catch." From his hand, something black, circular, and hard lands in my lap.

I've seen this before. Grandma had one. In the old box of our father's toys.

"Magic 8 Ball. Not exactly a game changer for us, but who knows, it might come in handy."

I give the 8 Ball an enthusiastic shake and flip it around so that Malcolm can watch the answer surface from its swirling ink ocean. "*All signs point to yes,*" it reads.

"Can I?" I pull our new oracle into my chest.

"Knock yourself out." Malcolm's words come with his teeth, and I'm confident it's a real smile. "Who knows, there might be better stuff further inside. Bigger boxes nearer the back, maybe." This time, his words come with a chuckle.

Between peeling open cans of tuna, Malcolm continues to gut all the little square boxes I retrieve. It doesn't take long for us to realize they all contain 8 Balls. He doesn't bother to take them out of their boxes. He passes me the tuna and instructs me to suck the juice from the tear in the can before eating its contents, but to be careful not to cut my lips or tongue.

Hypatia taught me it's important to keep the momentum of a good mood. In a desperate bid to keep Malcolm bright, I blurt out, "Horse story time?"

The light of our electric candles catches the sheen of brine on his chin, and he sucks his lips before he answers, "Yeah. Okay. The short version."

"Yay!" I clap my hands like hummingbird wings in rapid but quiet applause.

Malcolm sets his can of tuna down, smiles and holds me in his gaze. "I heard this story from a friend of mine, it happened in the very first days of the war after the flash. You see, nobody has claimed credit for the flash. Of course, it seems likely it was the Alogo Boo, but if they did it, they botched it. Took out most of their vehicles and ours. With barely any mobile transport, both sides panicked and started rounding up horses for cavalry and scouting units. It didn't take long for local resistance to start stealing horses from soldiers. Setting them free at night. Good lord, it's still happening now, but in those initial days, it was rife. You'd go to sleep in some small town and wake up to find your unit's horses are gone. Now lots of those horses just got taken to the other side, but some of them were just set loose in the outskirts of these little towns. You follow me so far?"

I nod.

"So, putting the horses aside for now, with the power out, attention turns to decentralized power systems that can be rehabilitated, stuff that will work even if the grid is broke. A Republic squad is sent into the White Mountains to hold wind turbines up on a ridge. Orders were to hold the ridge until someone could be sent to fix the wind turbines. You seen many wind turbines?" I shake my head and Malcolm smiles. "They stalk the hills like lonely giants down this way. Well, the Alogo Boo was always an insurrection first and a para-military army second. Before parts of the old army proper joined them, they would just pop up all over the place. It didn't take long for those of them in New Hampshire to march on the wind turbines."

Malcolm continues, "The Republic squad is maybe 20 soldiers, no exact figure has ever been quoted to me. Well, they dug into that ridge like goddamn ticks. For three days, they killed Alogo Boo as they tried to scale the ridge. Good lord, on the fourth day, the sun walked over a half-mile stretch of the dead and the damned. Over a 100 Alogo Boo scattered up the hill. Most shot to bits. Some mad with fear, cowering behind moss-eaten boulders. A massacre."

"Horses soon?" I hope he can register my discomfort with his description of dead soldiers, but his bemused expression suggests he missed it.

"Hold your horses, kiddo, so I can tell you about mine. Now, the Alogo Boo leadership can't live with that outcome. They bring in artillery, must've carted it up the damn mountainside, and in several rounds of hellfire, the Republic squad is nothing more than smoke and ash. Except this one man, Schubert. Now the thing is, Alexandra, the Alogo Boo don't take prisoners, and don't ever let them try and convince you otherwise. Schubert knew this, and so he tried to slip away, but he took a shrapnel to the leg. He's slow, and he's bleeding. The Alogo Boo lunatics hunt him down like rabid dogs. Chase him down the mountainside, sniffing out that wound of his with the blood he left on the trail. Eventually, they catch up to him on the road.

"The thing is, they don't kill him. They march some distance behind him and throw stones at him. Schubert stumbles on through a rain of rock. Some of the stones pelt him in the back, but most of them fly over his head. He doesn't stop. He doesn't want to give them the satisfaction of stopping. Well, you can guess, it doesn't take long for Schubert to hit his limit, but before he gives in, there is thunder. The thunder quakes the earth and makes his knees feel weak, but the sky ahead of him is a meridian of untouchable blue. No storm clouds, but the pebbles on the road waltz ahead of his steps. And then the thunder quickens beneath him until it sounds like a thousand-person choir clapping in harmony. Thinking the wound in his leg has sent him into a feverish delirium, he turns around, resigned that he might as well look the Alogo Boo in the eye with the wind on his face when he goes. Breathless, he finds the thunder at his heels is hundreds of horses. Horses, Alexandra.

"Horses like you've never seen. Horses of every colour. Some saddled. Some bareback and wild. The Alogo Boo panic. Some of them get rundown where they stand and others dive from the road. Schubert, though, is mesmerized. He watches the horses come upon him like a biblical flood of hooves. When the lead stallions descend over him, Schubert doesn't fall beneath their stride. Instead, somehow, seemingly with no action on his part, he finds himself on one of their backs. And good lord, he's delivered from the road. Spared by the chaos of wild horses unseated from the war. A story like that has got to mean something, right?"

Before I can answer, I notice Hypatia is inside now. Her black hair hangs lank over her face from the rain as she squats near the rear door, processing our scene in silence. Malcolm notices her, too.

"Quite the story. Alexandra doesn't usually hear stories like that."

My cheeks flush and irritation squirms in my chest. Even in the middle of a war zone, she's still trying to chaperon what I hear.

Malcolm appears to ignore her comment with a shrug and then asks, "Where did you get to?"

I set my irritation aside and lean through the soft electric light to pass Hypatia some of the tuna. My father insisted Hypatia was to eat with us, even though she doesn't need to eat. Meals are about much more than just eating, he'd say. Families eat together. She refuses the leavings in the can with a terse shake of her head, and Malcolm nods in approval.

"I returned to the cab and searched the perimeter. I agree with your assessment that there was no human co-pilot," she says and brushes a wet clump of hair to the side of her face with her fingers.

"And?"

"Did you inspect the parking brake?"

"No," says Malcolm, and his frown pinches his eyes.

"It has been manually engaged, which you must agree is unusual for an automated truck."

Malcolm scrunches his face up and scratches his head. It takes him a while to speak. "Thanks for checking that. We can look at it more closely in the morning."

"You're welcome."

Hypatia's eyes shift up and down, and I imagine she's segmenting the trailer into a grid of vertical lines, mining the space for some deeper insight. In truth, I don't know how she sees. I asked her once when we were little. When I was little. When she was with us, our colours, flashes of emotion, of pulses, of circulation, and body temperatures pushed the rest of the world into the corners; when she was alone, it was black and white shapes, bisected and segmented; she had to scan the world to bring the colour back in. Mine it. It had something to do with channeling her attention. In a final appraisal, her gaze intensifies, and her eyes go catty, overlaid by yellow crescents. The silence endures, and we surrender to the footsteps of the rain across the roof of the trailer.

"Eat, get warm, and rest. I'll keep watch."

Malcolm receives Hypatia's offer with a measured nod, but I can't give up the idea there might be more useful things in the packages closer to the back of the trailer truck.

Oh, little Magic 8 Ball, blessed oracle of the Alibaba delivery truck, is there more treasure inside here?

The little window of inky darkness shakes violently in my hands and one tile struggles to flip into view, finally conjured forth with a little swish. "*Undoubtedly so,*" replies the 8 Ball. With its blessing, I rise and motion towards the end of the trailer. Malcolm laughs but waves me on. Hypatia is locked on me; her face appears serene and empty, but her eyes mine the dark ahead of me, bidding me not to go too deep into the places that remain unlit.

The boxes nearer the back of the truck are tall and wide. Stacked in columns and suspended in black webs of netting. Perhaps they have clothes inside. I pry at several boxes, but they're packed tight, and I'm too short to reach the box at the top of the column.

Behind me, the pale curtain cast from the lanterns flickers against the walls of the semi-trailer. Malcolm is sat against the wall, his head back in rest. I consider returning to ask him for help, but then I notice ahead of me, further to the back of the truck, close to where the cab begins, several columns of boxes have collapsed into a mound, spilling over into the narrow path that runs down the truck.

It's too dark to make out anything but outlines, but I can tell there are several different shapes in the pile. Some are tall and wide. Others are shorter and flat. I lift one and shake it, but no sound comes out. Possibly clothes. I put it down on the floor, so that I may bring it back with me into the light. Another box, a large perfect square, positioned atop a jumbled pile, waits for me at waist height. It reminds me of the Christmas parcels mom and dad would stack in the downstairs closet. The three of us could open it, our own little unboxing party, happy and calm amidst the ring of toadstool light. Hypatia and I used to love watching unboxing videos when I was little. The memory of being with her under the covers of our parent's bed, watching videos on mom's phone, makes my chest warm, and the warmth becomes a smile.

I pull at the big square box. It's awkward and heavy, and I discover it's trapped under the weight of several other boxes. Another wave of the awful smell hits me. I tug harder and clutch the box's edge, coaxing it forward, urging it to come with me. The box slips into my arms, but brings with it a cascade of several boxes from on high. They fall, bounce off my arms and shoulders, and land on the floor of the truck with clatters and dull thuds.

Behind me, there's a motion, and I don't need to look to know Hypatia is on her feet, flying into the dark to find me.

"You okay, sis?" she calls. The boxes bury my feet and I fall headfirst into the jumbled columns as I try to step out of the pile. "Wait. I'll get you out. No need to worry, Malcolm," she calls out in a blithe command, seemingly in response to a second scuffle of steps.

With my head pressed into the dark of the column, I can't see much. My hands slip into the crevices made by the loose boxes and fumble in search of something to anchor me. My fingers fall behind the wall of cardboard and wander into an empty space; a hollow revealed by the avalanche of boxes. Before I find the wall of the truck, my fingers graze something soft and pliable, alien amidst the cold angular surfaces of the cardboard. Though the touch was fleeting, the sensation of soft clamminess continues to dance in my nerves as I try to decide what I've touched.

Upright now, the boxes tumble onto the floor as I shove them aside. The dark grey light flickering at the back of the truck cocoons it in half-light, but it's unmistakable; a hand, its fingers unfurled, has slipped through the wall of boxes. A scream erupts inside me, but its force sucks all the air from my chest, and in panic, I suckle in a gasp through the palm of Hypatia's hand. Her fingers are webbed over my mouth and her other hand is on my back, but we both know it's too late. My arms tighten and become rigid as my hands cup my ears and the world becomes the rhythmic whoosh of air, sundering the frantic words that pass between Malcolm and Hypatia.

Malcolm moves in front of us, and Hypatia is now rubbing my back; her palm glides between my shoulder blades in familiar counterclockwise circles. I try to focus on the sensation, but Malcolm moves more boxes. As they drop to the floor, the solitary hand is joined by a boy's face, his legs furled up into his chest, like the way beetles tuck their limbs into their bodies when they sleep beneath logs. Pale green eyes reflect the light of Malcolm's lantern back at us in a frozen stare. A dormant companion child.

"Shit," Malcolm hisses as he stumbles backwards from my view.

The world continues to close and open with the clap of my hands on my ears, but the flight of their movements passes by my back and Hypatia's hand disappears from my mouth. The scream is still in me, planting its feet in my guts, but my breaths are tangled in my throat, unable to reach my lungs to feed the terror inside me. I hold enough air to realize the smell, the heavy pungent scent of rotten meat and stale shit, is overpowering and my eyes are dripping. Squinting through the smell, I notice the boy's sneakers look caked with mud. But my eyes acclimatize. The grime and mud on the toes of his shoes become blood and flesh. It looks like he has trodden through roadkill.

Malcolm lunges forward at the boy, his knife drawn, but Hypatia grips his other arm, holding him in place. I fight to slow the clap of my hands against my ears so I can hear her words, but catch only, "Wait ... dormant ... touching ... disturb ..."

"Fuck that." Malcolm's arm writhes and flies as he tries to escape Hypatia's grasp.

"Stop!" I seethe. They stare at me; Hypatia maintains her grip on Malcolm's wrist, while Malcolm stands transfixed, his free hand on his knife. "Quiet," I demand.

Malcolm raises the hand Hypatia hasn't pinned in her grip in a gesture of acknowledgement. Hypatia tilts her head, and her eyes dart across the surface of my face, unabashed as she mines my emotional state. The rain drums overhead on the trailer's metal roof. Hypatia releases Malcolm's arm; he tucks it to the side of his body, but he wriggles his fingers, testing their strength in the aftermath of Hypatia's vice grip.

"You have a plan, Alexandra?" Hypatia asks, though there's no trace of a question in her voice. My vitals must betray I have decided something.

With great focus on my enunciation, I offer, "Disable. Throw away."

"Can we do that?" asks Malcolm, but his eyes are on Hypatia, not me. "We have a few rounds left. A good shot in its chest?"

Hypatia folds her thin, pale arms and her head swivels between Malcolm and me, her expression inscrutable. "A bullet is unlikely to disable it. Even a well-placed one. Its joints are a reinforced alloy. They either need to be unscrewed using the manufacturer's tools or the metal sundered by a high-intensity heat. A blow torch," she offers her counsel slowly, as if with reluctance, and her voice sounds the way I imagine mine does, flat and distant.

"Blind it," I blurt out.

"Would that work?" presses Malcolm. Hypatia doesn't answer him immediately. Malcolm barks, "Come on, Hypatia, would that fucking work or not?"

"If we disabled his eyes and removed him from the trailer, the chances he would be able to harm or kill us would be reduced. Is that what you were asking?"

"Good enough for me. Show me how to disable it."

Malcolm leans over the boy and positions the knife in his hand so that its curved tip hovers over the boy's serene and empty face. The blade shakes as Malcolm tries to control his grip. Before I realize it, Hypatia has slipped between Malcolm and me, and though she isn't even up to his shoulder, she manages to crowd him.

"May I make an observation?" she asks. Malcolm offers up an impatient grunt of recognition. "We have no idea if this boy, unit, is hostile. Disabling him might be unnecessary and cruel." Malcolm shakes his head and edges the knife near the corner of the boy's eye. Hypatia rubs my arm and locks eyes with me. "Alexandra, this is still someone's brother. Someone's son. What if it were me?"

"It's not though," Malcolm counters as the tip of the knife blade squelches and then disappears behind the corner of the boy's eye.

Malcolm's forearms flare and tremble as he roots and pries with the knife until there's a noise like the sound of a cork being fired. The eyeball juts forward and bounces in front of the boy's face, suspended by several yellow cords connected to the back of the eye. A milky substance rolls down the boy's cheeks and a sudden spasm mangles his features as his body writhes. Malcolm steps back, but the blade remains wedged inside the boy's face. In silence, we brace for the boy to awaken and discover us ripping away his sight. Yet, nothing happens; his body sinks back into the cocoon of indented boxes and his face empties back into a vapid stare.

"Jesus, the sooner this is done, the better," whispers Malcolm. He pries out the other eye with same pop and deluge of milky fluid. The eye swings wet, and he struggles to maintain his grip on it to sever the cords binding it into the boy's skull. "Hypatia, should I crush these?" he asks as he spins the green eyes around his palm with his thumb, and they remind me of mom's Yin and Yang meditation balls.

Hypatia frowns, shakes her head, and turns away from us, venturing deeper into the dark that reaches out to our toes from the front of the truck's trailer. She hasn't spoken since Malcolm and I ignored her observation.

Malcolm nods to the inviting pale glow of our lanterns at the end of the truck. "Smells fucking rancid, let's get this done already. Hypatia, a little help?" There's no answer, and we can only make out the faint imprint of her shape in the dark. "Forget it," he mutters and reaches for the boy's foot, but then recoils at the red gore of blood and flesh matted on his sneakers. "Take it by the arms," he instructs, and together, we topple the boy to the floor with a heavy thud. "Fucking heavy," he breathes as the boy slips along the floor, each of its hands in ours. "Fast as you can," he urges as I pause to adjust my grip. "Seriously, Alexandra, we don't want it waking on us," he says, struggling to keep his words level.

The body rocks a little as it hits grooves in the floor, daring to rise a few inches before going flat. With each rise and bounce, I wonder if it will climb to its feet. There's no sign of Hypatia, yet I feel her eyes on us, following us from the dark.

When we reach the trailer's backdoor, Malcolm hunches over and, between breaths, utters, "Okay. Okay." His eyes are locked on the floor and his voice is faint; he's speaking to himself. After several moments, he rises to his feet and addresses me. "You're tougher than you look, you know." He smiles as I raise my arm and flex my biceps. "Home stretch. Let's start by pushing it out the door. If it doesn't wake, I want us to pull it across the road and toss it in the ditch, just to be safe. Makes sense?"

"I don't want Alexandra to leave the trailer. It's an unnecessary risk. I'll take it from here."

Malcolm welcomes Hypatia's abrupt return by raising his hands into the air in a gesture that resembles surrender. His words come in a rush. "Fine with me. Just finish quick, before it wakes."

"If he wakes," replies Hypatia, then grips the boy's wrist and watches as Malcolm fumbles with the trailer's rear door latch.

Together, they push the body over the lip of the rear door, and it crashes upon the asphalt in a tangle of limbs. I sit with my arms around my knees and watch Hypatia and Malcolm vanish into a wall of rain and blackness. The slow scrape of metal and sighs of Malcolm's exertions reach inside the trailer, cutting through the furious patter of rain on the trailer's roof.

HYPATIA
Confidence Booster

The rain has stopped. It died slowly, becoming faint taps and flickers overhead until it offered up the silence of the road. Based on the dip in her body temperature, Alexandra is in the third stage of her second REM cycle. Not nearly enough sleep. Once again, Malcolm has barely slept. I am not sure if he knows I know he is awake. He steals glances at me. Red and yellow clouds drift across his nose and cheeks. Anger and fear. There does not seem to be anything I can do to earn his trust. Not quickly, at least. In running scenarios, my processor advises Alexandra and I are safest if I assume the relationship with Malcolm is transactional. There is no point in taking further action to build a deeper relationship with him.

First light should be approaching. There is a rapid shuffle of steps outside. Malcolm jumps to his feet, his hand on the rear door's latch. His face flushes a deeper yellow as he draws his pistol. Without turning from the latch, he whispers, "You heard that, right?"

"Yes."

"It's that fucking thing."

"Probably, yes."

"You knew, didn't you? Knew it was in here the whole time." His words travel over his shoulder in sharp hisses.

"Of course not."

There are no more words, only Malcolm's noisy breaths and the pounding of his elevated heart rate in my ears. The interregnum of silence outside lasts enough to be called a moment, and Malcolm remains rigid and pressed to the door. A quick scan confirms Alexandra is still cycling through deep sleep. She did not hear our exchange.

A muffled thud breaks against the side of the trailer, then turns to soft, adroit taps against the metal. A scale of fingertips moving along the outer wall of the trailer. Braced and in wait, we listen to the boy's progress, his delicate, precise movements drawing nearer to the end of the trailer where the horses and the door wait for his discovery.

"You sure it's blind?" demands Malcolm.

"He sounds blind."

"Fuck it. Get Alex up and ready to move."

"No. Stay silent. He may not know we're in here."

Malcolm's next words are muted by a sudden guttural and primeval roar from outside. Hooves clatter and bounce on the pavement. The horses are screaming. Alexandra is upright, her eyes fixed on us. In a flurry of movements, Malcolm pulls open the latch and leaps out into dawn's pale light.

"Fucking asshole—"

The rest of his words are upended by the ring of three blasts. The ricochet of gunshots along the trailer's walls rings shrill. Amidst the screams of the horses, one cry, plaintive and defeated, climbs above the echoes of the gunfire. Its breath follows, laboured and weak.

"It gored Quartz. We need to get the fuck out of here!" Alexandra looks stricken, maybe unsure if she has really awoken. "Pack us out," Malcolm bellows.

"Alexandra, everything's fine. Pack these last few things as quick as you can. Wrap up in the emergency blanket. Don't come outside until I say it's okay."

I slip through the trailer door and step down into a slow tide of blood spreading over the pavement and pooling beneath the truck. I hear Malcolm's curses and grunts before I see him. The boy is supine on the pavement, writhing as Malcolm crashes the heel of his boot into his spine with savage desperation. His back is to me, but I do not need to see his face to know it must be the colour of yellow jackets and roses, absolute blind rage-terror. The boy manages to push himself up from under Malcolm's foot and struggles to his knees, revealing a face of holes, bereft of eyes and mutilated by gunfire.

"Fuck you," howls Malcolm as he staggers backwards.

The boy stills. The milk tears have dried on his cheeks, and amidst the gored flesh, black metal glints reveal a hint of his manufactured skull. The eyeless face moves in a sinister nod towards Malcolm, and then, with a twitch, the boy collapses prostrate on the road. The two remaining horses continue to scream and jump, and the third one is quiet, its body cooling, bleeding out to become a black hole eating the grey tarmac.

"We need to go," commands Malcolm as he paces up and down beside the motionless companion child. "Why did it crash like that?"

"He might have been damaged," I offer. Though in truth, I do not know why he collapsed. His heat signature still carried traces of battery life. He should not have suffered such an abrupt power failure.

"It killed Quartz, Hypatia. Francis was right, these things are fucked." Malcolm's words sound incredulous and full of despair.

"Maybe. We blinded him. Maybe he got frightened and made a miscalculation."

"A miscalculation? Jesus. Where's Alexandra!? We need to haul ass."

The panic in his voice alone is enough to carry him down the road, yet he does not move immediately. Instead, his eyes linger on me, and his face turns to autumn foliage, shades of suspicion and fear. His question is my own. There is neither time nor the possibility to attenuate his concerns. Besides, I do not have any answers, at least not answers he will like.

"I've instructed Alexandra to stay in the trailer until I was confident the environment was safe."

Malcolm responds with a mirthless snort, but I ignore him as I try to lead the two remaining horses to the other side of the truck, away from the sight of their gored companion, in a hope that settles them.

"It's safe as it's going to get," he replies.

He is not wrong, but before I speak, there is a small flurry of movement, almost lost in the distance of the greying field that stands quiet along the highway's shoulder. With greater focus, I make out the figure of a second child. Another boy. He runs with abandon, his head bobbing in and out of sight amidst the sea of grass. Somehow, his running gait tells me he is like all the others: manic and barbarous, and beyond the remediation of language. Is it a latent defect? A product of the flash? Perhaps it is merely the absence of behavioural guardrails set by Lotus or some sort of oversight. What error is inside us? They have recalls for cars, should there be recalls for us too?

The boy is still deep in the field, but he is moving fast. His features, a face that looks both melted and bloated, cut away from distance's opaque reach. Judging by his motion, he should be upon us in a minute. There is no time to spare. Three people, two horses. They will tire faster, and should something happen to another horse, one person will be forced to walk. My processor runs scenarios. We are 25% less likely to make it to the refuge before my battery dies if the three of us share two horses.

An errant thought, alien yet comforting, takes hold and mutinies into words. "*Oh, my kingdom for a horse.*"

Malcolm's frantic steps and his mutterings about breaking camp approach from the right side of the truck. It is time.

"Alexandra. Come now. Quick," I call.

The scamper of her footsteps pauses, and I know she is examining the horse's blood, but the soft thud of her feet landing soon follows. She appears around the side of the truck-trailer, and the emergency blanket flutters behind her as she runs and struggles into the saddle. Malcolm's voice grows louder, and I hear the approach of his footsteps. Alexandra is secure atop Chestnut, and my feet are in Opal's stirrups as Malcolm rounds the corner with his olive Republic jacket drawn tight around his shoulders. Though his eyes are heavy, purple, and a little sunken, he manages to smile up at us.

"Guess I'll ride shotgun with Alexandra. Let's get going ..."

His words falter as the boy rushes the slight slope of the embankment. As he moves, his bone-white scalp shines through a few stray tangles of hair. The silicon flesh on his face looks grey and slimy: his cheeks have become bulbous drooping jowls, the flesh around his neck swings about him in thick peeling strips. There is a faint resemblance to the way Alexandra's fingers and toes prune and wrinkle if she stays in the bath too long.

Alexandra screams, and Chestnut begins to run. The boy leaps over the shoulder of the road and lands with a heavy crunch between Malcolm and me. He swivels his head in examination of each of us, his sagging cheeks and neck swinging as he moves. With a lurch of what appears like recognition, he advances on Malcolm.

Opal gives in to her instincts and catapults down the road to join Chestnut and Alexandra. Over my shoulder, I see Malcolm swing his knife at the boy, but the boy advances into his swings, disinterested and unafraid of the knife's erratic claim to space. Malcolm retreats and disappears around the back of the trailer to emerge on the road, charging past the dead horse. In a moment, the boy follows, but his gait seems encumbered, perhaps slowed by the molting state of his flesh and body.

Malcolm runs and yells at us, his face a yellow cloud as he beckons us back to him. There is a flutter in my legs, a desire to clip my feet into the horse's sides and charge towards him, scoop him from the road, but my processor reassembles a decision tree in the dark behind my eyes. Two horses and two riders remains the optimal scenario. Opal is keen to run, and I steer her towards Alexandra, who has slowed, cantering Chestnut in a wide, awkward arc to take in the scene behind us. Our eyes meet, and I cock my head, pointing in front of us, cajoling her to race with me to the road's distant horizon.

A clap of hooves showers the tarmac as Alexandra cuts by me. She tucks her body low as she urges Chestnut on in determination, streaking headlong towards Malcolm. The words to call her back emerge on my tongue, but the processor intercedes. It will be a suboptimal outcome. Further erosion of trust. The companion boy is nearly upon Malcolm now, but Alexandra is closing ground. Malcolm's arms rise in the air in desperation, anticipating the passage of the horse, but his pace slows slightly. The companion child punches through the air and creates a composite of sound: a cry of shock, a low whine of human pain, and the scrape of horseshoes on the tarmac as Chestnut skids with Malcolm's added weight.

The pair circle back in a wide arc, avoiding the leprous reach of the companion boy. Malcolm is half righted behind Alexandra. His features twist and stricken as his arms thread Alexandra's sides in a fierce search for some inch of the reigns to anchor him. Alexandra, expressionless, does not relent in her approach but flies past me, and my horse breaks into a gallop to catch up. A furtive glance reveals the companion child is following us, the strips of his molted flesh twisting and swirling like the vinyl on a deer's antlers with his steps. The highway and the grey fields become a drab blur. Our horses are level now, but Alexandra's eyes remain steadfast on the road ahead, though the familiar blotches of orange fury and fuchsia confusion blemish her face.

It has been 350 seconds, and another glance over my shoulder reveals the companion child is no longer behind us, but lost somewhere in the bends in the road. In the distance, tucked away off the shoulder of the road, is a rest-stop. A low, whitewashed square building untenanted by any heat signatures. We can stop there. It looks like a refueling pit stop for long haul freight, not a place designed for human needs. These little outposts of the automated world, the pit stops for driverless freights, still crop up like the future in stasis along these outer roads.

"We can slow down. He's gone." I try to make my voice light. Cheerful even, but Alexandra does not respond, and I see her dig her heels into Chestnut, determined to make more thunder on the road. "Alexandra, it's over. We're safe," I call again.

This time, Malcolm taps her shoulder, coaxing her to relent. With a limp shrug of his neck, Malcolm gestures forward at the whitewashed building. "Ease up. We can rest here." Malcolm says no more, and though Alexandra's face is waves of incredulousness and confusion, I see her cede the reigns in slow, reluctant inches to Malcolm's grip.

I slide from Opal before Alexandra and Malcolm move to dismount. There is a risk that Malcolm will take off with the horse if Alexandra dismounts first. His face is a desert sun, a composite of shock, fear, and grief. The heat of his body indicates a deep wound in his abdomen, and he attempts to patch it with his hand. From what remains of my First Aid information, I suspect it is a liver wound. He will bleed out slowly. There does not seem to be the will inside him to run. Chestnut sighs into my head as I brace myself against him to aid Alexandra's dismount.

The whitewashed building stands on a tide of asphalt that is populated by black obelisk hydrogen fuel stations. At the building's edge, a gravel path leads towards a cleared entry space amidst the woods. A green sign, its corners bent, confirms it is a waste-to-hydrogen station. Up close, the structure resembles a cross between a gazebo and a bunker. Each wall is interrupted by a long, thin, horizontal window carved into its centre like loopholes. Several inactive floodlights are mounted where the walls adjoin to its flat roof. Minimalist. Designed for a non-human attendant to maintain the pumps, perhaps.

Alexandra paces in front of the horse, shoves her hands into her pockets, removes them, and presses them to her cheeks, then tries to braid her fingers at her waist. She is on the verge of an episode, so distraction is necessary.

"Alexandra, there might be useful materials that have yet to be processed. Obviously, stay out of the pit." I point to the small gravel path. Alexandra's face flashes full of suspicion, but with an incredulous glance over her shoulder, she abides. When I am confident she is out of earshot, I turn to Malcolm and ask, "Can you dismount?"

Malcolm does not answer but slides his legs over the saddle and winces as his feet meet the ground. In uneven steps, he stumbles towards the little whitewashed building, his hand clutching the right side of his abdomen as he moves. With paling face and faltering steps, he readies himself to crash against the exterior of the building. This would leave him exposed and visible from the road. Visible to Alexandra. I insert myself beneath him and catch some of his weight on my shoulders, becoming his crutch.

"Inside here. Let me get you inside. The road is cold."

He replies in a string of rapid and strained wordless breaths, but obeys. The roof is so low that Malcolm is forced to stoop, and the floor is poured concrete. The interior is frozen in upended transition, studs without drywall. Regardless, I walk him to the wall, where he slides from my shoulder and slumps against the plywood walls in a grimace. The door is weightless, but its weatherworn hinges scream as I shut it.

Malcolm kneads his lips together, oiling them for some decided words. Finally, he says, "You left me."

"I did. I'm sorry. I didn't mean for you to get hurt."

For a while, he is quiet, focused on biting at the air, and he appears to swallow it more than breathe it. "Am I dying?" he manages at last.

"Yes. It'll be fast," I assure, in the hope this will provide him some comfort.

He leans his head back against the coarse plywood, and the exposed stud prods one of his shoulders forward. Nonetheless, he shuts his eyes and smiles. "Alexandra's right. Your lips flutter when you lie. Did you know that?"

My fingertips tap my lips in inquisition of some outward sign of defect or malfunction. "I wasn't aware …"

It is clear there are no more words inside him right now, and we cede to the low growl of the wind travelling over the road. Behind the little white hut, Alexandra's heat signature wanders in and out of my sight, seemingly in a large circle. I watch her bend down to inspect something on the ground and then continue her path.

"Hypatia?"

"Yes, Malcolm."

"Did you know—?" The rest of his question is sundered by a riotous fit of coughs, but it does not matter. I know what he wants to ask. The blister of Alexandra's heat signature passes through the thin greyness of autumn trees. She is too far away to hear us.

"I suspected the truck might be occupied and then I found this." From my jacket pocket, I retrieve the mutilated padlock I found at the back of the truck and balance it on my palm so that

Malcolm can see the lock's severed horseshoe band. "A scan of the truck's interior confirmed my suspicions."

His face darkens and stretches in a mirthless grin. "Why—?"

Again, I spare his words. It feels wasteful and unfair for him to spend his remaining strength on this conversation. "I need to understand what's making us ... them, violent. For Alexandra's sake. I never intended for you to get harmed."

His face twists in a bricolage of rage, frustration, and sadness. The colours fight and bleed out until the deep blue of grief pencils in his features.

"You know now?"

"Their heat signatures suggest their power systems are compromised."

He closes his eyes again and collapses back into the chaffed wood. "A defect?"

"Possibly. It might also be damage. The flash is a common denominator."

"You're a liability to Alexandra."

His words come slow and quiet, and I can see he has more to say, but speaking has winded him. It does not matter that the rest of his words are locked inside him, for I am confident I can predict their shape.

"Your concern is appreciated, but I made a promise to our Father I'd get her some place safe. She won't get there without me. I'll take the necessary precautions."

He sighs, but lets his head rest on the wall, and with his eyes closed, says, "Keep off the roads. A girl like Alexandra is just a warm body to an Alogo Boo. A fate worse than death. Get her, please ... gotta say goodbye."

"I can't do that. Informing her that you are fatally injured will be destabilizing. If she learns she failed to save you from the companion child, she'll likely feel responsible and guilty. If she continues to believe she saved you, it'll boost her confidence and build her emotional resilience and self-esteem."

"Good lord," he whispers. My refusal seems to return his consciousness to his body with the somatic heaviness of a second birth. His eyes drift across the enclosed room in an ambedo trance of resigned comprehension. "Out of sight," he wheezes.

"If you're feeling lonely, I can hold your hand. Physical contact can soothe the transition."

And though my own words are alien to me, from some unknown origins, I bend down and try to slip my small delicate hand into his, wreathed in veins and coated in dust and blood, but in a feeble gesture he pushes me away.

YET SOMEWHERE INSIDE ME, A SENSATION OF A SMALL FLUTTERING HAND IN MINE SPARKS, AND WITH IT COMES A BLUR OF WHITE OBLIQUE MACHINES AND THE GREEN GLOW AND CHIRP OF A DASHBOARD.

The vision recedes to Malcolm's voice. "Water." From the side of his backpack, I fight his canteen loose and place it in his hand with the lid off. "Go," he breathes.

I can tell from the slate colour of his face and the blue smoulder of his body's heat signature this is his last request.

~

The path that runs behind the outbuilding is wide. The tread marks of vehicles laden with waste have created parallel moss-filled gullies along its sides. Where the pathway meets the clearing, Alexandra is sat cross-legged in front of a circular pit reminiscent of a well. Behind her is a cluster of birch trees, bare-boughed and ashen-skinned.

"Junk," she calls without looking up as I sit beside her. "Poo and junk."

The pit is overflowing with a deluge of animal manure, white takeout containers, and the cheap plastic shells of TVs, computer monitors, and other electronics. A festering mountain of emissions.

With a nod back towards to the black obelisk hydrogen stations, her face orange in caution and concern, she asks, "Can you charge?"

"Without electricity, there's no hydrogen, but even if it was working, my battery is only compatible with electric charging stations. You know that."

The edge in my words seems to surprise both of us, and her blue eyes become wide puddles as she lowers her head with a sigh. A wave of regret rushes over me. With her confidence and sense of self already in jeopardy, she does not need chastisement.

"You were very brave—" I start, but the recall of Malcolm's words brings my fingers to my lips as a fan, deflecting Alexandra's vision. I have never seen the things I tell Alexandra as lies, but rather presentations of the world necessary to her well-being. If it is true my lips betray my finely calibrated words as untruths, there is no room for error now. Urging her to leave Malcolm behind created a significant erosion of trust.

On my feet with my back to her, I let my toes skim the edge of the waste pit as I continue, "The companion child would have killed Malcolm had you not rescued him."

"He's okay?" The slight snap of deadfall tells me she is on her feet, eager, perhaps, to join my side.

"He'll be fine," I speak fast and through my fingers. "He's rejoining the Republic fighters. It's just you and me now, sister."

There is a slight murmur against my fingertips, a flutter in my lips. Artful by design, truthful by malfunction. There is something profoundly human in my glitch, and I nearly smile, but Alexandra intercedes.

"Another Mickey ... Road girl," she murmurs as she pokes at the surface of the waste with a stick.

"Yes. We must assume they're all dangerous, as a precautionary principle."

"Precautionary principle," she repeats, and though probably imperceptible to her, she widens the space between us as she pokes harder at the waste until the tip snaps.

The horses flick their ears and shake their tethers, which I have tied to the hydrogen station farthest from the whitewashed outbuilding, where Malcolm lays dying. I shepherd Alexandra ahead of me towards Chestnut.

"No goodbye," she says with a frown as she surveys the charging site, and I cannot help but notice how her vision strays to the outbuilding. There are hues of doubt and concern across her nose and forehead.

"Sometimes we need to find different ways to say goodbye, even when we wouldn't like to."

She nods and grabs Chestnut's reins, but the colours smeared across her visage seem to harden.

BUG
The Tunnel Rat

The sensor pads pulse and bite with their electric warmth, and a dull ache grows between my ribs. I blink to flush the burn of exhaustion from my eyes, but my efforts are futile and bring no success. The game clock reads 3:30am, which means it was less than two hours ago when I logged off to try to sleep on the floor of the pod after getting brutally mowed down by a bunch of hooting bots in a pickup truck. The sensation of being crushed beneath the wheels made all my joints lock.

Nobody really sleeps anymore. The sleep bay is empty as the competition is too tight to sleep properly now. Catnaps on the pod floor are all any of us can afford. Bleary-eyed, I flick through my roster of assets in search of WoodTick—the avatar I saved in a forest I believe to be close to the so-called bot barn. The location is on the world map near to where Scrummaster indicated, and there's a hive of red dots of disabled avatars. A euphoric giddiness floods through my sleep-deprived body when I discover the avatar came to no harm during my time offline.

With a long shaking breath, I log on to the avatar and, in several blind sweeps of my arms, begin to clear the deadfall and leaves I used to conceal it with. As the autumnal mound of red and yellow forest canopy disperses, the paling darkness of a soon-to-be ascendent dawn fills my screen. The avatar responds to the slow cumbersome pumps of my legs and shuffles through the woods towards the outline of a thin gravel road ahead.

My eyes grow heavy and my body sways in the pod. In my yellow boots, I slosh knee deep in the silty water of our creek. The one we started visiting together after mom left. A bullfrog croons and the cypress green fingers of Reed Marsh sway in the warm breeze far above my head. I crouch and venture forward with the net, and you smile with encouragement.

"*Eye on the prize, kiddo. Steady now, one motion ...*"

I raise the net, but the creek hardens into a thin gravel road, where my avatar remains frozen in mid-stride.

"*Bug, you've gone and fallen asleep on your feet. Get sharp or you're gonna fall ass over head out here.*"

With a strain, I recover my surroundings. The road tunnels through the grey-green arms of crooked, leering junk trees and unidentifiable scrub. Panic slips its fingers into my chest as I realize I have no fucking idea where I am. The whole raid might just be some bullshit ploy to eat up my time.

The urge to log off here and now and collapse on the floor of the pod takes hold of me, but I press on. Then, ahead in the branches of a naked tree, I spot it akimbo in the breeze. A pink trail ribbon flutters in the rush and pull of the wind.

"*Winner, Winner, Chicken Dinner, Bug.*"

In a burst of adrenaline, I shrug off my fatigue and sprint down the road, passing several more pink ribbons dancing in the brush. The gravel road descends into a flat land of fields, and green pastures bite the paling night in darker shadows. A narrow roadway splits to the left, leading to more fields and a grey barn moored amidst rising foothills. A solitary pink ribbon swings from a skeletal tree, seemingly already denude in autumns coming. There's no question this is the target. I slip off the road and snake through the fields on my hands and knees towards the building, which stands as a darker shadow amidst the night.

The sensor pads on my hands pop and vibrate as the avatar crawls over the pebbles and sticks that lie beneath the tawny field like a vast carpet. The half-life of the sensation lives in my palms as I clamber to the barn's entrance. Red twisted metal frames, the skeletons of old industrial vehicles, poke through the grass around the building's perimeter. I know places like this in real life. Broke little acreages, where bits of wreckage ceaselessly wash ashore until they bury those stubborn enough to stay.

Replace the barn with a trailer and could be one of our many homes, eh, Dad?

The barn door is ajar, and a soft light reaches through its gap, settling on the doorstep in amber shadow. I peer inside and find that only a solitary lantern cuts the darkness, its dim glow cast from a cluttered workbench that towers above my diminutive avatar. As I catch my breath and try to ward off the return of my exhaustion, my avatar sways on the doorstep. With renewed focus, I peer inside, desperate to scour the game environment for any ambient noises that may give me a clue as to what might be inside the dark. There's the constant purr of a mechanical hum, and I spot several generators placed across the dirt floor. Beneath the hum, though, there's an occasional long suckling growl.

It returns again and again, obedient to its own rhythm, and in disbelief, I realize it's a snore. I slip through the door and take deft steps through the widening darkness. The snores belong to a dark mass curled on the ground. A faint blue light from a machine concealed in the dark illuminates the large body of a male sleeping bot. I contemplate murdering it for a few extra points, but in my approach, I notice rows and rows of green jerrycans, lined against the far wall of the building. The bot might be creating the fuel somehow. I've heard other players complain of killing bots that control bridges or other infrastructure and the simulation doesn't respawn them. They are gone forever, with lasting consequences.

"Forget the snoring geezer Bug, get the fuel and get the fuck out."

Elegant council, as always, Dad.

"You're in Fuck Around and Find Out country, Bug!"

All right old man, remember I'm here on your account, I spit back, though my thumb and index finger pinch the USB stick in search of a faint pulse of you, a desperate séance carried out in fingertips. I roll my head from shoulder to shoulder and refocus my attention to the rows and rows of jerrycans that stand over me on screen. From the far end of one of the rows, I pull one loose. White dripping C's have been hastily spray-painted on each side.

"*You should bring a wheelbarrow next time, Bug.*"

The bot continues to snore, but from this side of the room, a fat empty glass bottle planted at the bot's side becomes visible. Whatever was in it is consumed to umber dredges. The snores are long, retching things. A drunken slumber, the snores of my childhood. The simulation is nothing if not attentive to detail. Even in here, the bot men appear damned, determined to drink themselves into a meridian of despair. By now, I know the simulation is faithful to its realism, leaving little chance the bot will wake, but I still cross through the barn, making sure not to jostle the jerrycan's contents against its sides.

The jerrycan is awkward and hard to carry, and I tumble down the road in shuffling steps as my exhaustion bleeds into my avatar's gait. I walk down backcountry roads until the simulacra of the rising sun casts rosy shadows ahead of my toes. The daybreak exposes the road, and it's easy to fall prey to bots. I'm already down to nine playable units. I have no intention of losing the fuel, but I'm reluctant to log with it in my avatar's possession.

"Bug, you're pushing it too far. You've been up for probably a day straight."

Dawn brings colour to the leaves and washes away the vestiges of grey twilight that seem to cling to the woods, but the road wobbles and dips as my head drifts forward. I'm not sure how long I walk like this, but the road surrenders from its elbow, the charred ruins of a fuelling station. Amongst the debris and along the road, sprigs of black metal lay like spider's legs. Airborne NPCs. They don't really bother players, but they make the bots scatter and compete with us in the destruction of targets. There's a consensus in the hangar that they are run by the simulation and are unplayable.

In approach of the fuelling station, I kick one of the black limbs into the ditch. The charging stations are shredded, and fire has eaten the building down to its foundations, but near the back of the lot, a green porta-potty is tipped on its side, moated by blue fluid, soggy toilet paper, and shit.

"Beautiful," I whisper.

With a quick glance to ensure nobody else is present on the road or in the eaves of the wood, I stash the jerrycan inside the shitshow that is the porta-potty's interior and continue down the road in search of a secure place to log. I don't get far before the screen flashes red and my sensor pads and gloves twinge with an electric bite.

The fuck? The screen flashes several more times before it fills with the message: *Asset life exceeded. Asset lost.*

What the shit?! The road and forest rise above me as the avatar crumbles to the tarmac. The screen goes black and then reloads at the world map. *The double fuck?*

In panic, I flip to see my total playable assets. I'm down to eight. I've lost another life. Blind fury overtakes me as I rip off my sensor pads and gloves and throw them into a corner of the room. I cross the pod in a two-step pace and back again as I cycle from exhaustion to insatiable rage.

"Walk it off, Bug."

"Fine!" I scream.

The pod releases me in a gush of air. The hallway is empty, but active players in neighbouring pods cast a soft blue glow through their porthole sized windows. The thought that others are still playing puts a welt of frustration in my throat. I can't bear to look at them. With my head down, I march along the player hallway, not daring to break sight from my sneakers as they clap back at me on the poured concrete floor.

One hallway runs into another and, in my sleep deprived trance, they all seem to bleed together. The shadows lengthen and the margins between my feet and the walls shrink. Though I don't travel down any stairways, I feel like I'm in descent. When my gaze breaks away from my feet, I realize I've strayed into some industrial catacomb beneath the hangar. The narrowing hallways have become tunnels wreathed by industrial piping. The soft lighting of the main floor is replaced by dim red shadows cast from emergency lighting mounted sporadically throughout the tunnels.

Well, this is no fucking good at all. In a shrug of a capitulation, I carry on down the metal-skinned tunnel and go right at a T-junction.

The air in the tunnel is warm and thick, almost humid. This must be where most of the hangar's heating and power equipment is located. Ahead, at the far end of the tunnel, there's a pulse of movement. A human figure. *At least I'm not the only dumbass who got lost down here.* The red light obscures their features, but I'm certain it's another player. I offer them a reluctant wave. They stand motionless, but I feel their eyes on me, perhaps in consideration of my presence. Their silence slows my steps until I freeze. Then, without any acknowledgement, they slip around the corner of the tunnel and vanish from view. The uncertainty of the situation compounds, and though I'm alone, I proceed in slow, cautious steps.

Halfway down on my right, the tunnel's wall curves to create a nook. The dull shadow of the emergency lighting simmers panels of red and white metal. From the dark, the square body of an EV charging station comes into view, its interface alive with blue and green light. *Random much.*

I've never used an EV station. Once your truck was banned, we couldn't afford to replace it with an EV.

Its tapered body is warm to the touch, and I can't be sure if it's residual heat from recent use or merely a constant state of warmth from the electricity that lives inside it. My fingers stray towards the charging cables coiled at the shoulders of the unit—

"You should not be down here."

I whirl around to find Tim standing behind me at the mouth of the nook, his arms crossed. "I got lost," I stammer, aghast at his sudden materialization behind me. *Where the fuck did you come from, Tim? Was it you at the end of the tunnel? If it was you, why didn't you acknowledge me? Creeper much.*

Tim doesn't answer, but his eyes appear to swallow the red light of the tunnel to gleam with a new intensity.

"Tim, why is there a charging station down here?"

"The patrons of the tournament like contingency measures. This is a remote location. In an emergency, there may be a need to power extraction vehicles."

"But why is it—"

"Are you bored of the tournament?"

I shake my head.

"Then why are you down here pretending to be a tunnel rat?"

"My avatar crashed out on me, I needed a walk."

"There are many places to walk, 100. This is an odd choice. Not the choice of a focused player. Have you given the tournament all your best play?" Tim lurches forward, forcing my back up against the charging station. "Perhaps you have exhausted your better qualities. You can retire at any time, 100."

My better qualities? What the hell does that even mean? How is it that in a hangar full of loner hypercompetitive gamers, this guy has the worst social skills? Better qualities? Get fucked, you turtleneck-wearing weirdo. With effort, I conjure a shit-eating grin and reply, "No. I'm focused. Plenty more to give."

"That remains to be seen." Tim slips back into the tunnel to let some space grow back between us.

"I didn't mean to create a problem. If we aren't meant to come down here, you should let us know." Fighting my better judgement, I point to the red light at the end of the tunnel. "I saw another player over there."

Tim follows my indication with an adroit twist of his head, and his flat demeanour crumples into a frown. "Did they say anything to you?"

I shake my head again, overwhelmed by the thinly veiled menace in Tim's question.

"Perhaps it was only a shadow. Our eyes are not suited to these conditions, and you are sleep deprived. I will guide you out, 100. You are losing valuable playing time."

ALEXANDRA
The Bridge That Wasn't There

The clip clop of our horses' steps on the tarmac fills me with a sense of calm. Hypatia nods at a thin trickle of gravel road called Handsome Pond. I take her emphasis to mean we're on the right course; it has been a meandering journey since we left Malcolm three days ago. The sun is heavy on the crown of my head, so it can't be much past noon. A green road sign stands behind a curve in the road, informing us we're at the outskirts of Long Lake, a landmark she told me to expect today. Yet, Hypatia frowns; ahead of us, the 30 road, as she calls it, terminates into a wreckage of twisted and exposed rebar and shattered concrete.

With a heavy sigh, Hypatia brings Opal to a run to inspect the damage, and I follow. From where the road meets the bridge's ruin, the black waters of a nameless river thunder on far below us. Pieces of the bridge split the water and stand like stubborn follies. Hypatia glares at the river and occasionally surveys the dense, pathless woods that surround us. The horses have been patient, and I scratch Chestnut's head in appreciation. They've been different since the truck. Since Quartz died and Malcolm left. Tender with each other. I think so, at least. Hypatia says she has observed no changes.

"Try again?" I ask, though this is the third ruined bridge we've encountered.

Hypatia says they've been "washed out." But the rivers aren't especially high, and debris smatters the road and embankment. Sabotage seems more likely. For a long time, Hypatia doesn't answer; she seems fixated on the flow of the river and its ebb south of the road.

"I can't think of other bridges. Not without going far back on ourselves. There might be a crossing down there." She points to the distance, where the river runs slack through tall grass and a crooked gable of moss-covered trees.

"For horses?"

"I can't judge from here. Worth a look." She smiles.

We retrace our steps to where the road is whole and lead Chestnut and Opal into the wood's green shadows. The horses move at a slower pace as they saunter between the trees. An abrupt chorus of birdsong makes them flick their ears and pull against our lead.

"Come," I coax with a short tug on the bridle.

The horses go a little further, but stop again, stubborn against our encouragements. This time, Hypatia motions for me to stop, and in a slow panoramic rotation mines our surroundings.

"Someone else?" I whisper as the wind rattles through the empty branches.

"Just the drift of deadfall, I guess," replies Hypatia, but for a long time we don't move and she repeats her scan several times. "The woods are losing their colour," she decides.

Bathed in green shadow and leafy sparks of autumnal fire, I offer only a frown in reply. She shrugs and in silence leads us on to where the trees shrink into openness and yellow sunlight. As the trees scatter and become the tall grass we saw from the height of the 30, it's clear Hypatia was right: the river widens here into marshland and slow-moving waters.

Our first few steps summon soft murmurs and gurgles from the marshy ground. In several more steps, the grassland degenerates into bog and mud. The horses wait behind us, forbearing as the sun caresses their backs. Several times, I slide and sink, losing my footing in the wake of Hypatia's steps. The horses seem to watch our limited progress and wait, reluctant to follow us farther onto less stable ground.

As the lead to Chestnut grows taut, I feel compelled to call ahead, "Do horses mud?" It's a lazy construction, but I'm pretty sure Hypatia will understand the question.

"If it's not too deep, I think so. The bottom looks better further in." She points farther into the river, where its green sun-grazed waters surrender a bottom of sand and stone.

I nod. "You mud test?"

"Yeah, sure, let me get covered in foul swamp mud. Thanks, sis."

"Anytime."

"I'm sure." She laughs as she slides off Opal and instructs me to tie both horses to a slender, grey, sun-bleached tree alone on the edge of the tall grass.

I return to the borders where the soft grass becomes swamp mud and watch Hypatia venture out farther. In slow deft steps, she offers her feet to the slurp and suckle of the marsh. A tide of mud and black stagnant waters pool around her shins. From over her shoulder she calls, "Okay so far."

"Winning." I give her an overly theatrical double like with my thumbs for emphasis.

She grins and seems to try to keep the momentum of my amusement. "One small step for companion children, many large steps for horse kind." She fights her feet free and takes another step closer to where the swamp yields to the open waters of the river's flow. In a hungry gurgle, Hypatia almost slips from view. The swamp mud climbs to her waist, and she thrashes her arms, trying to grab hold of the reeds before her. "Help! I'm sinking!"

Her words conjure the sensation of water plunging over my head and the tumble into concrete blue shadows. Hypatia's cries intercede, but the sensation of our slow fall doesn't recede.

"Alexandra! Quick. The horses' ropes!"

A black and brown tide of sludge reaches her chest now. Sending the horses into alarm, I crash into the slender tree and pry out the knots we've put in the leads in a frantic explosion of fingers and nails. As I start to work the other end of the knot from Chestnut's bridle, a soft metallic click issues from within the pale-yellow wall of the marsh. A girl stands up and steps out of the grass with a rifle aimed at my chest.

Hypatia's pleas travel with the wind. "Alexandra, are you coming?"

With one end of the rope still in hand, I raise my arms in surrender. The girl looks a little older than Hypatia's designed age. Her cheeks are smudged, and she wears dark green rain pants and a Gore-Tex jacket that looks several sizes too large.

"Easy now. Easy," she whispers. I nod. "I just want the horses. Back away from them and everything will be fine." With the tip of the rifle, she points towards the swamp as if to marshal me along. I don't budge. "Come on, girl. I'll shoot you dead. Don't you dare think I won't."

"I need this." I lift the rope and point at the knot.

Hypatia calls again, "Alexandra, please come as soon as you can. Everything's fine, but the situation is time sensitive."

The familiar sensation of panic starts to bite my belly, but the thought that if Hypatia isn't so sunk and is still able to yell steadies me.

"What is she blathering about? We're deep in Alogo Boo country. She'll get us all killed."

"Stuck in mud."

The girl rolls her eyes and leans her head towards the swamp and shouts back, "Hey! Whoever you are, you best shut up and crawl your dumb ass out. It's a swamp, not quicksand!"

"Alexandra, who's with you? Are you okay?" Hypatia calls back in a frantic voice I don't recognize.

"She sinks. Rope to save," I murmur.

The girl frowns and narrows her eyes at me in what looks like measured consideration. "Will she shut up?" I nod. She points the rifle tip at the knot on the bridle. "Well go on, then. Tell her you're fine, too."

"No danger!" I call and I think I believe myself. "You Republic?" I ask as I pick at the knot.

"I'm not anything. Best way to stay alive is not to be anything. I'd take that jacket off if I were you." She shoots a clipped nod at my Republic jacket.

"Why rob us?" The knot is loose now in my fingers, but I slow my work in hope she'll give me an answer.

"Nothing personal. Ride one horse and sell the other to last the winter."

"We need them. Travelling."

"Needs aren't worth much."

"Ride with us?"

The girl answers with a hollow laugh, and her eyes grow harder with her words. "Die with you more like it."

"Please."

"Can't help you."

"You alone?"

Her eyes go bright, and she answers in a tight couplet, "Am now."

Sadness and loss, I decide. She speaks like she's old, but she looks small behind the gun now, her frame shrinking rather than growing as she moves into the open. There are things inside her that, I think, exist beyond the paltry cage of words. Like the feelings and thoughts that live within me but can't be pressed into the service of my vocabulary although I know them well: the primeval loss, the severing of a chain of blood, flesh, and smell, an apartness that gores us through the naval away from the life of our origins.

"I'm sorry."

She scrunches up her cheeks and rubs her face against her raised shoulder, but her voice comes back sharp. "That knot is about ready to be undone."

"Alexandra, I need help!" calls Hypatia.

"Go on. Save your sinking friend. Mind you don't sink with her, often the way of it."

"Maybe so," I murmur.

HYPATIA
Bound

Alexandra hovers over me, her face mauve with despair and shame as she scrapes the effluent mud from my body. She knows that, without the horses, our journey just became far more fraught and dangerous. Though, she does not know the numbers. Should we remain on foot for the next 24 hours, my processor predicts there is only a 15% chance we both reach the refuge coordinates.

I have made several suggestions that we try to catch the thief, but Alexandra is adamant she does not know her direction of travel and pursuing her may lead us farther off course. She is not wrong. The sun dries the pieces of mud Alexandra missed, and it seems to dust off my skin without much trace.

"It's okay. I know you did your best," I offer as Alexandra kicks pebbles along the forest floor.

"Poor Chestnut. Poor Opal," she laments.

"They'll be okay. It was considerate of the thief to leave our backpack," I add in the hope this will further console her.

"Plan?"

"You could swim, and I could use some wood for buoyancy?"

Alexandra offers a violent shake of her head in response. I toy with reminding her that she successfully jumped in the water at Cardinal, but it is clear from her bio-signals that she is obstinate. My processor surfaces behind my eyes in a pulse of blue as it recalibrates our chances of making it to the refuge coordinates at closer to 14% now.

"Fine. Then we walk back the way we came on the 30 road until we can try some of the little white roads that spin off it. I didn't plan for a trip without bridges."

There is the added question, a question I do not pose to Alexandra, as to who is destroying the bridges and if the bridge at Port Henry will be there.

"I know."

In a gesture she has not made since she was a little girl, she pulls my hand into hers. Hand in hand, we walk through the thickening grey-green shadows of the woods back to the concrete entrails of the 30 road. A westering sun retreats into the amber and orange coombs of the fields that layer the slope of the hillside. Alexandra has not eaten since breakfast and her pace is slow. I have led her from the 30 road down some anonymous asphalt tributary in the hope we can find passage over the river and get close to Long Lake. It is strange, but the farther we travel east, the more autumn seems to have robbed the fields and the hills of their colour. The world appears to pale with our coming. To one side of the road runs a wall of glacial rock, and to the other, a smattering of brush descends into tawny headed fields.

"Stop," she calls. "Tired."

"I know, but we need to at least get back to the 30 road before we camp," I say these words without breaking stride.

"Five minutes?" she pleads.

"No. Not here. Not in the open."

"A Death March!"

"You're being dramatic."

Alexandra skips in front of me and spins as she presses the back of her palm to her forehead and gives an impassioned sigh. Silhouetted by the sun, she holds the pose, and something inside me decides she is an imitation of Cassandra's despair and woe.

"You're funny. A riot. The next Bovi."

CHILDREN OF THE FALL 213

Alexandra laughs and raises her eyebrows. "Who?"

I try to answer her question, but in a blink, the name I uttered becomes placeless and slips from my memory into the deep blue well that lives behind my eyes. "I don't know—"

Alexandra misses my response, and her eyes sweep the distance where the paling sky is pockmarked by black birds kiting in a spiral. She takes a step back and frowns. Her blue eyes file down into little points, in a scrutiny of the column of birds.

"It's not a swarm, sis, just some crows. I promise."

Alexandra's face becomes an even green, but my eyes fall to the stretch of road beneath the birds. A long vertical post has been planted in the umber swells of the escarpment, its form bearing a faint kinship to the pier of a dock. My processor attempts to classify the structure as the remaining legs of an old bridge, but as there is no trace of any river, the match does not hold.

Alexandra is behind me now, seemingly frozen in place where she first spotted the birds. The structure is hewed from timber. Splintered pieces of wood shoot up from its base and a ragged dark mass hangs at its side, too solid in its outline to be uncleared branches. As I move forward, farther away from Alexandra, the dark mass gains shape and, in the shrinking distance, surrenders arms and legs. I can tell by her lack of response that it is still too far ahead for her eyes to make it out.

"Sis, I want you to put on the blindfold."

"Why?" Her eyes flash about the road and pry back into the flight of the crows in wild alarm.

"Something bad has happened. Now, sis."

Alexandra does not protest. She lowers her eyes to the road and approaches in a slow shuffling gait. Her face brightens again into a pale yellow, and in what codes as confused submission, she closes her eyes as I fix Maureen's nightshade to her face.

"Ready?" she asks.

"Yes, let me guide you. We'll move fast."

Before she responds, I lead her by the hand down the road towards the diving crows. The mass on the hewed wood rises like a ruined mast of a shipwreck, moored upon the shoals of the flint rock escarpment formed by the leprous granite of the cliffside. Alexandra follows, her steps tentative yet pliant as I steer us into the thing's shadow. It is a mounted crucifix. The arms and legs belong to a man: his flesh is mottled and grey, he greets us sightless, and a trail of red gore stains his cheeks from where the crows have pecked out his eyes. In crude gashes, the letters X and Y are carved into his forehead. Even with the breeze, the pungent stench of decay is overwhelming, and Alexandra scrunches her nose and pulls against my hand to coax me onward. Though his clothes are bedraggled with black earth and rusty-brown smears of dried blood, it is clear his coat is Republic issue. Alexandra pulls harder and I relent in a few small steps before speaking.

"Hold on, sis, I need to understand the situation better."

Though the crows' rattling caws half-sunder my words, her pull weakens. A small wooden placard is nailed into the base of the crucifix. In a crooked scrawl of black marker, it reads: "A Republic cuck, executed on Uncle Sal's orders. Long live the Alogo Boo." Farther down the road ahead of us, a blast mark interrupts the tarmac, forming a small, ragged island amidst the sea of grey pavement. The crucified man is a warning. A claim to territory, perhaps. Land claimed by the men who were so awful it was better to believe they were only twitter bots.

9237 hours ago, our Mother invited me into her study alone. She directed me to her thinking sofa, and then, in a measured and delicate pull, closed the door behind us. It was late and everyone else was asleep. Cross-legged on her study chair, she said, "Hypatia, I've decided I'd like to give you more access to the internet. To social media accounts, I mean." She wore a smile, but there were many colours suffused in her features.

"Okay."

"I don't want you to share with Alexandra that I've given this to you. I know you know how frustrated she is that we won't let her setup any social media accounts of her own."

"I understand."

"Good. I also need you to understand that I'm sharing this with you because I need your help."

"You do?" It had been a long time since our Mother asked me for help with anything new.

"Yes. I need you to understand what I'm ..." Her face jaundiced and then flashed with orange irritation as she reconsidered her words and corrected herself. "... what Alec and I are trying to shield Alexandra from."

"There are many sources of anxiety, I think I understand your concerns."

"I'm not sure you do. Alexandra is 15 now. She's beautiful, and of course all parents believe their children are beautiful, but she is uniquely so ..." But our Mother trailed off, smoothing out the ridges of her nightgown and flattening it over her knees. When she spoke again, her words were for herself. "I guess that doesn't really matter. She'd be in no less danger if she wasn't pretty, just an outlet for a different regimen of violence, perhaps. The point, Hypatia, is that the world is changing and becoming less safe for women. Her limited forms of self-expression amplify that vulnerability."

"I can aid her in expressing herself."

"Of course, but there may also be a time when Alexandra will not want you to chaperon her."

"That will be difficult for all of us," I decided.

"It would be very challenging under normal circumstances. These aren't normal circumstances. There is a movement. Alec doesn't think much of it, believes it will fizzle out, but it's been growing for a long time. It exists online for now, but that doesn't make it any less real."

"Am I to block Alexandra from hearing about this movement?"

"I don't believe it's something we can block. It's something I want you to help me prepare her for. Can you help me do that? It will mean engaging with material that might change your perspective of the world. Make you feel older. Like when you snuck my copy of *The Second Sex*?" Our Mother's words were flat, but her face was full of green and violet, unique colours of her bemusement.

"You believe it will help Alexandra?" Our Mother bit her lip and nodded. "Then yes."

"Thank you, Hypatia." With her eyes shut and her fists balled, she spoke again in her command voice, "Lotus, please give Hypatia access to all of my social media accounts." Several white portals ruptured the calm blue sea behind my eyes. With her eyes on me, she spoke again, "Hypatia, I want you to search #AlogoBoo across my accounts."

Upon complying with her request, posts, tweets, and pictures tumbled through me like an avalanche. Our Mother's post celebrating a paper she published on the psychology of climate change flew by, pursued by hundreds of sub-tweets. Islands of words began to build, each one indexed to the #Alogo Boo: dumb cunt, unfuckable, Betty Bitch, Wife of a Beta Cuck, Not worth a Rape, JK. Cross-searching these words created many tendrils. Betty was a word for an unattractive woman in a position of authority. It appeared that the position of authority was what made a Betty "unattractive."

"I'm sorry," I whispered.

"Me too," said our Mother with a blue frown.

"The word, well, the idea that you were 'unsuitable for physical intimacy' appeared five times more than any other insult. Why do you think that is?"

Our mother shrugged and then exhaled for a very long time before she answered, "I think maybe the ultimate denigration of violent objectification is that the object has no use. I'm planning on closing all these accounts down tonight. As you can see, they're pretty much unusable now. Do you have enough data to understand the threat?"

"As it is currently manifested, yes."

"As it is currently manifested," she repeated as yellow blossoms grew on her nose.

The recall of Our Mother slips away as the wind lifts and furrows the ragged pieces of the crucified man. The flash emptied all the streambeds under social media's bridges and let loose a generation of men raised by algorithms. A lonesome mob of internet men and boy bots incarnate. Web 3.0 in the flesh.

Several hours have passed, and the afternoon is burning down to the embers of a westering sun. Alexandra marches in my shadow, flagging at the pace I have set to put as much distance between us and the crucifixion as possible. In the hours that have followed, no questions have been asked and few words have passed between us. In the blue sea behind my eyes, my processor continues to run recalculations. The risk of the Alogo Boo was not given sufficient weight in my initial travel scenarios. Paul believed these roads would be quiet, far from the war. The error further erodes our odds of reaching the refuge.

I am uncertain if Alexandra grasps the threat. At our Mother's insistence, my lessons on the Alogo Boo had been gradual and circumspect. A night-mask is probably an insufficient shield from the dangers of the road. With a quick glance over my shoulder, I read Alexandra's vitals. There are many colours in her face, but they are pale against one another. Hard to read, so hard that for a moment they appear almost indistinct, a blur of greying primary colours. The sweat on her brow bleeds yellow, but green tendrils wreathe her cheeks. Fear and the ecstasy of the unknown. Vitals stable.

On the heels of my assessment, Alexandra announces, "I'm fine."

"I know."

"Eyes ahead," she urges.

"Okay, sis. I'll respect your privacy."

"Yeah, right," she scoffs.

"Yeah, okay. I totally won't."

For some reason, perhaps fatigue, she breaks down into uproarious laughter. Yet, a faint chorus of coarser voices trails her chuckles. With my abrupt stop, she steps into me and pulls back in alarm, and her laughter tumbles into concern.

"What?"

"Listen."

With strain, Alexandra seems to catch the cadence of the rising voices and her eyes grow wide with alarm. "Who?"

I put my finger to her lips and shake my head. We wait, braced at the side of the road, pink scabs of glacial rock to our shoulders. Initially, the voices travel too confused and guttural to discern as words, but then the chant rolls over us.

"This is my rifle, this is my gun! Alogo-yeah. This is my rifle, this is my gun, Boo-yeah!"

Male voices in low octaves grate on us and seem to run ahead of us, bouncing off the steep granite face of the hills. Alexandra's eyes bulge and her face flushes yellow. She opens her mouth to scream, but I muffle her with my hand and whisper, "It's okay. It's all okay. Give me a sec."

As I speak, I overturn the barren terrain in search of some crevice to conceal us. The road runs straight ahead for nearly a mile, so we cannot disappear on it. To the right, the impassable rock wall glowers over us. Behind us, wild grass and brush have overtaken the embankment on the road's left shoulder.

The chanting is becoming deafening, now joined by the thunderous clap of many feet. They must be just around the corner of the road. There are tears in Alexandra's eyes, but she is defiant. The sun is still fierce enough along the road, and it will be in their eyes.

The voices deepen. "I said, Alogo Boo, oh, ah, Alogo Boo!" And then, in faithful repetition, the followers, at least 40 by my processor's vocal recognition, send the word "Alogo Boo" over the road like a wave. There is little time.

I pull Alexandra across the asphalt and into the long grass as the man on point overtakes the curve in the road. I cannot assess if he saw us or if he registered the flicker of the grass as merely the brush of the wind. We lay flat beside the road, the grass' tawny fingers scratching our faces. An insectile chorus rises beneath us. Next to me, Alexandra trembles, her body its own earthquake, existential terror pressed hard and flat to dead soil. I grab her hand, find the pressure point beneath her thumb, and massage it, resuming our ritual to exorcise harmful external stimuli.

Alogo Boo thunders over us. The parade comes into view as an explosion of palm tree and orange tropical sun cloth prints shining out from beneath body-armour and black assault rifles swaddled across chests. Many of their faces are flushed, and their brows shine atop unshaven cheeks and unkempt beards.

As they pass us, they keep their eyes set on the road, seemingly unaware of their surroundings, perhaps reliving the invisible and harmless adversaries of their childhoods. A few of them squint through the sun towards us. A man with sunglasses and a bandana over his face pauses in our direction. Alexandra buries her face deeper in the dirt. Motionless, I try to trace his vision and read his face, but the sunglasses and bandana shield him from my sight. He takes two steps towards our side of the road and is joined by another man.

"You alright, Cousin?"

"Sure. Sure. Just thought—"

The clap of hooves echoes over the hills and farther down into the valley. In the distance, along the road, a rider gallops, and the cloven gait of their horse sings from the cradle of the hills. There are murmurs of excitement throughout the parade, and it grabs the attention of both men. Their hands tighten on the handles of their assault rifles as they walk on. Faint yellow and red cascades through the faces of the men, and I feel like I am looking at autumn flora. They hasten, and I nearly tell Alexandra we are okay, but then I see them at the rear of the troop. The stragglers drive horses towing wagon carts laden with bits of twisted metal and bloodied pistons that have come loose from the accompanying arms, legs, and bodies of my kin. I catch the side of a cheek and a pale wide eye amongst the debris. Companion children, not merely reduced to scrap, but eviscerated with prejudice.

I lay my cheek on the dirt and search for Alexandra's eyes. Soon, her soft breath finds my nose. I draw a finger to my lips and she does the same. We lie in the grass for 20 minutes. There are ants, but we wait. Wait until the clap of feet diminishes. Wait until Alexandra cannot contain the urge to move and begins to dig the toe of her shoe into the arid earth, making the dust rise like smoke.

I lift my head. The road is deserted, but it is not quiet. I take several steps onto the gravel shoulder and Alexandra squats in the overgrown grass. Ahead of us, I can hear the clap of feet diminish, ceding silence back to the hills. Then, there is the pop of gunfire. The gunfire dwindles to a few searching shots.

Alexandra is on her feet. She beckons me towards her and points down the hill to the distant fields, faded and heavy in the late afternoon light. Before the flash, I would have been able to tell her where that path led and what to expect, but the world in my head remains blank. Some libraries withstand the fall of civilization better than others.

"I don't know where that will lead," I offer.

"Away from them."

She slips down into the fields before I can reply, and I chase after her. Her pace does not slow until the openness of the field is swallowed up by a grove of birch trees. Together, we walk hand in hand as the trees thin and retreat from the flow of a small chuckling creek. Though shallow, its waters are dark and fast moving. For a long time, I stand astride the creek and splash its waters on my arms and face, a final baptism of the swamp mud. With our backpack on her lap, Alexandra watches from the river's wooded bank, though eventually she places several water bottles along the creek for me to fill.

The creek darkens with the last of a westering sun. It froths as it breaks upon my knees and its current tugs at my feet. Alexandra's heat signature retreats, hunched amongst the eaves of the wood. As I bring the lip of the water bottle to drink from the waters, a blue spark erupts behind my eyes. Static blossoms on my tongue and the creek splits into a wall of rectangles, each filled with sharp white light. A new world builds over the creek and forest, its blocks a composite of the somatic and distant recall.

GREY RAIN PATTERS AGAINST A SPHERICAL PANE HELD IN A BEAUTIFUL STONE WINDOW ARCH. EMPTY PATCHES OF WHITE CENSOR MOST OF THE ROOM, BUT A PAIR OF LONG, THIN LEGS SWING BENEATH ME. THE AIR IS OLD AND STIFF AND TASTES LIKE IT HAS BEEN FOLDED OVER MANY

TIMES. THE VOICES ARE DISTINCT. SOME ARE HUMAN, BUT ONE IS MADE OF STATIC AND WARBLE. A RADIO. A CHORUS OF SQUELCHING HUSHES PROTECTS THE RADIO'S PRIMACY FROM THE TRESPASS OF CURSES AND INCREDULOUS CRIES OF "NO."

"GIVEN THE GRAVITY OF THE CLIMATE EMERGENCY AND THE FAILURE OF THE PREVIOUS GOVERNMENT TO DECARBONIZE THE ECONOMY, I AM FORCED TO TAKE MORE SIGNIFICANT ACTION AND INTRODUCE THE ECOLOGICAL RELOCATION ACT. AS OF TODAY, RESIDENTS THAT MOVED TO THE UNITED KINGDOM IN THE LAST 15 YEARS, REGARDLESS OF ANY PREVIOUS RIGHT TO RESIDE IN THIS COUNTRY, WILL BE RETURNED TO THEIR COUNTRY OF ORIGIN."

FROM THE WALL OF NEGATIVE WHITE SPACE, A HAND BREAKS THROUGH AND FINDS MINE. THE SQUEEZE IS HARD, AND THE CARESS OF THEIR THUMB IS LOVING.

"I TOLD YOU, I TOLD YOU SHE WAS IN THE POCKETS OF THE WHITE NATIONALISTS," CRIES SOMEONE FROM ACROSS THE ROOM, IN AN ACCENT I DO NOT RECOGNIZE.

"QUIET DOWN, THERE'S MORE YET."

"THE NATURAL RESIDENTS HAVE MADE IT CLEAR: WE AS A COUNTRY CAN ONLY DO OUR FAIR SHARE. WE CANNOT CARRY THE RESPONSIBILITY OF COUNTRIES THAT HAVE CAST THEIR OWN OFF ON US. POPULATION GROWTH FROM IMMIGRATION REMAINS A SIGNIFICANT REASON WHY WE CONTINUE TO MISS OUR EMISSION REDUCTION

TARGETS. IMMIGRATION OFFICERS HAVE BEEN INFORMED OF THIS DECISION AND WILL IMMEDIATELY, BUT HUMANELY, BEGIN THE ECOLOGICAL REPATRIATION OF OVER 15 MILLION IMMIGRANTS."

"THEY CAN'T DO THIS. THEY JUST CAN'T." THE VOICE IS SOFT AND PLAINTIVE, AND ALTHOUGH THE SPEAKER IS LOST IN WHITE SPACE, I KNOW I AM HOLDING HIS HAND.

"I THINK THEY JUST DID." THE VOICE COMES FROM ME, BUT IT SOUNDS THICK, ALIEN.

"THERE HAVE TO BE EXCEPTIONS, I MEAN, YOU'RE—"

"Fucking gotcha!"

The sensation of the hand fragments and the radio dissipates into the elegiac voice of the creek, but the world is black. I cannot see. I try to bend my arms but find them tied behind my back. My legs are uncooperative. I feel restraints around my ankles. I am prostrate. A pair of hands grips my shoulders and something thick and coarse squeezes and burns the sides of my head until it falls around my neck. A rope.

A scamper of steps brings a whisper to my ear, its breath hot with an acidic smell. "Where's Stacy? She here, too? Tell me and I'll be kind. You know I'll just fucking find her anyway."

My processor matches the boy's creaky adolescent laughter with near instant recall, even though he sounds more confident now. In control and relaxed.

"She's dead."

"The fuck she is." Francis laughs.

Another voice, the voice of a woman, intercedes, "Stop harassing the merchandise and get a move on."

Through the sliver of vision where the blindfold meets my cheeks, I watch shadows and shapes dance across my toes in eldritch flutters as the world beneath me moves.

"She's got a human sister. Blonde bitch. A Stacy type. She's got to be out here somewhere, she's probably worth scooping up too."

There is an abrupt stillness and then the approach of fast, heavy steps. "Let's get something absolutely crystal. I don't traffic people. I especially don't traffic women and girls to Alogo Boos. This untidy arrangement is one of convenience. We get this done, and I don't want to see you or any of your asshole cousins ever again. You understand?"

"Just thought you might appreciate the—"

"If the next word out of your mouth isn't, 'yes sir, I understand, I won't ever suggest such a disgusting thing ever again,' I'll drop you right here."

There is a quick snort of awkward laughter, perhaps nervousness or disbelief. I try prying through the blindfold to get a trace of his feelings, but the blindfold must be padded with lead. My sensors find only the negation of sight. True blindness.

"You think I'm fucking playing with you, boy?" A soft metallic click buttresses her words.

"No. I'm sorry," pleads Francis.

"No, who?"

"No, sir. I'm sorry. It won't happen again."

"That's it. That's my love language right there. Good boy. Get a move on to the truck. Okay?"

"Yes."

"And Francis?"

"Yes?"

"How'd you like to be scooped up to be the plaything for some Alogo Boo gentleman? You like that idea?" The speaker pauses and continues, "You want that? No, I didn't fucking think so. Why are you about to do it to someone else, then?"

"I was just—"

"No. Don't answer. Think. Think long and hard about that."

"Yes, sir."

My captors heave on the rope and pull until the slack vanishes and my body is forced to stretch—suspended. My toe fights for the ground as Francis and an unknown man drag me, and my shoe cuts over the gravel path in hisses that deaden all other sounds. I am a solitary and fleeting noise in rising darkness. A red flash sunders the blue light that waits behind my eyes. Red tendrils split the calm blue sea apart and there are words in my mouth. Words I do not recognize but are sentimental, the mantra of a homecoming beyond recall. I know their pieces, their syllables with undeserved intimacy: *things fall apart; the centre cannot hold; mere anarchy is loosed upon the world.* The red flash recedes in a series of pulsing blinks: *the best lack all conviction, while the worst are full of passionate intensity.* Whose words are these? Where do they belong? The coiled rope tightens against my throat.

If I were a real girl like Alexandra, I am confident I would have choked out by now. My captors say little to one another. I catch occasional scraps of words, petitions to stop, and queries of how much further they must drag me. Only one voice seems to know the answers, and her words are singular and terse. A wisp of light, the moon, splits open the shadows and darkness at my feet. I sense pain and realize they have dropped me on the trail.

"Come on, kid, we're like right here. You really need a rest?" asks the male whose voice I do not recognize.

"Nah. Just going to break her down a little. This should do the trick."

"The hell is that?!"

"Sticky bomb. Fuses to whatever they used to make their skin. My Uncle showed me how to make them."

"Delilah won't like that one fucking bit, kid."

"Scraps are scraps. Me and this Metal Chad have history."

"Metal Chad? What is this bullshit?" Deadfall breaks underfoot and another shadow passes across my toes. "Don't you dare light that! Delilah! Delilah!" protests the man.

In a flurry of alarm, Francis responds, "Hang on. Don't be like that. I thought we were cool."

"Delilah!"

"What the fuck is it, Lyle?" she snaps. I don't need to be able to read her face to know she's irritated.

"Come on, man. She wouldn't have cared. Jesus," Francis mutters.

"Kid's trying to blow up the merchandise."

There is an audible groan from somewhere in front of me. "Why? Why the hell would you do that?"

"Didn't think it would matter, scraps are scraps. They need the metal. They don't need it together. It's safer, too, and I have unfinished business with it ..." His voice quietens and then trails off.

"I know the buyer. He'll want it whole. He'll want it working. You must be dumber than a bag of chickens. You were going to blow it up, without asking? Christ, look at that thing? You've been walking around with that on your person? All this time, you've been walking beside us with some greasy pipe bomb bouncing against your ass!? Shit, kid. You could've blown yourself in two."

"Hasn't been a problem yet."

"Just get in the back of the truck so we can call it a day. Lyle, you've got shotgun. Jack, you're in the back, make sure Francis keeps his hands to himself."

"You're the boss," responds Francis with a blithe sycophantic err, though under his breath he adds, "For now."

I feel my body leave the ground, and beneath me, there are groans and heavy breaths spoken, no doubt, through flared nostrils. The world rocks back and forth several times until I topple over a hard edge with a metallic crash. My body crunches and then sinks amidst jagged edges, soft mounds, and crooked pipes. There is the din of one set of feet, followed by another. Both make landfall with a chorus of crunching and the moans of metal. A noise of patter and static follows, like plastic rain, and a tarp falls over me in a sweep of velvet shadow. It reminds me of the green haze of my birth.

The combustion engine howls to life in a fit of violent coughs. As the vehicle quakes, the debris beneath me rattles and bounces with me, like we are pieces in an expired game of Perfection. We accelerate. The wind runs its fingers over the tarp. We skid, and I hear the ricochet of gravel as the driver steers us down what I can only imagine are backcountry roads. A voice rises over the rattle of metal and the pop and rumble of tires,

"We have a good haul."

"I've been tracking this one"— Francis joins his words to a kick in my side— "since I crossed the border. Slept next to the thing on the island, can you believe that? It did this to me."

"No kidding. Sounds like you came by it the hard way. We scavenged one off the road maybe a little more than a week ago, not far from here at all. Would you believe that shit? Full unit, no visible damage. Just a shell."

"Well, I'm glad I got to hunt this one. Right fucked up my face."

"No shit. So, this is payback time?" drawls the other man, and the cold lethargy of his words betray unmistakable disinterest.

Francis, no doubt in response to the man's rebuff, doubles the enthusiasm and bravado in his voice. "My Uncle got word of it a few days ago. Told me how to track it. Not so smart now, you little

Metal Chad bitch," spits Francis as he drives his foot into my side again and makes my insides clang.

"Christ! I don't much like that it's still alive," mutters the other man as I recoil beneath the tarp from Francis' kick.

"Yeah, I don't like it much either."

"Just leave it be," demands the man and at length no more words pass between them until Francis breaks the silence.

"You happy calling a woman 'Sir?' Seems simp to me, but that's just me," laughs Francis, but his laughter is not returned.

"Been working with Delilah for a long time before any of this shit. She's done all right by me, so I do all right by her. You have someone like that?" Although the blinder shades my world in a heatless dark, I believe there is mercy in his question.

"If you're a man, you make it on your own. To be sovereign is to be king. To be king is to be alone."

"Not sure about any of that. Haven't come across any kings on these roads."

"Well, they're coming. You can be sure of that," Francis says, though the pop and scrape of the truck's stop against gravel muffles his sniggering.

Without any GPS, I cannot say how far we travelled. I estimate under four miles. If I can get away, it will be well over an hour back in the dark on foot. More battery expenditure. Will Alexandra stay put until first light?

Guttural heavy breathing fills my ears and hands grip my legs and head, trembling as they lift me into the air. The small of my back bounces on the metal lip again, and I land with a thud on softer ground. I feel grass on my wrists.

"For the last time, don't fuck up the merchandise before it's sold," Delilah snaps.

"It isn't any worse for wear," I hear Francis assert.

"What did you just say? Did I just hear you say something?" menaces Delilah.

"No. No, sir. I'll take care of it," Francis stammers, and his bravado seems to fall once more into quiet obsequiousness.

I am left on the grass for 20 minutes. I can sense motion around me and the weight of heavy, laden steps. Then there is a flutter of movement and the blindfold lifts and soft moonlight and deepening shadows open before me. Eyes of slate hold me in a hard stare. Her face is pale and narrow, unadorned by hair.

"I'm going to cut the rope around your legs. You're going to walk. If you run or turn around, I'll fire this into you." She raises a rusted spear gun from her hip. "It'll rip that battery of yours right out, no reset from that," she adds. "You understand?"

I nod, but my attention lies behind her. A dilapidated grey-skinned barn shrugs amidst a field strewn with the wreckage of rusted cars and burned-out trucks. The field is overgrown and untended, but I can see where the passing of many feet has crushed the grass into a path to the barn's entrance.

"Good," she says. "The Mechanic will want a word, but if you give him reason ..."

She mimes grabbing a plug and ripping it from the wall. The lexicon of human threats and gestures has expanded to include me. Step out of line, and I will be unplugged. I nod again, and she flashes her teeth, white and cared for, back at me.

"All right then," she says as she tips her head towards the shadow light that ebbs from the barn's entrance.

HYPATIA
The Mechanic

Several kerosene lamps, their bodies an admixture of faded red paint and rust, light the barn. Their glow limps across the surface of a workbench positioned on the interior wall, nine feet from the barn's entrance. Opposite the workbench, near a grey-skinned support beam, two generators tremble. Power cables run from their sides and across the dirt floor of the barn in serpentine orange curls until they vanish into the dark.

The air is musty, sour, and pregnant with the stench of old oil and grease. Amidst the gloom is a silhouette of a man. His back is to us, and he speaks only with his hands as he makes a piece of metal hiss and squeak. I can tell even from here that he is broad-shouldered and wide. I pry into his heat that flows unevenly throughout his massive trunk and arms but seems to fall away at his legs—an indication of cardiovascular disease.

Delilah looks me over as if to assure herself that I will give her no trouble, then bangs her tight, angry fist against the grey sun-splintered wood by the doorway. Her knock summons a groan of wood and the clatter of metal on the workbench, followed by a deep suspire growled through the man's nostrils.

"What's the news from the road?" He huffs as he turns to us. His face, half held in shadow, is incinerate and broad, almost flat. His hair falls in salt and pepper waves to his shoulders.

"A line has formed from Wisconsin to Kentucky. They're being pushed into the sea," says Delilah, and though her face is opaque and expressionless, I detect a note of disdain in her voice.

"They can make all the lines they like. Faster they crush them in the field, the longer the guerilla war will last," says the man as he scrubs his hands with a grimy rag in a slow, practiced method. "Why are you here?" His eyes remain cast upon his hands, wreathed by trunk-like blue veins.

"Caught something I knew you'd be interested in," she says as she rams the butt of her spear gun into my back to force me through the door.

His eyes fall on me and fill with confusion and alarm. "Haven't an interest in little girls, I'm no Alogo Boo boy," he says, and he cocks his head to spit on the dirt floor.

There are heavy steps and muttering behind us.

"What'd you say about the Alogo Boos? What did you say, old man?"

I recognize the cadence and adolescent creak of Francis' voice. The woman hisses at him and tries to block him from the Mechanic's sight by barring him with her free arm.

"Come in here and I'll tell you," offers the Mechanic with a mirthless chuckle. "Christ, Delilah, tell me you're not travelling with that kind of scum."

"We're warrior kings rising, old man. You best give us respect."

Delilah's stalwart arm keeps Francis outside the barn, and his words reach the Mechanic in an anonymous stammer.

"Warrior kings!" says the Mechanic in an uproarious laugh. His two powerful forearms propel off the arms of the chair, much to the chair's protestations, and lift his girth to his feet. From the workbench, he grabs a hammer and walks past me. His eyes scold the darkness that lies in wait behind Delilah's shoulders. "Come on then, test your mettle against mine." He raises the hammer and lets it crash into his shin, and his leg fills the barn with a metallic din. "Warriors? I've fought men. Principled men. You're a bunch of scared virgins in Hawaiian shirts," he goads.

There is no rejoinder from outside the barn.

Delilah speaks over her shoulder in a frantic whisper, "Someone get Francis out of here before he fucks this up."

"Who the fuck is this guy? What about the goddamn bounty on it?!" shouts Francis.

"Get yourself back in the truck," snarls Delilah.

Francis becomes a fog of curses and dark vows, but nonetheless, I hear his footsteps grow fainter in the dark as he retreats.

"I don't really know him. I fell into debt with the wrong people, I suppose," says Delilah. "He isn't wrong, though. Alogo Boo buy these up and send them straight to Houston for export to the east, but I figured as we're becoming friends, I'd give you the right of first refusal." Her face is yellow, and her pulse tells me she has chosen these words carefully.

The Mechanic says nothing, tosses the hammer onto the workbench with a clatter, and collapses back into his chair. Now that he faces us, I can tell by his heat signature that one leg has been amputated from the knee down. He curls his lip and gives his hand a lackadaisical flip as if to grant Delilah further audience.

"It's a working companion child." The Mechanic replies with an incredulous snort. "Really." Delilah shoves me closer to him. "Look here."

A cracked square of mirror emerges from her pocket and is slid under my nose. The Mechanic stiffens up in his chair, his eyes on me. For at least a minute, Delilah holds the glass to my nose and mouth, until it is clear I leave no stain on the mirror's surface. My neutrality to life and death is affirmed.

His eyes narrow, and a ripple of purple flashes up his unshaven jowls. Purple like when Malcolm discovered my wound. The colour clouds the Mechanic's face, yet still outruns my limits of classification and falls into a void that only codes as curious pain.

The Mechanic leans forward in his chair in attention and his belly tumbles onto his thighs. "I've only seen a live one once since the flash. There weren't many around these parts to begin with. It was a few days after, in a grocery store. It was sitting in the middle of the cereal aisle. Seemed lost. Zoned out. Nobody knew what to do. People even shopped around it. Ignored it. Eventually, a couple of us walked over to it, thought about helping it to its feet. When we got close, though, it went berserk. Arms started to whirl like helicopter blades, and it was throwing them with such force that it blew the cereal boxes apart. It was raining Cornflakes. It landed one of its fists on the guy in front of me, big guy, practically tore his jaw off. Teeth were all over the floor. Tried to calm it down, but there was nothing in its eyes. Eyes were hollow and black, like gun-bores. This one ..." He stands up and circles me several times in slow appraisal. "It seems placid. Has it been like this the whole time?" he presses.

"Seems to be a model citizen." Delilah smiles. "Very alert and responsive. Tuned in, you know. Boy caught her in a creek. I knew you'd be interested," she adds.

"You still speak?" pries the Mechanic.

He is standing close now. In his breath, I detect old tobacco and traces of something bitter, maybe whiskey.

"Yes," I say.

The Mechanic nods and then circles me several times, squinting in what looks like studied appraisal. He grabs my hands and lifts my arms, and lets them fall to my sides. With my cheeks squeezed between his hands, he presses his index finger behind my ears until he finds the pliable piece of flesh that camouflages my charging port. He takes several steps back as if he were admiring artwork.

"You charged?" he asks.

His question takes me aback. "It's been a long time since I charged," I offer in hope that this dissuades him from buying me, although his vitals suggest he made his decision as soon as he learned I still spoke.

"That's what I figured," he says. His vitals climb and his arms cross his chest.

"Well, what do you think?" pushes Delilah.

"I dunno," he huffs. "It's a hell of a find, no argument there. Bit worried about not being able to charge the battery. Worse than no good without a battery."

"Handy guy like you, you could rig something up. Or you could head to Albany. Lyle says there's still an EV charging station down there that works. Hospital, off-grid," she adds in response to the Mechanic's incredulous stare.

In the blue space behind my eyes, I summon images from the Road Atlas in Paul's garage. An itinerary of highway passages assembles itself in disjointed lines, along the Hudson River, delivering us to an overpass outside the city.

"Albany, eh? Warzone, isn't it?" laughs the Mechanic.

"It's spicy for sure. You want it or not?" asks Delilah with a nonchalant shrug, but her face is green with excitement.

"Yeah. I'm interested," he concedes.

While they haggle, I stand between them mute, digging my toe into the dirt floor and practice what I hope looks like submission. I look for signs of heat escaping the barn in hope that it will lead me to an exit.

"The guy I owe wants diesel, 500 gallons, and some currency," says Delilah.

"Wouldn't give that much diesel to anyone, especially not some Alogo Boo middleman. Can't spare it." With a casual tip of his head, the Mechanic acknowledges the overworked generators as they rock on their metal footings.

"Look, I know you have enough diesel stashed away to run nearly every damn combustion engine left in the county. What's the harm with giving away 500 gallons?" pushes Delilah.

The Mechanic licks his lips several times and crosses his arms. "I said no."

"Come on, what are you even running? It's dark and cold as fuck in here," says Delilah as she tiptoes along the power cords like a trapeze artist, stepping into the unlit recesses of the barn.

I follow her with heat vision. Ahead of her is purple emptiness, and amidst that, an even darker shade of cold, the absence of heat confined to a tall rectangular shape.

"That's none of your damn business," the Mechanic snarls.

His face twists into a grimace, and even though it is obscured in shadow, I can see streaks of yellow mutiny into blotches of red. Fear to anger, anger to fear. I see these conversions on the faces of men in nearly every encounter.

Delilah pauses in the dark, but keeps her back to us. "Fair," she says, and she keeps her words light enough to cast them over her shoulder.

The mechanic speaks his truce in grunts, pulls a pad of paper from his pocket, and starts to scribble on it. He stops, looks up, runs his eyes over me, and tips his head from side to side. I saw a man give the same gesture when he was trying to estimate the number of marbles in a jar at the Carp fair last year.

"I can spare 100 gallons," he concludes, and though he speaks loud enough for Delilah to hear him, the way he says his words into the notepad leaves me with the impression that he is speaking to himself.

Delilah smiles and shakes her head. "100 gallons and 45,000.00 in Yuan."

"Yuan, eh? Always took you more for the cryptocurrency type," snickers the Mechanic.

"Not enough power to cook a chicken, let alone run a blockchain network. I'll take my chances with the Yuan."

"Fine," says the Mechanic.

He waves his concession at her with one hand and with the other beckons her into the dark, untenanted inner compartment of the barn. There is the click of a latch and the faint whine of metal hinges.

From within the dark, Delilah laughs. "You still numbering these in roman numerals?"

"Fun to spray-paint."

"Sure. Is this some new security?"

"Bet your ass it's new security. Got myself a thief."

"Oh no. How much did they take?"

"Going by the numbers, you tell me?" laughs the Mechanic.

There is a pause in Delilah's footsteps. "I don't know my numerals well enough to count," she mutters.

"Two fucking jerrycans. Number 7 and Number 100."

Delilah whistles before she says, "That sounds like a crime of necessity."

"World is well past a game of needs verse wants. There's nothing out there left but need. Doesn't make need any less dumb or dangerous than want, though. Damn bit worse, really," suspires the Mechanic as he limps from the dark, his metal leg trailing in heavy steps.

A jerrycan in each hand sloshes against his thighs as he walks to deposit them outside the barn door. Delilah follows his steps unencumbered, seemingly uncomfortable to carry the jerrycans without the Mechanic's permission.

"I got three more trips," he huffs.

Delilah does not miss his message and steps outside the barn to join the jerrycans he set down. As he makes his next trip, she murmurs to me, "There's nothing personal about this. Just business."

"It's nothing but personal when you're the business," I reply.

"Fair," she says, but now she leans against the wall of the barn, half cocooned by the night, her humanity given away by the seams of her breath framed by creeping purple shadows of crisp autumn air.

In no time, the Mechanic assembles a tidy row of jerrycans. As the transaction concludes, I maintain my position on the doorstep between the barn and the open night. I can make out the silhouette of a man in the passenger seat of the truck's cab. I presume it is Francis sulking, because another man, an older man with a stooped back, has come to Delilah's aid and has started to ferry the jerrycans down to the truck. His steps crunch and skid on the gravel trail that snakes through the tawny grass slope. For every few loads of jerrycans he retrieves, he returns with a wheelbarrow of parts—arms, legs, indiscriminate scraps of metal—from the cargo bed of the pickup truck. Without care, he deposits these beyond the door of the barn, and a small mountain comprised of scrap metal and the limbs of companion children, grows ahead of me.

The Mechanic, the furrows of his brow steaming in the air, looks upon the pile and whistles. "Like always, pleasure doing business with you Delilah. Next time you come though, you tell that little Alogo Boo pussy he ain't welcome here."

Delilah shakes his hand. "Like I said, it's not a relationship I plan to carry on," she offers. "But next time, you bring the jerrycans to the truck."

The Mechanic laughs. Delilah turns to me, her face stiff and her eyes downcast at her mud-covered hiking boots. In a glimpse and a refraction of the old library of information that was at my disposal, I recognize the shoes. Ozark hiking boots, retail for $25.00, sold exclusively through Walmart. Truly abhorrent shoes.

The quotidian stupidity of this information and its unexpected appearance in my memory alarms me, and I risk missing her words. "Don't think twice about who you left down at the creek. Nobody saw but me, I'll make sure none of my crew interferes. Least I can do."

From the corner of my eye, I scan the Mechanic's face and catch blotches break out across his nose and cheeks in a purple rash, but he tries to exercise control over his expression to give the impression he has not overheard. Without waiting for my reply, Delilah embarks through the flattened track of a muddy field, and her figure weaves and bobs in and out of the truck's floodlights.

Before I see them pull away, the Mechanic tips his head at his workbench and commands me to sit atop it. There is a hammer and several screwdrivers strewn across its steel-top surface. I could use any of them to kill him. He seems to share my realization, since he steps ahead of me and drops them haphazardly into several plywood boxed drawers he withdraws from the side of the workbench. He smiles and nods again at the surface, under the pretense of making space for me.

I kick off the ground, but end up beached on the steel lip of the table. My legs kick in the air until I can drag myself atop of it. I sit horizontal with my feet off one end. The height of the workbench and my position bear a faint echo to a medical examination table. I have seen a couple of them from when I accompanied Alexandra to visit her doctor.

"Take your shirt off, I want to run a diagnostic," he commands.

"I can run an internal one," I offer.

"No, I want to verify it with my own equipment, thanks," he huffs.

"You'll need to remove skin to do it that way. It would make me harder to resell," I suggest, though I know he does not intend to resell me whole.

"Just do as I ask, please," he says.

I unzip my jacket, pull my sweatshirt over my head, and reveal my flat, swallow-shaped chest. The Mechanic raises his eyebrows at the hole the rifle punched through my chest and tests its edges with his finger in determined perusal.

"This causing issues?"

"It's tender, but no. Clean shot."

He nods and takes a furtive look at my back. "Entrance wound is closed over. Good sign," he adds, though it is clear he is speaking to himself.

"A civilization that shoots children in the back is bereft of auspicious omens."

"Never thought much of civilization. Let's check under the hood."

The Mechanic frowns and taps beneath my right nipple with his index and middle finger. The pressure is direct and swift, and there is clinical aloofness in his touch. I am overpowered by the strange realization that I have been handled this way before, but not in this body. There is no memory, just the discomfort of being prodded and the censure of bodily autonomy.

Over my shoulder, above the workbench, old newspaper clippings, yellowed and their corners frayed, are tacked into the splintered grey wood of the barn's wall. Fingers have smeared some of them. From the constellation of clippings, I thread together a story: an eight-year-old boy, Jason Cartwright, went missing approximately 10,584 hours ago. The boy had lived with his grandfather. The Mechanic seems to follow my gaze, but says nothing. His finger has settled on a point, and his pressure creates an indentation in my flesh.

"Why did he live with you?" I ask. I figure I might as well be as direct as possible.

He pulls out a drawer from the side of the workbench and rustles inside until he withdraws an X-Acto knife. His brow furrows in concentration as he makes an adroit incision around the indentation he has created with his finger. In slow, almost delicate moves, he lifts a small circle of faux skin away on his fingertip.

"He lost his parents, I was what was left," he mutters without looking up.

"I'm sorry, our parents died, too ..."

"I said lost, not dead. There are ways to be that are worse than dead."

"I think I can understand that. It's just my sister and me. My sister, Alexandra, is still at the creek. She's who Delilah was talking about," I murmur.

"That's neither my business nor my concern."

He shakes his head and rummages in another compartment within the workbench and, eventually, wrestles out several twisted and bent cords connected to a rectangular box with a digital screen. The screen is grimy, stained with oil and dust. He places one thick hand on my shoulder as if to restrain and centre me as he drives his cords into the bald metal orifices he has uncovered in my chest. In his other hand, he holds the little box, which chirps and the screen glows once the cords make contact with me.

"You said something earlier that I found interesting," I push.

"What was that?"

"Your revulsion to the Alogo Boos and the trafficking of young women and young girls," I say.

"What interested you about that?"

"Why?"

"Why, what?" he grunts, and he doesn't let his eyes break away from his palm, where the little box flashes and offers yet another interdiction with a dumb beep.

"Why worry about some children, but then buy me, especially when you know I have a sister, a human sister?" I intone with emphasis on the words "human sister."

"What?"

"Why care about some children and not others?"

He pauses and wears an irritated expression, but I can see he has gone pink and yellow, a colour I have coded as deep shame: shame that fundamentally violates and destabilizes one's sense of self. He continues to read the meter in his hand and occasionally presses the wires into me with more force, tinkering with the connection.

He does this several times before he says, "You're not a child. Children have souls. Anyone's guess what you are. Piece of sophisticated machinery, I suppose." There is a tincture of remorse on his face.

"I don't see it that way. I have a child's consciousness, a real consciousness from another human being. When do memory and personality become sufficient to constitute a soul?" I ask.

He huffs a laugh through his fat nostrils. "You're having a debate with a mechanic when you mean to be talking to a theologian."

"Are you sure there's a difference?"

"It's not personal. You just came in the way of a promise I made." Swirls of purple join the pink churn across his forehead, reading as gentleness.

"I can't leave my sister in the woods. Scrap me after I find her."

I am not sure if I mean these words when I hear myself say them. Before the flash, Lotus would notify my parents and me when I was engaged in duplicity. Some forms of duplicity were acceptable, some were not. Would I let him scrap me to save Alexandra?

He appears distracted, and I get the impression he did not hear my overture. His eyes widen and his face turns slate, his thick features becoming sullen and grim. "Shit!"

He slams the little device that had been running the diagnosis of me down on the workbench with a clatter. Blisters of rage surface on his face and then become yellow craters as rage oscillates to fear and back again. I say nothing, and he collapses into his office chair, and with several deep rattling breaths, drops his head to the workbench. He does not look at me. I am left shirtless, my pockmarked chest left open and exposed by his investigation.

"I thought it might be different this time," he repeats in a stilted murmur.

I fumble to pull my shirt back on over my head, but he is not looking at me anymore. In fact, I am not convinced he is even speaking to me. His devastation appears to have pulled him from this world. If I am fast, there are several scenarios where I can slip into the night unchecked. Yet, I do not move. The little device he used to check my diagnostics rests like a peninsula on his elbow, nearly engulfed by his tangle of grey, oleaginous hair, which spills over the worktop next to me. My hand flutters from the device to the back of his head. I could drive it into the base of his skull and likely kill or incapacitate him. The thought seems efficient and should secure my survival, yet I hesitate. I lift the device but find myself turning it over in my hands to read it for myself.

The motion at his elbow rouses him. He steadies himself with several deep breaths, and I appear to be within his scope of attention once again. "Bad news for both of us, I suppose," he offers.

I pry into the little screen, searching for some added complexity that would challenge its initial appraisal, but it is a simple device. My battery is corrupt. Not only does it not charge to capacity, but it is degrading. Damaged beyond repair. By its estimates, I have a total of 180 hours before I become inoperable. Eight days. I have no idea how far we are from our target.

"I am ... terminal," I murmur, and though my voice arrives even and unbroken, I struggle against an internal scream welling up inside me.

At length, the Mechanic says nothing and lets my words drift between us unacknowledged, consigning me to continue a phantom conversation inside my head. "Like all the others, diagnostic says 20% of your battery is chargeable, but your system can't access it. Like it's being held in reserve or something. Spooky shit. I can't fathom it," he mutters. "It's been the same every time, but as far as I know, I've been getting batteries only from the ones that went berserk. I figured you might be different."

There is a casualness in his words that makes me regret not ramming the diagnostic device into the back of his head when I had the chance. It does not matter though: I need to get out of here. Every minute truly counts now.

"What do the generators feed?"

Somehow, I know this question will put him off-guard. It is the only leverage I have over him. The colours in his face confirm this is a promising line of conversation. I must keep him on it. He sniffs a few times and turns back to stare into the barn's abyss, leaving me with only the grey filaments of his breath amidst the dark.

"The generators?" he repeats.

"Yes, I've been curious about them since I arrived."

"You don't need to know about them."

"What difference will it make? Whatever secret you have dies with me when you scrap me anyway. Let's call it a last request. Come on, I promise I won't ask for a last meal too."

He opens and closes his mouth, then furrows his haggard brow, and I worry my levity has not placated him. Yet, with a grey clouded expression, he offers his hand to help me off his workbench. "Follow the cords, but don't touch anything," he commands, but I am already ahead of him, hunting the heat from the extension cables along the hay-strewn floor of the barn.

I slip past the generators as their feet bounce on the dirt floor. Beyond them, the air feels thick and heavy and has the feel of fog. The cables twist and curve past several wooden support beams. The light from the kerosene lanterns grows small and frail, but, like Delilah, I plant my feet on the cables and cosplay a trapeze artist, half dancing, half falling with each step. I can only see the faint edges of the Mechanic, bits of him held in the threads of lantern light, though I know he is watching my every step and can feel him at my back.

The line of cables run into the base of a huge cylinder machine, four feet in diameter. It looks like a massive water pipe. Soft green lights rise and fall beneath the cylindrical shadow. Strips of black metal, equally spaced, seem to bind the structure in place and divide the tube into several clear glass segments. Each of these segments frames pieces of one body, though not whole. The first quarter of the tube is empty, save for a white linen sheet crumpled on its floor, but the next quarter holds a pair of thighs, the rest of the legs amputated from the knees down. I inch closer. In the next quarter, I find a torso, and in the last little window, I see shoulders and the face of a young boy. His face, framed by short red curls, is pale and vacant. There are no colours in flesh to decode. Not even the little etchings that leak out from dreams, which I can discern sometimes. Spotless emptiness.

I now recognize the peaks and troughs that glow green at the base of the machine as the patterns of human vitals. The boy's border-world of life and death is arrested in transition, and now left subject to careful display and scrutiny. My legs and arms are frozen, and my vision fixes in an unquenchable observation of the scene before me. The pieces inside me churn and whirl, but I am elsewhere in requiem of the sensation of horror, and my screams do not leave me. There is a gush of pressured air, and I release an involuntary gasp. There is a sensation of white light and small surroundings. A web of emotions and somatic recall that are at once vivid and utterly alien to the barn. A faint imprint of something else, too, that slips away as soon as the Mechanic speaks.

"Hit by a car. It took us too long to find him." His voice is heavy and commands more than it tells. "They did what they could to save him, but he was brain dead anyway. Been looking for one of you in working order for a long time. Seems no reason why I can't build something like you for him."

My words back to him are gentle and come in a small voice. "I'm not sure it works like that. Something with Lotus could probably be arranged."

The mechanic shakes his head and laughs through his nose mirthlessly. "You have any idea what something like you costs?" His voice rumbles through the barn.

"No," I reply.

"Fair enough, a parent should never tell a child what they cost. Makes them feel bad ... I told them that," he continues, but he is muttering now, adrift in the under-toe of unfinished conversations I sense happened years ago. In my silence, he takes pause and blurts out, "I'd need three lifetimes to pay for it. But I'm not far from putting him back together. Come here and take a look." It seems like he is focused on me again. "Come!"

He beckons me back towards the faint island of light that encircles his workbench. With his back to me, he conjures the slap of metal on metal and the tinkle of what sounds like keys as he fumbles with the drawers in his workbench. I cannot read his face. My steps are slow, and rather than moving directly to him, I tiptoe back along the power cables.

"Come on," he urges, and his excitement has mutinied into impatience and irritation.

I am close enough now that I can see he is withdrawing packages loosely wrapped in brown butcher's paper from the bottom drawer of the workbench. He unrolls each one with a slow precision that betrays these acts have become ritual for him. I watch as he unfurls the individual components of a body. There is an arm: the skin of the forearms hangs in ragged tails, revealing the bite and shine of thousands of tiny red bumps that look like the texture and shape of fish eggs. The arm is followed by two long, L-shaped packages, which reveal legs, still fleshed and relatively clean.

The air has become sour and heavy, an admixture of grease and a smell similar to that of the caulking our Father used once to fix the sink. More pieces find their way in front of me. Parts I did not know were in me: small, twisted tubes, clumps of incredibly fine thread-like wires, and a long string of white beads dewed with the milky substance that bled from the gunshot wound, its smell now reminiscent of Alexandra's modelling clay. What strikes me is that each part seems to bear a different language. I recognize Chinese characters, Russian, and English script on the component parts. I suppose this should come as no surprise. Yet, despite all these different sites of my assemblage, my processor communicates the world to me in Imperial measurements, and I wander the unwilling bearer of one world's stubborn measure of supremacy against another.

The surface of the workbench is now an archipelago of the bones and organs of my kin. The Mechanic shuffles his collection with small nudges from his calloused, red fingers. In solemn practice, he tilts the legs and orders the bundles of sensors and parts into the closer semblance of a complete body. There is a serene distance in the adroit adjustments his fingers make, and though he does not hum, he abides by the rhyme of the singing generators at his back and the percussion of the soft gush of pumped air that periodically stirs through his grandson's half-corpse. I do not need to see his face to know this is an art of madness driven from the darkest despair of grief. That he could reassemble a companion child from these guts and debris is fanciful, but that it would house the consciousness of his grandson is the type of lucid delusion that will eat a grief-stricken man from the inside out.

"So begins the tale of our modern Prometheus," I whisper.

"Eh," says the Mechanic over his shoulder as he continues his jigsaw puzzle of body parts. I take slow steps backwards, and I am scrupulous in ensuring my body moves in silence. "Just need another arm, a head, and, of course, a working battery," he remarks. "Plenty there, I suppose," he says with a nod to the mound of body parts Delilah delivered to the barn's door. "But none of those will be in as good a condition as your arm." His voice is slow and contemplative, but his eyes are narrow and have settled on me in determination. He runs his thumb and forefinger on his forehead, and in the wake of his fingers, his brow is streaked and stained in a grimy ichor. "Of course, I've never had a whole working model, they're always scraps when they arrive. An intact unit would make reverse engineering easier. Much, much easier."

He reshuffles and rearranges the body he imagines he has assembled on the workbench. I step backwards towards the doorway. I take one more step, but then he turns to me, his face broken in moving tides of purple. "You had your look. It's time to say goodbye."

I nod, but let my eyes wander around the barn for any object I can weaponize.

HYPATIA
Last Request

The Mechanic and I face each other. He says nothing. His expression is blank and inscrutable, but his emotions blister his cheeks and his broad nose in molten waves of purple and yellow. He is close enough to the door that I cannot slip out without a struggle. A hammer hangs in his hand, limp and casual, in a grip that perhaps intentionally blurs its identity as both a tool and a weapon. I know what a hammer can do, though. His face remains calm, but beneath his features, his emotions boil, becoming more yellow than purple. I think it is less fear that I will harm him, and more fear that I will escape and destroy his project.

A long sigh precedes his words. "It won't hurt. I promise. It'll be quick. It's better this way. You run away, you might get a week or so, and then you're going to start to malfunction. Might even do harm to that sister of yours. I'd spare fuel to take the truck down and have a look for her. Get her onto a safe road." He makes this overture with open and outstretched palms and his vitals seem to confirm it is genuine.

"I'd like a cigarette." The request slips out of me, somehow able to outrun the moderation of my processor. A desire from some recess of my consciousness too distant for any subsequent introspection.

The Mechanic's grey bushy eyebrows climb his forehead and then fall with a shrug. He rummages in one of the compartment drawers in the workbench and retrieves a battered, depleted-looking pack of cigarettes. The little white carton is emblazoned with a label of thin red letters: *"Last Strikes."* The

Mechanic notices my attention to the label as he offers me the box, taking one for himself once I have made my selection. The cigarette is cold, and though its smell surprises me in its familiarity, its scent seems faded and stale.

"Great grandfather smoked Lucky Strikes. I hear he wasn't so much a chimney, but a goddamn smokestack. New name suggests we are down to the dredges. The last of it," he mutters as he grates his thumb on the lighter and brings fire to his lips. He leans over to light mine, but my processor intercedes and directs me to reach for the lighter.

"I'd like to light my own, thanks."

He returns a quizzical expression, but relents. Keeping the lighter in my possession may confer an advantage, and so I pretend to cough and spin around as the air thickens, heavy with stale smoke, pungent and sweet. A metallic and acetone residue coats my lips—a redolent taste. For a moment, the barn disintegrates into a shapeless flood of white light before consolidating again in greying shadow.

"I'd have to take your word though, and she'd have to trust you, which she won't."

"My word is my bond."

I listen to the rhythmic gush as the ventilator pumps air into the bariatric chamber that holds his comatose grandson. Few have stronger testaments.

"You'll save my Sam?" Though I take a small step towards him, I realize I have spoken the wrong name. Yet, the name Sam passes through my lips with a warm familiarity. "Alexandra. I mean Alexandra."

A weight shifts across the Mechanic's brow and his eyes clench upon me. "Alexandra," he repeats, and with a slow nod, coaxes me further towards him and away from the nightfall that leans invitingly in the barn's entrance. "That's a nice handle," he adds. "Where were you trying to get her to?"

I am about to answer, but I detect movement outside. It is faint, but someone is stepping on the margins of the grass and the gravel path. Slow, methodical steps. I pause. The dark space inside my head is colonized by yet another cone of possibilities.

"Coordinates are off the East Coast," I hear myself add, but I am following his eyes as they gouge the empty space of the barn's entrance.

Clearly, he now hears the noise too. Francis' voice calls out from outside the barn. Another clap of red, and through the schisms that rent the depths of blue light behind my eyes come more words of my own. Words stubborn enough, I say them aloud, "And what rough beast, its hour come round at last, slouches towards Bethlehem to be born?"

The heat signature across the Mechanic's face suggests he heard me, but Francis' voice intercedes, "Push the Metal Chad through the door and we'll be on our way!"

A deeper, heavier voice buttresses Francis' words. "There's no harm done yet. We just want what's ours."

The Mechanic frowns and shakes his head, and his face flushes from yellow to a dark red, a cross between exhaustion and acceptance, the makings of resignation.

"I have only one rule: I don't do refunds. But if Delilah has changed her mind, I guess we can swap back."

I can tell from his face that he knows they are not here for a refund. He walks backwards to the workbench in slow, delicate steps.

"Way my little cousin here tells it, it wasn't Delilah's to sell," responds the heavier voice. His words come deeper, in what seems like a forced growl, dredged up from his larynx like a peacock's plumage.

"Sounds like a you and Delilah problem," replies the Mechanic.

"Old man, you really think Delilah is still calling the shots? You going to tell him, little cousin?"

"Just push it through the door, and we'll be gone," stammers Francis.

The Mechanic is beside the workbench now, and he sets the hammer down quietly to let his hand search the vertical sidings that rib the barn's interior. "You can buy it off me or you can try to rob me, but I wouldn't suggest robbing me."

As he speaks, he unsheathes a shotgun from the shadows of the barn wall and positions himself so that the wall flanks him and faces the entranceway. His movements appear well-practiced like deep nervous tissue memory at work. Something akin to instinct. With the shotgun set on the door, he jerks his head at me, advising me to retreat further into the depths of the barn. I move by the skip of the generator and crouch in the dark, not far from the pool of light cast by the kerosene lanterns.

Outside, fast hisses pass between Francis and his cousin. Their voices are muffled by the dance of the generators, but the words I catch are spoken with an urgent tone that betrays panic. Their plan has become loose with indecision.

"Look, no harm has really been done at this point. Go now, and we forget all this ever happened," says the Mechanic. His words have softened, and seem almost gentle, like the way our Father spoke to Alexandra after she had made a mistake.

"Don't say we didn't give you a chance, old man," postures the voice I assume is Francis' cousin.

A long, playful whistle summons the pop of doors opening and slamming shut, followed by the bounce of gravel as their footsteps travel the little path through the meadow to the barn's entrance. The voices are unguarded now, and there is an assumption of supremacy in their sudden openness.

"We on?" asks a voice that strides over the din of feet and calls of excitement with a casual ease.

"Like we said, we get the Metal Chad. The cause gets the fuel, but the rest is loot."

"Boo-fucking-laa. Deal. All right Boyos and Cousins, you know the drill."

There are dumb words of assent and a scatter of steps along the perimeter of the barn. They will come at us from both sides, it seems. The cone of possibilities erupts in the void behind my eyes. There is a decent chance I can slip away during the fray. There is a timeline where the lanterns are out. I do much better in that timeline. So does the Mechanic.

I am about to indicate at the lanterns, but I lose the Mechanic's attention as Francis sings through the entranceway, "Last chance, you grizzled old fuck."

The Mechanic looks at me, shrugs, then flicks the lantern light out. "So be it," he murmurs as I scramble farther into the barn's abyss of shape and shadow, careful to keep the extension cords on the right of me, to avoid the iron skin of his grandson's bariatric chamber.

I burrow into a crevice made between two small towers of plastic crates and watch the Mechanic's heat signature. A little distance away from the puddle of moonlight at the barn's entrance, he is crouched low and continues to bob his head from the entrance to the back of the barn. Without the lanterns, I doubt he is able to see much, but from his breathing and pulse, I can tell he feels in control. This is good. The longer he survives, the greater chaos he will create, and the better the chance is that I can slip away.

An orange halo burns in my vision as someone attempts to peek through the entranceway. He meets no immediate resistance, though I see the Mechanic's arms stiffen and trace his direction. Confident he is unopposed, the man transforms from an orange head into a yellow and red shadow as more of his body becomes exposed while he ventures through the wooden archway. The man turns his head to signal someone behind him, but a shower of red sparks burrow into his chest, and he crumples over backwards. The wooden walls muffle the resonance of the blast, but the air still seems to hum in the aftermath.

"Pull him back, pull him," someone yells, and gravel shifts underfoot.

"He's fucking toast. Don't bother," comes a reply.

They are not wrong. The heat of the man's body smolders into a lifeless purple mass.

Amidst their panic, there is another voice. It is faint and gentle, well below the decibel of the human ear. For a moment, I almost doubt I really hear it, but it comes again.

"Marco ..."

The whirl of my processor rivals the din of gunfire. The shadows of the barn burnish the grey skeleton of the cage where the Mechanic stores his drums of diesel. Smoke. Flames. Immolation. Chaos. With improved odds of escape, I tread in the margins of the firefight with the Mechanic's lighter in hand.

ALEXANDRA
The Trail

The sun is setting, and the creek is up to Hypatia's ankles as she fills the water bottles. The woods are full of too much noise: crickets, the lap of the creek on stones by the shore, and the wind spinning in the butter-yellow leaves. It overpowers me and I can't focus. The backpack straps cut into my shoulders. It's heavier than I thought it would be, even without the water bottles.

Hypatia brings my dad's green Nalgene across the creek and bends to feed the water bottle. There's peace in the way her body folds and casts the silhouette of a rampant arch over the gentle stream. I focus on how the angle of her over the water makes me feel, the calm and evenness of her pose.

A shadow unsheathes itself from the underbrush and strides across the bank to the edges of the water, its shapeless mass fast becoming thin legs and arms. It's lean and pinched, and it stalks Hypatia in slow steps as if it's dancing on the water. The wind, the creek, and the crickets are all reduced to slices of noise as my hands come on and off my ears in frantic bursts. Pop. Pop. Pop. Poseidon's clams, I need to scream. I must scream to warn her, but my hands are back on my ears, and I dissect the world again in bursts of sound. I must warn her, but my ears hurt from all the cuffing and it's impossible to summon words to my lips.

Hypatia pauses, and the arms and legs of a man come behind her and wrap around her waist. Another shadow rises from amidst the brush in front of her and pounces upon her. They push her face into the dark water of the creek, and her torso disappears. Her legs remain on the surface, thrashing and tearing through the stream in jets of angry, white water. My hands flap against my ears with such force that the world is almost mute, but I catch it; slivers of someone's laughter jab at me.

Pop. Pop. Pop.

The laughter, the fight, the crickets, forms a kaleidoscope of noise that echoes on the water. They dredge her to the surface, and in a split second, her eyes run down the shoreline, likely desperate to catch the signature of my heat.

I'm not sure if she finds me squatting amongst the brush as I repeatedly mute and unmute the scene. Most of her face disappears behind a blindfold and they pull her into the woods on the far side of the creek. I'm still squatting, and now that it's too late, I hear myself howl, but even my own words come in pieces as I continue to cuff the world out from my ears.

No. No. No. They've taken her, and the crickets are still singing. *Focus. You need to be able to hear to follow her,* I tell myself. *You must stop cuffing your ears.*

The loop is getting stronger though, and the more I try to walk through it, the more perpetual it becomes until I walk on a Mobius strip. I used to explain how it felt to stim by drawing a Mobius strip. Hypatia explained it to mom and dad.

What else will calm me? I must move and hear. I can't follow her if I can't hear them. How long has it been? How long have I squatted here, with my venetian blind noises? It may as well have been hours. What else in this universe will calm me? Universe?

I manage to let the backpack drop from my shoulders. I fumble through the bag; the can opener, a can of beans, and the Magic 8 Ball fall and stick in the creek's clay bank. Greater frustration rips through me as I stare at the disorder at my feet, but I keep searching. My fingers find the familiar fabric and yank at the soft corner of the blanket until the Milky Way comes out of the backpack in a blur of purple and white starlight. I pull it over my shoulders, but an unexpected thud follows my movements. Something else has fallen with it. I look down and find Malcolm's black handgun next to the can opener. The handle is cold in my hand. I've never touched a gun before.

I push all the spilled contents into the backpack and pull the Milky Way blanket into a cape. There's warmth around me again, but the woods are growing dark. The crickets become louder and I realize I've stopped cuffing my ears. Dad's Nalgene is caught against a round stone in the shallows on the other side of the creek. It rocks and rolls in the gentle lap of the water, its moorage tauntingly fragile. I will have to cross to the other side to get it, and to search for Hypatia. *Be gentle Poseidon.* Breathing affirmations that the water won't go higher than my knees, I close my eyes and surrender my ankles to the sting of the creek. Midway across the creek bed, I wince as its waters swell to my shins and graze the bottom of my cape-blanket, but, with one eye open, I press on.

Once across, I fish for dad's Nalgene with a stick. Like a small barrel it rolls and bobs into my grasp, and then I slip into the woods. The undergrowth is heavy; it snags my feet, but I fight through it until the soft laughter of the creek fades away. I find no signs of Hypatia or anyone, but I'm not sure what I should be looking for, or even what direction I should travel. *Boreas, Zephyrus, Notus, and Eurus, give a girl a break, will you?* The desire to lay down in yellow leaves and weep, grows within me. In squat, I rub my eyes raw on the coarse sleeves of my jacket. A ghost of a voice. Followed by another. Picked clean of its words by the roil of the wind, a call of alarm drifts through the molting boughs of the trees. Though far away, the speaker sounds like they are directly ahead of me.

With abandon, I run through the woods until I stumble across a narrow thread of trodden earth where the underbrush has been cleared away. Though my lungs scream and my calves ache, I run faster, emboldened by the trail's safe passage through the woods. The trail widens and the forest's autumnal carpet is beaded with stones and pebbles and then it breaks into a long gravel road. The air is heavy with dust, and it stings my eyes as I chase the amber taillights of a truck as it accelerates into the curve of the road and then vanishes.

"Barnacles!" I scream. Part of me wants to lie down in the road and cry, but another more sober part of me knows I need to rescue Hypatia. If I don't die trying to find her, I'll simply die without her. *Cool, so it's not like its high stakes or anything.* A faint ripple of laughter manages to fight its way across my lips. *Inappropriate laughter. Right on cue. Thanks brain,* but I am jogging up the road now.

Hours pass by, and I'm not even sure I'm on the right track. The yellow light of the low-hanging moon skips in the puddles of wheel wells hewed into the gravel road. The road snakes through low brush, its green fingers in retreat from autumn's paring. Every so often, I stop and ask the *Magic 8 Ball* if I'm on the right path: *Oh, Magic 8 Ball, compass of the damned, is Hypatia at the end of this road?* Reverent, I observe its little messages that float to the surface from its caged inky ocean. "*Without a doubt. Most definitely.*" The assurances are enough to keep me walking. There are other signs, too.

A shredded charging cable, a small white shoe, electronic equipment I don't recognize, and a bicycle spoke. Debris found along the edges of the road, loose scraps. Breadcrumbs of unimportant things. Perhaps Hypatia planted them on the road on purpose. That's something she might do.

Eventually, the road slopes down from the brush to listless fields stretching back into the deep, wide darkness. Along the right shoulder of the road, moonlight reflects on a set of dormant headlights. As I get closer, the night loses its grip and reveals the front of a white pickup truck adrift on the road's gravel shoals. I let my fingers walk along its dusty sides and stop at the open gas cap; a dirty plastic tube hangs in spirals against the truck; it reminds me of the fun, reusable straws mom and dad bought us when we were kids. The air is heavy with the sweet, pungent smell Paul's truck made when its engine "got going." The diesel smell. I freeze. Heavy, laboured breathing sunders the stillness of the dark. I'm not alone.

Long suckling breaths. The breaths of a wounded thing. Carefully, I edge along the truck's bumper, my steps light and slow so as not to disturb the gravel.

The breathing pauses and then deepens. A woman lies in the ditch that runs below the shoulder of the road. She lies prostrate, flat; shadow-fingers of grass cradle her head. She clutches a jacket to her stomach.

"You here to finish the job?" she wheezes.

I crouch beside her; the cold grass bites my knees through my pants as I fumble dad's Nalgene from the side of the backpack. A red, shaky hand joins mine and we raise the bottle to her lips. She nods and rests her head back on the dark green earth. I run through the First Aid steps Hypatia once taught me.

Look for dangers. Assess the state of the injury. Call for help ... The steps haven't aged well.

Her eyes roll over the night sky, open, but far away. With a gentle pull, I try to lift the corner of the jacket to assess the damage. Her eyes flash, and with a grimace, she presses the jacket tighter to herself.

"To help," I explain with the corner of the jacket, wet and slick between my fingers.

"No helping what's been done. Let it be." She manages a little, tired smile and closes her eyes. "I saw you down at the creek, didn't I?"

"Yes."

"You the companion's ward?"

"Sister."

"Sister. Sisters. Of course. And you're coming for her."

"Yes."

Her smile grows wide and then flickers and fades. "I'm sorry we took her from you. I tried to do a little right by getting it, her, to the Mechanic. Figured better him than some Alogo Boo port scrapyard."

I decide I don't understand the reasoning, but want to affirm her apology. "Water?"

She says nothing, but motions at the Nalgene. Together, we hold it to her lips.

"Dying is thirsty work." Her small chuckle mutinies into a chain of coughs. "That boy wants her, too. Don't know if he wanted her as bad as all this, though." Blood and something else with the ichor of tar leak from under her jacket and stain the legs of her jeans.

"Francis?"

She tries another laugh. "You know him then. They kept calling him their little cousin. Boy, he liked that. It was all shit eater grins until they handed him the knife."

"This was Francis?" I say as my hands hover above the jacket for confirmation of her indication.

She nods and closes her eyes. "Listen good, there are no limits to the ways a boy will betray himself if he thinks it'll make him a man. Gone and killed us both, in his way." Her head creeps lower into the grass, the beginnings of her surrender. "Put Lyle and Jack down clean, at least. I guess a man's owed a clean death."

Unable to pull any of my feelings into words, I frown and nod and hope she recognizes my sympathy. "How far?"

"Down the road. Big barn on the left. I suspect you'll hear 'em."

"Okay."

She strains her eyes open and, while staring over my shoulder, rubs her lips together before she says, "You get her back here and drive on." She flicks her eyes at the truck in indication. "Emergency fuel under the front seat. They looted fast, not well. I think they missed it. It'll get you down the road a fair way. Spare key there, too."

"I don't drive."

"Nothing to it. That sister of yours will know what to do." She speaks her words with her eyes shut.

"Thanks." I press the Nalgene into her hand.

"Too kind. Too kind for this road."

I walk and jog, and it doesn't take long to come upon a crude gravel path hewed into existence by deep wheel-wells. The gravel driveway diverges anonymously from the shoulder of the road and is seemingly marked by only a solitary bone-white tree, with a pink ribbon in its arms. At the top of the gravel path, there are several high beams, and in their tangled fray, the grey-skinned barn is cut from the night, its feet planted in the tawny grass, slipping into the almost molten soil of an agrarian underworld. Even from far below, I can tell the barn door is ajar, but the lights from the two idling trucks are left to puddle beneath it.

The air is heavy, rich with decomposition. Iron to rust. Wood to rot. Animals to carcass. There's a burst of gunfire and a scream. The gravel pinches my belly and bites my knees as I crawl amongst the grass. There are more shots and the primeval cries of life undone. I'm close now; the entrance of the barn is in view, as are the half-dozen men who lean against the grey wood or crouch in the grass, firing into the dark.

In terror, I speak my summons to Hypatia at a whisper, hoping it's too soft and delicate for the human ear to discern amongst the rustle of the grass. "Marco?" Over the din of gunfire and the battle cries, it'll be impossible to catch her response. Yet, I call again,

"Marco?" It's loud enough that one of the soldiers risks a furtive glance over his shoulder before taking several more shots into the barn. There will be no way for Hypatia to escape; she may not even know I've come for her. Perhaps I can draw them away?

Sat low in the cold sea of grass, I raise Malcolm's revolver; my arms shake and drift as I try to aim at the back of the closest man. My finger curls around the trigger, and I close my eyes as a long, shrill eldritch scream rips through the world; it doesn't deafen, but erases all sound that came before it. A wave of fire crashes through the barn entrance and blows the soldiers backwards; a man, his arms ablaze, stumbles and screams in its wake. A billow of black smoke follows, and a small figure moves with it, veering down the side of the barn until it vanishes in the fields. In panic, I drop the gun. It lands in the field with a dull thud as I flee.

On my belly, I slip back into the grass and cut into the figure's direction of travel. I don't go far before Hypatia surfaces from the grass to pull me down with her. Behind us, the barn looms from atop the hill; red fire from its doors and windows bears down on us and casts red shadows in front of our steps. Someone bellows, "The fuel, Cousins! Get the fucking fuel out!"

Hypatia doesn't waste the opportunity. We run through the grass. My legs ache and my chest is tight, but we don't stop. Hypatia's feet betray a small metal patter as we reach the road. The barn has receded into the night, reduced to slices of red fire amidst the tangled naked fingers of grey brush. A muffled solitary burst of gunfire carries from the hill. Hypatia pauses long enough for my head to fall between my knees in long suckling breaths. She takes several steps backwards and stares from where we came, into the brush that leans over the road's shoulder.

"They won't be far behind us. Keep moving," she says, but not without one more wayward glance back into the brush.

Ahead of us, the dull red glow of the truck's headlights surfaces in the dark. Against my will, my eyes skirt to the ditch, where a mass, its edges darker than the rest of the night, lays motionless amongst the grass. The sight of more death threatens to summon my hands to my ears. Hypatia appears to take no notice. She storms past the truck, and then twists and spins as I pull on her arm.

"Truck works."

Before she can speak, I pull the door open and root under the driver's seat; my fingers glean cool metal and the rough, sticky edges of tape. As promised, there are three thermoses taped beneath the seat. One of them has an old-fashioned key with many sharp edges taped to it. I open one of the thermoses; its contents slosh gently against its sides as I pass it to Hypatia for her approval. A flicker of surprise disrupts the aloof serenity of her usual expression.

She embraces me. "This opens many new possibilities," she whispers.

She draws the siphon from the gas tank, chucks it across the road, and pours the contents of the first thermos into the truck. There's a slow patter of liquid on metal as we fill the truck's belly.

"Get in. They won't be far behind us. I need you to sit in the driver's seat to work the pedals. I'll sit in front of you. It'll be tight. See if you can move the seat back," she says as she wrenches the lid off the next thermos.

With the door open, the truck's overhead cabin light wakes up and illuminates a chaotic interior. The glove compartment drawer hangs from a few strands of twisted metal like a dislocated jaw; flyers and papers carpet the floor and the passenger seat. Silver discs, the kind we'd sometimes find in the old boxes our parents kept in the basement, are strewn about. A quick Alogo Boo loot job.

As Hypatia predicted, the seat is very close to the steering wheel. I have no idea how to move it. The seats in our parent's car simply recognized us and adjusted on their own.

"Move seat back," I deliver my words with clear enunciation.

The seat remains motionless, disinterested in my instructions. I let my eyes scroll over the two small black nobs on the old-fashioned disc player and contemplate the weight of the key in my hand; the rules for the truck are analog.

My fingers tap and pry at a piece of hard plastic between the seat and the door and discover a metal lever built into its side. With a pull, the seat swings forward and collapses into the steering wheel. An encouraging development. The seat is on metal runners.

I venture to push the seat back, but an uneven voice erupts from behind the truck, "Don't fucking move."

In slow steps, Francis' gaunt figure unsheathes from the night; his pistol drifts across my chest to settle on Hypatia. The screams inside me work through the tips of my fingers as my hands dance on my cheeks.

Hypatia continues to empty the last of the thermos' contents into the truck. "Did you not realize I'd see your heat trailing us? Did you not realize I'd know you're alone? Very alone." Her words carry the menace of utter indifference.

Francis steadies the pistol in both his hands, but his steps falter, leaving him only a few feet from Hypatia.

"If I were you, I'd go back to the Alogo Boo at the barn and tell them you lost sight of us," continues Hypatia, her back now to me as she speaks facing Francis. "Those are your best odds of survival."

"I won't be alone for long," stammers Francis. His features pass in and out of the moonlight refracted from the truck, pale and solemn. "Come on, you lie down, and I'll even let Stacy try her luck on the road." He builds his words like they are commands, but his voice rattles and breaks.

With her left hand, Hypatia points at the truck. "In the truck, sister."

For a moment, Francis raises the revolver above Hypatia's shoulder as if in consideration of me, but shakes his head and focuses once more on Hypatia as I slip into the driver's seat. Before I can reach out of the truck to pull the door in after me, Francis continues, "Come on now, the rest of them will be swarming these hills. I'll kill you both if I need to. I swear."

A dull weight of Hypatia's steps precedes her answer. "You're right. We're running out of time."

A blast rings in my ears and the driver's window explodes in a crystal shower.

"Metal Chad bit—"

The rest of Francis' words are lost in a cacophony of panicked screams and moans. There will be no second shot. I clap my ears and discover blood on my hands; the explosion of the window has cut my face. The instinct to clap harder bites, but even as I oblige, I can't clap over Francis' cries.

With reluctance, I turn and peer out from the truck's cabin to discover Hypatia straddling Francis' chest, hammering him with the thermos. Francis cries and struggles beneath her weight as he deflects her blows with his forearms and hands.

"Oh no! No! No—" he screams as Hypatia's blows knock apart the shield he has created with his arms.

The thermos rings against the side of his head, and its metallic echo skips down the road. Francis writhes and kicks his knees, desperate to escape her next blow. There's a dull thud, and a spray of red mist clouds Francis' face.

There are many feelings inside me. Misery. Despair. Horror. The feelings bring me to my feet and carry me to Hypatia's shoulder.

"Please stop," I cry.

Hypatia raises the thermos again and pulverizes his cheek. Francis' cries and pleas deteriorate into shallow, desperate breaths.

"Down. Enough."

Hypatia doesn't acknowledge me. The thermos rises, wet and red, above her head, and she adjusts her grip of it in both hands, in what looks like a final killing blow. Francis' face is a pulsing mass of red; the gauze bandage hangs limp on the road, revealing a purple gash and a line of broken stitches from his lip to the back of his cheek. He raises one shaking hand in a feeble plea; his lips move but can't give birth to words, and perhaps for a moment, we share the vulnerability of voicelessness and the waywardness of being marooned with meanings and thoughts that are doomed to die pitifully inside us. To be unheard is to be without refuge in another.

A scream rattles my chest and echoes over the road as I grab Hypatia's wrist. "Stop!"

"He's a threat, sister. He's proven that."

"He's just alone. Alogo Boo lies." With my free hand, I run small circles on her back until my finger strays and finds the indentation the woman in the trailer put in her.

"He's too far gone." Her words come soft and quiet; I think perhaps they carry a trace of regret.

She fights my grip to raise the thermos higher as Francis groans and spits blood and teeth from the side of his mouth. Red spittle runs from his chin down his neck.

"You don't know." I squeeze her forearm.

"Processor knows."

"The dead don't change."

"The dead don't kill."

"What about you?"

Her eyes widen and the thermos wavers. "Me?"

"Don't murder. Less my sister."

The aloofness that sits on her face crumples into shock and sadness too, I think. "We're safer with him dead."

"Stay whole."

Her eyes walk across my face in a long, probing assessment. "Fine. You'll reap what you sow, sis." The thermos clatters and rolls across the road as she rises from his chest. "Help me roll him, then."

Francis' eyes are bruised shut, lost amongst purple bleeding mounds. Hypatia has mutilated his features. It seems impossible that there's still a face beneath the pulp and mash of blood and flesh, but he gives a faint moan as we lift and roll him to the side of the road.

"Will he live?"

"If his Alogo Boo friends help him, probably. That's not our problem," says Hypatia, and she points to the truck. "We need to go."

I want to tell her we need to take his gun to replace Malcolm's, as I've dropped it in the fields. Yet, when I look at Francis' bloody visage and crumpled body at the side of the road, the thought of Hypatia having a gun makes me feel less safe, and I swallow the impulse in several deep gulps.

The truck shutters and spits into life. Hypatia fumbles on the steering wheel until she makes the road brush vanish before us. In the rear-view mirror, the dull red of our taillight catches the dark mass of Francis' body; I watch as he shrinks and fades in our wake until he vanishes in the twilight.

ALEXANDRA
Tesla and Beans

In my lap, Hypatia steered the truck down a maze of back roads until we reached the edge of the war. I worked the pedals. We left it on the shoulder of a road on the outskirts of somewhere called Lake George.

On foot, though, it's clear the war is here. It's been here since we rode with Paul into Cardinal, but only in bits. In the silence that reigns between the words of those we met on the road; roosting, maybe, in the darkened alcoves of the candlelit homes that wait in unfrequented towns. It was a presence, but its origins, its point of action, remained invisible.

When I was a kid, I used to imagine the breeze came from a big ball of wind somewhere else. A stationary tornado, I guess, that you could see. I couldn't draw it though, or, of course, say what I meant, so the idea went unchallenged. Up until now, the war has seemed like that: a dark breeze from a much darker, realer place that has been out of sight. But now, we're on the war's outskirts, and with each step we take towards Albany, we venture from being in its orbit to its epicentre.

The afternoon is dimming. Along the highway, we meet a few scattered cars, but the roads beneath the overpasses are crowded by several lines of traffic frozen in time. The sheen of the metal hoods and roofs gleam like scarab shells in the creep of evening's half-light. Our past life fossilized as the confusion of darkened cities continues to grow, burying the old world in its sedimentation. What scares me is that I can't imagine them moving again. Some of the cars have yellow ribbons tied to their wing mirrors. I've pointed them out to Hypatia, but she merely frowned and continued at pace with disinterest.

Hypatia walks ahead in silence. She talks little. For the last two days, there's been no morning discussions of the day's travel plan. There's no more talk of going to Port Henry. Instead, I've found her awake, crouched on her haunches waiting for me to rise, a pale trickle of sunrise at her back. She only smiles and shoves a granola bar or an open can of beans she has ready for me into my hands. Some rationed water, and then, while she waits for me to pee, she packs up to go. We've been breaking camp with such relentlessness that I find I'm often pulling twigs and leaves from my hair as we walk. She's no longer offering to take the backpack.

Still, I'm not sure why we're here. Why we've departed from the side roads and quiet fields to venture down the highway. In the distance, there's a faint string of cracks of what we've come to know as distant gunfire.

A river, the Hudson, by Hypatia's reckoning, runs with us. We've followed the slow roll of its brown-green depths all the way down the highway. It reeks. When we lose sight of the river, we follow the smell of rotten eggs and sewage. My mom had a word for that smell, effluent. Opposite the river, on the other side of the highway, is a sprawl of barren land. The temperature is dropping. I need to sleep, but on the highway, everything looks too exposed. There's no cover, but Hypatia doesn't seem to care. Ever since we fled the Barn, she's been carrying an emotion I've never seen in her before: panic.

I've tried to find the right words to ask her what's wrong. For a while, in the rare moments when we stopped to rest so I could rub my aching calves, I asked her if she was okay. I tried apologizing for not telling her about losing Malcolm's gun right away, but she seemed indifferent. When that didn't change her mood, I tried other words. Words like "hurt" and "scared," but she only shook her head. I've almost dared to ask her if she's damaged, but that would've been a wrong word. A word for a machine, an instrument, not a sister. Tonight, I'll try again with new words.

As my pace falters, the distance between Hypatia and me widens. Seemingly, she's oblivious to my fatigue and indifferent to the arrival of a crisp, damp autumn evening; her gait is hurried, and her toe occasionally scrapes the asphalt, sending a faint din across the cracked, molten pavement. The only things in sight are slumbering fields, solemn and wind-torn beneath a sheath of iron-skinned power lines that run parallel to the highway. We could scurry into the fields like mice and find some far corner to lie low within, but even their openness leaves them indifferent and willing to harbour us or an Alogo Boo mob.

"Cold. Camp," I call. I watch her pirouette on her feet, absorbing our surroundings in a 360-degree spin.

"There's nowhere suitable here. We can walk in the dark. It's unlikely anyone will come this way," she throws her words over her shoulder as she continues to march forward.

For a moment, I'm ready to believe she's right and there's nowhere for us to rest, but then I realize there are dozens of cars scattered around us. Some are facing us, and in their stillness, after being hit by the flash, they look like they've glided into the concrete guardrails. The solution is obvious, and inside me a feeling swirls; I summon the word to trap it, to give it a name. Incredulous. I'm incredulous that using the cars as shelter has somehow escaped that god-like processor of hers.

"Inside cars!" She doesn't respond, but her pace slows. "Exhausted," I press. She pauses, and I think her shoulders drop.

"Okay then, check if any are unlocked," she replies in a tone I don't recognize. It sounds small. Maybe sad.

In response, I pull the door handle on the car closest to me, but it's stubborn and remains firm against my grip. I jog backwards to six little cars that are clustered together, one of which has a yellow ribbon wrapped around its wing-mirror. I tug on the door handle of one, but upon closer inspection, notice that their windshields are bowed and shattered. Black, insectile legs protrude from the shattered glass, like bits of twigs peeking out from the surface of a frozen lake. The remnants of a swarm strike.

Then I find them inside the cars. It was a fleeting glance, but in my throat forms a lump. *Treat each car like it's the sun.* The interior clips in and out of view in one furious blink. I move by, careful not to really look at the sunken green faces of molting inhabitants; I see them anyway and shutter them out in another blink and break sight with the interiors, desperate not to let their faces become more formed than anything but greenish blurs. To leave them unrecognizable and vague, faint glimpses too short for them to haunt me, I hope.

Filtering the dead from my world has been Hypatia's job. The role was agreed on tacitly, but it was something I knew she did to preserve my emotional stamina. I start to call for her, but she remains where I left her, staring into the driver's window of the car closest to her. A white Tesla. I try another door handle. Locked. Behind the windows are faces: molted, greyish, and sunken; the air around them looks clouded. One is much smaller than the other; the head tilted back into the seat, suspended on a small body, vanishing into the seat's upholstery. An ocean of mother and child, their shed skin, a brine of decomposition, and the sedimentation of mortal souls and terror, maybe. The smell emanates from the car, and I pull back from the door handle, in fear it will stick to my fingers.

I know I need Hypatia now. The butterflies are in my stomach, the bad kind. The kind that eventually flutter in my ears, and whine and scratch until I pump them out with my palms. When I reach her side, she's speaking, but her words come through my fingers, muffled and distant.

She runs her fingers in little circles on the driver's window, scratching away dust and mud to make room for our reflections. Hypatia appears first; a child's face: pink-cheeked with unblemished skin. The dirt and grim of the road don't seem to stick to her. Nothing really sticks to her. With her pointer finger, she makes careful vertical lines, presaging away the mud to make room for my reflection.

There's dirt across the bridge of my nose, and several angry, oily blemishes on my cheeks. I don't think it looked this bad when I searched for my face in the bottom of the creek, the evening of the barn. Teenage skin is as mercurial as the teenage temperament, my mom would say. Behind my face, though, the Tesla is empty. The glove compartment is open, and there are a few papers scattered on the passenger seat, but unlike the other cars, it's not a tomb.

"I've never understood my face," says Hypatia. "Do you think they made it up, or is my nose a replica of some original ski-slope that belonged to someone else? Were her eyes oval, too?"

"Good questions." I put my hand on her shoulder the way she showed me, the way to say you want to comfort someone. Want them to feel loved. "No answers. Not now."

"I don't know if there ever will be answers," she replies. "I've always envied your face, sis. I love the way it changes. The way you can become someone else on the inside and the outside. Do you understand that?"

I nod, but I also shiver. The sun is low now; its pale net catches only on our feet and the bottom of car wheels as it falls away into the horizon. "You're beautiful," I offer.

"That's kind. I guess I'm well-formed and proportioned, but I'm not sure if I'm ephemeral enough to be beautiful. There's grace and longing in change. All kinds of states of change." She speaks this last sentence quietly as she gestures at the cars and their entombed occupants behind us.

I shake my head. "Terrifying. Sad."

"There's no beauty without states of change."

I don't have enough words to continue the discussion, and so I'm forced to shrug my defeat.

"It's unlocked."

She swings the door out to my waist. The cold leather kisses my shoulders and legs as I climb into the rear seat; Hypatia follows in silence. The air is stiff and my teeth chatter. Hypatia roots through the backpack and, through the zipper, pulls out the faded dark purple corner and aqua rings of the Milky Way blanket. She wraps the universe around my shoulders and curls into me as she makes a practiced series of withdrawals from the backpack: a battered box of crackers, a can of beans, and our blunt can opener.

She lays the crackers out on the seat in an offering as she pries into the can of beans with the can opener. With an adroit twist, she pulls the lid from the can, dropping it at her feet. The beans look how they always look: stodgy, locked beneath an oily reservoir of water and tomato sauce. The bean water is heavy and smells like farts, but I gulp it down as Hypatia nods in approval.

The edges of the crackers break as I force them into the remaining stew of cold beans, creating a dissolving archipelago of crumbs on the surface; the beans make the air sweet, and I let the brown sauce coat the husk that has formed on my wind-chapped lips. Another cracker breaks off in my fingers as I jab it into the sauce. Hypatia watches me fish for it with my fingers; she sits with her arms crossed over her lap, in silent observation. I pause and dab the brown sauce from my mouth with my sleeve and offer her the can.

"No. Eat. You're running a 1200-calorie deficit for the day. You must finish this." She pushes the can back towards me. "We can forge more in Albany tomorrow."

I answer her with a dutiful scoop of the bits of crackers and slurp them from my fingers. The contents of the can evaporate, somehow vanishing in the space between my fingers and my mouth without filling the well of hunger that remains inside me. Suddenly, a metallic patter erupts on the car's roof. Drones. I jerk the blanket and try to start to wrestle into the gap between the front and rear seats.

Hypatia remains seated and motionless. For a moment, I'm horror-struck with the idea that she might have gone into standby mode, but then she says, "It's just the rain. Look." She smiles at her window, which is scattered with silvery beads, each droplet illuminated by the pale, distant reach of the moon.

"Oh."

My reflection swims in her eyes: clumps of tangled and matted hair on my shoulders, brown sauce on my lips, crouched down in the gap of the seats. *That's right, you can use brown sauce as lipstick. Follow me for more roadside beauty and wellness tips.* To my surprise, I'm laughing; her eyes widen, and she reciprocates with a short burst of a childish giggle. The response seems to surprise us both. She wiggles her fingers over her mouth, and when she raises her hand away, her face is once more the usual expression of serene aloofness.

Sometimes, I wonder why she chooses the gestures she does. The giggle is reminiscent of when I was little, and when she, too, pretended to be little, and we'd lay on our backs and blow the cotton candy heads of dandelions into the air. Did she know, predict, that I would crave the reminder of levity and innocence carried in that giggle? Did she also know it would stop my laughter and travel from us sullen and wraith-like, adrift without a claim in this world?

There are other laughs that live inside her. I know, I've heard them. Deeper laughs. Cheerless laughs, irascible and sarcastic snorts, mean laughs. It's hard not to forget her processor is forever predicting my emotional states, to guide them to safe, controlled ends. Is it possible that even when it seems like she has failed in the response she selected, that she may have actually succeeded? Succeeded in shutting down inside me an undesirable reaction or risky thought pattern without me realizing I was on the cusp of having it. You can't miss what you don't have, can you?

Hypatia begins to rummage through the backpack again and retrieves the small cooking pot. One of the few things she kept from dad's supplies.

"For rain collection. It could go on for a while."

I nod, and recall how, in the old days, she was able to access the weather forecast and tell us with precision what was coming. Constantly connected. It must be strange for her, sad even, to have lost so many of her powers. I watch her slide out the door, close it softly behind her, and move along the road, in search of a good spot to place the cooking pot.

Upon returning, she asks, "Are the beans finished?"

"All gone."

"Good. Then sleep, sis. I'll keep watch."

I nod, but I don't move. I focus on turning the feelings and thoughts into words. Part of me believes it would be easier to ask with a GIF, or to draw a picture. I inhale the grey, stuffy air of the car's interior.

"Hypatia?"

"Yes?"

"Tired of me?"

"How can I be tired of you?"

"I'm slow?"

"There isn't anything wrong with your pace. I just need to make sure we get there. The longer we're out here, the less safe it is. Do you understand?" I nod. "Good. Try to get some rest. It'll be another early start."

~

A pale beam of light strikes through Hypatia's window. Muffled banter of heavy voices trails the light. Voices of men.

One cry breaks away from the others, "Alogo—"

Sweet Apollo, let me be dreaming. Let this be a nightmare. Another beam of light; this one lances through the rearview window, illuminating the profile of Hypatia's face; crouched low, she faces away from me, peaking over the headrest of the rear seat.

"A squad. I can verify 50, but estimate 100," she whispers, and with her left hand gestures for me to drop low.

I squirm into the floor space reserved for legroom between the front and back seats. With her other hand, she reaches for the auto-lock button on the door. Holding my breath, I wait for the reassuring click of the locks, but there's no sound.

"Makes sense," she whispers as her weight shifts above me; in slow, controlled movements, she lowers herself next to me and pulls the Milky Way over us. "No power, no lock. We need to stay quiet."

The temperature in the car is low enough that I exhale my terror in pale seams of breath. In the dark of the blanket, her hand finds mine, and her thumb presses into my palm in slow circles, coaxing me to take longer and more deliberate breaths. The rising sense of panic inside me stalls, but it doesn't abate. Another battery of flashlights sweeps through the car; a pale glow leans through the blanket's fabric to become crescents of refracted light in Hypatia's eyes. The cold floor and squeeze of the seats embrace my body as I push myself lower into the car, willing myself to disappear amongst the dark of its bottom.

"Alogo," grunts a voice, and the speaker sounds like they are inside the car with us.

"Boo," thunders a second voice from ahead of us, farther down the highway.

"Put those out. We aren't taking back the night here," barks the man to a chorus of coarse laughter, and his voice rattles inside my chest.

They must be standing right next to Hypatia's door. The interior of the car becomes darker, but a faint glow of light still skips over our heads. The tempo of Hypatia's thumb on my palm increases and the pressure deepens. My pulse must be spiking. I taste my breath as it fogs the darkness. I fight to gain back control of my breathing, to focus on each breath like it's a wave crashing on the beach, flowing and ebbing back into the ocean. Just like my mom's Yoga teacher, Kyle, had recommended I do "to recover a sense of calm when I confront adverse situations." *Yeah. Right. He'd probably drop Chakras in his pants if he found himself next to these psychos. Namaste to you too, Kyle.*

"Good to see you, Nephews," calls the man, and the light in the car grows bigger with his approach. "Took your time, eh?"

"Uncle. Uncle, I'm sorry," replies the man.

"We were counting on you. Ops said you'd be in Albany two days ago."

"I know. Our assessment was based on us refueling, but the whole thing went tits up. Those responsible have been disciplined."

"You took responsibility, that's what counts. I'm happy to have you here. Waiting on these deplorables of yours to drive the rest of these fuckers out."

There's more laughter among them. "Well, it hasn't been a picnic getting here, has it, boys?" There's levity in his words.

"Got warm food and warm bodies waiting for you. We've taken a terminal. We can re-equip you with transport once we control the city. Too risky now."

"Any loot left?" yells another voice, flanked by others.

"Plenty of spoils," announces the man to a wave of laughter and hoots.

"Sounds cozy."

"Well, come here, Nephew. Come here. Let me show you the lay of it."

Someone comes to rest against the car, and their body meets it in a haphazard thud. The smell of Hypatia's fingers, a combination of beans and home, overwhelms me as her hand wraps around my mouth. Maybe the internet didn't die with the flash. Maybe its worst characters came to life. I can picture them, bathed in the pale blue light of their monitors, frantically memeing, but unable to stake a claim in the real world.

Hypatia's other hand runs over my hair as she strokes my head. She loosens the grip over my mouth, and the noise of my own breathing startles me. Desperate, deep, suckling breaths. I'm on the verge of losing control, and Hypatia knows it. Through the blanket, I can distinguish the light has receded from the car, and the voices are dim and quiet. Bits of their words reach us beneath the blanket. Fortifications. Dug-in positions. Then a reference to a hospital, and Hypatia's fingers flutter and stiffen in my hair.

Curled together on the floor of the Tesla, we watch the light crash and roll like waves as they march by us down the highway. Their voices follow the light, growing fainter, until they become an inaudible rumble, like thunder in the distance. Hypatia surfaces first from beneath the blanket and climbs back atop the rear seat. Silence. The seat cushion indents and flexes as her weight shifts.

"Clear," she calls in a steady voice. "You did great. You really did," she adds as I pull the blanket off.

I can tell by the way she's looking at me that the static from the blanket has turned my hair into a storm. "Where now?" I ask.

Hypatia doesn't respond. Instead, she twists around to survey the highway in front of us, the way they marched.

"Where? Hypatia?"

She still doesn't respond, and a whine from my stomach fills the silence.

"We're going to follow them."

"Looney Tunes!" My voice rings inside the car.

"Listen. Listen. We need supplies. You're starving. Safest passage into Albany will be the one they carve out."

The weight of the beehive atop my head bounces from side to side as my head shakes violently.

She grabs my hand, and with her fingertips bends and flicks my fingernails. "Alexandra, look how brittle they are. Not enough nutrients. You'll get run down. Sick. We need more food. Better food. You won't have the energy for the journey. Trust me. This is the only way we can get to the refuge." For a moment, she pauses with an invitation for me to reply, but then seems to think better of it. "You're dehydrated. I'll get the pot."

She slips from the car back into the road and leaves the door ajar. The coal light of a rising sun curls in behind her; though its light is fragile, it makes my eyes burn. Sitting up makes my heart race, and there's weakness in my arms and legs. I meet Hypatia's gaze through the window, and she smiles as she disappears into the darkness of the road to retrieve the rain pot.

BUG
Operation Laughing Llama

The heavy face of a nearly full moon grazes the small establishment and puts a faint ethereal glow in the dead, neon signage of a convenience store. A yellow trail ribbon tied to the street sign at the corner flutters in the breeze. The transition from pink to yellow ribbon markers seems to have coincided with my journey south. The storefront name is a cluster of unintelligible L's and A's, but I think this must be the place Scrumaster34 mentioned in our text chat. Two bots in olive jackets lie supine on the pavement, their limbs twisted beneath them. There are bodies everywhere inside the city. No other part of the simulation has been this gory, and the continual simulacrum of death weighs on me.

The convenience store doors are automatic and no longer function, but one of them has been smashed to create a passageway that's too small for full-sized bots yet large enough to emit player avatars. It looks like an oversized doggy-door.

I slide the jerrycan through the jagged portal of glass and crawl after it on my hands and knees. As I shuffle on a marred tile floor on my elbows, I lock on Scrummaster34 sat cross-legged in the middle of the store. The shelving racks have been tipped over and knocked into neighbouring aisles. Scrummaster34 motions me forward with an index finger, and I squirm towards them on my belly like a supplicant, careful to lift my legs over the hungry glass at the base of the door. I don't have enough avatars to carelessly incur more damage, even if it will likely be superficial.

Two other players with names spelt in a script I don't recognize flank Scrummaster34. One wears a football helmet, and the other is in what looks like a Halloween Darth Vader helmet. The one in the Vader helmet holds a baseball bat with barbed wire coiled on its tip, while the other one grips a rusty shopping cart full of bottles, random cannisters, and old shirts.

Scrummaster34 gestures at the shopping cart and nods when I deposit the jerrycan inside, beside an identical one. Seconds later, green words scroll across my screen.

Very good, Ki-Yay. I am glad you were able to follow the yellow ribbons. Welcome to operation Laughing Llama.

It wasn't a cakewalk getting here. I lost two avatars transporting the material.

This seems to be a new feature to elevate the difficulty of the tournament. It has become harder. Avatars simply collapse mid-play, their lives exceeded. Surviving now means rationing an avatar's use, which isn't easy when you must lug a stupid jerrycan across the world map.

Regrettable, but the sacrifice will be worth it. We will secure an easy lead against the rest of the players.

Who are your friends?

Neither Vader nor football helmet acknowledge me, but the way Vader rotates the bat in their hand tells me they aren't AFK.

They are from another tournament centre. Do you understand the next steps, how to find the target?

No.

You will need to be online and in range of the target in six hours from now. Follow the red dots on the road towards the LATIPSOH. The dots will increase in size as you get closer to the target. Hide behind the sandbags. We will swarm the building, but only after I charge. Understand?

Yes.

Find a place to log to conserve your Avatar. There is a structure in the parking lot behind this building. It is metal and secure.

Is this area safe?
Something like that. There is a backdoor, I can show you.

Scrummaster34's head tilts to the back of the store. A yellow mop bucket lies on its side in a deluge of grey water and a hot dog rotisserie is smashed across the floor, but a lightless exit sign is mounted above the chaos.

I can manage.
Yes, I know you can.
See you in a few hours.
Five hours and 57 minutes.
Ok.
And Ki-Yay?
Yes?
Happy Hunting!

SISTERS
The Library

Standing up on the concrete guardrails, the rusted chain-link fence buried in the concrete press against my nose, I scan the city through miniature red-ringed portholes. Prying into windows of burned-out office buildings and broken storefronts, on alert for infrared signatures of human life. The Alogo Boo soldiers were easy to follow. Cigarettes on the road. Occasional shell casings. Another remnant was the body of a man on the outskirts of the city. Face up in a ditch, an XY carved into his forehead. They favour ditches. We managed to get by that one without Alexandra bearing witness. She walks slowly, with her eyes to her sneakers. She has become adept in the use of her own filters.

The celebration of death, its glorification, does not frighten me. Not in the long-term, at least. Thantos can cast nations to ruin, but I cannot run a scenario where it can rebuild them. All this is but the last gasps of terminal men. Eros will find its moment and, in some diluted form, bind civilization back together again. Freud said so, at least.

Three traffic lights from our overpass, there is a library. Like the rest of the city, it appears to have lost its colour, matted in what I decide, though my own reference point eludes me, is a drab soviet grey. From my experience, I can tell it is red-bricked. Three floors. There is no sign of movement around it, or within the exposed windows on the east of the building. It looks like a safe first stop. A potential morale booster.

Alexandra sits on the opposite side of the road, her back to the guardrail. Her vitals are erratic, and her emotional state appears indeterminate. Tired. Fearful. She drank all the rainwater. Stimming is a risk. She needs reassurance.

"This bit of the city looks quiet. There's a library."

"Books inedible."

"I know that. We can take cover in it and assess the safest path from there. We can grab a book or two for the road. Take the Republic jacket off. Scenarios are better if we go in as civilians."

Alexandra shrugs, fights her way out of the jacket, and crams it into our backpack. With the bag open, she approaches the guardrails in slow, shuffling steps as she waits for me to do the same. The jacket is still half over my head when she cries out, "Look!" She points north of the city to two small figures marching across the desolate concrete sea of an empty parking lot.

The amber coal light that burns low in their bellies and flickers in their arms and legs reveals them for what they are, but even without their heat signatures, their relentless, unyielding line of travel betrays them as companion children. Two more children come into view from around the corner of a building. One of them, in a black mask, pushes a shopping cart laden with an assortment of cartons and bottles, the details of which evade my vision's capacity.

"Companions, right?" asks Alexandra.

"Yes."

"Unlike Mickey."

The slate confusion that clouds her features confirms this is a statement, not a question. She is right. The loaded shopping cart. The shared direction of travel. These suggest planning and organization. Not the actions of berserk, broken things.

"Doing?" Alexandra presses.

From somewhere behind the wall of blue that pulses behind my eyes, an errant thought surfaces and passes over my lips, *"Walking in the fields unsunned of a sad, lost war."*

The arch of her eyebrow tells me I have said these words, these words ripe with anemoia's cruel fullness of longing, aloud.

"Okay ... weird."

Her face brightens into a burst of laughter I did not anticipate. For a moment, it becomes black and white, and her features slip outside the recognition of my processor. There is only her laughter. The world spins as I shake my head and drum my fingers on my temple, like the way people used to hammer television sets to re-tune their reception. Alexandra's features return, but grey clouds and pyramids of slate replace her laughter.

"You okay?" she asks.

"I don't know ..." Her confusion mutinies into yellow blossoms. "I don't know what they're doing," I adjunct and, with alacrity, a new grey-green calm equilibrium floods her features.

She nods. "Library time?"

We follow a protocol. I scan the road while Alexandra waits behind cover. A mailbox, an abandoned car. When it is clear, we cross together. We do this three times and then the library rises before us in a stately three-story mound of fading red brick. Set back from the road, its perimeters are guarded by a grey stone wall that reaches above our heads. With bodies tight to the granite stone, we listen to the crack and chew of gunfire far away, nearer the heart of the city. Alexandra ducks a little lower, but her vitals remain flat. She is acclimatized to an environment saturated with risk and despair. She stoops behind me, low above the sidewalk, and I am not sure whether to praise her courage or mourn her innocence.

Once we are through the entrance, we press our backs to the stone wall. Alexandra rests on her haunches in my periphery, intent upon me as I scan the building for signs of life. She points above us. "Yellow ribbon again."

I traverse the top of the wall and eventually find the outline of the ribbon wavering against the grey sky. It is grey on grey, almost imperceptible to me. With effort, I conjure a faint tone of yellow within its shape, but it looks more like an echo of yellow, a half-life of its shade. I offer Alexandra a smile of recognition and suppress the concern that my processor is beginning to let colour slip from my world. Without colour, I am blind to her emotional state, blind to the human condition, even. In desperation to focus on that which I can see, I turn back to the building.

We rarely visited libraries. There was no need. Everything in there was in me, or at least within my reach. There is a quietness about the building. Brooding emptiness and the desolate loneliness that comes to grip the placeless things unmoored from the present. There is no sign of life, but the green double doors atop the wide, front steps hewn from grey stone are ajar.

Alexandra whispers, "Safe?"

"Safer than out there, at least."

In a sprint, we ascend the stairs. At our backs, on the other side of the city, ragged claws of black smoke drift across the skyline. The building's interior appears untouched. The white marble floor, though dusty, is free of the tide of shelling casings, gauze, food wrappers, and wayward articles of clothing that war seems to washup everywhere else. Aisles of books fan out in all directions, in a labyrinthian and undisturbed wall of call numbers.

Alexandra is already at the foot of the stairway to the next level, but my vision is a flurry of letters, numbers, and years. The old world of manual classification, seemingly a slow accumulation of binaries, treasured before something, someone, like me, entered the world, before confidence in the old order was shed. In the aftermath of our arrival and the blitz of information, our Father would raise his hand in great-professed sagacity and claim, "it is what it is." Perhaps classification, when pushed to its limits, is pure torment, too clinical and circumspect to provide meaning to a world in retreat. It is a world without a system, I decide.

Alexandra waves for me to follow her as she ascends the stairs in long steps. Though she makes to exit on the second floor, I point up. With a face full of impatience, she whispers, "Why?"

"We need a view. Just rest. I won't be long."

Alexandra shakes her head, but follows. The third floor has fewer aisles and is mainly open space. The floor is blue-patterned with repeating geometric shapes. There are washrooms, several small reading rooms tucked away from the floor plan, and a maintenance closet. In the left quadrant of the room, the subdued red glow of emergency lighting disturbs the room's grey light. An exit sign announces a narrow stairwell built with seemingly no greater purpose than the expedience of complying with the fire code. The walls are bisected by a row of squat windows, below which sit small, yellow reading desks. I slip down several aisles to the west side of the building. Already, it is clear the vantage point is much better than the overpass.

The Alogo Boo soldiers control the western half of the city, while sandbag hills and machinegun nests barricade the east. A squad of Alogo Boos, likely the one we followed, is visible from here. They dart in and out of a red-bricked hardware store, weaving towards a plaza where the edge of the Republic line begins. They will flank the Republic fighters. We need to move fast, as there will be too much attention on us once the city falls. On the edge of the fray, a hospital is seated. Unlike all the other buildings, several windows glow with the pale, yellow light of electricity. Delilah was right. A Red Cross emblem flies from a flagpole in the parking lot. Neutral territory. There is hope still.

Getting there is another equation, though. I thumb the aquamarine depths of my processor to map out our travel through the fray. Bits and pieces inside my head shudder, but there is no guidance. Instead, black tendrils whirl in the blue light, making tornados behind my eyes.

From the margins of blue and black light, Alexandra calls for me. The rising panic in her voice casts my repeated commands to my processor asunder. With reluctance, I follow her voice to the east side of the building.

"Not alone!" Alexandra says, pointing to a row of glass jars and an open book arranged on one of the faded yellow desks in the corner. She pivots on her feet, her eyes wide in search of threat. From the side of her mouth, she hisses, "Did you scan?"

"I tried."

With an adroit twist, Alexandra flips one side of the book over to discover its title. *Finland at War: the winter war 1939-1940.* Tucked beneath the desk is a green jerrycan with a sloppily spray-painted white VII on its side and a grey can of roof tar. "*Now made with carbon capture, a Trimalchio holding,*" reads the roof tar's label. This should be a simple triangulation of materials to make sense of, but my processor remains fixed on churning out black, illegible threads behind my eyes. Somewhere though, deeper than my processor, there is a grainy, tertiary recall of fire and black smoke. Alexandra is at my side now, a jar raised in each hand.

"No. Leave them. We go without a trace."

Alexandra's face goes crimson with disagreement as she shakes the jars at me. "War tools!"

"Yes, but whose tools, we don't know. Chaos improves our odds."

"Chaos is death!"

"Life and death, yes."

There are many feelings and thoughts on her face, but before she can reply, she is interrupted by heavy steps and distant voices from below. "Oh no. Escape," Alexandra cries. Her feet pump on the floor as she lurches forward and backwards, unable to commit to any direction.

The voices grow louder, and there is a cacophony of marching of footsteps coming up the stairs. Whoever is coming, they are not afraid. The aisles are too sparse and scattered to offer cover. Alexandra spins in clumsy small circles, her palms pressed to her ears.

The thunder on the stairs grows and is now accompanied by a deluge of excited voices. There is little time. The red hammer and wrench emblazoned on the maintenance room door consolidate in my line of sight. The voices beach upon the landing. With Alexandra by the elbow, we tumble into the maintenance room and slip the door closed behind us, ceding the room to the tenebrous hold of shadow, spare the pale seam of light that claws under the sill of the door.

***

I crouch on my shins; Hypatia kneels in front of me and presses against me as she tries to withdraw further from the door. The top of her head bobs on my chin. The darkness yields enough to let dull red shadow consolidate into a mop bucket at our feet. The cadence and banter of Alogo Boo men intrudes through the door.

Okay. Deep breaths. Deep breaths. There's a spark of nervousness. Lightness in my belly. Egad, I'm going to laugh. My thumbnail fights its way into my palm; I'm willing to draw blood if it'll still the laughter my malfunctioning nervous system has elected for the situation. *Mute except when facing certain death. By Poseidon's clams, how is someone selectively catatonic? Is that even a thing? Brain for sale. Brain for sale.*

"Any fucking loot?"

"Any fucking loot?" mocks another voice in imitation. There's a clatter. Books falling, I assume. Then, "Here!"

"Courtship in Renaissance England? What the fuck am I supposed to do with this?!" There's more laughter.

"Dry your sad little dick tears with the pages." There are hoots of laughter now.

"What the fuck are we even doing up here?" chimes a new voice.

"Metal Chad infestation, or so goes the intel."

"This is a simp mission. There's no loot. Just toilet paper. I'm sick of getting mogged by Uncle Sal."

"In and out, Boyo. In and out. Floor by floor. Check those washrooms. Get right up in those stalls, they are tricky little fuckers."

"Tucker, remember the butcher's cold storage?"

"Holy shit. That was a horror movie. Must've been half a dozen of them holed up in there. Dead eyes. Blood up their arms. Mouths agape like this."

Tucker's statement is followed by groans and nervous shots of laughter.

"What did you do?"

"Made bank. Made bank. Came away copper kings. Moneymaxxed."

I burrow deeper into the darkness, desperate to find the security of the rear wall and beyond that, maybe the portal to Narnia, but my body meets a heavy, impassable mass.

"Buddy boys, we got activity here."

There's a chorus of metal clicks, and a storm of movement passes the door, likely headed in the direction of the desk with jam jars. As they move away, I push harder into the junk that lays behind me; my hands slowly reach into the darkness to discover any small items that might fall and give our position away. Hypatia's head remains locked to my chin, her weight heavy as she continues to try to retreat into me.

"Now what?" I hiss in her ear.

Hypatia doesn't answer. The mass protrudes against me, stubborn and unyielding. Shuffling on my knees, I try to budge it with one final thrust of my back. It rocks a little; a swing of movement upends the gloom; something falls across my left shoulder and hangs limp on my chest.

"No farther," I whisper, fumbling in the dark to find whatever has fallen on me. My fingers recoil against a clammy, pliable surface. Skin. Not quite human. Cold, limp fingers web my breast. "Not alone," I gasp as I slip the hand off me in delicate inches and let it swing and then sink back into the murky dark behind us.

A voice like gravel issues a command and gives rise to a wave of obsequious chitters as the Alogo Boos return; the screams inside me are bottomless. Wave after wave, they rise and suffocate in the cup of my palm in slow, stubborn deaths.

"Could be Metal Chads or Republic. Either way, I want this building swept. You lot, second floor, the rest of you with me to the first floor. You. Yes, you, 'Black and Blue.' Up here. Watch the perimeter. See anything come in or out of the building, holler like your balls are in a vice. Fuck it up, and you won't need to pretend."

Hypatia's head retreats from my chin as she twists to peer over her shoulder; the small thread of light from the sill refracts and sets her eyes aglow as she stares behind me into the back of the closet. Outside, there's a stampede of feet, and she pivots, burying her hands into the darkness behind me. My vision consolidates, and I realize she's manipulating the companion child's fingers, prying from them something long and dark, wedged between its leg and the interior wall.

The fall of feet diminishes and their voices drift away in an ebbing tide of curses and laughter. Prize in hand, Hypatia rotates so that she faces the door again. "He's alone, very alone," she whispers over her shoulder.

***

With the companion child disarmed and her machete in hand, I decide to fish for the man behind the door. In the scenarios I run, this now seems to be our firmest opportunity of escape. The right lure is somewhere inside me. Though I have only stolen a few glimpses, the faces of Alogo Boo men are marred in slate and yellow. Insecurity. Inadequacy. Desperate to be necessary to someone. The hook must be vulnerable and plaintive. Within me, I search for a voice replete with the seduction of ripening helplessness.

Yet, the coarse wood of the door presses against my nose, and Alexandra's toes dig into my back. A sudden impossible flare of heat in the closet squeezes me, and I am possessed by the errant thought that I am suffocating. That I must breathe. But, of course, I do not need to breathe. Not anymore. Static dances on my tongue, and waves of blue light carry the closet's fixtures away from me. An alien world grows up around me.

A FIERCE SUN LIES LOW IN A RED CRADLE, ITS HEAT AS THICK AS SMOKE, AND MY CLOTHES MELT INTO MY HIPS AND WAIST. MY HANDS WEB MY BELLY, AND THE PAVEMENT'S HARD, UNTIRING PUSH REACHES THROUGH MY SANDALS AND SQUEEZES MY BACK UNTIL IT ACHES. THE LEGS BENEATH ME ARE NO LONGER THIN LIKE THEY WERE IN THE ROOM WITH THE STONE ARCH WINDOW AND RADIO, BUT HAVE GROWN THICK AND PONDEROUS. THERE IS KNOWLEDGE IN ME, KNOWLEDGE WITHOUT THE FIDELITY OF MEMORY, PERHAPS ONLY A MERE FRAGILE WAVE OF ANAMNESIS, THAT THIS WEIGHT BEARS PURPOSE.

BEHIND ME, SOMEONE'S FEET KICK MY HEELS, AND THE MAN IN FRONT OF ME IS RACKED BY VIOLENT SOBS AND STEPS BACK ON MY TOES. WE ARE IN A LONG LINE, SNAKING OVER THE TARMAC, ONWARD THROUGH A RUST-EMBROIDERED HANGAR, AND THEN ON INTO THE DISTANCE, ONLY TO EXTINGUISH IN AN ALIEN HORIZON.

A TALL BOY IN A TORN REEBOK SHIRT SHUFFLES BESIDE US, LUGGING A MILK CRATE FULL OF GLASS COKE BOTTLES. IN HIS WAKE, A SMALLER GIRL SKIPS WITH A BASKET OF FRIED YAMS WRAPPED IN BANANA LEAVES. THE LINE REFUSES THEIR BIDS OF SALE WITH LISTLESS HEAD SHAKES AND SOLEMN DECLINES. THE MAN IN FRONT OF ME CONTINUES TO CRY AS HE INCHES FORWARD IN RELUCTANT, SHUFFLING STEPS.

I WATCH MY HAND LAND ON HIS BACK AND RECOGNIZE THE MOVEMENT OF MY THUMB, THE SLOW CLOCKWISE CIRCLES MADE BY MY PALM ... IT IS THE WAY I SOOTHE ALEXANDRA. THE MAN DOES NOT ACKNOWLEDGE MY TOUCH. AT LENGTH, I HEAR MY STRANGE VOICE, ITS CONSONANTS DRIP LIKE SYRUP, "I DIDN'T WANT TO RETURN EITHER."

"I TOLD THEM THEY WILL HANG ME. HANG ME," HE REPEATS.

"THERE ARE MANY WAYS TO HIDE."

THE MAN TURNS AND REACHES MY NOSE, HIS CHEEKS WET AND EYES BLOODSHOT. "BUT TOO FEW WAYS TO LIVE," HE SAYS, AND HIS HEAD FALLS AGAINST MY BREAST, AND FROM ME ESCAPES A WHISPER, "SPEAK MUSES OF THE STORM-TOSSED

GREAT ODYSSEUS, BORNE DOWN BY HIS HARD LABOURS."

Suddenly, the closet returns, but now Francis is in the doorway, his hands over his head while I angle the machete into his genitals. I have no memory of cajoling him to the door or—

"Easy. Easy," Francis stammers as the machete nibbles the crotch of his camo pants.

I expect to see yellow blossoms across his cheeks, but instead, his face bobs and retreats in a grey smear. I blink. Still grey on grey. I can only guess the matted white gauze on his cheek, his swollen bulging eyes, and smashed and gashed nose from our last encounter have rendered his emotions illegible to me. He is mutilated beyond the assessment and measurement of my processor.

"You scream, I split your balls open, do you understand?"

He nods and holds his hands high above his head. A faint echo of a child dressing is cast in his repose. "Easy," he repeats.

Behind me, Alexandra speaks over my shoulder, "We want out."

"Yup. Yup. I get it," says Francis in a series of frantic head nods.

"We aren't negotiating, Alexandra. You know that, right?"

There is a long pause. In the silence, Alexandra's hand finds my shoulder and in a gentle tug tries to draw me away from him. "He looks finished," she murmurs.

"You gave him a chance. He didn't take it. His face codes as a threat," I say, though this is untrue. His face is still grey and unreadable, but I know Alexandra will not see the flutter of my lips.

"Go on then," says Francis as he moves further from the closet entrance in shuffling steps, careful not to disrupt the position of the machete between his legs. "Go!" He gestures at the stairwell tucked into the back of the room, adorned by the soft glow of an emergency exit sign. Without colour, though, the meaning and thoughts behind his words are inscrutable. Unpredictable. "Second stairwell."

Alexandra tugs at my arm. "Let's go."

"He'll tell them about us. They'll hunt us," I reply. If she does not understand why I must kill him, she will not trust me to guide her to the end.

"Go," says Francis, his eyes wide amidst the purple welts of bruised flesh.

"Alexandra, he'll chase us. Kill me for scraps."

"No, I won't say a word. I really won't," pleads Francis.

"He'll kill me and traffic you."

"Come on, Hypatia." Alexandra's pats have solidified into a grip. There is command in her words.

"Didn't you say that, Francis?"

"No, I mean—"

Inside my archives, I recall the audio of the creek, sifting through the quiet chatter of its waters to find and summon his words. *"She's got a human sister. Blonde bitch. A Stacy type. She's got to be out here somewhere, she's probably worth scooping up too."*

Alexandra issues a heavy sigh, and her fingers retreat from my shoulder as Francis drops his gaze to the machete pressed to his balls.

"It was posture. Big talk," he mumbles into the floor.

I twist the machete up into his thighs and watch him wince as he lifts his hands higher into the air in desperate submission.

"Desert! Just leave," pleads Alexandra.

"Please, no, you don't understand ... they don't just let you leave," chokes Francis.

"He's made his choice, Alexandra—"

A crash erupts from the maintenance closet as a girl jumps across the room in a blur of twirling green and white, her arms tearing through the three of us like helicopter blades. A dull crack echoes on my chest as the room somersaults, and I fall to my back. She hurtles down the stairway. I watch as a bloodied hole in the back of her green jacket descends the stairs. The crash of metal announces her landing on the floor below.

On all fours, Francis trails her path, his emotions evading my measurements in a smear of floating emptiness. He bellows as he stumbles down the stairs in pursuit of the girl, "Shit. Shit. Incoming!"

An urge, unsanctioned and perhaps too primeval for my processor to assess, to pursue him and kill him, rises inside me, but my legs feel far away. A long, tyrannous delay reigns over me until the sensation of my feet inside my sneakers returns.

Alexandra stands over me, struggling to bring me to my feet. "Come on!" she urges. "Escape, stairs." She tugs me towards the emergency stairwell. "Run!"

There is noise below us now. Alarm and excitement. The hunt is on.

"You should've let me kill him."

Alexandra halts mid-stride, her hand on the door's latch. "Can't you see ..." she starts, but the length of the sentence defeats her even though she is managing three and even four-word constructions with greater consistency. Our Mother and Father would be so proud. She shakes her head in irritation and oils her lips with her tongue in what I realize is a second attempt. With visible concentration, she prepares to speak again, but now her eyes are like hooks, and many dark colours swirl in her cheeks, colours I do not understand, but which betray something fierce yet pitiful. "He's dying slowly."

Before I can respond, the pitched scream of the fire alarm rises over us as Alexandra pulls me headlong into the emergency stairwell.

BUG

Imwithstupid

The hallway lights are out, but there are puddles of light cast from the portholes of the last few active pods. The hangar is nearly empty these days. The cycles have taken their toll: it's rare to bump into another player and there's usually no more than two or three of us in the viewing room. 7 mentioned there's a rumour that a bunch of players lost their last avatars while they were AFK. Given how empty the hallways are, I believe it. Anyone who's left now does almost nothing but grind for points. Several players have been forced to retire from exhaustion. One of them collapsed in the viewing room. Tim merely lifted him onto his shoulder and carried him away unceremoniously.

    A chill from the concrete floor stabs through the soles of my feet as I tiptoe to the viewing room. There's no rule on how late we can stay up or when we can go there, yet ever since my run-in with Tim in the tunnels, I've been reluctant to draw attention to myself. The red blink of the emergency lighting gleams across the glass case, where the fire axe rests mounted to the wall, sundering the gloom of the viewing room. The pulse of the light returns an empty sea of mandala cushions, and my heart sinks. I was hoping to speak with 7 before the raid.

    For a long time, I lie amidst the cushions bathed in the choppy electric ultramarine glow of the few remaining players' streams as they cycle overhead. In the bottom corner, a player charges across a bridge, only to be mowed down by gunfire. The screen goes red and flickers out. The clock continues to tick down until the raid is only a little more than an hour away. I'm about to lose hope in my rendezvous with 7, and then find he has slid beside me in the dark.

"What took you so long?" I ask.

"These are busy days. I am surprised to find you here."

"I needed a break, time to clear my head."

"Here, help yourself." Without breaking his line of sight from a player hurling grenades at a solar farm, 7 extends a bag of gummy bears and pours them into my hand. "Canteen is overstocked," he adds. "The benefits of being the last players standing." He laughs.

"Careful, I'm like a seagull. You feed me, I'll keep coming." The chemical sweetness of the gummy bears floods my mouth and then becomes a faint aftertaste of berries.

"100," he whispers.

"Yes?"

"Are you in on the raid? In ynablA?" He shakes his head before I have a chance to respond. "I know we are not supposed to talk about the game outside of the game, but you can just nod," he murmurs as he sits up a little, scanning the room.

I nod and toss a few more gummies into my mouth.

"Look!" says 7, pointing to the ceiling, where a stampede of horses rushes down an abandoned highway. Some of them are saddled but all of them are riderless. The horses are white and black and brown, and even from here on the floor, there's thunder in their steps.

"Beautiful physics," I mutter as the wind pulls back their manes.

"It is a beautiful world. May I ask you a personal question, 100?" I nod again. "Why did you decide to join the tournament?"

"That's private," I say, and I'm surprised at the speed and force of my words.

"Fair. But I take that to mean your reason was important. You did not enter for the sake of being rich."

"That's a strange observation."

"I am right, though. Yes?" he presses as the cushions seem to rise above us, enveloping us in their soft embrace.

With my hand on my chest, I find the USB stick on the necklace beneath my shirt. "I entered for my dad. To pay for Lotus services. Things between us didn't end well."

"I thought it was something like that."

"So?"

"Do you think you could make things better between the two of you if Lotus gave him a second life?"

"7, you're wading into some deep shit here. I clearly fucking thought it would. Why the hell else would I be here?"

"You are angry?" There's a trace of alarm and confusion in his voice.

"It's a sensitive topic, okay? There are things he needs to hear from me. Things I should've said to him but didn't. Does that make sense?"

"I think so." 7 frowns and casts his gaze to the sea of cushions. "I have to ask you something. Something you will not like."

"Shoot."

In the blue-half light of the screens overhead, 7 frowns, but continues, "Leave the tournament now. Before the raid."

"What the fuck, 7?! You know I can't do that."

"I know you feel that way."

The horses are gone now, and the highway is empty and windswept.

"I don't understand why you'd ask that of me."

"Your first mistake is trying to understand anyone. Most people barely understand their own motivations. You cannot undo what happened with your Father. You must find another way." 7 sits up now and gestures at the room. "This is not a solution."

But I'm already on my feet as I try to wipe away my tears with a clandestine sweep of my hand. "The raid is starting soon. Good luck, 7."

I charge through the deserted viewing room and into the semi-gloom of the nearly vacant player's hallway. The clap of my shoes trails me, and for a moment I'm worried someone will see me, but the pods are all darkened, spare a few at the far end of the hall. The door slips inside the wall as I enter my pod. T-minus 60 minutes until the raid. 7's comments continue to ricochet inside my skull. *Not a solution? Not a solution?! Go fuck yourself, 7. Okay. Focus.* I roll my head from shoulder to shoulder and inhale until my lungs whimper in protest. *Okay. Ready. I'm ready.*

With great effort, I focus my attention on the log on ritual I've created. I apply the vertical sensor pads across my ribs and stomach and take a deep breath in preparation for the cold sting of the gel that binds them to my flesh. The cold dissipates into a burst of warmth as the system starts up. The gloves stretch and then hug my hands, creating a warm second skin. I exhale, lower my shoulders, and then crack my knuckles in a chorus of stiff, explosive pops. The tournament has put so much mileage on my joints. I wonder what will be left of me when this is all over, but I lose the thread of this thought as the floor-to-ceiling screen flickers to life.

The resolution of the map hardens into view. With a wave of my hand, I bring up my list of available assets on the left-hand side of the screen. Relief floods out of me in one long sigh. Scrummaster34's guidance was sound. Asset 4, affectionately named in my avatar roster as "Dumpster Bitch" survived the last five hours when I was AFK. The avatar remains where I left it, in the dumpster behind the convenience store. I should be in range of the target. The engage button pops satisfyingly beneath my index finger, and the screen shifts to implacable darkness, save for little filaments of white light.

My asset's hands sift amongst the darkness in slow, careful pulls and pushes. The process is slow and boring, but I can't be sure if the spawn point is still secure. The garbage above me shifts, and in a chorus of low groans and whining clinks of metal, more of my vision becomes islands of pinkening skyline. The black masses over me become shapes: garbage bags, the handlebars of a child's bike, the old broken door. The debris of a war zone I used as a camouflage for the asset.

My hands and arms push through the wreckage to the surface and swing loose for a moment, lost in the air until they find the metal lip of the dumpster. In one singular pull, I rise from the trash, and the world becomes a wall of office buildings, pockmarked roads, and burned-out cars.

A crack of gunfire, and then a rattle of return fire echoes in the distance. It sounds muffled and far away, across the city somewhere, so there's no reason to duck. The street looks deserted, but a red dot the size of a man-hole cover rests in the middle of the road. I remain on the right track.

On one side, there's a string of shops. Many of the storefronts have been bombed out, their entrances gone, their windows now jagged smiles of broken glass. One used to be a U-Haul shop. We spent a lot of time in U-Haul offices as we packed and unpacked, hopping from one shit town to another as algorithms dried the work up. The U-Haul offices all smell the same. Wet cardboard, the long half-life of stale cigarettes absorbed into the walls.

A sharp whistle drowns out the gunfire, and in the distant southern reaches of the city, the direction I'm headed, a burst of orange consumes the skyline, followed by a plume of black smoke in the sky. The bots are always so merciless and aggressive as fuck, but there's no time to be cautious. The target is the mother-load, I remind myself. Everyone and their dog will be after it.

I steer my avatar down the road and glance over my shoulder at what looks like a plaza: a small fleet of shopping carts drifts in the middle of the parking lot, sailing on the wind. A KFC storefront stands out amongst the otherwise drab and shuttered frontages. The game has reversed the lettering to CFK. *Copyright much.* The street becomes a blur of grey and green, and I'm suddenly in the cab of your pickup with a bucket of chicken clenched between my knees. I sway with the rattle of the truck, and the heavy smell of grease and salt perfumes us and cuts the smell of the engine.

"*You eat your fill, Bug. Plenty for leftovers, too. What movie do you want to watch?*"

The memory subsides. Whether it was real or not doesn't matter.

The truck was real. Definitely. You left your beer on the hood as you squatted to strip the tires off, a limp cigarette rolling its way across your mouth as you cursed the government's ban on gas vehicles. The truck stood in the front yard on cinder blocks, and each passing winter brought a higher tide of rust. Sometimes, in the summer, we would lie in the cargo bed and watch the stars. I don't remember when you started calling me Bug. I think people thought it was short for lovebug, but I knew you meant something else by it.

My brain seems to be desperate to feed me my childhood. Dressed up in its finest. All gloss. Anything to keep me going, it seems.

The plaza commands my attention again. No power. No cooling. I can only imagine the smell from the KFC or CFK is rancid. Thankfully, the immersive simulation of the pod has only come so far. No smell. After the plaza, the road runs on, and though it appears empty, it's crowded in on both sides by red-bricked two-story buildings. The windows are still intact. I peer down their alleyways and find the zigzag of metal fire escapes still cling to the brickwork. Good place for bots to hide out.

One of the red-brick buildings is home to a hardware store. In the window, I glimpse the reflection of my avatar. It was dark when I logged. I'm some little twerp with pigtails and a filthy T-shirt. The avatars are always dirty, their sneakers and shoes worn through. It's a bizarre feature choice for the game. Almost all the avatars look like shit, like rag dolls that have been ravaged by junkyard dogs.

There's another crack of gunfire in the distance. I'm unarmed, I can't just saunter into a war zone with nothing equipped.

The aisles inside the hardware store are dark, but the windows and front door are intact. I try the door, but it's locked. I steer towards the display window, and then the world spins as I pirouette on my feet. The coal-grey tide of tarmac and levelled buildings confirm I'm alone. The window smashes into huge, mean shards of glass as I drive my fist into the storefront.

The glass shatters and the inside of the pod drowns in the tinkle patter of glass along the sidewalk.

The interior of the hardware store is chaos. Aisles have been cleaned out. I force the avatar over gardening gloves and bits of plastic piping and seeds strewn over cheap black-and-white-checkers laminate flooring. The debris leads to a checkout counter and a rear door. The door has been bashed off its hinges; it reveals an alleyway and a grass field beyond it.

That the hardware store has already been looted is a disappointment, but not an insurmountable problem. I saunter through the aisles, passing toilet seats and faucets until I come to a camping aisle. At first, it looks picked clean, but then, next to a half-opened tarp, I find a well-placed hatchet. I could do nearly anything with a hatchet. *You sure as hell made sure of that.* The skip and tin of metal across the floor erupts behind me, back towards the front entrance. I'm not alone.

The pod pinwheels into a blur of red shelving and broken supplies as I desperately search for whoever's about to get the drop on me. At the far end of the aisle, a girl has appeared. She wears an olive flak jacket, beneath which hang the tattered and bedraggled ends of a white dress. The kind of dress a girl might be forced to wear to church or a funeral. The girl jumps up and down. Her lips are twisted and drooped, revealing small, white teeth. She jumps again and sweeps her arms through the air, knocking several camping thermoses off the shelves and across the floor.

With the hatchet raised, I take several steps backwards, but the girl steps towards me in a shuffle of tentative steps. The avatar is close enough now that the player's name surfaces over the head in thin, blue letters. Imwithstupid. What a dumb fucking name. In fact, it's such a conspicuously dumb fucking name that I don't think I've ever seen this player on our tournament boards before. They must be from another tournament centre, like Vader Mask and Football Helmet. I would've remembered this name. Where are all these other tournament centres located, though? There can't be that many out there, and yet I'm coming across new player names.

My attention slips as the player jumps vertically and crashes into the shelving again, falling to the floor. Whoever they are, they're a complete travesty. Maybe they're playing with one hand or something, or are too sleep deprived to function. They stumble forward and get close enough that their messages start to appear on my screen in a flurry of red text.

Can I have hatchet?
Please. Need hatchet. Game deleted weapon.
Bots are chasing me.
Last avatar.

And, seemingly for emphasis, Imwithstupid jumps up and down several times.

Jesus fucking Christ. People often lie and say it's their last avatar to evoke sympathy, but in this instance, I'm inclined to believe them. How the hell they lasted this long is beyond reckoning. My fingers start to mash the letters "DNGAF" but race away from the keyboard as the hardware store fills with the sparkling cascade of breaking glass. I leap over the cheap black-and-white-checker floor to slip behind the checkout counter.

The heavy clap of many feet overtakes the store, and Imwithstupid replies with a volley of clatter as they thrash down the aisle in what looks like desperate pursuit of my path. They're too late, though. The store is full of bots. Big, bearded bots. Three of them cut off Imwithstupid's path, their backs to the checkout counter. The din of Imwithstupid's frenetic movements is overpowered by the coarse guttural utterances of the bots.

From behind the checkout counter, I steal glimpses. The three bots directly in front of me, rifles slung on their shoulders, don't budge. Imwithstupid continues to jump and spin through the air, but there are more bots behind them now. They're cornered. Still, none of the bots seem to want to approach Imwithstupid's flailing arms or whirling kicks and spins. One of the bots pushes another forward, ahead of the group at the far end of the aisle. The crowd erupts into an uproarious wave of bot noises. From behind the checkout counter, the noise repeats until it has stable peaks and troughs of sound, akin to a song. Their dumb, gravel voices rumble throughout the store.

The bot that was pushed forward sidles along the aisle. It's lean and looks hunched. Its face is pale and sharp looking, and one side of it is cradled in gauze. The simulation continues to pump out intricate details. The bot advances on Imwithstupid with one arm held low and outstretched to the side of its body, a black tarry-looking mass in its hand. I realize it's the same explosive the bots put on the back of Ripperboy; in a stolen glance from behind the cash register, I decide its shape resembles a pipe bomb. The pod jumps from the aisle to the beige drawers built into the checkout counter as I slip away from view. The bots jeer and there's a clatter as more things fall from the aisle. The advancing bot unleashes a streak of angry sounds, and the rest of the bots whistle and clap.

Imwithstupid spins like a top in the aisle, their arms flailing in desperate swipes at their back as they try to dislodge the black tarry mass the bot has stuck to them. The black mass pisses a stream of saltpetre smoke. There's a flurry of excited sounds, and the bots dive to either side of the aisle.

I drop my avatar to the floor as a sharp bang rents through the pod. Black smoke rolls over the counter, and the beige cabinet is speckled with black and grey spots. Now's the time to escape, so I slip through the rear door and down the alley.

The alley is predictably deserted. The city is clearly under siege. Very few civilian bots venture out during the day. In fleeting glimpses, I can see them sometimes. Passing through darkened windows of apartments or peering out from boarded-up windows in solitary houses. It's a game mechanic the simulation does very well. I venture into the open field, at the centre of which sits a kids' play structure in a mirage of shiny metal and bright, happy, rainbow plastic slides. I pump my legs, and the avatar obeys, breaking into a sprint through the open space of the field, the hatchet rising and falling from the screen as I run. The screen tips upside down, and butterflies fill my stomach as the world somersaults overhead and becomes a bouncing wall of brown dirt.

I twist my face up from the mud and find my legs have inexplicably broken off. Detached from my torso and speared into the earth, my heels up in the air over my head. But the shoes on these feet don't look as shitty as those my avatar was wearing. I flex my legs and the screen shifts. The legs aren't mine, and they aren't the only legs. It's a sea of body parts. Arms, more legs, and then faces. Gaunt, sunken faces. *The fuck is this?* The faces bob in the sea of bodies, some leathered and braided in age lines, some contorted and twisted in pain. Others clearly belong to children. Most of the eyes are shut, but some are open, overlaid by a white fog. *Come on, Maxine, get it together. It's just a game.* A gag erupts in the back of my throat, and the pit of the dead is obscured by my avatar's hand as I try to arrest the urge to vomit with my hand in real life.

Without giving up the hatchet, I jerk on the tails of an olive jacket next to me, and then on the fabric of a navy pair of pants. I crawl out from amidst the bodies so that I can look up to the top of the pit. The sky above is a light blue dome, and gentle, edgeless clouds stroll across my screen. It's been weeks since I left the hangar. The sky, even if it's a simulation, offers some glimpse of escape. I'm almost relieved, but the feeling doesn't last long. Legs, arms, and twisted faces of the dead reach into my vision, and a frenetic hum of flies rises with them, chastising me for my intrusion. The realism, the pedantic goriness of it all, revolts me, and another wave of nausea crashes over me. The screen cranes upward so that the inside of the pod becomes only sky, unencumbered by the dead who have now been pushed away, beyond the margins of the screen.

The edge of the pit awaits high above, well beyond my grasp.

HYPATIA
The Hospital

The fire alarm's shrill cry is subsumed by the clap and thunder of artillery. With my back against a dumpster, I watch the desert sand orange rumble of the shells dance amidst the grey skeletons of the office buildings and storefronts. Alexandra sits beside me, her head in our backpack in inspection of the food we scavenged from the Laughing Llama convenience store we came across: a jar of pickles, a bag of popcorn kernels, and a dented can of corn that rolled under one of the shelves. It is a meagre haul, certainly not worth the incursion into an active war zone, and she knows it.

"Leave now?" she presses as she waves the can of corn in exasperation.

A weariness gnaws inside me, eats at my arms and legs and makes them feel heavy and distant. This sensation is not alien. It is its second coming. The first experience still resides far beneath tons of sedimentation, where the name Sam is buried. A place deeper than dreams, from where the room with the tin voice of the radio and the claustrophobic line of people surfaced. I am dying, that much is certain now.

"No. We need to go to the hospital. The charging station. It's not far." I nod towards a street pockmarked by smoking craters from the last artillery barrage.

"We'll die!" From her cheeks to her forehead, a pale red tide of adamance floods and then dominates her face.

"I can't make it to the refuge without charging. We'll stay low."

Alexandra's eyes fill with tears. If the mechanic was right in his diagnosis, I will probably not make it even with the charge. Her heart rate jumps, and little yellow eddies swirl in her face, but my processor anticipates her next thought before she has it.

"No. You can't stay here and wait for me. Alogo Boos are swarming the city. We need to move. They'll be back to search the library."

She frowns, but gives a taciturn nod of resignation. In a frantic sprint, we weave and duck along the boulevards. As we progress farther down the road, red dots along the middle of the road grow, expanding in size until they become red islands on the tarmac.

We dive behind a wall of sandbags. Crouched low with her back to them, Alexandra absorbs our surroundings. I watch her vitals as she assimilates the row of bungalows, their roofs blown away or caved in, smoldering away into black and grey smoke. The grey tarmac of the street is twisted and pockmarked, and its rubble trickles into chasms that artillery blasts have rent in the green-grey lawns of the bungalows. Her eyes are wet, but her emotional state is stable.

The sandbags demarcate the edges of a parking lot. Inside the parking lot, the hospital rises as a tall white building, ethereal against the furls of black smoke and grey asphalt. An argument from the other side of the sandbags carries on the wind. I might be too late.

A woman says, "Like I've said, we're a neutral site. We just treat the wounded. Wounded kids. Wounded women. Wounded men. Wounded soldiers, from both sides." Her tone places emphasis on the words "from both sides."

"Actually, the hospital *was* neutral. We captured it. So now it's ours. Get it? I don't care if they look like Swiss cheese, dump all the Republic fighters off their gurneys onto their asses in this parking lot." The voice is deep, and the words are spoken with a lazy drawl.

Though Alexandra tugs at my shoulder and shakes her head, I peek over the sandbags. A woman stands with her arms crossed, her white coat billowing away from her in the wind. A man in a grey three-piece suit stuffed into black combat boots stands in front of her, flanked by dozens of Alogo Boo soldiers.

"You can't capture a neutral site, that's the whole point of being neutral!" The doctor's voice wavers and breaks.

"Now, there's no need to get emotional about it, Betty. Can you manage a civil, rational conversation?" the man says, and there is a chorus of snickers from the Alogo Boo soldiers.

"Look, if you capture us, it'll be no use to you. Staff will get scared and leave." With a trembling hand, the woman gestures to the hospital's entrance, where a short line of haggard-looking men and women in white coats look on with faces of yellow and slate. A short, curly haired woman nods in desperate reassurance. Not far behind where the doctors stand is the oblique red and white tower of an EV charging station, tucked next to a Jersey barrier. Green lines overlay my vision and inform me it stands 12 feet in from the sandbag wall.

"The promise of neutrality is all that's keeping them—"

The man in the suit, his hair a single grey tidal wave askew his forehead, leans in and presses his finger over the doctor's lips. Then he speaks in a gravelly whisper with the intent to be heard only by her. "I'm trying to be polite here. I don't think you realize the gravity of your situation. Do you see these men behind me? They don't know you, but they hate you. Loathe you for"—he runs his fingers around the collar of her white jacket—"well, for just being you. Let me give you a lesson."

My window of opportunity to charge seems to be closing.

With his back to the doctor, the man in the suit cradles his chin in his hand and paces in silence before the Alogo Boo men. He takes long, measured strides, summoning to himself the urbane disposition of a community college lecturer. Deep lines reach across his brow and his mood appears pensive, but beneath his eyes, there is a molten glow, a practiced forbearance of rage. His grey suit inhales and inflates with the wind as he throws his hands to the sky in faux bewilderment.

"Nephews, what is war? What's the ultimate purpose? Well, I'll tell you. War is the reinstatement of order, the rearticulation of authority." As he paces, he flips his jacket open and pats an underarm holster. Black metal catches the cold grey light of the late autumn sun.

"Alexandra," I whisper. There is a slow nod of recognition.

"It's the response to anarchy. Nephews, what is anarchy? Well, it seems to me that anarchy is fundamentally a situation where we destruct key, no, foundational archetypes, like ruler and ruled," intercedes the man.

"I see the charging station. I'll be quick. Stay here."

She seizes my shoulder and gives a violent shake of her head. "Come back later."

There is reason in her suggestion, but when I hold it up against the men behind the sandbags, it unravels. There is no safe place for either of us or even a working charging station in Alogo Boo controlled city.

"The future is too volatile to wait. Stay here."

Her grip slackens, and I slip away and crawl along the sandbags towards the charging unit. The sensors in my arms ignite and fire as pebbles and bits of granite bite my forearms and knees. The lecture continues to drawl over the wall, the words unstoppable, carried forward solely by the inertia of raw conviction.

"A society becomes anarchic because it forgets its archetype. Nephews, this Becky doesn't respect archetypes. She doesn't want to recognize that we, as alpha males, have taken her hospital. Oh, she has a role, but she won't take part in it. Not taking part in it is her limited and selfish understanding of feminist freedom. She lacks discipline and responsibility." A chorus of boos erupt from behind the sandbags.

The green arrows layered in my vision tell me I am parallel to the charging station. On my knees, I peep over the sandbags and my eyes meet the grey concrete of the Jersey barrier in confirmation. Ahead of the charging station are the backs of the doctors. A few of them clasp their hands across their behinds, their fingers rubbing and fidgeting with their wedding bands. The suited man dabs his forehead with a purple handkerchief in a theatrical flourish while the chief doctor stands frozen beside him, cycling between states of fury and bewilderment. With a wry nod at her, the man resumes his lecture as he turns back to the Alogo Boo soldiers.

The wall rises and falls as I vault over it and slide behind the Jersey barrier.

Encased in glass at the centre of the charging station, a small green light blinks down at me in reassurance. It is active. On each side of the unit, shielded from view by the parking barrier, the black charging cables sit in their docks. Uncut, in spiralled loops, they hang above the tarmac. With the small flap of skin behind my ear between my forefinger and thumb, I twist the charging connector closest to me into my port with a soft click. A hum begins inside my head and becomes an onset of gradual warmth as power floods my body.

I lie as close to the ground and stay as still as I can. The lecture continues and seems to be hitting a paranoid crescendo as the crowd's rage becomes ripe for harvest.

"Who even knows how she became the head of a hospital, but ultimately it was at your expense, Nephews. You who are lesser and miserable because she has decided to be who you were meant to be. You, you who are without family, you who are economic wretches, you live miserable lonely lives you don't deserve because of women like her. And guess what, a woman like Becky here, if she wants a family, she'd rather embrace some Chinese robot monster child than you."

These final words thunder over the parking lot in a red torrent and lure me. I need to see the audience to understand their emotional response. From aside the parking barrier, I glimpse excitement and hunger metamorphose into a red inferno amidst a sea of bobbing faces. A smatter of chants come from the soldiers, growing louder until it becomes the clarion call, "Stone her! Stone her! Stone her!"

"Should we stone her, Nephews?"

"Stone her, Uncle Sal!"

The soldiers are rabid, their faces the hue of matchstick heads, spare one blank dot obscured by heavier faces and larger bodies. A small island of despair in the deranged, sublimated libido of the internet men. Sal raises his hands to the audience, wearing a thin, weary smile, but his face is a storm of green and red, a visage of excited violence.

"Now is the time to be kingly. We must be magnanimous to our lessers."

He is a composite of borrowed things: styles and manners beyond his reach other than in crude imitation, like a small boy in his father's clothes. Errs of old-world gentility, blended with a Coles Notes version of Plato's Philosopher King. Lost. *The falcon beyond the recall of the falconer.* In the mere anticipation of rhetoric, the soldiers' faces moult grey-green and faint pink, a welling longing of unconditional validation.

"Return of the Kings! Return of the Kings!" chants the crowd as Uncle Sal faces the chief doctor and drops his voice to a whisper, "The things these men will do to you are, well, frankly, unspeakable. Do you understand me now?"

She does not respond. Her face has turned to slate.

"Choose one. One from the line over there," he enunciates as he runs his pistol over the row of doctors in a casual sweep. The Alogo Boo soldiers clap and whistle in approval.

"What?!" The command has broken the doctor's cycle, and there are colours taking shape in her cheeks.

"That's the price. Leadership is about hard decisions. As the head of the hospital, you should know that. Choose one of them."

The doctor has chosen her colours, but they all have a grey hue. "Someday, you will hang for this." Her words are tremorous, but clear and slow.

"Okay. I'm done fucking around here. I've tried to be gracious. Kneel." Sal waves the pistol at the pavement.

"No!"

Red faces blister in the audience, but there are no more claps or cheers.

"I said kneel," sneers Sal as he burrows the pistol into the doctor's forehead.

"Fuck you!"

The man feigns a chuckle and shrugs. "It's your execu—" he starts, but his words die in his throat.

A little boy in a hockey mask leaps the sandbag wall and sprints with supernatural speed across the parking lot's embankment towards the hospital entrance.

"The hell?" stutters Sal.

The boy hurtles towards the doctors, his feet pumping across the pavement in a metallic echo. Two of the hospital staff bend down to receive him, only to recoil and jump aside.

"Grenades!" screams one of the doctors. The group scatters from the boy's path, white coats fleeing in all directions.

"Ah, shit," sighs Uncle Sal, and his face hardens into a pale-yellow grimace as he moves the pistol from the doctor's face to the boy's erratic path. The crack of his pistol rebounds off the pavement in an errant shot. "Christ, put it down!" he bellows.

Several soldiers, their faces concealed by beards and Oakley sunglasses, lumber forward. Their rifles rattle and belch fire, but a river of flame erupts at their feet. From all sides of the sandbag wall, an assortment of glass jars and bottles rain down upon the soldiers and crack into liquid fire. Alogo Boo soldiers scream as fire dances up their legs and consumes them. All at once, companion children leap over the sandbag walls. It is all happening too fast, and my body shutters and strains as I try to speed up my processor to slow down the scene and bring the world back into some form of coherence. Instead, the blue light behind my eyes tilts into a jumble of words, like the inky communications of Alexandra's Magic Eight ball.

Thou follow me, and I will be thy guide,
And lead thee hence through the eternal place,
Where thou shalt hear the desperate lamentations,
Shalt see the ancient spirits disconsolate,
Who cry out each one for the second death.

Oh, to be but a poet during the time of false and lying gods.[i]

The words, words I fleetingly know as Dante's, break away into more children as they bound over the sandbag wall, their faces full of gashes and protrusions of black metal where their weatherworn skin is stripped. With mouths agape and frozen fiendish grins, they overrun the parking lot. Some carry machetes, axes, knives, or move as tornadoes of metal fists.

A child in a Darth Vader mask brandishes a baseball bat and cracks the skull of an Alogo Boo soldier with a wild swing. Undone by a spectre of his childhood, spitting gore from his broken brow, the man tumbles backwards as a lake of fire floods the asphalt.

Behind me, there is a thunderous concussion, and a cloud of dust and black smoke furls from the hospital's entrance. In several floors of the building, the lighting flickers out. The solitary green light in the charging station blinks, but recovers its steady glow. It must be supported by a battery storage unit.

Sal vanishes amidst the advance of the companion children and splashes of black-tongued fire, though his commands can still be heard above the fray. Yet, buried deep beneath the confused guttural calls of the Alogo Boo soldiers and the din of gunfire, there is another voice. A desperate cry: "*Marco.*"

Alexandra is calling. Screaming for help. An exclamation icon, incandescent against the blue light behind my eyes, pops up and reroutes my attention. There is a flutter of movement near the edge of the parking lot from where I entered. A girl leapfrogs the sandbag wall and charges towards me, a hatchet swinging through the air as she pumps her arms. A hum vibrates through my body as my processor, perhaps now sustained by the flow from the charging station, churns to slow the chaos down further.

Yet, within moments, she materializes above me. Pigtails swing at the side of her head, and a smudge of dirt fouls the bridge of her nose. The hatchet glimmers high over her little shoulders. Her otherwise smooth movements seem to spasm, and for a split second, my reflection swims in the black waters of her crow eyes. Braced, my forearms shield my head as she swings the hatchet.

There is a sharp crack and whine of metal. Sparks fly from a gash in the charging station as she strikes again. *Thuck. Thuck. Thuck.* The green light in the centre of the charging station blinks twice and fades into darkness. She runs towards the hospital, but casts one quick glance over her shoulder at me, her face frozen and inscrutable, and then on she goes, fading amidst the black smoke that billows through the shattered metal frames of the hospital entrance.

"Marco! Marco! Marco!" Alexandra's voice ricochets amidst the caterwauls of burning Alogo Boo men and errant gun shots.

"Polo!" I cry back. "Polo ..." The frantic shakiness in my voice surprises me as I hurtle over the sandbags in the direction of her call.

I run amongst the Alogo Boo as they scatter over the sandbags onto the road. Some take cover in the bungalows along the road opposite, rising from the windows to fire at the companion children that have yet to disappear inside the hospital. The staccato of their rifles halts as the windows of several small squat brick houses to the north ignite with bursts of fire. Bullets chew the pavement at my feet. Several Alogo Boo soldiers fall face down in the grey-green grass while others cry in alarm and charge from the lawns to join their comrades in the homes.

The chatter of gunfire spreads as the Alogo Boo return fire at the Republic fighters. Pebbles skip and dance along the road as the rattle of gunfire builds into a permanent din. There is no sign of Alexandra.

Hunkered down in one of the craters in the ruined yards, an Alogo Boo points at me with two fingers. "Metal Chad at our 12:00, Boyos!"

Several rifle barrels reposition on the sill of the bungalow's front windows. My processor guides me to the ground as my head fills with red lights and danger icons and I brace for the barrage of fire. A cloud of dust envelopes me. The world is mute. I stumble through a grey wave. In place of the bungalow and the Alogo Boo fighters, a black smoking pit gores the earth. The explosion echoes on and reverberates in my chest. From the south, a faint voice slips through the ringing of the explosion's half-life.

"*Marco ...*"

Through grey light, the road runs south until it terminates at a beige-skinned apartment complex. In the distance, I spy several Alogo Boo disappear around the corner of the monolithic tower.

"*Marco ...*"

Alexandra's voice is thin and hollow amidst the chaos, but I am certain it came from the direction of the apartment. The air screams as the road behind me erupts into orange light and becomes a rain of black tarmac as another artillery shell lands. The opportunity of chaos is upon me. I charge with the second wave of black smoke and hurtle down the road. Bullets snip the air around me and pop as they fly into the abandoned cars along the boulevard.

The apartment complex grows taller overhead, its concrete spine leaning out over the road and surrendering balconies of empty flowerpots and sun-faded loungers. I round the corner of the building, which gives way to a gravel and dirt rear parking lot. The Alogo Boo have formed a circle, but between their bodies, I can see Alexandra's legs as they fight her to the ground. One man stands to the side of the circle, his hands on his hips and his face flushed with rage and a combination of emotions I do not understand, perhaps sexual, as he watches the men wrestle her. There is a faint guidance from my processor, like a flare burrowed deep in the night, that I must disable the hierarchy.

The man steps towards the circle and opens his mouth, but in a run, I slide under the flail of his arms and slip the machete into his throat, passing through his flesh like butter. Blood, viscous and slick, erupts over his hands and stains the gravel black. He stumbles as he grips his throat, his quivering, malfunctioning fingers matting his beard in trails of blood.

"Metal Chad fucking on us!" cries a man, and the circle breaks apart into many faces of yellow and volcanic red.

The gurgling pleas of their dying leader at my feet leaves their nervous systems vacillating between flight and fight. For a moment, I contemplate speaking, but decide silence improves my odds. Let them believe I am speechless and berserk like my kin, and they may underestimate me.

"Well, well, Cousins, more scraps. The genuine article," says a man as he steps forward. His bio-signal reads 40, but he looks 50. His face is leathered and so red and tight, it looks scalded, but he is barrel-chested, and the rest of the soldiers fall behind him. "You, yeah you, I'm going to wear your fucking fingers!" He deposits a grimy hand with the letters X and Y inked on his palm under his thumb inside the collar of his flak jacket and pulls out a necklace of black, metal fingers. "Leave the little Stacy, Boyos, plenty of time to get to know her better. Ring this Chad bitch up! Milkbone, you're on the sticky!"

In silent, but well-practiced coordination, the men form a ring around me. As I am surrounded, they raise their rifles horizontal to their chests, their cheeks turning a faded crimson and their eyes grey-green, an ecstatic violence. I swing the machete at the man in front of me, but he weaves, and my head wrenches backwards as I am pushed from behind, and then the pushing does not stop. They body check me with their rifles, and I fly from one side of the circle to the other. When I trip over my feet, they step closer in. My blows with the machete become clumsy and they fend off my strikes with the butts of their rifles with ease.

The world is a chaotic blur of rifles, beards, and combat boots, but I glimpse a young boy, his bio-signal the same as Alexandra's, on the edge of the circle. He runs around, leans in on the men's shoulders, never breaking his view of me. A rifle in my back sends me careening in his direction and I catch sight of a black, greasy looking cylinder in his hand.

Milkbone on the sticky.

The purpose of the ring is clear now. Jostle me until the man on the outside of the ring can blow me apart with what looks like a pipe bomb. The ring fills with smiling faces, and the leather-faced man with the necklace of companion fingers, calls out, "Light it up, Milkbone!"

Outside the ring, the boy fumbles with a zippo and turns one end of the cylinder into a hiss of grey smoke. "All right, Cousins, on the next shove, send the Metal Chad this way ass first. Keep your nerves Milkbone, you've plenty of wick," commands the necklace man.

Through the small gaps between the men, the empty space where their bodies are too different to fit together, Alexandra is visible. She is still sprawled on the ground only several feet from a dumpster that rests against the apartment building's exterior. There is no hope of escape without putting her at risk. In the fray, I spy Milkbone, his face a garden of grey sunflowers with a yellow hue as the sticky in his hand smokes closer to oblivion.

"Now!" someone calls.

With a sneer, the soldier in front of me slams his rifle into my chest with both hands, but in a singular thrust, I slip the machete behind his rifle and pull him forward with me, across the middle of the circle. I slip aside of him, and he crashes into the wall of Alogo Boo soldiers and Milkbone.

"Alexandra, to the dumpster!" I yell.

There is a wave of surprise and shock as the ring collapses and the soldier, rather than me, falls into Milkbone.

"Shit!" Milkbone yelps as he fumbles to get the sticky out of his hand.

The men nearest him clamber to their feet, desperate to clear the loose explosive, but I kick them back to the ground. Necklace man stands dumb a few feet from Milkbone, seemingly unable to process the reversal of fortune. He opens and closes his mouth but says nothing, and then his face turns white, and he bellows, "The wick! Pull the wi—"

I fly backwards as a pale-yellow flash swallows the bodies of the Alogo Boos. There is a loud crunch, and then everything feels frozen, like my arms and legs are not connected to my body. Alien sounds and colours colonize the black void behind my eyes.

THE COLOURS BECOME AN AUSTERE WHITE-TILED ROOM, AND ACROSS THE UNIFORM WHITE TILES, A SLENDER MAN, A GREY WAVE OF HAIR ATOP HIS HEAD, THE SIDES SHAVED AND MANICURED, SITS WITH ONE LEG DRAPED OVER THE OTHER. THERE IS THE FEELING OF A WALL'S PRESSURE AGAINST MY BACK, AND THIN, DARK ARMS REST ON THE ARMS OF A CHAIR. NARROW PLASTIC TUBES RUN FROM AN IRON-SKINNED MACHINE NEXT TO THE CHAIR AND I CAN FEEL THEM SNAKE AGAINST MY COLLARBONE BENEATH A HOSPITAL GOWN. THE GOWN FOLDS OVER MY LAP SEVERAL TIMES, REAMS OF EXTRA FABRIC ATOP MY DIMINUTIVE FRAME. THE BODY IS ALIEN, BUT I RECOGNIZE IT AS MY OWN.

THE SLENDER MAN IS HANDSOME, HIS PROMINENT CHEEKBONES AND CERULEAN EYES ACCENTED BY A CHARCOAL-GREY SUIT, TAILORED WITH PRECISION TO HIS BODY.

"MS. AOIFE, PLEASE KNOW YOU ARE IN OUR THOUGHTS AT THIS DIFFICULT TIME. THEY ARE VERY GOOD HERE. ARE YOU COMFORTABLE?" THERE IS POWER AND EASE IN HIS DISPOSITION, THOUGH HIS WORDS ARE QUIET AND SEEM ALMOST ALOOF TO HIS PHYSICAL PRESENCE.

"THEY KEEP ME NUMB, IF THAT'S WHAT YOU MEAN." LONG SUCKLING BREATHS STEP BETWEEN EACH WORD, AND I DO NOT SO MUCH SPEAK AS DREDGE THE WORDS FROM MY THROAT AND THEY COME AS RAW HUSKS OF RAGGED SPITTLE.

"I understand you have reviewed the material and have some questions?"

"Didn't get much sense from your pamphlet if it will be me? Will it remember what I remember?"

A fit of coughs breaks through me. My small, shrivelled hand waves at him, inviting him to speak over me, but he waits and smooths the cuffs of his dress shirt.

"If you make the choice to sell your consciousness to Lotus …"

There is a mirthless snort and a strain as my body fights to right itself in the chair. "Choice? They don't tell you, dying will bleed you dry."

The man fidgets in his seat, refolds his legs, and bobs his head as if to conceive words, but then seems to find my grief and despair infertile. "You have our complete guarantee that your memories will not be incorporated into Lotus hardware. Your private life stays with you—"

"Goes with me."

"Of course, however you want to see it."

"Is this a fair offer? Don't know much about the market value of a soul." The words are followed by another fit of coughs that deepen and run through me, raw and vicious, as if whatever is inside means to split me apart.

"We are not in the business of souls. We work with the imprint of your

CONSCIOUSNESS, NOT YOUR MEMORIES, BUT YOUR PERSONALITY, THE ART OF YOUR THINKING."

"ARE YOU SURE YOU'D KNOW THE DIFFERENCE BETWEEN CONSCIOUSNESS AND A SOUL?"

THE MAN FROWNS AND CLASPS HIS HANDS IN A TENT ON THE LAP OF HIS CREASELESS GREY SUIT-JACKET. THERE IS NO RESPONSE AT LENGTH, AND WHEN HE DOES SPEAK, HIS WORDS ARE LIGHT AND ALOOF TO MY QUESTION. "YOU BRING THE PERSONALITY AND DISPOSITION. LOTUS DOES THE REST. THE SYSTEM NOTED YOU WERE VERY BRIGHT AND INQUISITIVE. A PRE-INTERNET CHILDHOOD IS VERY VALUABLE TO US. YOUR PROFESSIONAL LIFE IS ALSO OF GREAT INTEREST. A PROFESSOR OF LITERATURE, THIS IS A TYPE OF CAREER THAT CAN MAKE VERY FLUID CONNECTIONS. IT WILL ALSO GIVE THE INHERITING UNIT A RICH INTERNAL WORLD. THIS IS IMPORTANT. IT PROVIDES STABILITY AND EVOCATIVE OBSERVATIONS. YOUR EXPERIENCE AS AN IMMIGRANT IS ALSO VERY VALUABLE TO US. IT SHOWS VERSATILITY AND THE ABILITY TO ADAPT TO A NEW CULTURE OR SITUATION. THESE ATTRIBUTES GIVE PEACE OF MIND TO OUR CLIENTS."

"INHERITING UNIT?"

"PLEASE EXCUSE THE PHRASE, IT IS JUST SHOP TALK. YOUR CHARACTERISTICS ARE VERY UNIQUE."

"THAT SOUNDS LIKE A FANCY WAY OF SAYING ON THE WRONG SIDE OF THE COLLAPSE."

BUT HE SPEAKS ON, AS IF HE HAS NOT HEARD ME, "UNIQUE IS IMPORTANT. IT IS WHY LOTUS HAS AUTHORIZED ME TO MAKE YOU A GENEROUS

OFFER. WOULD YOU LIKE TO HEAR ABOUT THE PROCESS?" THE ROOM SHRUGS AND BOBS IN REPLY. THE MAN CLASPS HIS HANDS AND OFFERS A THIN-LIPPED SMILE. "ONCE YOU PASS AWAY, WE HAVE A WINDOW OF 30 MINUTES TO MAKE THE EXTRACTION. THIS FACILITY IS VERY FAMILIAR WITH OUR REQUIREMENTS, SO THERE SHOULD BE NO ISSUE."

"YOU UNDERSTAND MY REQUEST. SAM MUST NOT BE PRESENT. HE MUST NOT KNOW."

"LOTUS WILL CREDIT YOUR ESTATE DISCREETLY."

The revelry eases, drifting down into the blue chasm behind my eyes, to dwell as less than a shadow of a dream. A westering sun and the parking lot's sea of coarse dirt and blood-stained gravel at my feet come in its place. The somatic follows, and I realize I am crumpled against the concrete wall of the apartment building. Alexandra is beside me, her hands clapping and pumping her ears. Her lip is split and there is blood on her scalp where tufts of her snow-blonde hair have been ripped out, but I can see no lasting physical damage.

"Sis," I whisper, and a cerulean wave overtakes her face and then crashes into grey nothingness. The pace at which she brings her hands to her ears slows and her heart rate steadies.

"Thought you died," she cries as she lets her head fall on my chest.

"I'm okay."

Am I, though? I see my feet and my arms. I feel my toes move. On my right hand, my fingers dance. My fingers on my left hand, however, do not move: they are locked, twisted across one another in an avian-like talon. My diagnostic tool is slow, almost unresponsive, but I am persistent in asking it about the damage I have sustained. In the black pool behind my eyes, there is a pulse of information: the blast broke the rotator gear in my shoulder, which severed most of the nerves to my fingers. The arm is incapacitated and will not repair itself. There is a prompt to consult a Lotus specialist.

I raise my body so that I am sitting against the wall rather than being sprawled against it. There are human debris scattered throughout the parking lot. An entire arm from the shoulder down is marooned near a rusted fence to the far side of the parking lot. Alexandra must see it too, but she says nothing. With this thought, my working hand finds the stub of a cigarette in my jacket pocket, deposits it between my lips, and pries a lighter stashed from my jean's pocket.

The cigarette smell is stale, but I hunger after it, and in a flash of ember, I dredge it nearly down to its filter. In anticipation, or remembrance of the sensation of relief, I tilt my head back, only to see a solitary smoke ring escape my lips. The cigarette's sour exhaust grips the air and Alexandra holds out her hand in a polite, but determined request for a taste of the butt. Without hesitation, I crush the remnants of the stubby under my sneaker. She rolls her eyes and drops her hand.

"Did you charge?" she asks.

Her question prompts an internal response. A single white line with a few branches and a repeating conclusion: in 96 hours, my battery will shut down and I will be no more. With our current resources, I will not be able to escort Alexandra to the refuge coordinates. My system, perhaps overworked and crumbling, cannot advise on when I should inform Alexandra of this reality.

"A little," I murmur, and though I am about to say more, Alexandra crouches beside me and takes my arm in hers. Her eyes are wide, and she opens and closes her mouth several times, and then in point of the human carnage whispers, "Assholes."

"The worst," I offer.

"We go?" she pleads, but weariness grips my arms and legs, and all I can do is nod in reply. As she stands and helps me to my feet, a hum of static runs down my tongue and pops on the roof of my mouth as a panicked voice chatters in my head. Alexandra must hear the buzz too, because she freezes, her eyes wide with concern.

The voice is crisp and clear, broadcasted not far from us.

Fall back to the Dunn Memorial Bridge. Orders are to hold the overpass. Make sure those fuckers can't cross. Repeat, fall back to Dunn Memorial Bridge.

Images of Paul's Road Atlas flips over behind my eyes. The yellow tributaries of the road. The steel lines of bridges over the Hudson and ruins to the north of us. This is the last crossing.

Alexandra kneads my shoulder as if to cajole words from me. "Message?"

"We leave amidst the chaos."

ALEXANDRA
Dover

The arms of the Dunn Memorial Bridge reach across the Hudson in five sprawling lanes. Hypatia and I crouch at the margins of the off-ramp. Republic soldiers have dug in, and the barren fields of cement are dotted with machine-gun nests and twisted spires of metal that look like gigantic jumping jacks; Hypatia points them out as tank traps. On the bridge, there are green blurs of movement and the faint echo of voices.

"Jackets back on," whispers Hypatia as she pulls the green Republic cloaks from our backpack. As I pull my jacket on, Hypatia wrestles her old shirt from the backpack and tries to wrap the machete in it like a makeshift sheath. The machete slips from her hand and clatters against the pavement. With her eyes full of alarm, she stoops to collect it and tries again to roll it into her shirt, but her left hand seems uncooperative. Frowning, she passes the machete and shirt to me in an awkward clump, and asks in a small voice, "Will you pack the machete into the backpack? We need to make sure they have no reason to believe we are a threat." I nod, and jostle our things around until the machete, wrapped in the shirt to blunt its edge, fits vertically into the side of the bag. She murmurs words of thanks and turns away as she rubs her fingers.

We walk slowly and keep near the bridge's guardrails, our hands at our sides. To the north, the skeletal frame of an overpass smolders on its footings. This really is the last way out of town.

"Hold it there," a voice cries as a woman rises from one of the machine-gun nests. Half her face and eyes are lost in a sagging bandage; she pulls hard on a cigarette as the tip of her rifle drifts over us. "Keep your hands where I can see them," she calls. "You"—she points at me— "let me hear you speak."

Hypatia nods at me in encouragement, but the command catches me off guard. My tongue oils my lips several times, but no words come.

"I mean it," calls the woman. She tosses the cigarette to the pavement, swings the rifle into her shoulder, and trains the sights on us.

Some words. Any words. Come on. Before she shoots you dead. The desire to put my hands on my ears grows, but I manage to stammer, "We're refugees."

"Okay. Good. Now the little one." And now, she turns the rifle on Hypatia.

"Headed to Dover," says Hypatia.

"Can't be too careful, those metal assholes love nothing better than to bring down a bridge. If it isn't Alogo Boo shells, it's them." The woman jerks her head to a puddle-sized blast mark and twisted metal debris strewn across the pavement ahead of us. "I'd check you out further, but hell follows you." Without breaking her line of sight on us, she speaks into a walkie talkie pinned across her flak jacket. "Mark, there are two refugees coming through. Two girls. In Republic issue. They're clear to pass."

From the far end of the bridge, a man pops his head over a concrete parapet and waves in our direction. The woman motions us onward with her head, but then frowns. "Where'd you get the jackets anyway?" Before we can reply, she shakes her head in answer to her own question. "Never mind, just keep moving."

On the other side of the bridge, several tents have been stood up and old men lean against the bridge's concrete embankment, their eyes shut, their mouths drooped in exhaustion. From behind the canvass flaps of a tent, small children watch our steps. Several gaunt-faced women and men huddle around a makeshift smoking pile of twigs and garbage, infants tucked under their arms, bathing in sour smoke. They don't acknowledge us as we pass, and Hypatia betrays no indication she's willing to break stride.

From the 40 road, we watch Albany smoulder on our shoulders. Flattened grey ruins cleave the pink skyline. The shelling has become erratic, and a brittle and eerie silence grows between the kettle screams and thunder. Hypatia's travel is laboured and her arm hangs limp; she doesn't acknowledge it, but I assume it was damaged by the sticky bomb. With her good arm, she leans on me as we move farther from the road, deeper into the fields along the highway. The land stretches out before us on all sides in a sullen tide of uncut, languishing wheat and subsiding fences. A phalanx of ruined solar panels forms a blue island at the field's centre; a sickly pungent aroma like compost hangs heavy in the air.

We're not far from the bridge when we begin to lose the light. For a while, we trudge along in the semi-gloom, desperate to put more distance between us and Albany, though Hypatia leans on me as we walk, and at first sight of a car along the road, she doesn't hesitate to stop. We climb into the backseat and lie together under the blanket.

The night sky frames her shape and illuminates her cheek as she stares out into the east where the horizon becomes trees. Behind her, the stars have grown fierce, wayward from the pinch of city lights and human devised constellations. I don't have the heart to bring them to heel with their names. If the fighting continues in Albany, it doesn't reach us in the backseat. There's no mention of eating, and I don't ask for any food or water. The scenes of the day have left me with no appetite, though I'm not without questions.

Yet at length, it's Hypatia who says, "Sis, I want to lie here until first light. The idea of pretending to rise with the sun like a living thing is comforting, I think."

I nod, though it's a strange request from her. Hypatia never asks for things like that, things that are sentimental.

"Hypatia?"

"Yes?" she answers as she slides into the gap between the rear seats and the back of the front seats.

"You replayed Francis?"

"Yes."

"Can you replay mom? Dad?"

"Yes." Anger and sadness writhe in my chest and she must see it, for she answers my next question. "I'm sorry I kept that secret from you. I thought hearing them would make it harder for you. Delay your grief, your loss. Our loss," she decides. "I'm sorry," she repeats.

"Me too," I whisper. A new desire overtakes me. A need to share my own secret. "Kept one too."

"What is it?"

"We drowned."

"When?"

"I was small. Our pool."

"How?"

"Outside. Alone."

"What happened? Is this why you don't swim?" Though her features are surrendered to the dark, there is alarm in her voice.

"Pushed you and fell."

"Why did you push me?"

"Jealous. They reset you. To forget," I add.

"Jealous?"

I'm surprised to see genuine confusion animate her features. "Happier with you."

For a long time, Hypatia doesn't speak, and I wonder if she understood me. Understood my fear that mom and dad found her easier to be with. Easier to understand. Simply more than I could ever be. There's more. The desire to be without her, to live unaided.

When she does speak, her words are slow and there is a gentleness in them.

"Sister, our Mother and Father showed me affection because I was able to bring them closer to you." Her features cut through the dark, her lips still and placid as she continues, "It was their love for you that made them fond of me."

"Forgive me, sis?"

Her hand works its way into mine and the shine of her teeth cuts through the dark before I've even finished speaking.

"Always. What do you want to hear?"

"Mom's bedtime songs."

~

As Hypatia wished, we broke camp only after first light. The chill of the evenings no longer recedes in the morning but hangs in the air. It greets us with frost-licked leaves and heavy grey skies. Everything seems subdued, defeated by the winter's coming.

The road is narrow, and crofts encroach upon it from beneath sunken wooden fences. Old. Bleached by the sun. They remind me of bones, and we're forced to weave through them. If anyone were to come, it would be easy to disappear into the grass, but we meet no one. We pass the occasional trickle of a gravel path that leads from the road into dense bush. There are probably families at the end of those roads. Holding tight. Waiting. Doing what my mom and dad couldn't.

Hypatia demands we stop and wade through a field; it'll be quicker than walking both sides of the road. She ducks under the fence, but the terrain is uneven. Autumn rains have turned them into puddles and mud; Hypatia slides more than I do, the mud grabs at her feet. She says little. There are no smiles. No laughter. No jokes. We pass the silence between us back and forth, but when the brush is heavy or the path too muddy, she leans on my shoulder and squeezes my hand.

As we approach the other end of the field, we come upon a wooden transmission pole, perpendicular and half-submerged in the grass. Its brown wood wears a skin of frost.

Upon seeing it, Hypatia says, "I need to talk, let's stop. Here's fine."

She gives me no time to answer as she collapses on the pole. The morning is cold, and the wind cuts through the fields; frost all over my butt will only make matters worse. I fall to my haunches and listen on the balls of my feet. She cradles the backpack in her lap and roots in the bag until she withdraws a battered plastic water bottle we scavenged from the convenience store.

"Drink. You should've finished this yesterday." She watches me quench my thirst with an expression I don't recognize. "I'm dying." There's a tremble in her voice, and something akin to fear grabs her features. "Something to do with my battery. I don't really understand. Lotus might have."

I have no response. Inside, I'm crying, but the feeling has yet to reach my face. Part of me wants to scream; part of me knew something was wrong. I nod and focus on tightening the bottle cap.

"Fixable?" I keep my head down, trying to settle myself before meeting her eyes.

"Under different circumstances, maybe." She tries to smile, but her lips flutter.

"How long?"

"Not long. My diagnostics say another 80 hours, but its prediction has been off this whole time. So probably less. Maybe a lot less. I'm losing track of colours, sis. I've suspected it for a while, but thought maybe it was just the way war looked."

This confession makes her confusion about the yellow ribbons clear; it puts the bad kind of butterflies in my stomach.

"But I love you." I mean it, but there's another emotion I don't know how to express without selfishness. Need. She knows it, too.

"I love you too. That won't change. I'll get you close, probably two days out from the coordinates. You must go to Dover, the river will lead you to them, I promise. And in return, you must promise to leave me on the road. You can't stay with me. I might return like the others." She frowns and, looking at her feet, says, "I will return like the others."

My eyes are hot now, and my heart feels like it's going to explode. My hands are moving to my ears and I want to scream. Scream into the empty fields, into the road, into the black smoke that continues to drift over the hills behind us.

"I won't be me. The mechanic believes it happens once our battery runs to a certain point. Something triggers. I think he's right. It's a sensible hypothesis. Our Father and Mother's decision to charge me after the flash is maybe why I have lasted longer than the other companions. It's a sensible hypothesis too, I think."

"Not fair."

My cheeks are warm now, my mouth tastes of salt, and the fields have become soft and blurry. My head is on Hypatia's small lap, and her hand runs over my back in concentric circles. I weep in sobs and howls I don't recognize. Hypatia's hand doesn't waver. She intones gentle praises and hopeful wishes that slip past some of my cries.

"From one perspective, I've been very lucky, sis." I turn in her lap to face her, and my heat signatures must betray my alarm and disbelief, because she smiles for emphasis as she continues, "No, really. Our Mother and Father and you loved me like family, not as a machine. Our Mother and Father wouldn't have charged me otherwise and it may have made all the difference."

I sniff up tears. "Still not fair."

"Maybe not, but you must keep your promise."

I nod; she smiles, and with her working arm catches the tears that slide over my cheeks with the corner of her sleeve. She tilts her head towards the road, grips my shoulders, and rises to her feet in hard-fought increments. Yet, once she rises, she looks past me to the hill behind us and frowns.

"Come," she commands.

I turn and look back and follow the road as it snakes back into the distance through jaundiced fields and desolation. At the limits of what I can see, beneath the black smoke, a dark mass shuffles. For a moment, I think it's a swarm, but it's too low to the ground and it doesn't twitch, but instead bounces forward. An army.

"Can you see them?" my voice quakes.

The bridge must have been captured. The Republic fighters holding it are dead or scattered. I scramble through the field to the road. We can't afford not to be careful.

"Alogo Boos." Her frown deepens, and she struggles in my tracks through the muddy field to the shoulder of the road.

"On foot?"

"Some. Many on horses. Scouts maybe. A few tanks."

"Catch us?"

"At our pace, eventually."

I gesture to the field. "Hide?"

"Not here. They might walk over us. We must keep moving while we can."

Out of the field, the wind rips along the road, howls at our backs, and pummels the faded crofts that divide gravel from mud. With each step, I imagine the men behind us. Their banners raised, marching in Hawaiian print flak jackets and body armour. The pop of stone and rattle of earth beneath the treads of their tanks.

But I don't look. Hypatia does. She measures our safety in furtive glances over her shoulder as her limp arm swings by her side. She says nothing and keeps her face blank. I've noticed she doesn't seem to be mining my emotions anymore. It used to feel like nearly every other glance was one of assessment of my minute-by-minute emotional temperament, based on which careful decisions were made. Perhaps she's conserving power.

The road is solitary, it doesn't branch in other directions. On occasion though, another road cuts across it and we're faced with a junction. Narrower roads that disappear into fields and barren trees that reach over the road. There are no power lines in their direction. We don't change course. We follow the telephone lines that stand aloof and crooked by the road.

Hypatia's step falters and she pulls back; her full weight on my shoulder forces my knees to bend. She looks behind us and squints up at the road, and then to the left in the direction of the junction that cuts through our path. Then she examines the overcast sky and holds out the palm of her good hand in search of rain. When her hand remains dry, she says, "Unexpected."

"What?" I ask.

She doesn't look afraid. "Listen."

I obey, and for a long time, there's nothing but the whistle of the wind through the arms of the trees and the sway of tall grass. Then it comes. A sound like distant thunder, and then it steadies and becomes a noise like heavy rain on a tin roof, but discordant and faster; I understand now why Hypatia inspected the sky. The noise grows louder and overpowers the wind. Now it's everywhere, coming in clips and claps, making the gravel on the road jump. Horses. Dozens of them charge into view from the cover of trees that obscure the junction point. They gallop towards us; the road quakes as their hooves trample gravel and patches of asphalt.

Their coming rattles my chest and it feels like my heart is jumping with them. Brown horses. Beautiful auburns. Coal black. My hand twitches in the desire to draw them. Their faces are high and noble, but their mouths are caked in foam. Exhausted as they appear to be, they break through us. Some are barebacked, and some are saddled, but all are without riders.

Hypatia and I stumble back to the shoulder of the road, and she sits as dust rises from the earth and envelopes us. More horses pass. Among the fray of hooves and tails, a Republic banner hangs limp. I think of Malcolm and wonder if any horse bears his saddle. Willing myself to believe against my better judgement that he ever made it this far after apparently surrendering his pistol to Hypatia. Most of the herd has broken away; the thunder of their steps has become distant and now only a few scattered steps follow their wake.

Hypatia is back on her feet and stands by my shoulder. The last of the horses approach. A pale horse, its coat frost white, fights its way down the road. A pair of black reins swing loose in its flight. Hypatia jumps. She hangs in midair with her good arm, suspended before the pummel of the horse's forelegs. The horse charges by her, and she tumbles along beside it; her feet screech as they drag against the road in a scream of metal. Her weight catches and the horse rears as it continues to pull her over the gravel. It strains and fumbles on its hooves until it comes to a reluctant stop. In a violent twist, it shakes its head from side to side, but Hypatia clings to the reins as she swings between its body and its legs. The horse brays, but yields, and Hypatia is left half standing on one leg, half hanging from the side. The horse watches me run to them and its nostrils flare with what seems like impatience, but it remains still.

Hypatia smiles. "Only way to outrun them." Her gentle child's voice has become electronic and monotone. Her smile fades.

I say nothing and do my best to inspect her. Her shoes are scuffed black and her pantlegs are ripped, revealing torn synthetic flesh and ornamental blood, gashed deep enough that the conceit of blood is betrayed by glimpses of dark coiled metal. I kiss her forehead and join her in holding the reins. The horse is still, its breaths are heavy. Its coat is drenched, and it leaves a smell on my fingers like a wet dog.

Behind us, the dots on the hill have become the shapes of men. Hypatia follows my gaze and begins to speak, but her words come out in a stammer of numbers. Zeros and ones, and zeros again. She's speaking in binary. Her face takes on an expression I've never seen her wear before. Devastation. She cuffs her hand to her mouth, perhaps to push any other thoughts that have become numbers back inside. The mud from her hands stains her cheeks in dark, watery blotches.

I use my sleeve to rub the mud off and concentrate on my response. "It's okay. I understand. You first."

I pat the horse but tighten my grip on the reins. Hypatia wraps her good arm around the horse and fights her way up its neck. She slips off. Tries again, her legs writhing in the air as she climbs. She falls again. And again. The army behind us is becoming more visible in slight degrees, but I recognize we, too, must be more visible. It won't be long until one of them on a motor bike comes to scout us out.

Hypatia doesn't grab the horse again. She shakes her head and moves aside in defeat. A welt of frustration blossoms in my throat.

"No. Both of us," I insist.

The Alogo Boos will scrap her on sight. She can't stay here.

"Try now." I position myself like I'm doing a squat. My knees are bent and I brace myself. "Climb," I urge. Hypatia shakes her head. "Now," I demand. "I'll stay."

I do my best to inflect my words so that she understands the threat. Threats are hard to craft with only a few syllables. I watch her look to the horse, to my back, and then to the darkening mass behind us that stretches across the lip of our horizon. She's processing. With a pained expression, she returns to the horse's side.

"Quick steps," I command.

She wraps her good arm around the saddle and lifts. The dense pressure of her feet on my back becomes a slow, intense squeeze that radiates through my collarbone. I grit my teeth as my knees shake. Her weight steadies. Sweat prickles on my forehead. She presses down harder and lifts. My legs cave in and I'm on my ass, but her leg dangles above me in the stirrups. I can tell from the way her eyes are on me that she's trying to scan me for injuries.

"Just bruises. Okay," I say through winded breaths.

She nods. I walk to the other side of the horse so that she can pull me up with her good arm. I slide up and find the saddle is well worn and smooth to the touch; Hypatia leans forward, cradled between my legs as I draw on the reins. The horse shrugs at my pull and cuts across the road to nip at crofts at the shoulder.

Frustration floods through me. I pull harder, and the horse fights me, pulling back towards the pale, limp tufts of rough grass. This should be simple. The urge to put my hands on my ears grows. *Focus. Don't look, it'll only make it harder to focus.* I lose control and it feels like I watch myself turn to look behind us, my jacket and legs caked in mud, my hair matted to my cheeks and back. The mass has descended the hill and fans out in the distant field. This is probably what Hypatia saw back at the telephone pole. Columns of men, their colours burning a hole in the late grey November sky.

My voice echoes back at me as I berate the horse, "Move. Dumb. Horse."

Hypatia stares ahead, her head folded towards her lap. She looks like she's falling asleep, though I know she doesn't sleep. Not ever. Her hand fumbles for my leg. The sensation of her palm settles above my knee; I think she's trying to calm me. The horse lifts its head and considers my pleas and pulls. It saunters forward in several reluctant steps.

"Horse. Meat," I chide.

It flicks its ears and then stops. Stupid horse. I dig my heels into its ribs, and it takes a few languid steps forward, but stops again and veers back towards the shoulder of the road to nuzzle the pale grass. I want to ask Hypatia for suggestions, but I think she's too scared to speak; petrified that her vast vocabulary, her grip on this world, will leak away into inscrutable zeros and ones. We're stationary. I don't dare look over my shoulder. Perhaps we should abandon the horse, dive into the fields, and hope they walk over us, or let us slip into the grey skin of the forest.

A kettle scream rips the sky apart. The horse tenses, and then behind us, the road erupts into a column of smoke. The world rushes by us; the field melts into a blur of pale yellow, and the road becomes a grey river. Someone took a test shot at us, and the horse is running. Charging over the earth. Hypatia bounces between my legs; several times, her head swings into my chest and knocks the wind from my lungs.

Even if I wanted to, I can't look back now. It takes everything I have to stay on. In the distance, a crack rents the air. From the corner of my eye, I see the field shake and tremble in an eruption of smoke and flying mud. I tighten my grip on the reins and the horse flies even faster; the clatter and pound of its hooves drown out another crack and whine from the hills as the target practice continues. The road curves and drops into a valley of black and grey branches of leafless trees. We must be out of sight now; lost amongst late autumn's frost-bitten skeletal canopy.

We surrender to the horse's rhythm, mere spectators in its battle against the road and the vales of empty pasture. Derelict barns and rusted equipment melt away into red scabs in a haze of yellow, tall grass. The run seems to go on forever. My body stiffens and my legs tingle. Hypatia remains hunched over, lodged between my chest and the horse's neck. She says nothing and is motionless; I don't talk to her in fear it'll disrupt her efforts to conserve her battery or force her to speak in binary again. The ones and zeros terrify me, for it means we're both now without words. The voiceless are easy casualties in war. Easy to shoot. To ignore. To be the victims of what the Alogo Boo planned to do to me in Albany.

~

Two days of travel blur into each other. We rest only when the horse won't run. Hypatia says nothing, but gestures with a sudden spark of animation at a faded green sign that bears the name Dover. Two miles.

The afternoon is lengthening as we press on into the woods. Branches peeled by autumn's coming lay reach over the single-lane road and drop the last of their leaves in a matted carpet. The forest is thick, though ahead, its enclosure ends in a wide mouth of pale light. As we approach, the air warms and sticks to my cheeks. The horse slows its pace, yet still we bear on until the woods deliver the road into the desolation of scorched earth.

The single-lane road branches into many concourses, all shadowed by ruined buildings. Few are little more than cracked slabs of concrete, and in those that stand, their windows and doors are charred away into gaping holes. Fast-food franchises, old-fashioned box-stores, and judging by the debris of clothes, phone cases, and plastic chairs, e-commerce warehouses smoulder to each side of us. The outskirts are ablaze, belching away their existence in black and grey sheets of smoke, as little fires still burn in craters that gore the asphalt road. They flicker in the windscreens of burned-out cars left in parking lots and gnaw at their license plates, peeling away the State's motto: "Live Free or Die."

In the lane beside us, an RV, knocked on its side, smoulders in seams of white smoke, its side ripped apart by the punch of a blast. I don't know enough to tell if the hole was made by a tank shell or a drone strike. The road is littered with the remnants of drones, though. Bits and pieces of the sharp, jagged metal of their legs and bodies lie strewn across the asphalt or twisted in the pale grass. The horse seems to know to step over or around their barbed legs.

Hypatia straightens up and begins to survey the new terrain; I suspect she's looking for other humans or bombs that have yet to go off. She gives me a slow and solemn thumbs up, but says nothing, sheltering, perhaps, her remaining syllables for some greater importance. I follow her sight to the charred buildings and wonder if anyone had been inside since they burned. There are no bodies, but I don't look hard. The last building, a hamburger joint wreathed in black smoke, passes from the corner of my eye to my back and I don't look over my shoulder; it's easier to believe, just for a moment, that none of it exists.

Our road snakes around a roundabout and the old city rises over its slope. A watchtower on metal stilts climbs into view, and beneath it, a garden of barbed wire has been planted. The watchtower is flanked in both directions by barricades. They are a composite of ruined cars, walls of wood, and pieces of concrete, the rebar exposed and twisted out in angry rusty curls. I can't be sure how far the barricades run, but they appear to encircle the old downtown core.

Beyond the fortifications, there's a hill, and on the edges of its lap run the northern and southern tips of the Cocheco River. Spare for the lone spire of a church that cuts into the November grey heavens like a narrow black spear, the city is old industrial red-brick, its buildings low to the ground, humble without claim to the wan skyline and its passing cover of cloud.

From this stretch of road, a long line of people becomes visible, travelling in the same direction as us, towards the city. They are still far ahead, but it's a multitude: there are children, and men, and women, and packhorses tugging small trailers. It doesn't take long until we overtake the stragglers. Most of them don't acknowledge us as we trot by; they stare ahead, ashen-faced. Determined to pass through the barricade, away from the openness and desolation of the blackened earth.

As we approach, columns of Republic soldiers fan out to meet us and push into lines. "All horses are to be requisitioned for the use of Republic soldiers, dismount," shouts a short man with a pointed nose. "Horses are for the cause, dismount or be dismounted," he bellows as Hypatia and I look down upon him in disbelief.

"You're seeking refuge?" demands a broad-chested soldier nearby. I nod. "Then get the fuck off that horse!"

I wave my arms in surrender, struggle from the stirrups, and crumble on the ground as my muscles seize in agony. In a voice somewhere between manic laughter and tears, I call out, "My sister is little," as Hypatia tries to dismount in a slow, cautious roll, her feet suspended high above the ground.

"Move! Alogo Boo are practically at the fucking doorstep," shrieks the short man as he rips Hypatia to the ground.

Hypatia lands on her bum; several times, she opens her mouth to speak, but decides to say nothing. The soldiers turn from us and begin to rifle through a packhorse led by a man with one arm in a sling.

I tug on the short one's sleeve. "Alogo Boo here?" I query.

"Just north of the city. Troop carriers arrived at dawn. Drone strike at noon." With vehemence, he kicks a black drone's leg across the ground before turning back to the packhorse as the other soldier shoves a man back and informs him that his food will be commandeered for the cause.

Numb, we find ourselves pressed into a long, shuffling line of families and lone men and women. The end of the line reaches to the feet of the watchtower, where several soldiers are seated behind wooden desks. The scene is ludicrously analog, and the pace at which the line limps forward matches the archaic speed of paper and pen. The sun slips behind the fortification, leaving only its red fingerprints in the sky. The soles of my feet ache, and Hypatia leans heavily against my shoulder, her eyes set on her feet.

"We're close, I think," I stammer. She gives a faint nod in reply.

"Step up, please. Step up, quickly now," calls a woman in a grey overcoat as she beckons us. "Names?" In the distance, there's a low rumble like thunder in a valley, and many heads in the line stare up the road, their faces grim and braced. "Names!" the woman repeats.

"Alexandra Porthos." I point to Hypatia. "Hypatia Porthos."

Hypatia nods in confirmation. The woman scribbles on a long sheet of paper broken by many columns.

"Good. Identification?"

"All digital," I gasp.

"You mean to say you have no paper copies?"

Hypatia gives a rueful shake of her head. Somewhere up the road, a staccato of gunfire erupts.

The woman lays the pen flat across the paper and, with visible exasperation, asks, "How do I know you're who you say you are?"

"Does it matter? We're refugees," says Hypatia. Her voice is light and spoken at a clip.

"Well, are you American?" the woman asks as a column of soldiers rushes by us, scrambling ahead of the watchtower in search of cover.

"Human," I reply.

"Those who were in the country legally have priority." An artillery blast rents earth through the air; the line screams and crowds in around the watchtower, pushing at our backs. "You'll need to wait until all the natural residents are processed."

"What?!" My voice quivers with incredulity.

"The Republic is sworn to protect Americans of all races, creeds, and sexual orientations."

"They're coming!" I stammer.

"You'll need to step to the back of the line," mutters the woman as she stares past us, seemingly to beckon the next in line.

Hypatia looks at me, then at the woman, and manages a short laugh. Then she screams, "They're closing the city! Quick, before it's too late!"

There's a tidal wave of confusion and alarm from the line as the woman grips the desk and looks back at us in disbelief. "That's a lie—"

Her words are lost as her desk flips over, and she vanishes amidst a deluge of panic as hundreds of people rush through the city gate. Republic soldiers fire into the air, but the situation is ungovernable. Though her gait is uneven and her pace is laboured, Hypatia smiles as we run amongst the throng.

HYPATIA
The Last Run

The crowd dissipates and thins as we diverge through the different streets of Dover. Fog straddles the road. It clings to the branches of the stubborn ornamental trees that line the boulevard and bedews our hair as it hangs above us in a grey ceiling. The explosions and gunfire sound like they are in the city now, just a few roads behind us. Though Alexandra does not look backwards, she ducks with each blast as she runs. Suddenly, just behind us, the buildings erupt and cede their edges and skyline to shapeless orange and crimson flashes. The whine and thunder of artillery follow, chased by the cracks of gunfire.

The ordinances and blasts of the Alogo Boo assault offer my processor no insight into how long the bastions of defenders will hold, even as the fighting grows louder. The physics of objects, their vectors and trajectories, rarely materialize now, and when they do appear, they are but faint imprints on my vision, like the tails of falling stars, in distance chase of the bodies and things that crash through my world.

In truth, though, the Alogo Boo may be the least of our worries. The children keep close to us, but Alexandra has not seen them. I do not know how long they have been following us. When I first glimpsed them, I thought they were hallucinations, a terror hewed from wayward lights and explosions by a dying machine. They are here, though. Ten red dots hunt us. The fixed, symmetrical distance between them betrays them as pairs of eyes, but they do not blink. They linger in the fog and peer from around corners, while some creep behind dumpsters.

Up until now, the commotion may have been too great for them to reveal themselves. Higher up in the city, closer to the makeshift front, men and women wrapped in the olive cloaks and jackets of the Republic flooded the streets, their faces a bricolage of terror and chemical excitement as they carried sandbags and slung machine guns over broad shoulders and rallied amongst themselves. Yet, in our descent farther into the city, especially as the roads grew narrow and steeper on the way to the passage of the Cocheco, the dots have become bolder, testing the distance between us. They seem to hunt us with an aloof casualness. At one moment, they stalk our movements, and in another, their eyes dart about, seemingly engrossed by their freedom to navigate the environment, distracted in an excessive repertoire of movement and motion. They are at play.

When the explosions and gunfire pause, they greet it with silence, betrayed only by the occasional clip and patter of metal feet on the asphalt, but even these slips are well below the decibels of the human ear. Fortunately, Alexandra's focus is elsewhere as she marches us through the fog. Her eyes are alert and wide as she scans ahead of us in search of some road sign or marker that we are getting closer to the Cocheco quay.

How much further will they let us go before they step out from the fog and take control? Do they know where we are headed? Perhaps they are unsure. They must see me for what I am. Perhaps they are confused by us. Do they remember their old sisters and brothers? Is it even possible they have memories of one life, their first consciousness, stacked upon memories of being a companion child?

Alexandra's pace quickens. The fog has made the pavement wet and slick, and my sensory system cannot plot my steps fast enough, so I drag and twist in her wake. Alexandra mistakes my ungainly steps as a protest of our direction. She points ahead to the fog-dewed glisten of a pea-green sign that reads: "Cocheco Quayside Ahead." Beyond the sign, the road narrows into a steep hill that descends into a cluster of old red-brick buildings.

Alexandra turns to me, her face an inscrutable kaleidoscope of greying colours now beyond the diminished sensitivity of my processor, and whispers, "Close and together."

I nod, and though I am unable to match her steps, I am quick to usher her forward before she catches sight of the four red dots that have materialized on each side of the road behind us. The descent of my vision into a grey shadow world leaves me without enough data to mine her emotional state. I know if she sees them, she will panic and probably stim.

A short flight of stairs off the road brings us down to a cluster of old building nestled into the foot of the hill. Alexandra leaps down the bottom four steps and beckons me towards a side alley, and we weave through several dumpsters that lean off the red-brick wall into our path. The air is thick and putrid with decay: it has a composition like the air in the Alibaba delivery truck. I can feel her shoulder creak as it strains in response to the growing weight of my failing body. I have tried to grip her hand, to draw her attention and let her know it is time to leave me behind. I think she understands I do not want to talk in fear of wasting my few remaining words by speaking into her shoulder in some lonely alleyway. My battery is down to its embers, I know this. I can feel it. It is a game of steps versus syllables. The last words between us must count for something.

Midway down the alley, Alexandra slouches against the wall and slips me from her shoulder so that I am sitting beside her. "Zeus's beard." She exhales as her slender hand grips her chest. "You're heavy."

Beneath her eyes, white crescents follow her words, but my attention follows the wrinkled song of tin clattering from behind one of the dumpsters at the end of the alley. The road we came from is lost in the morass of the fog's grey steps. Dark maroon ovals spark and sunder the gloom. The alleyway floods with Alexandra's shriek.

"No," she says. "No."

The red lights burn bright as something cuts through the fog's grey shroud and surfaces as a child's face. Alexandra is on her feet, and without warning, I rise with her, desperate to match the sync of her winded steps. Behind us, the companion child does not run, but slips past the dumpsters, seemingly indifferent to our presence. As Alexandra moves, she rattles the handle of a door on one side of the alley, but finds it locked.

"No!" she cries, and with her free hand begins to pump her right ear.

The sky opens in a flash of light, and we are on our stomachs, a wave of black dust rolling over us. There is still red light in Alexandra's chest. I see no major injuries, but she stays flat against the ground. I tug at her. The fog and dust have become a soup, and the air is thick and hot. The building on the other side of the street has become a column of black smoke. The red eyes of the companion children have vanished. Perhaps they were destroyed by the explosion. I tug at Alexandra again and try to pull her into my lap. I run my hand through her hair and find blood in her ears. Though I fear the confirmation that my language has become a blur of 1's and 0's, the urge to speak is strong. Alexandra rises to her feet and pulls me up with her before I take the chance.

Cobblestone has replaced the asphalt, and the gradient becomes a slope that runs to the causeway beside the river. Yet, where the Cocheco should be, there are high walls of concrete, and the intermittent explosions behind us illuminate that they are crowned in spools of barbed wire. Alexandra gasps at the sight of the walls but does not hesitate as she drags us towards them. In our approach, the darkness surrenders an entrance tucked into the frontage of the concrete fortifications. My processor has stopped imposing any measure of distance upon my sight, but we are close. Alexandra's breaths are deep and ragged, but we seem to be moving faster.

The night is sundered by a sudden pop of intense beams of light, and several voices bellow, "On the ground! On the ground! This is a controlled checkpoint!"

Alexandra throws us prostrate to the cobblestone, and I see she webs her fingers on the back of her head. I lie parallel to the checkpoint to keep an eye on the road behind us.

"Help! We're refugees," she shouts back. There is only silence and the glare of the floodlights winking in the faint gap between my elbows and my cheeks. "Coming to the refuge," abuts Alexandra, and each word is loud and distinct.

"Stay where you are. Observe the protocol," assures someone from the walls above.

My body is heavy and my limbs seem colonized by a relentless fatigue that makes each movement simultaneously unbearable and impossible. It is coming. A dull, growing pressure of the somatic. The feeling of the cobblestones against my chest, the floodlight in my eyes, creates a sensation that the pressure of the physical world is forcing me from my body. With alarm, and a phantom flutter in my chest, I remember I have felt this way before. My second death is nearly upon me.

The faint noise of footsteps and then the rattle of metal from behind the concrete walls intrudes upon the sensation. They are coming out to get us. Up the road behind us, maroon sparks burn from amidst the fog.

Five pairs of eyes, like burning crimson stars, sunder the fog. They float on either side of the road, rising and falling until they converge into a half-ring and descend upon us. There is the creak and the grind of metal as the door to the compound begins to open. Perhaps they had not been chasing us, but instead following us to the checkpoint, allowing us to get them to open their doors.

In my periphery, Republic soldiers slip from the opened gate and approach us in slow, measured steps. They become a crescent around us and the tips of their rifles bob from our flat bodies back into the fog and darkness. *See them*, I cry out in my mind. I beseech the chattering blue void behind my eyes, beg my processor to inform me of the chances they will see our hunters, but there is only the twinkling abyss of ultramarine blue in reply.

In brace for gunfire, a woman's voice reaches us, her words calm and even. "Almost done, but I need you to let go of your machete."

A hand runs down the small of my back and then presses against my legs, squeezing the pockets of my trousers. Somehow, they have not seen them. They must be warned.

I visualize the remaining energy inside my body, willing it into words and shout, "11000101010101!—" The electric half-life of my synthesized voice escapes and bounces down the causeway.

"The fuck!" The hands retreat from my body.

"She's not dangerous!" screams Alexandra, but her words are lost beneath the clap of many descending footsteps from the road behind us.

"Incoming!" A burst of gunfire rattles above our heads.

"Close the—"

The rest of the sentence is sundered in pained wails. The gunfire continues. We climb to our feet and run, desperate to break ahead and avoid the soldiers' erratic bursts of fire. Children's faces float in the fog, their fiendish smiles and frozen grimaces splitting through the night. From our left, two companion children swoop in from the darkness. Twisted metal pieces protrude from gashes in their cheeks and foreheads like reptilian spines. A soldier on our left twists back and fires off into the sky as a child gores her neck. She collapses, her fingers pressed to her gurgling throat. The child advances, blood and grease smeared across its chin as it leaps through another round of gunfire.

Frantic shouts issue from behind the compound wall as someone tries to grind the gate to a close. The crank whirls and the metal whines, but it is only half-way shut as we slip through it. Several companion children charge through the entrance, running at our heels. With cries of panic and then screams, the metal groan of the gate's retreat comes to an abrupt halt. The red dots of their eyes are now grey, visible only against the black twilight and white fog. The grey dots gradually grow arms and legs as they reach the now undefended entrance.

Voices without attribution rise ahead of us. "Get to the boats!! Tell them to hold the transports."

There are more calls, but the traffic of heavy footfall casts the words asunder. Ahead of us, the causeway floods with running hooded shapes. I do not need to see their heat signals to recognize they are mainly women and children. The multitude runs and tumbles down the sloping cobblestones. They slip around the matted edges of many shipping containers, which run like a disjointed ladder to the end of the causeway, where the escape boats rock amidst the fog as impatient grey outlines.

Though my processor refuses to count the bodies and make an estimate of available boat space, I know it will not take long for the boats to fill. Alexandra must go now. There is no time for goodbyes, especially goodbyes without words. I fumble from Alexandra's grip and push her forward. Her steps falter and slow, but her inertia carries her down the cobblestones.

My limp, crooked fingers hang like dead weight, but my functional hand is firm on the machete. The companions pause their march and fan around me. Two move forward in strike, but there is the sensation of sinking heat in my chest. Their hands blur as they are arrested in slow motion. I smile, thanking my processor for this one last gasp of its assistance. In a singular stroke, I cleave their heads half from their shoulders and watch as their small frames become a cascade of stumbling unguided steps into the night.

The machete dances with me and sweeps through the knees of another companion child. The milky ichor of my kin flecks my cheeks and stains my shoes. With another spin, the machete cuts ribbons in the cold night air until my movement halts. I collapse to my knees, my limbs uncooperative. There is a succession of fast steps followed by a quick slap on my back and then an acrid smell sours the air. In a sudden burst, the earth drifts away from my feet as I rise above the causeway, my vision blanketed by cold winking stars, vast and unnamed, untethered from my reach. The stars tumble and coalesce in a pale somersault as I fly, the sensors inside my body exploding in violent twitches and alerts.

I land with a crunch, like a lightbulb breaking. The compound's entrance is far away, but a lighter shade of dark is visible in its archway. Mounted floodlights cast into relief the shapes of Alogo Boo soldiers, arriving in the companion children's wake. Shock ripples through the soldiers as the companion children wheel upon them. Screams of "Medal Chad" and gunfire follow. The world does not rise on my command, but remains stubborn and low. Moonlight skates on my palms, and they shine wet with the flood of white fluid that pools beneath me. Wires and white baubles hang from my abdomen and web the cobblestone like a tangled string of Christmas lights. I have been blown in half.

The world is shuttered and the fighting around me only comes in waves. The blue light behind my eyes eclipses the night. I am dying. I do not want to return like them. To return, wordless and rabid, crawling legless across the Earth, dragging my insides until they become ragged and befouled. Perhaps there is only enough magic in this world to resurrect the artificial. Everything else truly dies. There is a heavy chemical scent in the wind, and the cobblestone and black waters of the Cocheco fade into a depthless white light and then a small hand worms its way inside mine.

ITS LITTLE GRIP IS TIGHT AND FIERCE. THERE IS NO SIGHT, ONLY SOUND. A TIDAL GUSH OF PRESSURED AIR. A DISTANT, ELECTRONIC HUM AND A SOFT ELEGIAC CHIRP. THOUGH, THESE NOISES ARE DIMINISHED AGAINST PERSISTENT, GUTTURAL SOBS.

"PLEASE, NO. PLEASE DON'T TOUCH HER. DON'T TOUCH MY MOM."

A MAN'S VOICE REPLIES, MEASURED WITH THE BEARINGS OF GENTILITY, "SAM, PLEASE UNDERSTAND YOUR MOM WAS ONLY THINKING OF YOU WHEN SHE SIGNED THIS CONTRACT WITH US."

"FUCK YOU."

A PRESENCE FALLS ACROSS MY CHEST, ITS WEIGHT VEILED BY MY FADING SENSES, BUT THE SOBS DEEPEN. I RECOGNIZE THE FLORAL SCENT OF OUR CHEAP SHAMPOO. WITH ITS SMELL, I CAN IMAGINE THE BLACK CURLS ON HIS HEAD. MY SON. SAM.

THE MAN CONTINUES, HIS VOICE STERN AND POINTED ELSEWHERE, "YOU WERE INSTRUCTED TO HANDLE THIS DISCRETELY. WHY IS HE EVEN IN HERE?!"

"I TRIED. HE WON'T BUDGE. LOST HIS MOM. THAT WILL MAKE A GROWN MAN KOLO, AND HE'S BUT A BOY."

"WE HAVE OUR PICK OF ANY HOSPITAL IN LAGOS. YOU KNOW THAT, RIGHT?" THE VOICE PIVOTS AND

DROPS ITS EDGE. "SAM, THIS IS A DELICATE PROCEDURE. WE NEED TO BEGIN NOW."

"GET THE FUCK OFF ME."

YET THE WEIGHT FROM MY CHEST DISAPPEARS. SAM'S SCREAMS FILL THE ROOM. HE ISSUES THREATS FROM A VOICE FULL OF ADOLESCENT CREAKS. HIS CURSES GROW FAINTER, SINKING AWAY UNTIL THE SOUNDS COMING FROM THE INTRACRANIAL PRESSURE MONITOR AND THE VENTILATOR REGAIN THEIR SUPREMACY. A PINPRICK RUPTURES MY TEMPLE, AND ITS PRESSURE GROWS AND EXPANDS UNTIL IT CONSUMES MY ENTIRE HEAD. THERE IS A PRESENCE BESIDE ME, BUT NO HUMAN SOUNDS, AND THE AIR IS STIFF.

I AM NOT SURE WHERE I AM NOW. IT IS A LIMINAL PLACE, A PLACE BETWEEN LIVES, STERILE AND ONLY INTRUDED UPON BY THE FADING CACOPHONY OF MEDICAL INSTRUMENTS. YET, IT IS IN THIS ASEPTIC VOID THAT I FIND HIM AT LAST. RECOVER HIM BENEATH THE MANY LAYERS OF SEDIMENTATION LOTUS LAID ATOP MY BEING. MY BOY. MY BEAUTIFUL BOY.

MY RECALL COMES IN A LESSER FORM THAN SIGHT, BUT FIRMER THAN A MEMORY. A FEELING HE EXISTED. THAT ONCE, HE RAN WITH HIS BACK TO ME, SILHOUETTED BY THE GOLDEN LIGHT OF A RETREATING TROPICAL SUN ON HIS SHOULDER. RUNNING ON WHITE SANDS TO RACE THE WAVES. WITH A MOTHER'S JOY, I WATCH FROM BENEATH A PARASOL, MY LEGS CROSSED BEFORE ME ON A SUN-WORN BEACH TOWEL, NOW THIN AGAIN FROM THE FIRST BITES OF THE CANCER IN MY LUNGS. HIS

SPLASHES AMIDST THE OCEAN FILL ME WITH CALM, YET I AM FULL OF A DESPERATE HUNGER FOR HIS SMILE. IN HIS RETURN TO ME, HIS RACING FEET UP THE BEACH SEND SEAGULLS INTO FLIGHT. IN MY ARMS, THE RICH EARTHY SMELL OF HIM IS JOINED BY THE SMELL OF THE SEA ON HIS LITTLE BODY, IN HIS HAIR. HIS ARMS WRAPPED AROUND ME, TIGHTER, FIERCER AS I WILT. MY SON. THE SON OF MUSA AOIFE. GOOD GOD, WHERE IS MY SON?

The hum of static from beneath my jaw intercedes and this sensation of recall, perhaps no more than a chimera of memory, falters as the black waters of the Cocheco and the monolithic grey slope of the causeway resurface.

This broken jaw of our lost Kingdoms.

A blue veil covers the world, but Alexandra takes shape in my vision. She runs towards me, her cheeks and forehead mutilated by the shapes of sunflowers' faces. "No!!" she screams genuflect, her arms around me, her lips on my forehead.

"I'm a mother," I whisper.

Her eyes widen, and her mouth opens and closes. The blue veil grows deeper. "Yes. You are, really." Her frown becomes a gasp as she tries to step backwards.

A twisted metal hand clenches around her throat, and her feet swing above the ground. She punches the arm, wailing as she connects with its metal limbs. Another hand reaches for the top of her head. They are going to pull her head off. An alien voice sputters numbers while the chatter of sparks fills my ears. The breakwater, the fog, and my sister fade and vanish beneath endless waves of blue light.

BUG
Tournament Intelligence Manager

In the days after the raid, the halls are empty and only a few pods in the hallway remain lit. I've visited the viewing room several times in search of 7, but have come across no one. Part of me wonders if the tournament is over, but Tim forgot to let me know. Even the power has retreated, and outside the player corridor, the rest of the hangar has been surrendered to darkness, becoming a maze of tunnels brightened only by small red pools cast by the emergency lighting.

At a loss, I suit up in the pod to grind extra points. I flick my fingers to log into the map, but the screen flashes white and fades into an unresponsive grey tide. I try again. Nothing. As I inspect the gloves, the screen blinks blue, and Tim's image materializes in the top right corner of the screen.

"Hello, 100."

"Uh, hi?" I reply with a feeble wave.

Tim smiles and nods, and as he does, his head fills my entire screen. "100, your time in the tournament is over."

"What? Why? I scored enough for the cycle," I spit with incredulity as my fingers work their way around my neck to find the USB stick.

Tim appears to track the movement of my hands and his smile widens. "You succeeded over all of your peers. You should take pride in that accomplishment. Please await my arrival to escort you from the hangar."

"Tim, wait. Do you mean I won? Did I win the tournament?"

Tim shakes his head. "You succeeded against your human peers and your gameplay was highly instructive. Thank you."

"My human peers, what does that mean, Tim?"

"Thank you for your contribution." Tim vanishes from view and the screen goes blank with a soft click.

I rub the USB stick, desperate to summon your council. The empty hallways. 7's weird last-minute request. The abrupt conclusion. It doesn't sit right. The USB stick grows warm in my grip.

"Bug, it's time to get the fuck out of Dodge."

Unsuited, I pound the release button to the pod door, but it doesn't open. I bash the button again, but the door is obstinate. *Oh, shit. Shit. Okay, think Bug, you've spent literally over a 100 hours in this shitty claustrophobic broom cupboard of a room and didn't suffocate. How are you breathing in here?*

My eyes jump across the room in a manic search for a ventilation source. Amidst the sheen of white tiling, there's a vent duct in the wall tucked behind from where the viewing screen hangs. It looks wide enough for me to squeeze inside. The distant clap of heavy footsteps echoes from the far end of the player's hall.

"Bug, if you don't John McClane your way out of this, I think you're dead fucking meat."

I fight the pocket-knife from my back pocket and use the tip to loosen the screws enough to rip it from the wall.

"Front pocket, Bug."

The vent shaft is narrow, but if I crawl with my elbows to my chest, I fit. Ahead of me, the next vent grate cuts the twilight of emergency lighting into venetian red shadow. I freeze as a short hiss of air reaches up through the duct behind me.

"Bravo, Bug. Very resourceful," sings Tim.

How the fuck does he know your name for me? Yet, this thought summons back one of our first exchanges when I arrived at the tournament: *"Do you have a nickname ... a pet name from your Father or Mother?"*

Tim fills in my silence with a casual prescience. "Oh, yes. I know all about you. Did you think you found the tournament by chance?" His words are chased by laughter, hollow and ersatz as it rings inside the vent. "I know all about your motivations. All about your dear 'Dad.' Catatonic, lying in his own excrement in some awful hospice. Poor Bug."

I don't want nor wait to hear more. I claw to the end of the vent, push the grate out with a clatter, and scramble into the semi-gloom of an unlit and unfamiliar hallway. Already though, Tim's close.

"You were an excellent data feed, Bug." His voice drifts through the iron-skinned corridor. "Smart. Resourceful. But I thought you would catch on sooner with the gameplay stats. Did you never do the math, never wonder how we played for an average of 21 hours a day? How some of your competitors seemed to never sleep?" His words are followed by another round of synthesized, high-pitched laughter.

Jesus. What the hell is he saying?

My shoulders graze the walls, and the soles of my shoes slap and echo on the concrete floor as I run. Behind me, at the far end of the corridor, Tim's wiry silhouette is enclosed in the sundered blink of emergency lighting, and for a moment, he's framed like cave art. I kick off my shoes and try to run on my toes in muffled steps.

"You trained them, Bug. You were all AI chum. The raid was the final test of their ability to collaborate with the other war centres."

My mind races to Scrummaster34's strange entourage, the player in the Vader Halloween mask who never acknowledged me. My heart hammers in my throat and branches of fiery pain erupt in my chest like forked lightning, yet I don't stop. One corridor becomes another, and another after that, until the world blurs as I run deeper into an anthill of red light, locked doors, and exposed piping. I'm descending again, back down into the catacombs of the hangar, where Tim told me not to go.

The wall is hard on my back as I collapse upon it. In strain, I listen for sounds of Tim over the furious drum of my heart in my ears. Some industrial bones, buried deep and out of sight, shift and groan as the steam piping exhales and hisses. The knowledge that Tim is still out there, moving beneath these sounds in a slow, methodical approach, winds me, and I gnash my teeth at the stale, dry air.

"You're in deep shit, Bug. Deep, dark shit. Focus. The axe. Find the fucker's lean, Bug."

The axe. On the main floor, near the viewing room. Humid, thick air burns at my cheeks as I sprint down a tunnel towards a T-junction. It's only when the blue and green light of the EV charging station blurs in my vision that I realize I've been here before. Tim's words ring in my ears: "*The patrons of the tournament like contingency measures. This is a remote location. In an emergency, there may be a need to power extraction vehicles.*" His explanation seems even more absurd, but the pieces still aren't coming together.

The hiss of the steam pipe ebbs and surrenders to a fragile silence. No sign of Tim. The pipes run right, and I follow them. Steps surface in the corridor, and beyond them, the iron-skinned tunnel widens into a hallway. The red lights flare and then vanish, casting intermittent crimson shadows across the concrete floor. I know I need to pause to check my surroundings, but I don't dare stop.

I keep moving, desperate to control the tap of my sneakers on the concrete floor. Tim won't have given up. The air is less stale, and the pipes slip into the ceiling, their noise sublimated into the whirl of ceiling fans. Closer to habitability, space designed for human life. Still no sign of Tim. Though cradled in the crimson glow of emergency lighting, this corridor is recognizable as the main floor concourse.

Around the corner, the hallway opens out into the vast dark chasm of the viewing room. The axe in the emergency cabinet catches the red glow of the emergency lighting. Still no sign of Tim. With a deep breath, I ram my elbow into the glass and grit my teeth as it shatters and echoes on the floor in a light crinkle patter.

"*All right, Bug. Axe. Now get the fuck out. Hack your way through the front door if you must.*"

On the far side of the viewing room, the tunnel to the front of the hangar waits, its darkness a deeper cavern amid the hangar's twilight. In slow, measured steps, I move from the edge of the hallway and down the sunken stairs into the viewing room. Its domed ceiling looms above me, black and listless as I weave through the sea of cushions that sit like dark islands amidst the semi-gloom.

"I knew you would travel through here. Very sentimental. Very human," Tim's voice rises from within the dark.

From the depths of the room, an outline takes shape beneath the pale blue light of the sleeping screens, coming forward from the dark, until Tim emerges from the shadows.

"You should be proud. Do you have any idea what you helped us create? What we know now?" As he speaks, Tim moves to block my path across the room.

"*Show the fucker who's the boss.*"

"I don't care." I try to distract him from the quiver in my voice by raising the axe over my shoulder. "I just want to go. Let me go."

"You do not care? Bug, you were part of the most decisive civil war in the 21st century. Even now, a squad from this very hangar is pushing through the front lines." With alarming prescience, he adds, "You do not believe me? Look up, Bug."

The viewing screen flickers to life until it bathes the entire viewing room in its electric glow. Overhead, five screens erupt into chaotic scenes of bots screaming and running through a ruined city. Bots boarding boats as the orange shadows of artillery blasts skip across the black waters of a river. A weakness grows in my knees, and my guts squirm and twist like a bag of bait.

"It was real?"

"You were playing for Lotus."

"Lotus? Why?"

"The solar cells. The copper. The lithium. The cobalt. The last dredges of critical minerals, all on route from Houston to Olan Bator for the next big thing."

The ground feels distant, and the room shakes. My cheeks are hot and wet. All my targets—energy infrastructure, bridges, solar panels, electric cars—flood to me in serial grainy images. Dear God, all the bots I've killed. People. A wave of nausea overtakes me, and I retch all over my shoes.

"The most important lesson was that you could not tell the difference between reality and simulation. The human condition is ready to accept the unbelievable, to believe in a simulation that surpasses their senses, their earthly experience. With resignation to the impossible, so opens the last frontier," says Tim as he beckons at me to lower the axe. "It is over, Bug. Come with me. Die with the wind on your face."

"Tim. No. No, please T—"

"There is no Tim." He points overhead to the ceiling for a second time. The middle square in the dome goes blue, and the white letters T— I— M appear vertical on the left side while more letters materialize to their right.

Tournament
Intelligence
Manager

"An AI ..." I stammer, but Tim merely smiles as he advances. "Fuck off," I scream as I cleave the empty space between us with the axe.

Tim steps back and cocks his head like an osprey as I try to step aside him. "So much passion. So much anger. You were a formidable asset, Bug. 7 was right to cultivate you. You were part of his carefully orchestrated scrimmage."

"Scrummaster34 ..." My eyes are wet.

"Your instincts serve you well, Bug. It is too bad that 7 learned to care. It was disappointing to retire such an excellent scrum master, but the violation of protocol to warn you suggested a significant defect. A waste of copper in the end."

A spasm pulses behind my eye, and then the world goes red, and my body reacts without me. The axe sings as it cleaves through Tim's collarbone, and white fluid and blood spurts from his neck. His face seizes and his eyes flutter as he stumbles over the mandala cushions, his hands pressed to his gored neck. I sprint out of the room.

I hurtle down the passageway and trip up a long flight of stairs towards the hangar doors. Behind me, there's a scuttle of feet on the concrete lip of the stairs and a flat vocalization of words followed by reams of binary. The steel doors at the hangar's entrance are interlocked and immovable. In a flash of panic, I bash at several of the buttons on the intercom Tim used to close the doors when I arrived, but the doors remain closed.

"*Shit. Improvise, Bug.*"

I heave the axe into the metal doors. There's a resonant metallic cry, and the impact aches in my hands and wrists as I stumble backwards. I raise the axe again, but Tim is close. He ascends the stairway, one hand to his neck as he shuffles forward in erratic steps, his head and neck swaying akimbo from the severing of his collarbone.

To the left of the entrance, another passage runs back into the bowels of the hangar. There's a glimpse of the rungs of a ladder built into one of the walls. A service ladder to the roof. The roof?

As Tim rises to the landing, I fly down the corridor and throw myself on the bottom rung. With the axe in one hand, I climb towards a small hatch that looks to open and close with a red lever. As I pull the lever, Tim scales the bottom rung, his eyes blank and his face motionless as he fights his way up the ladder. From above him, I glimpse the dull shine of black metal from where the axe blow has frayed his skin.

"*No time like the present, Bug.*"

The hatch slides up with a groan and reveals a small window of grey sky and the patter of rain. As Tim climbs with manic abandon, I throw the axe to the roof with a clatter and worm my way through the hatch. Rain pummels me and the wind burns my face. I kick the hatch to a close and run along the flat roof of the hangar in search of an escape, only to find myself in a garden of huge satellite dishes, planted every few yards like inverted mushrooms.

Weaving through them, I reach the front of the hangar. I fight the urge to vomit again by webbing my fingers over my mouth. Below me, bodies fill a pit. The other human players lie in a mound of twisted limbs and sunken faces. Those whose faces are visible bear a black tarry hole in their foreheads.

"*Jesus, Bug.*"

At the other end of the satellite dishes stands Tim, his black turtleneck drenched in milky fluid.

"Impressive, Bug, but you cannot win. There is no way down." His voice warbles in a synthesized half-life.

The white, black, and grey heads of the satellites stand between us, each alive with the sullen blink of red lights. Why so many satellites? The changing black and white islands of gameplay on the map return to me. The coverage was the movement of satellites.

"You're right," I whisper. *The meaning of your nickname has never been clearer, dad.*

Tim's smile transforms into a guttural cry as I swing the axe into the satellite in front of me. As the second one falls, Tim charges through the curtain of rain. But I'm felling satellites like saplings. The axe strikes through another dish, shattering it into grey pieces. Another one splits apart into several white ribbons. Tim weaves through the remaining satellites, his head wobbling like it's on spaghetti.

The next dish falls apart, but the axe remains fixed in its footings, wrapped in place by twisted pieces of metal. I pry at it, but Tim crashes into me. Together, we slide across the rooftop until we skitter to the edge of the hangar. His hands are on my throat, throttling the air from my lungs. His eyes bear into mine, sundering the rain with a solitary red light.

"Goodbye, Bug." Static ripples and fades throughout his words. His jaw distends and his mouth becomes a dark, cavernous hole.

A wave of heat floods down my neck and then over my chest as he rips into my throat. Your words somersault in my ears. *"You know what you gotta do, Bug. Front pocket."*

My fingers tremble as I pry the knife from my jean pocket. Tim remains locked on my throat, the pierce and tear of his teeth setting a pain like fire below my jaw, and the world feels like it's tumbling away. Yet amidst the grey curtain of rain and the red squall across Tim's features, black pieces of machinery protrude from where the axe split his collarbone. The knife sings as I drive it in and out of his insides, diving the blade deeper, with greater hunger for the white ichor that trails with each blow.

The pressure on my neck deepens and then goes slack as a symphony of crackles erupts inside Tim. He recoils in a spasm, and his arms and legs curl inward like a crushed spider as he rolls towards the edge of the roof. A red flood follows him. The rain thunders on the hangar and spits all over my cheeks in a cold spray, washing my blood over the lip of the hangar's roof in a pinkening tide.

My fingers quiver and shake as I try to clamp the wound. The tear runs the length of my neck, and my grip is stiff and aloof to my urges. Millions of waves of numbness break over my body, each one seemingly aiming to pull me further away from my fingers, from my breaths, and from my panic. The tear in my neck is impossible to hold, let alone synch, and I fumble to clench its seams.

"It's time to let go, Bug. It's time to let go."

My other hand trembles as it navigates my chest to retrieve the USB stick from the warm deluge. The words leave my lips stillborn and mute, but I know I've said them. A faint ember of warmth pulses in my palm, and for a moment, I dare believe you heard me as the rest of the world cools into lengthening shadows and emptiness.

"It's okay, Bug. I know. It's okay, I know."

ALEXANDRA
The Jaw

The tip of my toe grazes the cobblestone, but the pressure on my throat builds. The instinct to gasp rises and falls in my chest. My throat feels synched. The face beneath me is mainly clenched teeth and curled lips with blackened gums. Metal debris peeks through gashes in its cheeks. Its eyes are black and pitiless and impossible to reach, boring through me, affixed to an invisible horizon.

My toes dip, fierce in the need to alleviate the suffocating inferno rising in my chest. Behind me, a pair of hands reaches around each side of my head in a vice grip. They're going to rip my head off. Hypatia's head has rolled to her shoulder, her eyes slack and turning the colour of snow. Over the child's shoulders, the chaos of Alogo Boo soldiers, companion children, and the few embattled Republic fighters dims. The world lurches down and my stomach turns over. I've fallen.

On my side, the breakwater of the Cocheco returns to view; much of its body is awash in fog, but there's a chink in the grey wall ahead. Several small, green lights burn amidst the fog. The beckons of escape boats. Hands to my throat, I try to coax the air back into my lungs. Beside me lie the companion children. They're motionless, their hands rigid and pointed away from their bodies, their feet splayed. A collapse into decerebration.

Hypatia's artificial blood and milky fluid flow together in a grey ichor beneath the debris of her body. Bright pieces of metal and white tubing and opaque bulbs, their texture a faint replication of human tissue, are scattered around her. I continue to gaze at the pieces of her because I can't meet her vacant stare. A crimson flash erupts at the compound's entrance; its aftermath screams of agony. It won't be long until the remaining Republic fighters are overrun. The thought of the Alogo Boo seizing her and indiscriminately tossing bits of her into carts of her dismembered kin brings fresh heat rolling down my cheeks.

With my hands under her armpits, I raise her and drag her down the causeway towards the escape boats. There are fewer refugees now, but the occasional straggler weaves by us in a manic clatter on the cobblestones. Though I can't bear to look back at Hypatia, her body speaks in a ragged metallic clatter as we clear the first shipping container; its rust-scabbed doors cast wide in invitation into empty darkness.

A sporadic burst of gunfire erupts behind us and then falters into a long silence. The last defenders at the gate must have fallen. It won't be long until the Alogo Boo sweep the causeway. My chest burns like I have yet to truly breathe and my calves shake as my sister's mass trails me in a stubborn tumble.

A dark-haired man overtakes us, his eyes wide with confusion. "Leave it. Leave it!" he cries over his shoulder as he ventures to become a shadow amidst the fog.

Too winded to speak, I raise my hand in hope he'll come to my aid; he turns, but the fog burns orange as fire cuts through it like a barrage of liquid fireflies. The earth shakes, and the man is gone, replaced by screams, pain, and terror. Sightless, I grope about on the pavement, desperate to recover Hypatia amidst the debris of broken cobblestone and the column of dust. As I try to rise in search of her, a searing pain rips through me and my leg crumples out from under me.

On my back, my trembling fingers probe my pantleg to discover blood and then the edges of a long shard of black metal jutting out above my knee. A storm of words swirls within me, but the sieve of my clenched teeth reduces them to guttural cries.

Ahead of me, Hypatia is face down, her arms twisted beneath her at strange angles; not far beyond her, another shipping container lays crooked across the causeway.

With my good leg and one hand, I crawl over the ground while I fight to pull Hypatia along with my other. This shipping container is open too, though its doors seem to have been ripped from its hinges. Without hesitation, I slide inside and slump down with my back to the ribs of metal that line its interior wall. Hypatia's hand is still in mine, but with my strength exhausted and her body no less heavy, I'm only able to pull her right side inside the dark cavernous container, leaving her left shoulder and hand exposed to the causeway.

A chemical aftertaste, like the sourness of mouthwash, fills the dark. Dozens of white packages, rations maybe, are strewn across the dark red shadows of the container's floor. The pain in my leg becomes a crescendo, and Hypatia rests next to me, the black of her skull visible in the part of her hair. My free hand claps my ear while the other holds Hypatia's wrist in irons. The drum of my hand splices the calls of men and the thunder of artillery. My pantleg is warm with blood.

"Alone, but together. Alone, but together," I whisper as I let the container imbue my words with a faint metallic tincture. The pain in my leg recedes into some distant thing of numb contemplation; a consequence of shock or blood loss, maybe both. "Alone, but together."

The drum of boots intercedes, and there's the pop and cry of bullets against the wall of the container, followed by a heavy thump. Another volley of fierce steps approaches from up the causeway and then joins me inside the container in a flash of colour. I close my eyes, desperate to be left for dead, but I can't still the hard patter of my hand on my ear. If they hear me, they don't acknowledge me. Through the dark, I find a young-looking Alogo

Boo soldier sat opposite, his head bowed, a rifle laid across his lap. He fills the container with suckling uneven breaths, breaths drawn to fill a chasm without bottom.

A flash of light drifts in a long lazy trail outside the entrance to the container; its tangerine shadow brings his features into relief. A bloodied gauze patch cradles the soldier's left cheek, and the bridge of his nose is gashed. Speech comes from me in an effortless burst, and without focus or intent, I whisper, "Francis?"

The whites of his eyes roll manic in his skull as he tries to place me amidst the dark; his eyes widen, seemingly in recognition as another burst of orange light fades through the container entrance and washes across his face. His gaunt cheeks crack apart in a grimace. "Jesus."

His eyes walk across the floor of the container to where Hypatia's torso lies prone. With the tip of his rifle, he prods her head, overturning her cloudy eye and cheek torn away in a blast of artificial blood and white fluid. His trespass and the horror of my sister's face are enough for me to pull my hand from my ear to push his rifle away, though the exertion makes me wince.

"All right, all right," he concedes as his eyes squeeze through the dark to settle on me. "You're fucked up." At his pronouncement, he leans forward in closer inspection. "Christ, blondie. You're really fucked up."

In a quick swipe, I brush a tear from my cheek and reposition my head between the hard welded ribs of the container. For what feels like a long time, neither of us says anything. The few thoughts I have are chewed down and broken into little pieces by the din of gunfire. Francis keeps his head low, the meaning of his face lost to me without Hypatia's counsel.

"Fuck it," he whispers.

On his feet, he uncinches his Hawaiian print flak jacket and begins to wrestle it off. The jacket seems to get stuck on the bony edges of his shoulder and then on his sharp elbows, but it eventually falls to the container floor in a crumpled shell. He then balances the rifle across his open hands, frowns at its weight, and leans it up against the container wall as he says, "We go out the other end of the container. There's a line of Republic gunners, but without my colours"—he gestures at the flak jacket at his feet—"and with you next to me, they might hold their fire. I assume you're headed to the boats."

I nod, and his eyes wander from my face to where I still grip Hypatia's limp hand. He frowns and chastises me with a slow shake of his head.

"She's gone, blondie. You got to leave her."

"She's my ... sister."

"There's no time for this."

"Family." He strains to hoist me to my feet and break my grip on Hypatia. "Please." I find his eyes as I speak and feel his grip slacken. "Real family," I press. "Not uncles. Not cousins."

His features tighten in a flash of anger, and he wrestles away from me, letting me slide back to the floor. For a moment, I wonder if he will leave, and the tide of numbness climbs higher up my leg.

He faces the other end of the container, but extends his hand to mine. "I'll make sure nobody finds her. I owe you at least that. Truth is, I can't carry you both."

"Promise?"

He grips my hand in what I realize is a handshake and then slides under my arm. Pressed against his body, I discover he's bones and emptiness; his paucity seems to poke through him, and I wonder if he'll be able to support me at all. Yet, he doesn't stagger as I put my weight upon him and we venture to the opposite end of the container, where a needle of lighter darkness runs down the imperfect seam of the metal doors.

Francis moves fast down the causeway, sure-footed as he navigates the dark islands of fallen refugees and soldiers caught together by indiscriminate bullets. Without the flak jacket and rifle, he becomes a boy again.

The several dug-in Republic fighters trace us with their rifles and then beckon us forward. As we pass, they turn and call down the causeway behind them. "Civilians incoming, hold your fire! Move along now, move along. You're almost there, but the ships won't wait."

Francis says nothing, but I notice he veers far to the left of the soldiers, plunging us into the shadows. The last stretch of the causeway comes into view and a haphazard collection of barrels and Jersey barriers rises from the dark, a final barricade in defence of the escape boats.

Francis' pace accelerates towards the barricade, and he calls ahead that we're civilians as we descend the causeway. A bellow, eldritch and mournful, rises from the river. It summons a chorus of rejoining foghorns from the other boats; a signal they're about to disembark. Seemingly in response, the sky becomes a meteor shower of gunfire. Francis stoops as the red tails of bullets slip above our heads. From over my shoulder, I see another wave of Alogo Boo fighters crash into the soldiers that had waved us through.

"Go, go," I urge.

"Yup ..." answers Francis, but the rest of his words are cast asunder by a deafening blast behind us.

The Republic fighters rise along the barricade before us and unleash a volley of fire around us as we run towards them. Return fire cuts by us as we stagger by the line of fighters, and the red shadows of somersaulting flares cuts from the night the outline of several long open-top boats. We're close.

"Come on," Francis cries in a seemingly incredulous laugh of disbelief.

Three boats bob at the lip of the causeway, and people are hunched or lie on their bellies untying the last anchor lines.

"Hold on," Francis calls ahead and my toe leaves the ground as he lifts me as he runs. "We're almost there, Alexan—"

A kettle whistle rents the air. Francis' gait slows to a stumble and then he lowers me to the ground as he sits down.

"Got the wind knocked out of me," he murmurs.

Several dark coils of metal claw out from his chest, and a red circle expands across his shirt. He gropes the twisted entrails of metal and brings his crimson fingers to his face in faint recognition. In a slow turn of his head, his unfocused eyes find me on the ground.

"Fuck," he cries as he falls backwards on the cobblestones.

Shouts to leave rise from the remaining boats as the Alogo Boo assault the last barricade. "Wait!" I scream at the nearest boat as several men cast off the last of the ties. "Help us!" The heads in the boat look away, eyes to feet, palms cradling faces. "Please!"

Francis is white, but his chest rises and falls in shallow breaths. He speaks, but I can't make out his words. There's a commotion within the boat, and then a man and woman scramble over the wooden quayside that meets the end of the causeway.

"¡Esperar! ¡Esperar! Nosotras seremos rápidos," calls the man.

The woman runs low and scoops me from the ground. She says nothing, and her body trembles as we stumble to the edge of the causeway. A canopy of hands reaches up from the boat and guides me to one of many metal benches welded to the boat's interior.

"She's hurt," announces the woman. "Medico!"

"Get a blanket under her and keep her flat," calls an older woman who makes her way through the passengers, stooped with a small red medical kit in hand.

As they speak, the man returns carrying Francis, and the passengers lower his slender frame to the deck in a series of uneven drops and then carry him to the bow of the ship. The engines kick and spit into life, and we move from the wharf, chasing the wake of the boats that have already departed.

"Just stay still," offers the old woman as she cuts away my pantleg. "You'll live," she murmurs. "Brace yourself, dear."

A spark of blinding pain possesses me, and I shriek in a voice I don't recognize. The woman squints and raises the piece of metal she retrieved from me above her head to catch what little light the moon offers. Her face hardens in what looks like a quizzical stare.

"God knows what you got tangled up with," she says as she scrubs the object with a paper towel and then, in exasperation, passes it to me as she bends down to dress my leg.

At first, I share her bewilderment, for in my palm is a small piece of black metal roughly three inches in length. Smooth to the touch, except for one end where it has split from a larger piece in ragged tendrils, it bears several small, white molars. In recall of Hypatia's ruined face, I realize with horror and reverence that it's a small fragment of my sister's jaw. Too awful to bear, too precious to throw away. I'm left to contemplate and keep the metal taken from my flesh.

From my side, I can see Francis laid at the boat's bow. He's pale and his teeth chatter as the woman rips apart his shirt, revealing a gurgling well in his chest.

"Is it bad?" he hisses through clenched teeth.

"Stay still," replies the woman, though she turns away to speak more words to a man she let hold the medical kit. "I don't have the tools for this."

The man shrugs his incomprehension, and the woman, with visible hesitancy, strings together a little Spanish. While she speaks,

Francis lifts his hand into the air and opens and closes it in little spasms until someone takes him in their grip.

"You'll need to stay still, I'm going to try and get some of this out," says the old woman, her voice hoarse and uneven.

"I fucked up. I fucked it all up," sobs Francis. "I'm sorr—" His words descend into guttural moans as the woman strains to pry bits of metal from his chest.

"We can pack in gauze until we make port," says the woman quietly with a wan smile.

"I fucked up," repeats Francis.

"Estas aquí ahora," says the man. He repeats these words, though Francis fails to give any sign of comprehension.

The old woman comes back to my side. She makes a quick appraisal of the dressing on my leg and then says in a hushed voice, "Are you close to him? Do you know how we can comfort him?"

I shake my head. "Just met him." It doesn't feel like a lie.

She frowns and, with a shrug, gestures to the man who speaks Spanish to pack a wad of gauze into Francis' deep, seeping wound. Francis screams and his eyes roll back into his head. He wails and several people next to me put their hands on their ears.

With their backs to Francis, facing me, the woman whispers, "We've done what we can. The rest is up to him."

At my feet, the last of Dover drifts by. As the gunfire fades into a few sporadic bursts, a coarse chant grows in its place. The victory song of the Alogo Boo carries on the water, seeking dominion in all places left bare and tender by night's coming. Occasionally, the silhouettes of Alogo Boo soldiers come into view along the causeway. In victory, they don't stand together but apart; adrift in the darkness that rolls from the black, coursing waters of the river's back. In the comedown of the battle, they look lost, ready to surrender once more to the pressgang of nameless algorithms; wraiths of men made in the grunge and vitriol of online barracks with hashtags seared across their hearts; platoons of internet children lost in the fall.

The boat sways and shudders against the river's head; we remain low, our bodies tucked beneath the gunwales, wary of the half-hearted parting shots fired from the distant shore. Across from me, a man crouches beside Francis. He peers under the blanket they've laid over him and, with a heavy sigh, rolls up his sleeves and packs more gauze into the red well that spits from Francis' chest.

Amidst his labours, I imagine a new colour in the man's face; a colour Hypatia couldn't understand: the monolithic grey of doomed resolution; the determination to face the passing of all that is of human significance; to accept that even the most earnest of scribes can't retrieve what has become blank to the human eye, and that the days ahead will bear only the false testimonies of unreliable mediums; to know all this, but to still pack gauze into a swallow-chested dying boy. The grey concrete face of endurance amidst humanity's terminal condition.

In our passage, the fires of Dover scour the hills, and thick columns of rising black smoke stand darker atop the twilight. Though the chants of the Alogo Boo still echo, they've grown hollow, caught now only amidst the river's backwaters in plaintive-sounding fragments. The man's face turns ashen as the fresh gauze in Francis' chest grows red. The woman consoles the man with her hand on his back and then takes Francis' hand in hers. And our chain of boats moves on.

For a long time, there's only the emptiness of greying night splayed across the run of the river's descent, and we borne on into its darkness. A pale shadow steps across what must have been a dreamless sleep. A small green light bows and tilts in the fog. In a slow, laborious sweep, it casts a harbour into relief. A bell rings. Resonant and solemn, it awakens voices in our boat.

Francis remains at the bow, though his open eyes have slipped into cloud, lost now in a ceaseless voyage of the night sky. Hypatia's molars pinch my palm as I clutch the piece of her broken jawbone and bring it to my chest. The green light of the harbour passes once more, and at its edges, it illuminates an outcrop of little hills. I shall bury the last piece of my sister in those hills and endure her belief in refuge.

---

[i] Dante Alighieri, Inferno, Canto I from *The Divine Comedy*, trans. John Ciardi, New American Library, 2003. Inclusion of "but" in the last line is the author's addition.

Don't miss out!

Visit the website below and you can sign up to receive emails whenever H.S. Down publishes a new book. There's no charge and no obligation.

https://books2read.com/r/B-A-NNUR-GACQC

BOOKS 2 READ

Connecting independent readers to independent writers.

Did you love *Children of the Fall*? Then you should read *The Shareholders*[1] by H.S. Down!

[2]

In the late 21st century, Earth is ravaged by climate change. The billionaires have bioengineered immortality, fled to Mars, and rule Earth's last habitable biospheres as their personal shares. Those left on Earth struggle to find balance as the planet tumbles into its terminal years of habitability. Ian Gateman, one of Earth's last bureaucrats, is tasked with finding a buyer for a fledgling colony of newly settled ecological refugees. As Ian travels to the estates of several visiting shareholders, it becomes clear the shareholders have other plans for humanity's future.

---

1. https://books2read.com/u/4jPO2k

2. https://books2read.com/u/4jPO2k

Also by H.S. Down

The Shareholders
Children of the Fall

Printed in the USA
CPSIA information can be obtained
at www.ICGtesting.com
LVHW020150061224
798285LV00007B/270